GHOSTWALKERS

First Published in Great Britain 2018 by Mirador Publishing

Copyright © 2018 by Edward J. McGee

First edition: 2018

Any reference to real names and places are purely fictional and are constructs of the author. Any offence the references produce is unintentional and in no way reflects the reality of any locations or people involved.

A copy of this work is available through the British Library.

ISBN: 978-1-912192-89-2

Mirador Publishing
10 Greenbrook Terrace
Taunton
Somerset
UK
TA1 1UT

Ghostwalkers

Unreliable memoirs of the Poor Man's SAS in Northern Ireland in 1976-1977.
The Unit the IRA (or anyone else for that matter) never knew about.

Edward J. McGee

Dedication

Dedicated to all the people associated with 'The Troubles' in Northern Ireland of whatever political persuasion. Be they security forces, terrorist, civilian, alive, injured or dead. Let us all hope that a future based on the foundations of those lost generations be forged anew in the arms of the young who, if given support and freedom, would be undoubtedly brave enough to put aside inherited animosity for neighbours who are, after all, exactly like themselves and, curiously, also in the same place.

Contents

Introduction

This book is a work of fiction, but the fiction is based closely on the stories of real soldiers who served in Northern Ireland during 'The Troubles' between 1976 and 1977. The NIPG as a military unit had in fact really existed and was based in Abercorn Barracks, Ballykinler in County Down, just below Belfast on the Irish coast.

The NIPG was started in about 1975 because the IRA changed their tactics and set up what became known as Active Service Units (ASUs). This terrorist structure used small groups that were independent of each other and because of this, intelligence on the players was hard to obtain. The Army, in response, changed its own tactics and started an information gathering war against the various terrorist groups in Northern Ireland. The Special Air Service was introduced on a more serious footing and 14 Independent Company was set up. However, the SAS and 14 Independent Company were just not enough resources to gather the amount of raw intelligence required, so the Commander Land Forces in the Province set up the Northern Ireland Patrol Group or NIPG. The NIPG, sometimes jokingly referred to as the 'Poor Man's SAS', was employed to undertake operations across the Province in a covert observation role taking clandestine photos of the players. Due to this, 'baddies' could be tracked by the 'squaddies' serving across the Province who had been issued with the pictures. On occasion these photos did get a bit raunchy and on others they were sad or even grisly, but they certainly did the job. The work was potentially very dangerous as the soldiers operated in very close proximity to their targets using advanced infantry field craft and sniper camouflage techniques to remain hidden. This was not plain clothes work but full combat dress, weapons and lots of heavy kit.

Three years or so after it was started it was disbanded as the unit was still not big enough to cover the Province. Due to the early success of the NIPG the role was expanded and taken over by the then newly created Close Observation Platoons (COPs) of the resident battalions. This provided the level of resources required to undertake the role effectively across the entire Province, using the tactics and skills adapted by the NIPG from those bravely pioneered at huge risk by the SAS[1] and SBS[2] before them.

In this book, I have made up a patrol of NIPG characters, amazingly similar to the team the author was in who are going through a twelve-month tour with the group. However, in truth, the book would be very boring indeed if we stuck to the facts, so I have basically fiddled with timelines to generate what I hope is an interesting story designed to give the reader a feel for what the NIPG, and the Army in Northern Ireland in general was like, but without the boring bits. All the bravery and action accounts as stated are based on true accounts and I am very glad to announce had absolutely nothing to do with me! The humorous bits and the cock ups are mostly actually what happened to me and the section I was a part of.

Regrettably soldiers and civilians did lose their lives or got seriously injured in N.I. and there are some darker parts of the story that includes this aspect. Out of respect for the families and friends of those departed who may not want to relive or be made aware of what happened to their friends or loved ones, these episodes have been changed quite dramatically to ensure no links can be made. I have also not included names of victims either.

Northern Ireland evokes memories that will remain with me forever. Blindingly green pastures on rolling hills framed with a light mist alongside dramatic coastlines with black angry seas. Pubs rich with the cráic and Irish traditional music soaked in the distinct dialects of the North of Ireland with a hospitality that ensnares and makes it hard to leave. The dark-haired beauty of the young girls who have spirits of fire welded to an intense love of life. Mix all this with a sincere generosity in a people who have an identity that is immense with strong ties to roots that not many outside truly understand. This is even more poignant when you place this into the context of roadblocks, armoured cars, street art, sangars and barbed wire. Soldiers patrolling the streets with loaded automatic rifles Bobbing about and 'hard targeting'. Not forgetting the bands and the parades followed by the demonstrations, riots, petrol bombs and rubber bullets.

Northern Ireland is indeed a land of opposites and contrasts that host a

---

[1] Special Air Service Regiment
[2] Special Boat Squadron (Royal Navy's equivalent to the SAS)

people wearied of 'The Troubles' but who carry on in their own version of the 'Dunkirk Spirit'. Singing their rebel and patriotic songs tinged with sadness and honour. Unionist or Republican, Protestant or Catholic I wish them all a peace they can live with in contentment and pride, placing their grief, ghosts and burdens behind them. Meanwhile my own memories will live on, good and bad, with no hard feelings towards anyone. Just a feeling of sadness for the dead, injured and the angry mixed with a strong belief that our little bit of history in the NIPG was worth it.

So, in true British Infantryman style, pull up a sandbag, swing a light and read on…

Chapter 1

Volunteering?

Maghera, County Londonderry, N.I., September 1976

'For fuck's sake, Kermit, wake up!' was the first thing Eddie heard that morning. 'Heard' would have been a slight understatement; it was more like a mad woman screaming accompanied by a series of violent wrenches. 'Kermit' was the nickname Eddie had been christened with during the first week with his regiment in Hong Kong after his two-year episode as a Junior Soldier in Shropshire. It had something to do with green and slimy, but he was too drunk at the time, having downed copious amounts of San Miguel lager, to recall the incident and as much as he asked nobody else seemed to be able to enlighten him. It had stuck though, whether he liked it or not, as nicknames often do in the military.

He blearily opened one eye and eventually, his brain now in a low level of consciousness, looked up and saw the animated face of 'Spoon' looking down. 'Spoon' was the night duty radio operator from the operations room and had obviously been sent to give Eddie an unexpected early wake up call. 'Spoon', a gangly and naturally anxious chap, whose own nickname had something to do with the intimate place he inserted spoon handles whilst masturbating, went on.

'Captain Johnson is outside and wants a word with you, better hurry up and get out of your bunk; he looks like he means business.'

The bunk that 'Spoon' was referring to was a three foot by six foot compartment in a holiday caravan that the Army managed to get hold of sometime in 1969 for the comfort of troops serving in Northern Ireland. Somehow this crappy, washed out, leaking and dilapidated, blue caravan had made its way into the car park at the back of the police station in the very small town of Maghera, County Londonderry. There it had been unceremoniously left to die. This same car park, by the summer of 1976, was a sprawl of other caravans and makeshift buildings looking curiously like a new world traveller's anti-bypass demo camp. Albeit a particularly untidy one where 7 Platoon, of the resident Army battalion for the area, were currently undertaking operations from to try and curb the over enthusiastic excesses of Republican and Unionist activists in the local area.

Eddie, like a bedraggled fly emerging from the larvae of an unworldly green maggot, uncurled himself and, with difficulty and awkwardly, undid the zip on his green army sleeping bag. This unleashed a wave of fetid air into the room that confirmed the fact that the good old army 'gonk bag' was never, ever washed.

He attempted to get up but just tumbled off the fitted bunk bed that was little more than a shelf, and fell onto the floor, not that you could see much of it. This was due to the military paraphernalia, empty beer cans, army green underpants and combat kit spread all over the floor giving the impression of an itinerant gypsy's toilet. This was, as usual, accompanied by the mandatory pornographic literature spread all over the walls exaggerating the lack of space. To make things even worse he shared this miniscule piece of purgatory with the camp cook. So, in addition to the mess and smell of rank sleeping bags there was an air of stale cooking fat, digested baked beans and stale sweat wafting about. But Eddie and mercifully the cook, no longer noticed it anymore. 'Spoon' opened the door and left the room hastily in what could only be described as a desperate attempt to avoid breathing in the toxic air that even the local cockroaches avoided.

Through the now open door Eddie could hear Captain Johnson walking up and down, bellowing that if he did not hurry up and get out of that polluted and grimy 'shit hole' of a caravan then Eddie's bollocks would soon be used as some form of novel decoration on the toe of his right DMS[3] boot. Eddie Johnson was a short and wiry, but well respected, captain and rugby winger who played for the Army. He was also the Signals Platoon Commander and Eddie's ultimate boss, so Eddie was well aware that Captain Johnson didn't joke about such things.

Eddie, after fumbling about like a deranged goblin within the dark lair he lived in eventually found the door, leapt out of the caravan into the light and instantly regretted it. He was unstable, unshaven and wearing a pair of sweaty and creased combat trousers accompanied by a green Army vest, and was still

---

[3] Directly Moulded Sole – Army boots were made of a kind of compressed cardboard with a directly attached sole. That said they lasted well and after a while were quite comfy.

in his bare feet. He was looking the worse for wear since the previous night he had gotten completely 'rat arsed' with some UDR[4] guys in their bijou but lively bar on the other side of the compound. Eddie's eyes looked like someone had viciously pulled them out and, having kicked them about a bit over a gravel road, slipped them back in again but without the benefit of any lubrication. Eddie found the captain by simply squinting into the light and picking out his silhouette from the dawn sun.

Dawn? thought Eddie as the light of the bright morning sun seared his senses and left red blobs in his field of vision as he tried to get used to the sudden radiance. He reminded himself that the sun rose at about 5am in September, so an audience with his boss right now was probably important and needed his attention – it also, and probably more importantly, meant he was in trouble again. Captain Johnson, in full combat kit, was standing there with his SLR[5] rifle held vertical, the barrel pointed at the ground aligned down one side of his body. He held it, almost nonchalantly, with his right hand cupped under the magazine with his other hand on his hip. He looked Eddie up and down and then addressed him in that crisp Sandhurst voice favoured by Army officers.

'Christ in a tent, you're a bloody mess, McGee. What happened to you last night? Did some violated daughter's father catch up with you and beat the living shit out of you or something?'

'Er… Yes, sir! I think that was it, sir!' Eddie responded, keeping with the honoured Army tradition that officers are always right!

'They dip you in alcohol afterwards as well then, McGee? You stink like a real ale brewery,' the captain said, whilst with one hand he removed his officer's beret and pushed it back to scratch an imaginary itch all with the same hand, his beret held expertly between finger and thumb.

Eddie smirked and replied, 'It was purely medicinal to kill the pain, sir.'

The captain looked squarely at him and whilst expertly replacing his beret again one handed, said accusingly,

'That's bollocks, McGee, but if you're not packed up and in that Land Rover ready to move in thirty minutes then you'll need another effing dip. Now piss off and pack, you're leaving.' To reinforce his words, he pointed towards

---

[4] Ulster Defence Regiment – Local part time soldiers who supported the Police and Army on internal security duties.
[5] Self-Loading Rifle – Issued rifle of the British Army at the time. Quite heavy it fired a 7.62mm round that stopped *anyone* if hit by it.

the long wheelbase olive green Land Rover he had arrived in that was now parked in the open area opposite the Operations Room. Eddie also noticed that Brian, obviously his replacement signaller, had already unloaded all his military paraphernalia and was leaning against the *Makrolon*[6] covered vehicle enjoying the spectacle of his half-dressed and, no doubt, half cut performance.

The captain then gestured to Brian to follow him across the small open area behind the police station, an area made up of odd bits of concrete apron and tarmac that was broken and cracked, to the Ops Room to introduce him to 7 Platoon's Commander as their new addition. At the same time Eddie stumbled away and ducked back into his special diminutive portion of Hell. Eddie considered going back to bed for twenty-five minutes and then use the remaining five to pack. However, Captain Johnson's reputation for getting his boot entangled in a squaddie's lower rectum when really pissed off, persuaded him that perhaps he should just pack up and get on with it. At that moment, the small door to his cell-like hovel was pushed open to reveal the Platoon Sergeant bearing a mug of tea. Eddie was surprised.

'Fuck me, Sarn't that was decent of you.' He took a tentative sip of the hot, brown coloured nectar, it was strong and sweet. 'Lovely cuppa!' he exclaimed.

The sergeant looked a little embarrassed and confessed,

'Well, Eddie, I felt it was the least I could do as you've brought me one almost every morning in my maggot for the last couple of months here. Any idea where you're off to?'

'Probably the pokey[7] at Ballykelly but I have no idea what I've done wrong,' said Eddie defensively.

'Well it's nothing we've said, Kermit. Good luck anyway and get word to us as soon as you know what's happening, okay?' He put out his hand and Eddie shook it.

The tea seemed to do the trick and thirty minutes later he was shaved and dressed in his kit with all his gear ready to go. This included his SLR rifle which was loaded up with the statutory magazine of twenty rounds. Whilst he was waiting by the Land Rover for Captain Johnson to return, a couple of the lads from 7 Platoon ambled up; the word was out that he was leaving so they all exchanged handshakes and the odd manly hug with him. In the usual manner of the Army they all told him he was useless and a waste of space

---

[6] Makrolon was a Polycarbonite resin shell that covered the vehicle to protect it from small bombs and small arms fire. It was very heavy.
[7] Pokey is the Gaol on an Army camp managed by the local Regimental Police

amongst a welter of swearing and expletives. The unstated message was that he was a mate and they'd miss him.

The Platoon Commander left the Ops Room and walked over to where Eddie was waiting. He had, coincidentally, also been Eddie's first Platoon Commander about three years earlier when Eddie had started off as a Junior Leader at Oswestry. When they got to Northern Ireland the officer had specifically requested Eddie as his signaller at Maghera based on his past experiences with him. The young officer stopped and looked him up and down approvingly then said in his posh Surrey accent,

'Farewell, young McGee and thanks for your efforts here. Here is a small token from the platoon to remember us by. You'll always be a friend of 7 Platoon and don't you forget that.'

The Platoon Commander handed him a single *Mars Bar* and then shook his hand in farewell. Eddie took the *Mars Bar* looked at it and almost lost his poise. In IJLB on their first ever expedition, a trip up Mount Snowdon, the young lieutenant had completely forgotten his own ration's haversack. Eddie had noticed that he had not eaten anything and knew he must have been starving. Once at the top Eddie offered him the *Mars Bar* from his own haversack stating he didn't like chocolate. The officer had paused and without much enthusiasm accepted it and seemed ungrateful. A few weeks later back in Oswestry the officer, unknown to Eddie, was some way behind him in the Post Office queue when he bought four *Mars Bars* amongst the Post Mistress' observations that perhaps Eddie was eating far too many of them. It seemed the Platoon Commander had not forgotten his small gesture of kindness many years before.

Eddie said his farewells and amongst much heckling got into the back of the Land Rover whilst the driver was revving it up ready to leave Maghera Police Station. Eddie had been there month on, month off for about eight months. He was, until a few moments earlier, their platoon signaller and had spent long eighteen hour days working in the small Operations Room using radios and such like. The problem was that due to this he was very unfit plus he was about two stone overweight and at almost nineteen years old, for an infantryman, that was nothing to be proud of.

He looked out of the back of the vehicle and up at the clear blue sky and sensed that today would be another scorcher like most of the summer of '76 had been. He could already feel the strength of the sun and it was only 6am. Once settled he was still uncomfortable in the dim interior of the Land Rover, with his SLR rifle placed across his lap whilst wearing the customary flak jacket that now felt unfamiliar and heavy.

The two escorts accompanying the captain were now leaning out of the back of the Land Rover with their SLR rifles at the ready to scan the area for baddies which, to be honest at that time of the day, was unlikely. The Land Rover moved off and drove through the gates turning left onto the road for Ballykelly. As it turned it swayed wildly due to the weight of the *Makrolon* shell designed to protect the vehicle from the worst of blast bombs and low velocity bullets. After a while of coaxing, the ancient Land Rover was eventually going at breakneck speed along the main road in the direction of Ballykelly. Above the whine of the engine, the road noise and wind, Eddie had to ask a question. He shouted,

'Sir, not wishing to be nosey or anything, but is there any chance of being told where I'm going? Am I in the shit again? I don't recall doing something really seriously illegal or anything like that recently, sir.'

'Oh!' said Johnson half turning around in the front passenger seat, smiling but also shouting. 'I think it's fair to state that you're in the shit as you so gracefully put it.'

'Any chance of letting me know what I've done, sir?'

'You're off to join the elite, the dogs' bollocks, McGee. You're off to Ballykinler!' The captain said it as if it was some mythical place of pleasure and something that Eddie would be pleased to know like a utopia for soldiers with poor drink habits. Personally, he'd never heard of the place.

'Ballykinler, is that some new nick or something, sir?' asked Eddie, a note of panic in his voice.

'No! Calm down,' the captain said, still shouting to defeat the racket in the Land Rover.

'You're off to join the NIPG, Clarke broke his leg during final training and we've had a look at the Signals Platoon and you're the only one suited to go.'

Eddie was absolutely gobsmacked.

Oh shit! Eddie thought. *The NIPG!*

The original five guys that had been chosen to go to the NIPG had been superbly fit even before they started the demanding SAS type training in preparation to go there. They had been training to join the NIPG for about three months now. Hard, twenty mile runs up and down small mountain ranges with fifty-pound large packs, full webbing with rifle, and other paraphernalia, type training. The closest he had gotten to that recently was lifting cans of Tenants lager from the bar to the nearest table in the UDR club. Even doing that he started to become weary close to the end of the evening to the point, it was occasionally known, that his legs would buckle. He passed a worried glance over the Land Rover bulkhead towards Captain Johnson, who was looking back at him with some amusement.

'Don't worry too much, young McGee, remember they can't shoot you and they can't give you a baby, even if they did you don't have to love the little bastard, so calm down, you'll be okay.'

'Permission to shoot myself, sir, to save them the hassle of course, not to mention the pain?' he retorted.

'Permission denied, now shut the fuck up or I'll shoot you myself.' The captain turned around and faced the direction of travel indicating that the matter was closed. The officer then turned to the driver and suggested that some music might be a good idea. Suddenly *The Who*, competing with the engine and road noise, iconically blasted out *We Won't Get Fooled Again*.

As the music played Eddie pondered the captain's kind offer and in doing so his body recalled the fragile condition that it was already in. So, despite the music volume and the noise of the Land Rover he leaned his body against the hard case of the C42 radio next to him and dozed off into a welcome, if troubled, sleep.

Eddie was a soldier, almost nineteen years old and still not quite grown up. His 5'9" frame was broad but over the last few months he had put on more than a few extra pounds due to sitting about with radios doing little physical activity. He was from Southampton with a strong local accent that always gave away Hampshire as his place of origin. Eddie had joined the Army, like most others, for the simple expedient of getting himself away from his home as soon as possible. The crushing poverty he had lived in whilst being looked after by a barely functioning schizophrenic mother, together with the physical abuse he suffered at the hands of his usually drunk and violent alcoholic Irish father, was telling in his blue eyes if you looked closely enough. It's not surprising as his formative years were spent looking after a sibling six year his junior, playing truant and shoplifting for food. His specialty was stealing lead or copper from old houses and then selling it to dodgy looking characters in scrap yards. But his bubbly and cheeky humour often meant that the damaged, deep and introvert boy inside the young man remained hidden and often slightly wary.

Eddie had seen a lot for a nineteen year old. He had joined the Army as a

Junior Leader at the age of fifteen having already, at his father's insistence, illegally worked on a building site from the age of fourteen. Since that tender age he had learnt a lot about the art of killing, soldiering and survival, although thankfully had not had any opportunity to apply what had been taught yet in earnest. He had lost his virginity tackily to a reasonably cheap Hong Kong prostitute during his first posting just after reaching the age of seventeen and a half. So, although experienced in many aspects of life he was still naïve and needed guidance in many others. Despite all this the teenager with the black plastic NHS glasses and short mop of brown hair slept heavily, considering the music, the road noise plus the number of bumps and jolts the Land Rover suffered on the journey.

He was abruptly woken by the vehicle bouncing up and down whilst negotiating the sleeping policemen embedded in the road in front of Ballykelly Camp. This was an unused military airfield that was inhabited by a large variety of differing Army units, only one of which could actually fly! Simpson, the driver, turned off the music and stopped the Land Rover by the Guardroom; a wooden single-storey building that looked like it had cheated the laws of time and space and had appeared suddenly from some tropical location from the old British Empire, complete with verandah. There the driver dropped off the captain and the two escorts. The escorts quickly and without fuss disappeared into the Guardroom eager to get some much deserved scoff and a cup of tea but the captain hung back and attracted Eddie's attention, who was now wide awake. Captain Johnson walked to the rear of the Land Rover and peered into the dark interior to discover Eddie peering back.

'Well farewell, young McGee and good luck. I'll see you when you get back from your tour of duty with the NIPG.'

Eddie said nothing but continued to stare back at the captain like a rabbit caught in the headlights of a speeding fifty-ton articulated truck. Johnson leaned on the side of the Land Rover's rear entrance created by the *Makrolon* where the rear tailgate should have been. He looked Eddie square in the face, and said conspiratorially,

'Kermit, go with it! We didn't put you forward for this without thinking about it.' He put out his hand and Eddie took it and they shook hands.

'I know you'll do us proud and we'll see you in just over a year's time.' He paused for a moment and then continued thoughtfully with a hint of menace in his voice.

'Of course, if you don't make it and they send you back, then remember that the hell of Selection with these guys is as nothing to what I can do with you in one hour with a rugby ball and a minimum amount of *Vaseline.*'

The gleam in his eye indicated that he may have meant it.

God knows what they put Public Schoolboys through, Eddie thought.

Eddie had been, on the few occasions he turned up, a comprehensive school pupil and from that point forward very thankful of it. The captain waved a fond farewell and then briskly walked away like a man on a mission. Rob Simpson, the Land Rover driver and a chap Eddie knew quite well from his past life in Hong Kong suggested that they drive to breakfast. He, having been up an hour and a half before Eddie, was hungry. Eddie suddenly realised he was starving himself and readily agreed, and after unloading his weapon at the loading/unloading bay he jumped into the front passenger seat like an armed robber during a getaway and off they both went.

Now that the captain had left, Rob using one hand, whilst steering the aging Land Rover with the other, lit up a cigarette and changed the music cassette for the short trip down to the cookhouse. Marvin Gaye singing his opus *Heard It through the Grapevine,* oozed smoothly out of the speakers as Eddie, not for the first time, pondered and worried about the NIPG and his future. Rob just pondered breakfast.

Army cookhouses are a very little appreciated art form. It's quite amazing but the only place a squaddie never needs directions to regardless of which barracks or camp they are at is the cookhouse. It exerts an aura, a magical sense of presence that all squaddies can detect instantly from the first day they join up. It cannot be explained. But to test the theory, ask any ex-soldier where a cookhouse was on any posting that they were at. They will respond with unerring accuracy as to where it was, the way in, the hot plate, how meals were served, the texture of the sausages etc. Then ask them where their pay office was, no idea! It's vague, like a tax office, we all have one but where is it? God alone knows.

Illegally they parked the Land Rover outside this temple to military cuisine and they ambled in. The familiar smell of burnt cooking oil, mothballs and body odour hit them as they grabbed some well-worn cutlery and plates whilst taking their place in the queue which, at six thirty in the morning, was not very long. After a short wait, they were soon shuffling along the front of the hot plate picking at the delights on offer whilst poking fun at Cooky Ellis, the Duty Cook that morning. Cooky was average height and, like most army cooks, slightly overweight. Cooky always looked and sounded miserable with his

Brummy accent emphasising his quite naturally pessimistic view on life. His whites had long lost that description and even up close he resembled one big grey shadow of depression. Everything allegedly edible was drowning in a slow-moving sea of grease. Taking a slice of bacon was like saving a writhing seagull stuck in crude oil on some polluted beach somewhere in the south of England. Cooky was perhaps the worst cook in the world let alone the Army. There were pygmies on islands in the deep depths of the Amazon Delta living on a staple diet of raw insects who could instinctively produce better fare for 650 men on a Bunsen burner than Ellis could using a whole Army kitchen. The refreshing part was that Cooky knew this.

'Call these sausages, Cooky? Poor fucking pig must have hitched hiked to the knacker's yard in shame,' observed Simpson whilst looking in amazement at a tray of sausages that were burnt on one side and almost raw on the other.

'No, I don't, arse face; they're shit on a stick fried in horse spunk as recommended by Mrs. Beeton. I would recommend, as a suitable accompaniment, the Chateau Tea de la Bromide over there to go with it,' he said, pointing his little finger limply towards the tea urns.

'Sorry I asked,' replied Simpson suspiciously eyeing the fried eggs that were moving about the hotplate apparently under their own volition.

'So am I,' sniffed Cooky.

'So how do you get the horses' spunk then, Cooky?' shouted another soldier as he swamped his meal in a mixture of baked beans and tinned tomatoes.

'Don't be fucking stupid,' the alleged chef responded dismissively. 'The RQ[8] gets it in bottles marked 'Horses' Spunk',' he said, whilst holding up both hands, his fingers acting like punctuation marks. Then he continued, 'Anyway, that's what it says on the label. Though I've often wondered what he does of an evening and he does smell of horses now and again,' he added, his face feigning a questioning look.

'That's his wife, hairy with a long snout and all teeth; she does have a funny smell,' said another voice at the back of the queue. They all laughed.

'Fair enough, but I just cook it. I don't know where it comes from.'

Cooky turned away and busied himself with another portion of something or other to terrorise the troops with. It was said that if Cooky Ellis was sent to the Maze Prison to cook for terrorist prisoners there, the threat of losing liberty would pale into insignificance against the prospect of spending years eating his

---

[8] Regimental Quartermaster.

food. The mere thought of this would scare terrorists so much that the 'Troubles' would end immediately. Then again, perhaps the appropriate authorities did threaten that, causing a hunger strike that removed the Government's responsibilities for certain well-known Republican terrorists whose deaths were distinctly linked to food, or lack of it.

The breakfast, once eaten and washed down with a cup of allegedly Bromide laced tea, was a good foil to the night of alcoholic abuse that Eddie had put himself through the previous evening; he was beginning to feel human again. Eddie and his companion paused for a short while and chatted to catch up with the local gossip whilst they both enjoyed another mug of tea. Eventually they left the cookhouse and Simpson drove him to his block in the lower part of Ballykinler Barracks and dropped him off. They wished each other a fond, if manly, farewell. Then Rob disappeared in a cloud of fumes, dust and crunching gears with the faint sound of Teddy Pendergrass whining about lost love almost undetectable amidst the clamour.

Shackleton Barracks, better known locally as Ballykelly Camp, was an ex RAF airfield that was made up of two distinct parts called Upper and Lower. These were about a mile or so apart. The barrack itself was a nice posting, going by Northern Ireland standards, apart from the fact that the place was huge. In the block Eddie found his bed space and unlocked his locker, a steel wardrobe that housed all his worldly goods. He felt a bit uncomfortable as it was eerie being in the room on his own, generally there was another twenty or so squaddies in the room bantering, swearing and playing loud music from four or five different hi-fi systems, all playing different songs of course. The silence made the room feel eerie as he sensed the presence of the legions of grey and khaki draped souls that had passed through this block over the fifty or so years that the place had existed. In front of these ghostly witnesses he quietly packed what he felt he needed for his upcoming sojourn with the NIPG.

The NIPG was a platoon sized outfit based in Ballykinler near Belfast that undertook secret 'sneaky beaky' type operations. The acronym stands for Northern Ireland Patrol Group, although some wag had suggested that they should be called the 'Poor Man's SAS' and in the military way of things the name had stuck. It was quite an honour to be chosen to join them. The Army would prefer the term 'volunteer', but Eddie did not seem to recall volunteering. The difficult part was that potential members were expected to be at the peak of physical fitness on joining as there was an arduous selection process to suffer. Each regiment that was on an eighteen month tour of the Province had to send five soldiers of which one would be sent back as reserve in case something happened to one of the four that were chosen. Eddie felt that the reserve slot would almost certainly be him as he was far from his physical peak, rather a trough. A trough, he feared, so bad that it was similar to the valley in the Himalayas between Everest and the next nearest peak. He felt that all his effort over the next several weeks would probably be a waste as he would almost certainly end up back at his regiment as the odd one out.

All at once he was ready to go with his shabby army issue suitcase, green sausage holdall, '58 pattern webbing & large pack with his SLR. He stumbled out of the block and waited as directed by the side of the road, looking like an armed itinerant bagman, for the transport to turn up. Eventually an olive green *RL Bedford* four-ton truck, gushing huge amounts of diesel fumes, approached him. It clunked down through its gears, its engine complaining and wailing, then stopped opposite him creaking and swaying on its high suspension. A corporal, a member of the RCT[9] as his cap badge announced, was sitting in the passenger seat in the cab. He stopped reading whatever was in his lap, lowered his window and looked down at him and then in a voice that sounded completely apathetic asked a simple question.

'Ballykinler?'

'Yep, that's what I've been told anyway,' Eddie responded.

'Best jump on then, all the other victims are already in the back,' and with that he slowly wound up the window and went back to whatever he was studying.

Eddie, with some struggle, pulled all his kit round to the back of the truck and started to pass it up to the guys sitting nearest the tailgate. They reached down and helped him to load it amongst a backdrop of jangling chains, clunks and bangs. After he had thrown his kit up to them he then heaved himself up the rear of the truck until level with the tailgate. Looking more like a three-toed sloth than a trained killer, he eventually and red faced from effort fell over the tailgate and into the back of the truck. For a long moment, the other passengers thought he was going to perish from the exertion, so did Eddie!

'What in the name of Beelzebub's bollocks are you doing here, Kermit?' asked Kevin, a short wiry man with curly black hair. Kevin was the kind of bloke you should never pick a fight with. Extremely physically fit he looked

---

[9] Royal Corp of Transport (or sometimes Rickshaws, Cabs and Taxis).

like an armed bank robber wearing ladies' tights over his head even though he wasn't. Many unsuspecting and larger men had fallen foul of this genuinely hard man who, after an initial and unsuccessful career as a professional boxer and bouncer, had escaped some shit hole in Stoke-on-Trent to join the Army. He was from Drums Platoon; he was one of the two in the Regimental Band who played the tenor drum and could be seen whirling their white pom-pom style drumsticks all about the place over their heads during parades whilst managing to not knock themselves out - very artistic! He had earned the nickname Gus, which was short for 'gusset' and was apparently prompted by his endearing compulsion to sniff the gusset of ladies' panties, obviously worn ones. Apparently, he had quite an impressive collection.

'Oh, nothing much, Gus, just off to join the fucking NIPG I'm told,' replied Eddie. Then he paused for a moment and added sarcastically, 'What are you doing here?'

Kevin gave him a look and Eddie's blood went cold thinking perhaps he'd gone too far and that Kevin would throw him off somewhere between here and Ballykinler. But Kevin unexpectedly lightened up and announced to all,

'You'll be pleased to know that we're all off to join the NIPG.' Kevin said this with an air of innocence whilst ignorant of the fact that he was stating the obvious.

'Fuckin' God help you, mate,' he added looking at Eddie, 'you're gonna need it if you find it this hard to get onto a bleedin' truck.'

Kevin introduced him to the others. There was Steve, this small group's commander and, by the grace of God, corporal in Her Britannic Majesty's Armed Forces (Army). Eddie had never encountered him this close before, but he was considered by some to be a bit weird. He had dazzling blond hair that was almost white, of medium build with a face that can only be described as 'questioning'. Very well-educated, it was always said that he should have been an officer but had socialist leanings that made his conscience preclude that option. He enjoyed ambushing unsuspecting officers who expected corporals to be thick. He loved quoting Shakespeare and Kipling and that kept the higher echelons nicely off balance. He treasured a small clump of hair at the base of his neck that he was constantly being told to shave off, but he always refused stating that it was in fact part of his chest hair. He greeted Eddie.

'Welcome to the team, Eddie. I know it was short notice, but Clarke broke his leg during training. We needed a replacement signaller and it looks like you got the job. We weren't sure we were actually going to get anyone.' He looked and sounded like a very enthusiastic vicar during a church fete. Eddie understood now why, generally behind his back, they called him 'The Pope'.

'I'm only too happy to be here when I could be sat on my arse in Maghera with sod all to do,' Eddie replied, a touch sarcastically.

The corporal continued, 'Well, as Kipling would have said it's "to the Legions of the lost ones, to the cohort of the Damned". I've heard a lot about you, Eddie and I hope that most of it is *not* true' He emphasised the 'not' like an infant school teacher telling little boys *not* to pee in the swimming pool.

Christ! thought Eddie, whilst hoping his latest boss wasn't a God botherer or something even worse.

The corporal pointed to another guy near the back of the truck barely visible in the gloom.

'Meet Pete, Pete is from B Company'

Eddie peered into the half-darkness and was greeted by a huge face smiling back at him.

'Hello, Eddie, pleased to make your acquaintance, I'm Pete. Medic in the section.' This was said in a deep melodious West Country tone. Eddie mentally noted that with a guy this big, he'd call him anything that Pete wanted him to call him and no questions asked. Pete must have been 6' 4" in his bare feet, seventeen stone and not an ounce of fat anywhere. A huge hand came up out of the darkness and Eddie shook it. Eddie was expecting a bone crushing engagement but was amazed at how tenderly he shook hands almost knowing that he could break Eddie's fingers at a whim. Eddie was grateful.

'A pleasure, Pete,' replied Eddie to the brown-haired giant sitting in the darkness.

He looked across the truck to a thin and very tall chap sitting by the tailgate, another one whom Eddie had never before met. Steve introduced him.

'This is Leather; he's the sniper of the team and 2ic[10] of the section'

'Pleased to meet yer, Kermit' he greeted Eddie in a blatant East End of London patois and Eddie reached out his hand. His actual name was Les and he was generally regarded as one of the best shots in the Brigade. He had even won medals at Bisley, the shrine of competition shooting. Les shook Eddie's hand whilst he went on.

'Came 'ere from Z Company, Mortar Platoon. Are you lookin' forward to the NIPG, Eddie?'

---

[10] 2ic – Second in Command of the section

'Not really sure I exactly know what the hell the NIPG is. I was only informed by Eddie Johnson at 5am this morning'

'Well, the less you know the better or you'd be off this truck in a second, mate, especially carrying all those pies, my son.' He poked Eddie lightly in the stomach and smiled sympathetically. Eddie looked at Les with his thin frame and found it hard to believe he was in Mortar Platoon. They were usually huge guys with very broad shoulders who carried loads of heavy equipment everywhere. In fact, the definition of a Mortarman was 'something to hang kit on'.

'Is it too late to just fuck off back to Maghera?' asked Eddie in a bit of a panic to nobody in particular.

As if to imply the answer the four-ton truck started up, stuttered a bit and then lurched off in the direction of the camp gates. The moment was gone, and he was now off to Ballykinler and apparent despair.

UK, Oswestry - September 1972 – First Ten Minutes in the Army

The blue train with white stripes had seen better years. The British Rail 'Sprinter', a contradiction in terms if ever there was one, entered Gobowen train station amidst a cacophony of howls, engine noise, brakes, creaks and squeaks, until it came to an eventual slow and grinding halt, its diesel engine thumping out a monotonous dour tune. Eddie, barely fifteen years old, hurriedly collected his few belongings and literally fell out of the train. He had travelled from Southampton to join the Infantry Junior Leaders Battalion (IJLB) in Oswestry, a very small town nestling in the Shropshire countryside that only came to life on a Wednesday when the sheep market took place. It nestled to the east side of the Berwyn Hills just outside of the border with Wales, a place in which Eddie would be spending a lot of time over the next two years. Eddie, looking for directions with luggage in tow, ambled up to a 6' 6" regimental sergeant major, his mandatory wood and brass pace stick perfectly balanced under his left armpit. He was resplendent in his immaculately pressed No.2 dress uniform wearing a string of medals with a Sam Browne [11] across his chest. His boots were so well bulled with polish you could see your entire reflection in them; he was the very embodiment of British military drill and discipline. Eddie stopped, looked up at him and asked innocently,

' 'scuse me mate, but I'm supposed to be meeting a bus or summat here to take me to some place called Ozwestree, ya know it?'

The sergeant major stopped his slow evenly paced walk, stunned as if struck by an unseen laser that gave the victim a moment of intense pain. His head quickly swivelled around until it was aligned with the direction of the question and then his face slowly angled downwards until Eddie slid into his field of vision just below his immaculate slashed peak cap. He spoke slowly and deliberately with a deep West Country accent.

'Did you just call me mate?' The whisper was barely audible and Eddie missed the unspoken threat.

'Eh? Yeah, mate...we do that a lot in Suhfamten.'

The sergeant major moved swiftly and before Eddie knew it, had pushed the sharp end of his beautifully polished pace stick up Eddie's nose and kept

---

[11] Sam Browne is the brown leather strap that goes across the chest with the accompanying waist belt. Designed to hold a sword if worn.

pushing until Eddie was on tip toe. For the next few moments all Eddie could see was a huge gaping cavern with teeth around the edges topped with a thin moustache.

'LISTEN TO ME YOU FUCKING BRAINLESS ARSE WIPE, MY NAME IS REGIMENTAL SERGEANT MAJOR HADFIELD OF THE GRENADIER GUARDS AND YOU WILL REFER TO ME AS 'SIR' WHENEVER YOU ADDRESS ME, WHENEVER YOU TALK ABOUT ME, EVEN IF YOU ARE FUCKING CURSING ME OR STICKING PINS IN MY FUCKING UGLY EFFIGY YOU WILL STILL REFER TO ME AS 'SIR'. WHEN YOU WRITE HOME TO THAT WHORE YOU CALL A MOTHER COMPLAINING ABOUT ME, YOU WILL RESPECTFULLY REFER TO ME AS 'SIR'! WHEN YOU WRITE MY NAME, YOU WILL SPELL IT CORRECTLY. PLUS, EVEN WHEN YOU'RE LOSING YOUR FUCKING VIRGINITY TO THE MOST STUPID AND GROTESQUE WOMAN IN EXISTENCE YOU WILL STILL NEVER LET IT LEAVE THAT PIECE OF BIRD SHIT IN YOUR STUPID FUCKING HEAD THAT I AM TO BE REFERRED TO AS 'SIR' AT ALL TIMES. DOOO YOOOUUUU FUCCKINNGG UNNDERRSTTANNNNDD ME?'

Eddie's face was literally dripping from the amount of spittle that had forcibly accompanied the words. His eyes were wide with fear; he gulped, wiped his face and said automatically without thinking,

'Sorry, mate!' The RSM pushed even harder with his stick and Eddie added alarmed,

'Argh! Sir, sorry, sir!'

The RSM looked scornfully down at him as if he was some form of disgusting insignificant insect that had been discovered scuttling around in a dog's turd. This, coincidentally, is exactly how Eddie felt.

'NOW FUUUUCK OFFFF!'

The interview was over and with a dismissive gesture of the pace stick Eddie was thrown off in contempt. Eddie staggered away to the station exit dragging his bags forlornly behind him. Luckily, he soon found the required green Army truck with a young corporal sitting near the tailgate accompanied by about twenty other shiny faced new recruits. Eddie was invited to climb up. Once on board the corporal gently touched Eddie on the shoulder, pointed at the RSM and said,

'I see you've met Tiny Hadfield then.'

'Yes, sir!' said Eddie immediately whilst rubbing his still bleeding and sore nose.

'No, lad, you call me corporal, not sir. Don't worry you'll get the hang of it, did he shout at you at all?'

'Eh? Yes! He was very keen that I should call him sir, Corporal, sir.'

'He would, lad, he is in the Guards, and they're all fucking tick tocks and a bit barmy. You were lucky lad, that one's alright.'

At that the lorry burst into life and started moving to take Eddie to a new life. The corporal continued, almost to himself, 'All the rest are right nasty shits.'

Chapter 2

A Whole New Level of Torment

Ballykinler, N.I., September 1976

The trip to Ballykinler wasn't long, just a few hours. It was situated below Belfast on the coast close to the seaside town of Newcastle. After an uneventful trip the truck announced its arrival and woke up its occupants by bouncing over the ubiquitous sleeping policemen. It drove through the main gates and, as expected, stopped by the Guardroom. The driver came around the back of the dilapidated *Bedford RL* four tonner and pronounced the evident observation that they had arrived and helped to lower the tailgate. The passengers pulled out their various bags, weapons, military gear and any other tackle they had and placed it all onto the veranda. Once unloaded, and to their astonishment, the truck immediately turned around and was gone in what seemed a blink of the eye. Eddie now knew how one of Cortez's men must have felt looking at the burning ships in the New World as the back of the truck, engine still howling with its exhaust belching fumes, rapidly disappeared through the main gate.

At that time, the regiment installed at Ballykinler as resident Battalion for the area was The Black Watch, the First of Foot, a famous Scottish highland regiment with an illustrious history and an impressive reputation. Steve and Les infiltrated the Guardroom whilst the rest of them lounged about outside trying not to look too conspicuous. The duty Regimental Policeman, dressed crisp and smart with all the right creases in all the right places, with his brown Tam O'Shanter jauntily placed on his head, colourfully adorned with a red hackle, greeted them. It seemed all was going to plan. They were expected and subsequently they were directed to their accommodation, which was a huge oblong red brick building. Ballykinler Camp was built in the Victorian era and the barrack blocks looked depressingly like the workhouses of old, where down and out families laboured in misery.

'You talk o' better food for us, an' schools, an' fire's an' all,' muttered Steve to himself, remembering his beloved Kipling.

They crossed the road and ambled in the direction of the block identified as theirs carrying all their kit at the same time in a way only soldiers can. Suddenly their attention was grabbed by what can only be described as a very thunderous cry of pain somewhere behind them. It was so weird and loud that they stopped and looked around to see what it was. In an instant, they were set upon by a small, stout Scot who, by his appearance, could only have been none other than the Provost Sergeant himself, the man in charge of the Regimental Police in barracks. The 'Provo' as they were usually known was usually an older sergeant who by the sole virtue of staying as long as possible in the Army and, having successfully dressed themselves daily, had by some quirk of fate, been promoted beyond their level of competency by what some people may refer to as 'Peter's Principle'[12]. In the case of most Provost Sergeants, 'Peter's Principle' was somewhere close to newt or even amoeba. This specimen could only be described as a particularly thick example and quite probably newts and amoeba everywhere would be extremely insulted at any comparisons. Immediately he was in amongst them shouting and screaming whilst gesturing with his pace stick like a crazed pygmy warrior.

'Whaya deeing yer feyng curd bench of linys ya arhells nid tay knoo wha ya boot.'

They all fell silent as they had no idea what he was saying and so looked towards their leader for inspiration.

'Problem, Sarn't?' enquired 'The Pope' tentatively.

'Fickin probim? Yer stitin aboot a fickin pribim. Yu werd fickirs canya nay ba kne ya nay lood tay wk on a s.'

The corporal looked at Kevin for help as he could do an excellent impression of a Geordie but on this occasion, he was just as stumped as they all were.

'Sorry, Sarn't didn't quite get that, can we help at all?' The corporal's southern and well-spoken accent must have really grated on the hairy anthropological specimen that someone had placed into a kilt before them. He bellowed like a wounded bear and at such a high decibel that some famous tenors hundreds of miles away at the time were known to have resigned over the incident. The Provo made a special effort to speak some proper English so slowly he said,

---

12 'Peter's Principle' is where someone is promoted beyond his or her level of competency.

'Yaaar ferkan stooped begurs do ye knay ken ye no loed tea wik on the griss or sammat?'

Pete caught the last phrase and mumbled to the group that he thought the Provo was upset that they were walking on the grass. 'The Pope' apologised profusely and they then all sort of ignored the Provo, again picked up their kit and walked away towards the block. He was shouting and screaming still but they thought it best to move away before a crowd gathered, after all they thought who knows there could have been more of these types hanging about and they may be hungry.

Provo Sergeants may not be the sharpest tool in the Army's toolbox, but they do make for very nasty enemies in camp. This Provo Sergeant mentally marked their card, albeit badly spelt and in childlike writing, and would wait patiently for an opportunity for revenge.

The inside of the Army red bricked block was unremarkable and, like most Army camps, depressing, but they soon found a room with a sign on it indicating it was an NIPG space, so they strode in and commandeered it for themselves. The room was quite large by Army standards especially for five guys to share. It had colossal windows overlooking the square and the NAAFI[13]. Inside it had parquet flooring with emulsion painted walls in a kind of washed out depressing matt light blue. The lockers were the wooden sort and quite new, almost humane. They started to unpack their belongings and wondered what time tea was as they had missed lunch. In a flash, Les had set up a small stereo player and within minutes *Thin Lizzy* was playing their *Johnny the Fox* album at high decibels. Without warning the door crashed open and there, stood in the doorway, was a giant of a man who was giving a very good impression of being in charge. He was a good six feet and broad with it. This Olympian was dressed in green denim trousers and a white PT vest with his rippling muscles giving a strong hint that he was obviously extremely physically fit. Les hit the stop button on the cassette player allowing the Herculean God to introduce himself. In the ensuing silence Sergeant Major Bruce informed them that he was the Senior NCO[14] in the NIPG and as of this moment they were his to toy with. He went on to explain that he was running the selection process for the next six weeks and that it started right now! He wanted them outside in ten minutes in T shirts and denims ready for a run with

---

[13] Navy, Army & Air Force Institute – An organisation that delivered tea and buns historically to troops, so much so that all breaks were referred to generically as NAAFI breaks.
[14] Non-Commissioned Officer.

rifles and full webbing; he then turned and left the doorway thus allowing light back into the room.

They rushed about and got their kit together, which was difficult for Eddie as his webbing was still in bits. However, after a mild panic and still running around like headless chickens they all managed to get outside and onto the square in front of the NIPG office just in time. It was then that they first got sight of the other patrols who had been brought together to start the latest tour with the Group. There were patrols from the Argyle and Sutherland Highlanders, the 9th/12th Royal Lancers, the Gordon Highlanders and the Black Watch (who had provided 2 groups), plus themselves. Thirty five guys in all, now ready for a run. Eddie wondered to himself what haggis tasted like as with this many Scotsmen about he was sure he'd be confronted by it sooner or later. The sergeant major shouted for them all to fall in and to shut up, and they obeyed. He then gave one of those talks that they wished they'd never heard.

'RIGHT LISTEN IN, MY NAME IS SERGEANT MAJOR BRUCE AND I'M YOUR BOSS FOR THE NEXT SIX WEEKS DURING WHICH TIME WE ARE GONNA WEEDLE SEVEN GUYS OUT OF THIS GROUP. I'M NOT A NICE MAN AND I'M GOING TO MAKE YOUR LIVES FUCKIN' HELLISH. THE NIPG IS A REAL HONOUR TO BE A PART OF AND ONLY COMMITTED, FIT AND INTELLIGENT SOLDIERS ARE ALLOWED. OK, LET'S HAVE A WEE LOOK AT YOU ALL THEN.'

With his formal introduction over he then came along the ranks asking names and checking the soldiers' webbing to see if they had enough kit in them. As he got closer, Eddie became aware of the fact that CSM Bruce was carrying in his webbing enough weight that it must have been close to that of a small hospital and that most of his own pouches were in fact empty. The CSM tested Les' webbing and gave a satisfactory nod. Les probably had half the contents of their room tucked away in his webbing just in case he needed a change of clothes or a wash in a proper sink. The CSM didn't speak much to him and Eddie concluded that his East End vernacular had defeated the muscle-bound Scottish six-footer.

The CSM winced as he got to Steve and asked him to empty his webbing for inspection as it felt a bit light. Steve assured the CSM that everything needed was indeed in his webbing. The CSM insisted and Steve showed him everything. After checking everything the CSM had to agree that all that was needed was indeed hidden somewhere in the few pouches that Steve had attached to his webbing. He indeed had everything. He looked Steve up and down.

'Are you that Doctor Who chap on the telly?' he questioned.

'No, sir, just a close relation,' responded Steve. The CSM laughed emptily and called him a smartarse, then strongly suggested that Steve should shave off that clump of hair at the base of his neck. Then he turned to Kevin.

'What's in your webbing, laddie?' the CSM asked whilst looking down at him.

Kevin looked up and said brazenly,

'My full CEFO[15] kit plus my complete personal selection of ladies' soiled panties, sir.'

'Has it taken you long to collect them, son?' queried the Scotsman seriously, raising an eyebrow and tilting his head.

'About six years, sir,' said Kevin proudly.

'Indeed? I'm impressed. Would I be catching some exotic disease if I were to put my hand in there?' asked the CSM.

'It's possible, sir,' Kevin smiled in reply.

'Christ in a kilt! A fucking spaceman and a pervert, what's next?'

When he got to Eddie he asked him his name.

'McGee, sir!' Eddie replied. The CSM's face lit up.

'A good Scottish name thank fuck. Where's ya family from then, lad?'

Eddie winced as he replied,

'Eh! Dublin originally, sir!'

The CSM ignored the response and took a serious interest in Eddie's webbing. By the time he had finished it felt like he was carrying a small semi-detached house on his back. The CSM then announced, sounding somewhat exasperated,

'Fucking Dublin? I canna believe it. I prefer the pervert there!' he stated gesturing at Kevin before he moved on and started to weigh down the next guy with the weight of a small corner shop. Eventually, after everyone was weighed down with enough kit to keep Camden Market in profit for some weeks, the CSM looked satisfied. He faced everyone and bellowed,

'RIGHT TURN.'

'DOOOUUUBLLE MARCH!'

So, Eddie, after a few diversions and near misses in life, had at last finally arrived in Hell.

---

[15] Combat Equipment Fighting Order – Better known as 'webbing'.

The run was a simple one, four miles long, running and walking, and even in Eddie's rather fragile and ailing condition it would have been almost manageable. But there was a twist, Ballykinler was near the coast and it had its own private beach. This beach was all loose shale mixed with pebbles and gruelling to run on. The weather was also unbearably hot as the heat wave continued without compassion over the British Isles. Eddie was convinced that if he hung back and dragged his arse then this NIPG thing would be a short-lived affair and he'd be off on the next truck. But it was challenging to hang back when a six-foot shaved Silverback Gorilla of Olympic proportions, wearing a vest, was yelling obscenities in your ear at such volume and with such malice that Eddie was sure CSM Bruce would have simply preferred to drown Eddie in the sea to put him out of his misery. To Eddie it felt like fifty miles of sheer torment whilst he slithered and slipped on the shale whilst mentally descending to Dante's seventh level of Hell.

He was barely able to breathe, sweating heavily, believing that his heart was beating so hard it would burst out of his chest and flop about on the pebbles until it expired. However, the gods were not in a humour right now to assist and his heart unfortunately remained firmly inside his rib cage. Eventually and thankfully the run came to an end and Eddie, bent over double, stopped himself keeling over from exhaustion by the simple expedient of using Les and Pete on either side to hold him up. His vision was blurred but his hearing was perfect. The CSM, who didn't have even the lightest amount of sweat visible, addressed them for the second time that day.

'RIGHT YOU PUTRID LOAD OF FUCKING TUBES. THAT WAS JUST A SMALL TASTE OF WHAT'S TO COME. NEXT TIME IT WILL BE SIX MILES AND THE TIME AFTER THAT EIGHT UNTIL WE GET TO TWENTY MILES, SHOULDN'T TAKE MORE THAN A WEEK OR SO, EH?'

CSM Bruce smiled broadly. Eddie hated him already and suspected that the huge Scots bastard was doing this all for his sake. The huge Scots bastard continued and Eddie could perceive if not see that the CSM was definitely at his end of the squad and probably looking precisely at Eddie.

'Oh, and if anyone thinks they can be a bit slack and not try hard enough, please keep in mind that being RTU[16]'d only happens at the end of the selection and not during it. Anyone not up to snuff physically does extra

---

[16] Returned to Unit

exercise with me in the evening. FUCKING UNDERSTAND, EVERYBODY?' He was especially careful to emphasise the 'me' part.

'YES, SIR!' they all responded.

'I DIDNA HEAR YE!' shouted the CSM.

'YEESSS, SSIIIRR!' screamed the squad. The CSM looked at Eddie, who was still being held up by his muckers due to his legs being too weak to sustain him anymore. The CSM cocked his head to one side and said in almost a whisper,

'I couldn't hear you, young McGee! Do you need extra PT with me?'

Eddie just rolled his eyes before mumbling something short and unintelligible that rhymed with 'uck' and 'uff'. Steve spoke up for him.

'Private McGee has only just returned from an operational tour in Maghera and not quite ready for this, but I'm sure he'll come up to snuff, sir!' The CSM looked 'The Pope' in the face and said,

'Or snuff it, eh? Captain Johnson and I have discussed the McGee situation, Corporal and I am well aware of the current condition of young arse wipe here.' He gestured at the almost unconscious Eddie and continued, 'I just looovvve a challenge.' He looked away to address the entire squad.

'Right listen in! I want you all back down here with a combat jacket on over your current kit with full webbing on carrying your personal weapon. You have ten minutes. GOOOOO!'

They all disappeared. They already had their weapons and webbing from the run so all they had to do was get their jackets. Steve's group had the additional problem of Eddie. Les and Pete literally carried him upstairs, stripped him and stood him under a cold shower until he regained some animation. Eddie salvaged enough consciousness to be able to dress himself and to amble downstairs in his kit. He felt absolutely awful and in dire need of some rest. He was the last to arrive and as he shuffled into the squad Kevin passed him his rifle. Immediately, two olive green four-ton *Bedford* trucks appeared from around the corner, their canvas canopies flapping and cracking in the light breeze. They stopped in front of the soldiers with their engines idling and simultaneously a beaming CSM Bruce emerged from one of the cabs. In a voice of almost normal volume he addressed them.

'OK, we have a slight operational issue in that we believe PIRA [17] scumbags, thugs, dipsticks and the like are going to pick up some stuff tonight

---

[17] Provisional Irish Republican Army – Republican hard-line terrorists who thought the IRA had gone soft.

from a hidden arms' cache and we want you guys to observe the site and see if the players turn up. If they do you are to arrest or shoot the bastards so that the hard working, law abiding folk of this Province can rest assured that their taxes are paying dividends! Section Commanders on me for a full briefing, 2ics[18] to the stores to get kit and you can take the rest of your squad to assist. Back here in thirty minutes ready to deploy. MOVE!'

Steve doubled across to the CSM and Les took the rest to the stores as detailed.

'Shag a badger in a bleedin' sack, Leather, when's fucking grub time? I'm famished,' enquired Pete biting his nails.

'Bollocks if I know, mate, but let's crack on and get these stores sorted, they have to feed us eventually, eh?' said Les somewhat uncertainly.

Eddie was stumbling along aimlessly mumbling to himself almost in a daze. He seemed to be burbling something to express the fact that he was probably half dead and needed hospital treatment, but nobody cared. Then again, he might have been mumbling some ancient Irish curse that would render the CSM infertile or probably even worse. The rest couldn't figure it out, so they just carried on pulling him along in the right direction. They all arrived at the NIPG stores in a chaotic jumble but the storeman responsible for issuing the equipment was archetypal of the genre and was unflappable. Dressed majestically in his pressed and spotless green overalls the Colour Sergeant ordered, bossed and bullied them all about until they had enough kit to invade a third world nation. However, just prior to Les signing the dreaded AF G1033 Army form for the kit the 'Colour', as they were referred to, had something to say first.

'Right, this stuff is clean and works and I want it back in clean and working order. Now listen in as there is one thing I will say about everything you're signing for.' He placed great emphasis on the word *everything* and then went on.

'Every single bit of it is arse bustlingly expensive so don't lose anything. If you do it's a court of enquiry and a bill that means no paying for blow jobs or any other of the disgusting things you lot pay for, for the rest of your natural lives. Plus, and more importantly, I will personally beat you to death with your own testicles if you attempt to hand in dirty or broken equipment or tell me you've lost something.' He gestured to Les with a pen that had magically appeared in his hand and pointed at the form.

---

[18] Second in Command.

'Sign here.'

The rest of the squad all looked at Les admiringly with that, 'Thank fuck that's not me' look then got all the kit together and sped back to the block. It took them another ten minutes or so to pack the stores into their Bergens and they arrived back to the trucks just in time. The CSM surveyed them all for a few moments like a tyrant reviewing his minions, and then, seemingly satisfied, he spoke.

'Right, your NCOs will brief you whilst en route in the trucks. Off you go!' He paused for a moment and then added, 'WHAT THE FUCK ARE YOU LOT STILL HERE FOR? GO AWAY, DISAPPEAR, PISS OFF!' At that they all bounded away into the two trucks which then sped off towards the gate like two frenzied giant olive-green beetles. Inside the trucks each section huddled around its commander. Steve briefed his guys above the noise of the truck as did all the other NCOs. Steve had to shout to be heard above the din. To any pedestrian the trucks must have sounded like some passing riotous pub quiz on a Saturday night on wheels. Steve commenced his briefing.

'Listen in you lot, we're going out to watch a house where they think a cache of arms is being picked up tonight by some PIRA guys. If we see them with weapons or explosives we are to approach and arrest them. This is not an exercise as I have ten full mags of live ammo in my webbing, two each. That said I doubt anything will happen as we are doing it on the training area just adjacent to the camp. This is just a test to filter us out. We have to build full hides and watch the site for twenty-four hours. Any questions?'

'When do we get food? I'm hungrier than a China man with no chopsticks,' moaned Pete. This was agreed by all to be a very sensible question.

'Didn't you lot get the stores? Were there any rations there?' asked Steve. They all shook their heads in response. He paused and then said dismissively,

'Then we go hungry for a while,' and then speaking to himself he recalled his Othello and said quietly, '"they are all but stomachs, and we all but food, and when they are full, they belch us".'

Steve considered the conversation over as they sat quietly in the bouncing and veering truck waiting for it to stop. Eddie was asleep already, Les was cleaning his weapon and Pete was picking his nose and eating it whilst still biting his remaining nails. The truck dropped them all off as individual sections all over the area about three miles behind the camp. They all trudged off to where their own hide was to be dug and got on with it. They were not all that concerned with being tactical as they knew they were on an Army training area and the house they were looking at was derelict. Any self-respecting terrorist would not be stupid enough to hide its weapons on a busy Army training area.

The hide, once completed, was quite snug and they all got in. A hide was a trench about three or four feet deep and six feet long and about three feet wide with a step left in it to sit on. The length depended on the number of occupants and time. This one was not very long but they could all sit down in it. It would be covered to look exactly like the surrounding ground and would be well hidden with slits left for observation. You got in via a flap left in the back of the camouflage. If done properly it would be almost impossible to see it unless you were almost on top of the thing. But it was exhausting to dig and build especially if you wanted a good one.

Pete was the first to notice that they had not got any sleeping bags with them; he was sure that during early September in the wee hours of the morning it was going to get cold even if they were in a heat wave of tropical proportions. To make it extra uncomfortable they all realised they still had on only their PT shirts under their Combat Jackets that were now wet with sweat from the run earlier, apart from Eddie who had, due to almost becoming a statistic, completely dry kit on. All this and no food either. They were all starving, but morale was, with exception of Eddie who was already deeply asleep, fairly high.

They roughly woke Eddie up to set up the radio; it was a *Clansman PRC 320*, a HF model used for long distance communications, so talking three miles away would be a doddle. Eddie yawned and reached into the pouches at the back of the radio and pulled out not one, but two tins of Oatmeal Blocks, refugees from some past 10-man ration pack. Obviously, the last owner had left them in there.

'Anyone got a tin opener?' enquired Eddie innocently.

They all looked at Eddie in amazement.

'How the fuck did you do that, Kermit?' asked Pete.

'Well you know, I thought they'd do something like this, so I brought a little something with me,' boasted Eddie.

'But you've got no tin opener, eh? "Else Puck a liar called",' coyly quoted Steve reaching over for the tins.

'Good job I have one though!' said Les and passed it over. Steve opened one of the tins and worked out that as they had twenty blocks that meant four each. He rationed them two now and two for later.

They feasted on the two oatmeal blocks like men possessed and Pete looked at Eddie in gratitude, his nose was empty, and his nails had definitely been worn very low indeed. Les pulled out a brew kit from his webbing so they were also able to have a cuppa to warm them up. They set up a rota and three got their heads down for a while whilst two stayed awake and watched to see if anything developed. That was unlikely as they had live rounds and only an idiot would pretend to be an enemy at that time. They carried on this routine until 3am in the morning when over the radio they were told to bug out and go to the road and wait for the transport. Eddie was on the radio when the order to 'bug out' came in.

'Endex[19], guys,' stated Eddie matter-of-factly and added, 'they want us to fill in our comfy hole. Such a shame as I was quite getting to like it in here with you lot snoring and farting.'

'Well, we can always bury you here in this shitty hole if you want to stay that much. I doubt the CSM would miss you, doubt he'd even care if you were missing actually,' observed Les.

'Yes he would, Leather, he'd have no one else to piggin' pick on would he? Scots bastard is a bullying arsehole,' countered Eddie.

Kev, whilst getting out his entrenching tool to start filling in the hole made a suggestion.

'I think the CSM is a bit lonely and wants some love… I think he fancies you Kermit, and probably wants to give you a damn good shagging! I'd strongly suggest you get him a kitten or something cute before he drags you off and tries to fuck you, mate.'

'A kitten? Poor bleedin' kitten. First thing the CSM would do is wrap it in cling film a few times before shagging it to death,' Eddie said feigning sadness.

'Why would he wrap it in cling film, Kermit?' innocently queried Pete. Eddie looked triumphant as Pete had fallen into the trap.

'It's to stop the kitten bursting when he fucks it.'

They were all completely knackered, hungry and cold and they hadn't been in the NIPG for twenty-four hours yet! They filled in the hole, finished the last of the oatmeal blocks, tidied up and left the area as if there had never been a hide in that spot. They then moved close to the road and waited in all round defence. After a short wait a truck loomed out of the darkness and picked them up. Other patrols were in the truck and were asleep already. Steve's group, in

---

[19] End of Exercise.

the standard cloud of diesel fumes, got their kit onto the truck, dragged themselves on and sat down. They dropped off to sleep almost immediately, if not sooner!

The next thing they knew was that they were being woken up outside the NIPG HQ office block by the CSM shouting at them to get off the truck and to get into the classroom for a debriefing. Wearily they got their equipment together got off the truck and trooped into the block. They were told to place their equipment at the end of the room and to sit in one of the chairs provided. The CSM got their attention and for the next ten minutes he thoroughly berated them for their lack of professionalism, laziness and general poor attitude. He then told them to listen in as they now had to take in an important lesson. Any individual who fell asleep would get special PT training from the CSM immediately at the end of the lesson. At that they were all awake instantly whilst a bespectacled captain entered the room.

'SIT UP!' bellowed the CSM.

'Relax everybody, my name is Captain Smith from the Army Catering Corp and I am here today to introduce you to the intricacies of differentiating between a fried and a roasted potato.' They all looked at each other in some confusion as it was roughly 4am in the morning and it appeared they were about to be given some cooking lessons. He continued. 'This will be accompanied by pictures and diagrams of the subject matter...' He had droned on for about five minutes when Eddie was woken by the CSM's smiling face.

'It's PT for you at the end of the lesson, laddie,' the CSM informed Eddie with obvious delight.

At that point Eddie almost told the CSM where he could shove his beloved NIPG but Captain Johnson's remarks about rugby balls and lubrication sprung to mind and he suppressed his preferred response. The forty-minute lesson did indeed go into the subject in some depth, with pictures of both roasted and fried potatoes, hints on textures, smell and even some samples, that were not to be eaten of course, passed about. This was obviously just another test of character that they had to endure.

Les took notes and even asked questions and was thoroughly engaged by it but by the end of the lesson ten guys, who were more normal, had nodded off at various times. The CSM punished those that succumbed to the mortal requirements of sleep with a thirty minute PT lesson that was hard but not as hard as it could have been. Eddie did have a moment when he thought that perhaps the CSM did have some feelings after all.

By 5.30am in the morning they were all back in their rooms with the CSM's last remarks still ringing in their ears that, as they were all crap, they had to be back on parade at 7am for a run. This was especially cruel as they were all starving and breakfast did not start until 6am. They all decided to wait until after breakfast before sleeping as they were so tired they'd probably sleep through breakfast, so they sat down and tried to stay awake. However, they were only human and to their surprise Kevin woke all of them up at 6am as they had all, to a man, nodded off. It was appreciated that Kevin had a knack for waking up when he wanted to, and this would serve them well in the months ahead. Bleary eyed, tired and hungry they all went across to the cookhouse and each had a huge breakfast, no insults about the food and no banter; they were all too hungry to delay eating. They breakfasted and having washed it down with huge mugs of tea they all rushed back to the room. Steve made them get into their combats and PT vest then to get their webbing sorted out, so they'd be ready for parade. He set the alarm for 6.45am which gave them about ten minutes' sleep and in an instant, they were all snoring. The alarm clock did its duty and went off as directed. Initially nobody stirred until Les threw a boot at it. It was bang on and the alarm clock flew through the air hitting the wall and was immediately silent. No one was impressed as Les was a trained sniper. Pete roused them all five minutes later by playing *Santana's* epic *Black Magic Woman* on his stereo at full volume. After a quick shave and a wash, they were ready in their Combat trousers and PT vests with webbing on, standing outside waiting for the CSM. At precisely 06.55 the CSM strode into view.

'Good morning, gentlemen,' he crooned.

'GOOD MORNING, SIR!' they bellowed back.

'RIIIIGHT TUURRN, DOOUUUUBLE MAAARRCH!'

Off they went as one, wrenching Eddie up to another level of fatigue and misery. The run was hard for Eddie and, after about two miles he reacquainted himself with his breakfast and the oatmeal blocks in a spectacular multi-coloured yawn. Very soon after that he lost the will to live and had to be assisted by the rest of his squad. Pete was a dab hand at this, superbly fit and immensely strong, he kept Eddie up by the simple expedient of holding him by his webbing and pushing him along. However, on this occasion, it was done at arm's length just in case Eddie decided to commune with God again without the help of the usual big white porcelain microphone.

This technique went on for several days until Eddie found that he could actually keep up and after a few more days was running with the best of them. The PT in the evening also helped as the CSM took a distinct interest in Eddie and made sure he got the full benefit of his invective. However, the CSM slowly stopped picking on Eddie and eventually the two held a kind of grudging respect for each other.

The training and selection continued on and for the most part it was hard work but very interesting. They were learning SAS tried and tested techniques for rural and urban patrolling. They were shown how to hide away and see but not be seen, be it in a wood, field, an attic or even someone's garden. It all seemed magical. Dodgy looking people taught them the rudiments of picking locks and opening windows from the outside, plus many other burglary techniques to gain access to a building without setting off the alarm. They were also taught the skill of observation and how to expertly look at people and places to see and interpret what was really going on using body language and facial expressions. As for weapons, they had a lot of fun learning about a variety of unfamiliar ones. The L1A4 Light Machine Gun or 'Bren' as it used to be known. This was an updated version of the original WWII classic using 7.62mm calibre rounds and a straightened magazine. The weapon was favoured by Special Forces for this work as it was so accurate. Kevin fell in love with it the moment he saw it and became expert at using it. However, with these new weapons they all had to learn and become absolute experts at using all of them.

They also had a choice of keeping their SLRs or being issued with M16s. The M16 with a 5.56mm calibre was lighter and a lot shorter than the good old SLR. Pete and Steve went with the M16, but Eddie decided to keep his SLR although he made sure he was proficient using the M16 just in case. Eddie knew that if he shot someone with the SLR, the 7.62mm bullet made sure they were not going to get up again. Les already had his personal L42A1 sniper's rifle and Type 32 Scope with him but decided that he needed another weapon for close work and personal protection, so he opted to have a Remington 870 semi-automatic shotgun as well – he often pondered if he could use it for the odd armed robbery.

They were also introduced to the L79 Grenade Launcher, a veteran American piece of kit that was very popular during the Vietnam War. It fired 40mm grenade rounds and was very accurate up to about two hundred yards and with a real expert, out to three hundred. It was a great leveller and was a lot of fun on the range as they fired rounds filled with coloured chalk. Steve commandeered this as his own much to the chagrin of Kevin. But it was the best decision as all the rest already had enough weaponry to put a small private army to shame. Finally, all of the team were issued with their own personal Browning 9mm pistol, also known as a Hi-power. This was their personal protection weapon and they were to always carry it in the field, sleep with it and take it everywhere. It was also to be carried when they went out of an evening to Newcastle, a seaside town near Ballykinler, or wherever, on their time off out of barracks in the Province. They were also issued with 'under the arm' holsters and so they all felt a bit like James Bond when out on the town in civvies.

The training settled into a routine and they went along with it. Fitness training with heavier and heavier Bergens was a large part of the regime and was always done in the mornings. Specialist training then took place, constructing hides for use in rural and urban areas. Discovering how to hide in plain sight in the city using techniques pioneered by the SAS, MI5 and also 14 Independent Company. This was coupled with intense focus on zeroing their personal weapons and improving their shooting skills and accuracy so quite a few days were spent on the ranges. They were also introduced to a number of technical bits of kit for looking at stuff at night or at a distance such as NITECH and TELETRON. These bits of kit were so good it was possible to take pictures of people using a normal camera on very dark nights. They were also expected to be expert with detection and listening equipment called Unattended Ground Sensors or 'UGS' for short. This range of devices were designed and used successfully by the US Army during the Vietnam War. UGS had a whole range of toys that could listen, tell the temperature of passing things, detect motion or footfalls and therefore how many people were passing it and even tell the difference between a car, a lorry or a tank. If they were used together in co-operation with each other the operator could build up a very good picture of what was happening. Eddie became very adept at using UGS and very soon quite the expert. Further along a lot of time was taken teaching them photography and how to be effective both during the day and night. This was linked to give them skills in the use of very long and very powerful lenses until working with lenses of 1000mm focal length was familiar and not uncommon. It was hard work but fun and interesting.

In addition to being experts with all the new weapons plus their own advanced infantry techniques they also had to improve their own particular skill that the NIPG had taught them and to learn and be the backup in another. Eddie was nominated as UGS specialist along with radio communications and therefore an expert in HF and Morse code, but he was also expected to become an expert medic.

Kevin's speciality was photography and the use of lenses, film and the use of light but he was also expected to become an adept at Premises Access and Insertion or in common parlance 'Burglary'.

For Steve it was accepted that he would be expert at command, control and navigation but he was also expected to build a full and complete personal understanding of the various terrorist groups and the senior personalities involved. He also developed a very good understanding and was the back up for UGS.

Les, apart from his sniper skills was also second in command and charged with knowing all there was to know about hides, selection of a site and building them so they cannot be seen and was also to be as adept as Kevin at 'PAI'. As he was a sniper he also became almost as good as Steve with the M79 plus he was also Kevin's back up on the photography front.

Pete, already an experienced and qualified medic was charged with learning radio communications and voice procedure, so he worked with Eddie and was a willing and able student. Steve however, felt that all should have at least a basic knowledge of all these skills and pushed them hard to achieve that. In the coming months ahead, they'd need all of it!

Kowloon Hong Kong, April 1966 - Star Ferry Riots

Private Bruce was feeling the heat and the humidity as he stood in full riot gear carrying his rifle and wearing webbing. On completion of basic training three months earlier he had been badged to the 2nd battalion the Queens Regiment. His original choice of the Black Watch, his local regiment, was a long-gone dream. However, he had the good fortune to be posted to Hong Kong, and up to now had enjoyed a great time in the old British colony. But recently the locals had all started to riot due to the price of the Star Ferry going up by fifty percent. The Star Ferry was the cheapest ferry in the world and the smallish two decked ferries in their famous livery of green and white appear in many a tourist's photo album. They are also the main means for the locals to cross the harbour and even a small increase in price would have a large impact, so those same locals wanted people in authority to know that!

The trucks they had arrived in were left in a now abandoned and cordoned off Nathan Road. The men were formed up as a platoon with about 30 men ready to deal with the 300 or so rioters that they had been told were at that point attacking the Star Ferry terminal on the Kowloon side. Formed in a square they had a mixture of soldiers with shields and batons, rifles and two had a huge banner that would get unfurled that announced if the rioters did not desist in said threatening behaviour then the soldiers would fire at them, written in Cantonese of course.

The trick to disrupt a riot is to show total discipline as a fighting force. They dressed off and at the word of command from the Platoon Sergeant, Private Bruce and the rest of the platoon stepped off as one to the rhythmic beat of the front rank banging their shields aggressively with batons. They wheeled right into Salisbury Road looking like they were the cream of British military drill and discipline. As they passed the YMCA they started to catch glimpses of the riot at the Ferry Terminal and the Platoon Commander, a very young and fresh subaltern, asked the interpreter to again ask how many rioters there were via the radio to the police. The answer came back again, about 300.

The noise alone was starting to be deafening and the Platoon Sergeant very soon sized up the situation as a huge wave of Chinese humanity, angry and inflamed, started to run towards the thirty or so troops who were now arranged in a perfect and now intimidating square. All of the rioters were waving knives, choppers, axes and machetes. The sergeant didn't hesitate. It appeared that the estimate of 300 might have been a tad light.

'FUCKING RUN! GET BACK TO THE TRUCKS **NOW!** *RUN, YOU BASTARDS! THESE FUCKERS MEAN BUSINESS. LEEEEG IIIIITTT!'*

Nobody needed a second order. They abandoned all pretences to discipline and duly legged it. However, they had radios and other such military trappings whilst the Chinese rioters were mostly carrying only one thing and that thing usually involved one sharp side so, unfortunately, they were catching up fast. The soldiers now in a less than polished 'panic and run' formation reached Nathan Road and the lorries. Instantly and as one man they started shouting to 'Get those fucking things started'. The engines luckily surged into life and the soldiers pulled the confused Royal Hong Kong Policemen, who were guarding the trucks, into the moving trucks.

A shower of stones and machetes hit the trucks and one or two squaddies were injured, but none seriously. After a short drive up Nathan Road and then right into Austin Road the trucks quickly arrived back at Gun Club Hill Barracks. The Platoon Sergeant leapt out the back of the truck and strode like a thunderstorm up to the Royal Hong Kong Police Commander, an ex-Metropolitan copper but now the equivalent of a colonel in the Army.

'Oi, you! I wanna fucking word with you, are you the twat that told us 300 people were storming the fucking Star Ferry?'

The senior policeman looked stunned that a mere sergeant would address him like that.

'Eh? Yes, but I got confused between the English and the Cantonese and I interpreted three hundred but they meant three thousand, my apologies.' He sounded not entirely apologetic.

The sergeant leaned over until his face was a millimetre in front of the policeman's.

'Well, you effing nark, next time you make a little bollocks like that with my boys I'm gonna stick my arm down your fucking copper neck, grab your fucking copper arsehole and pull it up through your fucking lying copper mouth and then shit in it, you almost killed us, you prick.'

From that moment, Private Bruce had found the role model that he was looking for and slowly but surely developed his very own style around it.

Chapter 3

Baptism of Fire

Ballykinler, N.I., October 1976

After six weeks or so it was time to see if they had learnt anything. The CSM got them together for a briefing by the Officer Commanding the NIPG. He was a major by the name of Twigge. He was a diminutive little man who had earned the Military Cross during hand-to-hand fighting in the Oman. No prizes for guessing who he used to work for and the last bloke you should mug in a dark alley! His Special Forces past made all present listen to him with a kind of awe, like a god passing out advice on how to actually give a girl a real orgasm whilst allowing you to know the difference between that and a fake. This was good stuff to know!

'Listen in all,' he began, he had no need to shout because the CSM had already done that. He was talking across a room so quiet that you could hear a cockroach checking its antennas for kinks.

'It's about time you all had a little test and we are going to do that starting tomorrow night. It's a kind of exercise but it will be *real*, in a *real* tactical setting with *real* baddies and *real* ammunition. Should be just the kind of shindig that you can all get your teeth into.' He spoke in that understated posh way that British army officers will, like they are discussing the Chancellor of the Exchequer's last speech or the whereabouts of Lord Lucan. He smiled broadly obviously relishing the moment and then carried on.

'A well-known PIRA thug has escaped custody from the RUC [20] in Londonderry and we understand he will be visiting his dear old mum over the next few days. His escape was positively encouraged and some of our closest friends are tracking him as we believe he will be more useful to us out of prison

---

[20] Royal Ulster Constabulary – The police in Northern Ireland.

than inside.' He paused picking up a wooden pointer and turned on an OHP. Projected immediately onto the wall was a square of luminosity that had embedded in it an image of a map depicting a portion of the County Londonderry countryside.

The major pointed at a spot on the image. 'His dear old mum lives in a dilapidated old shithouse on the edge of Kilrea, but we know that she is visiting this equally crappy farmhouse near Magherafelt and we are sure the two will have a lovely and touching family reunion right here.' He tapped the end of the pointer onto the depiction of a small farm. Next the projector threw up a picture of a face onto the wall; it was a mean face, ugly and angry.

'This miserable bastard is definitely the ASU commander for the Kilrea area but too thick to go any higher so not a very big fish. But his mother was the wife of a long standing and high-ranking IRA man who ran half the IRA many years ago before giving up the ghost to the big C. She'll have a lot of contacts and we suspect that there should be a lot of VIPs turning up to pay respects and kiss his murdering arse because he showed balls by escaping and because of who *she* used to know. That's what we want with lots of nice piccies of them before he pisses off and scarpers for the border. He won't make it across though as I have a funny feeling he will be captured just before he leaves the Province.' He paused and pulled down a canvas screen with a large-scale map of the Magherafelt area.

'OK! So, this is how it's going to go...'

The briefing lasted three hours and went into every single minute detail of what was going to happen and when. Afterwards they broke up into their teams and were given their detailed section briefings as to what they were all going to do. Eddie's team was chosen to be nearest to the target and, as the closest team, to do the close recce of the building and to place the UGS so they could catch some additional intelligence by listening to what was being said and perhaps place names to unfamiliar faces. In the current situation, this would be a dangerous activity, so they had to ensure all the other teams would know exactly what they had planned.

'Oi, Steve, you stubble hopper![21] Seems like the boss knows about your fetish for wearing older ladies' underwear!' Steve was being taunted by the Section Commander of the 9th/12th Lancers patrol, and the only other Pete in the group. He was a posh thirty-year-old tank commander who was, with the

---

[21] Tankie nickname for Infantry – refers to running over the stubble left after the harvest in Germany when the exercise season starts in earnest.

rest of his team, slumming it by acting as Infantry in the NIPG. He had a nickname 'Hardhat'; it had something to do with rendering himself unconscious in a tank in Germany when drunk at some point in the past. He was very similar in outlook to Steve and they got on well.

'That's only when I'm knitting Hardhat, not all the time like a Tankie would.'

'But we have to have something additional to keep us warm in those steel coffins, Steve. Anyway, good luck and we'll be watching your back so just give us the word and we'll even blow the little old lady away for ya, but we keep the underwear, OK?'

'OK, but just remember that it's not a tank so you may have to pull the trigger more than once, alright?'

Steve and Hardhat laughed and they waved each other goodbye. On this jaunt Steve only wished too much that Pete's guys were actually in a tank watching out for them. He watched Pete go back to his billet. Steve got his guys together and they all went over their kit again. He saw the enthusiasm in which they checked and double checked their equipment and then each other's. He was minded of Shakespeare and Henry V, *like greyhounds in the slips...* he thought, and he smiled knowing he was in good hands. He suggested that they all took a well-deserved NAAFI break. They slipped on their berets and sauntered out of the room to go and buy a pie or whatever other poison they fancied on the hallowed ground of the Navy, Army and Air Force Institute. The NAAFI was a distinct monopoly that could sell anything to soldiers from cheap tea in chipped cups up to the latest tax-free cars in Germany. The NAAFI was usually a dilapidated building built either during or before the 1960s, designed to look as depressing as possible both inside and out.

They ambled in and walked up to the counter to see what goodies were on display. They ordered their bits and pieces and found a table and some chairs to sit on. The chairs were uncomfortable and hard, but they sat there and waited whilst the lady behind the counter fussed about making their tea and microwaving pies. It made Eddie wonder what they would have done without the magic of the microwave in the NAAFI. *Everything* went into the microwave. He'd seen tea heated up that way because it was cold in the urn and the NAAFI employee just could not be arsed to make some fresh.

'I see that the pies are being ruined in imaginative and diabolical ways as usual,' exclaimed Les, whilst watching his Snake and Pygmy pie making small circles in the glass fronted box slowly becoming the pappy mushy mess he had gotten used to during his six years in the Army. He went on, 'I am sure that the tea will be a suitable vintage liberally doused with bromide and other chemicals designed to keep its shelf life up at around the thousand-year mark to match the longevity of the cockroaches in 'ere.' He spoke whilst gesturing in a way that he imagined wine connoisseurs did when discussing the finer points of a good wine.

The good thing about the NAAFI was that the food was really quite cheap and generally the same everywhere you went. So, a pie in the NAAFI in Germany would be pretty much the same in awfulness as a NAAFI pie in Belize or Kenya.

Soldiers the world over were always amazed at how the NAAFI managed to employ the ugliest and socially inept women that could possibly be found. Thus, the Fens of East Anglia, the concrete estates of Birmingham and Liverpool plus small towns in Wales were probably completely empty of such women. They had been spirited away by the NAAFI with stories of travel and horny young men desperate for their female company. At least the NAAFI got one bit right, they did travel a fair bit.

That night the CSM turned up with several cases of beer, compliments of the OC. The entire platoon gravitated to Eddie's room and almost immediately the sounds of ring pulls hissing and Alice Cooper screaming 'Schools out,' filled the room whilst a light rain started outside.

The next day, as they'd be going on Ops, there was no run so they all had a welcome lie in. Once awake and dressed they all ambled along to *Sandy's Homes Cafe*, which was a charity based servery in the barracks that prepared a superb full English breakfast and wonderful tea for next to nothing. It was a nice place if you didn't mind the odd dip into Christianity as it was heavily linked to the Protestant Church. Little was said whilst eating as they were still recovering from the celebration the previous night on the prelude to their first gig.

'Hello, boys!' was all the warning they got. It was said with a distinct Belfast accent as a Lay Preacher, a mature lady of about fifty, decided to try and save their souls. They in turn tried to ignore her as she grabbed a chair and sat in amongst them. It was expected.

'Are you boys well?' she enquired, her smile almost permanently carved onto her heavily made up face. She almost certainly realised that the squaddies she was trying to reach were most likely beyond saving and would probably try and act like she wasn't there. She was largely correct, but Steve fancied some fun, so he replied almost nonchalantly,

'We're fine, missus but we are gonna have to go quite quickly as we have to worship Ba'al at noon when the sun is highest, so we only have thirty minutes to get to the temple.' He said it completely seriously without hint of humour. They could sense her not quite comprehending Steve's sentence. She leaned forward on her chair towards Steve.

'Who? What did you say?' she queried.

'I said Ba'al, darlin'! He's the pagan god of soldiers, fertility and druids. We like to keep him happy as he has a terrible temper and we're out on operations later, so we'd like him to keep an eye on us.' Steve said 'Ba'al' slowly and deliberately so she would have no problem in hearing it.

'The god Bawl?' she repeated in her strong Belfast twang questioning whether she heard it correctly.

Steve continued.

'Yes, that's right. We're from Hampshire and we worship the god Ba'al at Stonehenge, I'm sure you've heard of Stonehenge?' Steve asked looking a bit exasperated.

'Yes, I have heard of Stonehenge but here we believe in God and we worship him. I don't think this Bawl sounds very good at all,' she replied, sounding somewhat sceptical in her acknowledgement. She then asked, 'Where is this temple you mentioned?'

Steve looked at her as if she was stupid and said,

'In the armoury of course, where else would it be? If you don't worship Ba'al then who do you worship, then?' he asked innocently.

'Oh. We worship God,' she replied almost patronisingly.

'So do we,' shot back Steve, 'but what's his name, what do you call him?'

She was a bit flustered at the question and after a short think she said,

'Jesus Christ!' a bit too quickly.

Steve then looked slightly surprised and responded,

'If you can't remember there is no need to blaspheme, missus. Just say you can't remember.' The lay preacher was obviously disconcerted to think that they thought she had said that as invective rather than the name of her saviour.

'No, no Jesus is the name of our saviour, the son of God,' she attempted to explain.

'Oh, I see. So what's your god's name then, this Father of Jesus?' Steve insisted.

She flustered a bit and then looked relieved as salvation dawned on her.

'Jehovah, our god is often called Jehovah,' she said triumphantly. But Steve had a surprise up his sleeve.

'Ah, you're a Jehovah's Witness then! Sorry, love but the chief druid has instructed us not to speak to Jehovah's Witnesses 'cause they make a pest of themselves knocking on doors and disturbing innocent burghers at their rest. So we're not allowed to talk to you, sorry.' He turned away from her slightly dismissively. Les almost pissed himself and was burbling into his tea whilst Kevin, innocently convinced by Steve he was a now Ba'al adept, wondered why they never mentioned this change of religion at the recruiting office.

'No, no!' she said, wildly shaking her head. 'We are not Jehovah's Witnesses at all; they call God the same name as we do. It's from the Jewish religions Yahweh,' she stated thinking they'd be impressed.

'You're Jewish then, that's OK with us I suppose. Anyway, what can we do for you love? Do you want to see inside our temple? Lots of ladies like to.' exclaimed Steve raising his eyebrows slightly and almost whispering the last part of his sentence.

'Er, why?' she asked in the same tone.

'Because Ba'al is also the god of promiscuity and fertility and is represented by a ten-inch phallus, women often use it to improve their fertility. Would you like to use our phallus whilst we pray? Might be good fun.' Steve said this looking her directly in the eye with a slightly lecherous gaze on his face then topped it by licking his lips slowly.

She gaped, suddenly understanding what was being proposed. She slowly raised her body until she was standing up, bestowed on Steve a look of total disgust and then flounced off to the other end of the room to save other more deserving souls from damnation.

Les looked at Steve and said, slowly,

'Steve, you're gonna burn in Hell.'

Steve nodded gravely in agreement, but he asked if they'd noticed how big her nipples were at the end of their chat. Kevin just wondered what kind of panties she was wearing and if he could steal a pair.

After their breakfast, they made their way back to the block to finish off their preparations and got ready to ruin a terrorist's day somewhere. There was a chilly nip in the air so it looked like the extraordinarily hot summer was definitely ending. Having got their webbing and combat kit sorted out, they drew up their weapons and the specialised kit they had trained so hard to master. At the appointed time, they were ready to parade in front of the civilianised box vans they all loved so much, with their weapons, webbing and Bergens. All in all, they were each expected to carry in excess of a hundred and fifty pounds of weapons, ammunition, food and kit. Eventually they were told to get on the vans and without question they did. Once moving it was obvious that the box vans were not going where the original plan stated so Steve asked the driver where they were going.

'That's a fucking secret and you know that, Corporal,' responded 'Mess Tins' their RCT driver. Steve rolled his eyes in exasperation, but the driver continued in his clipped Manchester accent,

'Any of you lot know the way to Lisburn HQNI? Never bin there meself?' Steve laughed and responded,

'It's very close to the Belfast/Liverpool ferry and looks a lot like a fucking big boat – let us know when you're close and we'll buy the tickets.'

'Righto, Corporal.'

So, they were off to HQ Northern Ireland for a briefing – *Must be a fucking bigger deal than the OC said it was,* thought Steve.

It was.

The moment they arrived they were very quickly taken to a briefing room and given tea and biscuits, not a good sign as this meant it was definitely a suicidal operation. All around them were maps and models. Eddie was impressed, it reminded him of the Second World War films he had seen about D Day or bombing dams. Perhaps they were going to invade Ireland or perhaps the IRA was going to write an inspiring piece of music about them. After about fifteen minutes and 10 or 12 biscuits later, there was a shout.

'ROOM SHUN!' They all sat upright. The Commander, Northern Ireland Land Forces, burst into the room like a gale, a man who knows he's the boss and typical of British officers throughout the Army. They are all probably given pills to take daily or given implants at Sandhurst. The brigadier gave a briefing but Eddie and the rest didn't quite understand the exclusive language, so they switched off and assumed that Steve, their leader, had some form of interpretation device that would allow him to gain whatever enlightenment the brigadier was imparting.

Eddie was amazed at how many biscuits Pete could put away, he was well beyond fifty. As quickly as it began it was over again and the brigadier was gone, it was almost as if they had imagined it. They all gathered around their

NCOs to learn what they were going to be involved in. Steve got them together.

'Well, boys as our divine leader just said we are going to get acquainted with some top knobheads in the organisation we know as OIRA[22]. It looks like some of them are going to have a bit of revelry at that farm. Our job is to surround it and get some happy snaps of these fuckers so that our colleagues around the Province will have nice piccies to track them about the place. We already know all that, but the brigadier is also very keen to get any information on what the fuckers are planning so the SAS can give them the odd surprise now and then. It goes without saying that if OIRA find out we're there then they probably won't be very impressed. The brigadier just wanted to emphasise the importance of this mission and he also added that if there are any Middle Eastern looking people then to be particularly creative at getting pictures.' Kevin tried to ask why people from Bradford and Birmingham were getting involved but Steve shut him up.

That night at about 11pm Steve's patrol was dropped two miles north of the target and the other three patrols chosen to take part were dropped off at various places around the farm at roughly the same distance. Two patrols would be in close at about one hundred yards and the other two would be in depth support about three hundred yards out. They would be placed either side of the target so that most of it could be observed but in addition anyone arriving or leaving would be seen. Steve's patrol had been chosen to do the close recce and this was because they were definitely the best at sneaking about and not being seen. This was attributed to the poaching links in the county where their regiment was raised. The other patrols latched onto this and they were nicknamed 'Tea Leafs'. 'The Pope' and his group were quite proud of that.

The 'Tea Leafs' patrolled with great care towards the site where they had picked their hide to be. This had been done previously at Ballykinler using maps and stereoscopic photography. This technique uses two aerial photos taken simultaneously but at slightly different angles and, when viewed through special apparatus of World War One vintage, showed the actual geographical features on the ground in a kind of 3D effect. In this way, you could choose where to build a hide and know if you could indeed see the target without actually being there. This was useful as an actual physical recce could not be done as it may alert the local AK47 Enthusiast Club (unofficials!) who may

---

[22] Official Irish Republican Army – the original and more formal IRA.

then be waiting to welcome you as a moving target or may leave some fertilizer for you to stand on that had been treated to ensure that it made a nasty bang that would ensure no more masturbating, roller skating or doing up shoe laces ever again.

Camouflaged up entirely, each one of them looked like some unworldly brown green zombie covered in thin rags with bizarre faces painted various shades of green, brown and black. Their weapons and Bergens were painted in matt paint and treated the same way with camouflaged cloth ripped and torn. In a hedge or lying down in grass a passer-by would barely notice them from ten feet away and at night they could literally stand next to you in a wood and be undetected apart from their breathing and perhaps the whites of their eyes. They had learnt and perfected techniques to 'ghostwalk' silently through woods and along hedgerows. Weapons always at the ready to dispense life depriving projectiles they moved dangerously and silently down the edge of a field and copse and eventually approached an RV about one hundred yards from what was to be their Final RV. They all felt the weight of their heavy Bergens and webbing digging in to their bodies.

They stopped, got down in all round defence and listened silently. The wind had just picked up slightly and Les was convinced it was going to rain again soon. They listened intently for about twenty minutes. In the dark, ears are the main defence so listening is an important skill for the long-term survival of any military team at night. It was dark with no moon, so they used their NITECH to scan the area. This used any available light to generate a sharp and distinct view of the area as if it was daylight but with a green tint. The quality was good enough to take photos with and had the ability to be attached to cameras. Once fully satisfied that there was nobody about who may or may not have had an interest in them, Steve and Les went forward and checked out the FRV[23]. This is the place that they would operate from whilst they were building the hide. From the FRV three would go forward and work on the hide whilst the other two would keep watch with the night vision kit and their ears.

Les was very particular about recce and took his time. However, time was also an enemy and they had to dig out and disguise a rather large hole, so Steve jollied him up a bit. Les and Steve returned from the recce and as a group they occupied the FRV. They cached their Bergens into one spot and got into good fire positions. Steve and Les would start the hide off so they went out first; it

---

[23] Final Rendezvous

was already one o'clock in the morning. At about two thirty Eddie saw a shape looming out of the darkness and quietly challenged it by saying,

'Halt.'

'It's me, Leather,' came the muted reply. It was distinctively Les, but they had practiced many scenarios one of them being that terrorists had grabbed one of them and was using them by sticking a gun or something to their neck. So, Eddie would ask a weird sounding question as a code word and they all knew two answers to it. One if they were in the clear, another if they were under pressure. This removed the age-old problem of forgetting the password and therefore getting shot.

Eddie asked,

'What is the size of Steve's prick?' he whispered.

'Not big enough,' came the reply. They could give any answer that was non-specific in any way and that was correct. But if they answered with a size or a measurement then they were in trouble. If they were in that situation they'd be told to advance anyway with the sentry knowing now that an enemy was also possibly with them. At that point, it was up to the sentry to try not to kill the team member and the team member was to try and get down or at least not get blown away as well.

'Is anyone with you?' he said quietly.

'No, just me to swap with one of you guys.'

'Advance.' He allowed Les to come a bit closer and whispered again,

'Stop.' Eddie gave him one last check over and looked at Kevin. Kevin nodded agreeing that Les looked alone as he'd been watching the whole thing via NITECH. If someone had been with him, Kevin would have shot that person without hesitation as it was clear that Les was of the view he was alone.

'OK, come in, Leather.'

Les moved into the hide whilst Eddie and Kevin watched the area where he had come from closely just in case he had been followed without his knowledge. Les was in no way upset that he was checked like that as that was how they'd stay alive, by being careful and professional. Pete opted to go next and he slipped out of the hide and was no doubt treated the same way by Steve when he got to the actual hide location. This was the routine and they kept it up and swapped until the hide was ready. When it was finished Les checked the hide from all angles whilst Pete and Kevin did a sweep of the immediate area to make sure they had not attracted any unwelcome attention.

Eddie fully checked the radio and technical kit. Once Steve was satisfied they were not compromised and they had made sure nothing had been left outside, they slowly moved into and occupied the hide. Eddie sent a radio signal using just a code word indicating they were in. Over the next hour three more code words arrived meaning all patrols were now hidden from view and open for business.

The patrol fell into their routine of three asleep and two on duty watching the baddies. The area of interest was a farm complex but a very small one. It was in a state of poor repair and had no livestock nor did it grow any vegetables, so it wasn't in all honesty much of a farm. There seemed to be two elderly people living there who appeared to be a married couple. That fitted in with the council records. Every now and then one of them would be seen pottering about and then they'd be gone.

Every night it seemed that the man of the house liked to sneak out for a few jars up the road and would come back quietly drunk. Drunk was not perhaps the precise word, apoplectic would be more accurate.

On the second night things started to happen. Three cars arrived in quick succession. The visitors were using older, filthy cars that would not attract any attention by the authorities. In the second car was the aforementioned mum, so it seemed the party was starting. Each patrol radioed back to the HQ the code words that indicated something was warming up and Steve decided they'd complete their close recce that night at about 2am. It had been agreed that it would be best to place the UGS whilst doing the close recce once the meetings had started as it was obvious that the longer the kit was around the house the more opportunities there would be for the house holders to find it. HQ agreed to their request and sent back the authorisation in the form of another code word.

It would take all five of them to do the task. Eddie would also take his radio and Kevin the Bren. At the appointed time, they crawled away from their hide and merged into the nearest hedge line. Then like wraiths they moved literally unseen towards the buildings whilst over the radio Eddie was informed that the other patrols had them covered if there was any trouble. When they were fifty yards out Pete stopped and took up a fire position covering their approach and their backs. The four others moved off towards the house soundlessly; it was a dark night, so they were very close for communications reasons. Les was in the lead with Steve, followed by Eddie with Kevin taking up the rear.

Ten minutes later they reached the hedgerow that marked the edge of the farm complex and paused. Kevin and Eddie remained there as close cover with the SLR and Bren whilst Les and Steve, leaving behind their heavy weapons, would actually deploy the electronics and UGS devices whilst listening to what was going on in the house using their 9mm pistols as personal protection. Pete would keep further out and watch the bigger picture and make sure nobody sneaked up behind them. He had kept the M79 with him and was heavy artillery support and had the IWS for looking about within the dark. The remainder of their kit was left in their hide and was covered by the Tankies' patrol who watched the hide and the farm complex. If anyone tried to pinch anything whilst they were out visiting, the perpetrators would find that the hide had a very efficient alarm system that entailed seriously armed squaddies firing lots of nasty things at them from one hundred yards away, most of which went bang.

The four of them were at the back of the house with only a thin hedgerow between them and the farmhouse kitchen. They were just about to split up when suddenly the door flew open and the hedgerow they were a part of was flooded with light. They froze immediately, but luckily they were in the shadow on the far side of the hedge. A small dog rushed out and started to charge around the yard yapping and making a fuss. They all kept still; although they were close to the hedgerow they were not actually a part of it, so they still felt a bit exposed. Steve had a depressing thought that the Tankies were almost certainly watching this and were no doubt laughing their bollocks off. The dog was now running along the other side of the hedgerow yapping and growling at them. The dog knew they were there and Kevin was not impressed.

'I'll strangle little Tutsi if it comes over this side of the hedge,' he murmured to Eddie.

Almost as if on cue the little old lady who lived in the farm came out and, as if talking to a three-year-old, shouted,

'Oh, Tutsi do stop barking you naughty little dog.'

Kevin was amazed at the coincidence and almost burst out laughing and as he was trying to contain it she said it again. Kevin could not hold it in and he could not cover his mouth without dropping the Bren. He was crouched down, so he stopped himself laughing by the simple expedient of biting Eddie in the calf muscle.

'Jeez, what the fuck?' whispered Eddie.

'Shush,' said Les quietly.

'Shush you, ya twat, Gus is biting my fucking leg.'

It was very painful, Eddie was tempted to remove the problem by just shooting him in the head with his Hi-power. Eventually Kevin overcame his urge to laugh and released Eddie's leg. Kevin leaned over to Eddie and whispered he was sorry and owed him a pint.

'Sorry? You stupid twat! That fucking hurt so you owe me more than a beer, you git,' Eddie whispered. Steve looked at both of them and his look was not very pleasant even if they could only see his eyes, so they regained their composure and carried on with their tasks.

It took two hours for Steve and Les to plant the UGS around the building and cam them up so they could not be seen. They were very conscious that they'd also have to get them back sometime later or the Colour would keep their bollocks as a souvenir, which meant a return trip. Whilst they were there they looked in the windows and took stock. It appeared that the escapee baddie had turned up as expected and was currently entertaining about six others with plentiful supplies of *Blackbush* whiskey. They also noted that they all were sporting pistols of various types. These vicious bastards were definitely players so the Military Intelligence guy's information had been bang on. Les discreetly went forward of the house and took pictures with the NITECH of the cars and got their make and registration numbers. All done they sneaked back to Eddie and Kevin and after pausing to check they had not been rumbled they all crept over to Pete and then did the remaining distance in their best sneaky style back to the hide.

They had already set up the listening and detection kit, so they could start monitoring straight away. They did have some hardware that they could use to tape record the conversations but it had only a limited capacity so that was reserved for very serious stuff, for the moment one of them listened in on a headset and wrote down what was being said in a log book. Eddie was first and he slipped the headset on. They were all watching him to see what wisdoms he'd write once he'd overheard them. Kevin couldn't wait any longer.

'What the fuck are they saying? Why aren't you writing this stuff down?'

Eddie looked languidly at Kevin and responded,

'I doubt our green bereted masters of intrigue would be interested in how scumbag number three in the house is doing on the gee gees; not well I'm afraid.'

'Write it all down, Eddie, you never know what becomes interesting, perhaps that info can be used to blackmail him or whatever those allegedly Intelligence people do in their spare time when not torturing poor innocent

terrorists. Anyway, that's what *An Phoblach* would have us believe, eh?'
suggested Steve.

An Phoblach was the IRA mouthpiece rag. Its weekly cover would have
bloodcurdling pictures of IRA heroes hanging off barbed wire looking like
skeletons whilst being tortured by Nazi looking well fed British squaddies with
wide grins. The stories inside were even better and could match anything
written by commentators discussing the horrors of Auschwitz or Buchenwald.
However, the serious narrators of the horrors of the Nazi era had documentary
and photographic evidence of those atrocities whereas the authors of this
pigswill only had their imaginations. Every squaddie who read it knew it was
total and utter bloody rubbish, and read it they did as copies were passed about
for intelligence reasons. However, it was always best to avoid giving copies to
Provost Sergeants and their RP staff as the pictures were quite distressing
whilst difficult to explain and could be upsetting for chimpanzees.

'OK,' said Eddie and he started to write down the drivel that such people
discuss.

The temperature, noise and motion sensors meant they knew where people
were in the house so if they came under fire from that direction they would
know where everyone was, more or less.

The next two days were boring with people coming and going, names and
registrations taken. Long range photos of the players with the cars they were
using. They were building up a picture of what they thought was a big
operation to be held over the next two or three days and HQ Lisburn wanted to
know every single detail of the arrangements. This meant that Eddie was
spending twenty hours a day converting key parts of the log into Slidex, so the
info could be sent securely. If someone was listening in to their radio traffic,
then it would be possible to link them with their patrol activities if it was sent
in clear. Nothing was sent that was longer than twenty seconds in length and
then at varying times so that a routine was not established. The IRA was known
to have radio direction finding kit and in fact a TV set up on the right channel
meant everything being said could be heard anyway. Radio communications
was a serious threat if compromised and Eddie had no intention of giving
anything away on a plate to an amateur radio guy with an interest in bypassing
the democratic process at the expense of their lives.

Another forty-eight hours passed and they were feeling the strains of little or
no sleep, and no hot food or drinks. The stress of keeping on watch, observing
the target and personal admin was telling and tempers would on occasion, fray.

Les was good at taking the anger out of a situation when the stress got the better of them. A short quip or a self-directed joke would usually do the trick, but now they had been on this job for six days and even his diplomacy was being pushed. Steve roughly woke Eddie.

'Kermit get the recorder out I think we need it.' Eddie was barely awake and told Steve where to get off and closed his eyes and was immediately back to sleep again.

'Kermit wake the fuck up and set up the recorder now.' He kicked Eddie.

'No need to piggin' kick me, you twat,' Eddie said in a whining voice.

Les piped up,

'We need it now, Kermit. Sorry, but Steve is a bit stressed, he wants a shit but his bag is full, and I won't let him use mine.' Les broke the potential confrontation. Kevin had one eye open.

'Whassat Leather? You say Steve is a bag full of shit?' Kevin giggled at his own joke and was back asleep a second later.

Steve rolled his eyes and thought about the M79 and how it would look stuffed up Kevin's arse.

Eddie set up the recorder and apologised to Steve who was also conciliatory.

'Sorry, Kermit, I was a bit harsh but these fuckers are talking about an ambush of a UDR guy and we best get it all down.'

Just to be sure, Les was getting as much down in the log as well. Eddie had the recorder working in a flash. Eddie took up a pencil and a spare log book and looked at Steve.

'I'll take scumbags one, three and five. You do the others, OK?' suggested Eddie.

'Good man, Kermit.' Steve was pleased Eddie had jumped in when he needed the help as Les' writing was bloody awful. In fact, most of the writing in logs was 'bloody awful' as they were doing it in the pitch black of their hide. Even during the day it was very dark in their hole, so writing did prove to be difficult. However, a technique for this had been evolved that meant using a finger to find the edge of the page and then writing everything in joined up letters with no breaks or grammar in between until you came to the other edge of the page. It all had to be written out again nicely at the end of the operation, but this technique did help.

Les was now busy taking some pictures as more baddies were arriving; it looked like they were preparing a serious moot.

'Kermit get on the blower and let them know we got something serious going on here, tell them the threat level has risen to 3 and get Sunray's[24] permission to go weapons ready.' Steve was getting anxious. It was possible that so many had arrived for the simple expedient to take them out. He was a bit comforted by the Tankies to his rear, but they were used to 120mm tank guns and taking out the enemy from two thousand yards or so. He had a thought.

'Whilst on the wire, Kermit, mention to the armoured arseholes behind us that we may need their help if this lot come out firing at us. Tell them to watch our back and sides.'

Eddie almost laughed and thought that Steve may have actually meant backsides.

Les informed Steve that one of Michael Collins' private army was unloading what looked like semi-automatic weapons from one of the cars. A few moments later they could hear them in the front room cleaning them and loading up magazines with rounds.

'They're talking about a UDR ambush, so it looks like they are bombing up for that,' Steve said to all of them.

Eddie butted in and confirmed that HQNI stated it was OK to go weapons ready.

'Make ready with the weapons and load up the M79,' Steve announced.

Kevin wrapped the Bren up in some Hessian and cocked it almost silently. The rest did the same with almost no noise. The Orders for Opening Fire in Northern Ireland were enshrined in what was called the 'Yellow Card'. Basically, you were not allowed to walk about with a weapon with a bullet up the spout unless you were in mortal danger and before shooting you still had to give a warning first. If perchance you did shoot someone accidentally or intentionally and they turned out to be innocent, then five years in Brixton getting habitually raped and becoming some old lag's bitch was on the cards. However, Special Forces were excused such rules when inserting or extracting and they did have their weapons cocked and were ready to fire. If they were ambushed at two in the morning it was pretty sure that it was not some old woman out for the night air. However, once in the hide it was considered to be safer to have magazines attached but to not have the weapon cocked. A negligent discharge with a high velocity bullet in a small trench, could well kill or maim two or even three of them in one hit.

---

[24] Radio Appointment Title for a Commander.

They set themselves up in case they needed to defend themselves and Eddie sent a code word to all patrols heightening the threat level. The patrol closest to the target was the unit that dictated the alert status. Eddie was now listening into their local terrorists and raised his eyebrows.

'Er, Steve! They said that they're gonna come out and test fire the weapons, zero them in etc.'

'What? It's dark and two in the morning how the fuck are they going to do that? The noise of the shots will travel miles.' Steve was incredulous and was starting to feel his sphincter muscles strain more intently.

All of a sudden, they heard two tractors start up and then trundle out of the barn and after negotiating the gate turned into their field and pointed the tractor lights literally directly at their hide location. From behind the lights two guys came walking up the slight incline of the field that they were at the edge of. Due to the headlights, all they could see were silhouettes, but it appeared to Eddie and the others that they were carrying a wood and board screen. Steve made a decision.

'Don't shoot but standby. It looks like we have found OIRA's official firing range. Eddie tell the other patrols to standby but to only shoot if we say so – be specific, only if we say so.'

The two OIRA guys carrying the screen huffed and puffed up the field and eventually about twenty yards in front and about ten yards to the side of the hide they set it up. They walked back down the hill and the tractors were adjusted so the headlights were bang on the screen. The shooters got down and started to get ready with their weapons. Then both tractors revved their engines and in the hide they could only just hear the shots from the rifles as they test fired and zeroed them in.

No shots rang out behind them so the Tankies had got the drift of the situation. Kevin was hunched over the Bren rocking backwards and forwards getting a bead on the bad guys below who were lit up like a floodlit football match.

'I can take them all out in two to three bursts, just say when.'

Steve realised that taking out a few guns and shooting them into a field at night was not on the face of it a serious offence. Killing them, although an attractive thought, was not very practical and they'd all probably spend the next few years bending over at Pentonville. However, if they started to take incoming fire that was potentially life threatening then they could blow them all away without a thought.

'Don't shoot unless you get a direct order from me. Assuming you do not want to go to prison and become some criminal's convenient arsehole on legs that is.'

The men in the field fired about twenty rounds and then consulted the screen. Not satisfied with the results they all pottered about discussing, and at one point arguing, the niceties on how to zero a rifle's sights. Eventually after another sixty or so rounds, and a few more gallons of agricultural diesel for the tractors, they seemed satisfied and they collected the screen and the tractors were put away. Once they all went back into the house silence crept back over the field again. Steve got Eddie to send a message standing them all down to a lower level of threat. Steve had definitely had enough and decided to go to the toilet. He borrowed Pete's bag and Les, as usual, held the bag for him as he did his business. Kevin kept watch and Eddie listened in to the radio.

'That's interesting,' said Pete who was reviewing the UGS console.

'What's interesting, my shit? Look on in wonder, boys,' said Steve proudly. After that he grunted, and the bag sagged a little more. Compo was hard stuff to get out once eaten.

'Not that, you twat, according to our UGS kit three or four guys were in the top of the house during that shooting match. From previous traces it looks like they were all carrying something that weighed about forty to sixty pounds each, but only two, possibly three, have gone back up again.'

Steve did not need to be told that those things were most likely not weapons as they were too heavy plus he was curious why they would have left look outs in a bedroom window.

'Why would they do that? Eddie go over the logs and see if we missed something that suggests they know we're here.'

Les passed Steve some toilet paper and once wiped he pulled up his combat trousers. Doing life's most personal activities in public had now become routine amongst them all, so much so that quite often it went almost unnoticed.

Composite rations or 'Compo' as it was known, came in one man or ten man packs and was designed to bind you up so that you went less often, which was just as well. They were also very high in calorific value. Most squaddies preferred the one-man twenty-four-hour ration packs as they were more personal, and you could swap stuff about until you pretty much had the sort of grub you liked. Famous dishes lurked in each pack that any seasoned soldier would well remember such as Chicken Supreme, cheese (processed), bacon grill and the ever-famous Oatmeal Block. Although squaddies would most likely remember it better as Babies' Heads in Spunk, cheese (possessed) and Sick Pig or similar. They had chocolate bars and sweeties, toilet paper and a wonderful little gadget that was a tin opener. One of the drawbacks that compo gave, apart from a lifetime's flatulence condition that no doctor could cure, was the fact that once you got back from operations or a big exercise where compo was the main fare, a big problem presented itself. The moment you eat fresh food you suddenly find yourself in great and dire need of a toilet. This was all well and good if there was just a few of you back from an operation, but if the whole regiment had just got back off exercise and all had just had a fresh meal then toilets were suddenly at a premium. The aroma of six hundred and fifty men all moving their bowels for the first time in several days or even a few weeks could not be explained or imagined, neither would it go away quickly.

Les was watching the house via NITECH and he could see the place almost as plain as day but through a ghostly green light. A camera was attached via a prism type fitting and, if anything interesting happened, they could take passable photos anytime day or night.

'Everything looks quiet at the house,' he stated in a whisper.

Pete nodded after checking the UGS kit.

'It looks like they've all gone to bed,' he said just as quietly, as Les checked the place over with the IWS.

Steve was perplexed and was wondering what was going on. If they were all tooled up and they knew they were there why did they not take the advantage? He concluded that the guys upstairs were just a coincidence and probably looking on in the warmth of the house.

'I don't think they know about us, but I think it is time we got ready to leave, food's low and the shit bags are getting distinctly high!'

Eddie got on the radio and sent a coded message, by return they were told that if they wanted to move out now that was okay but not to forget to get the UGS back. If the scumbags found the sensors and microphones they'd know about the whole deal. In addition, although the military now knew about the UDR hit, they didn't know who or when or where. Outside of that the commander of the NIPG left the decision up to Steve as they were the ones taking the major risk.

'What do you think? Stay or go?' Steve asked.

Kevin spoke for all as he gestured at their mini armoury.

'No problems in staying, Steve. If they attack us we're dug in and heavily armed with serious support behind and to the side of us. We'll wipe them out, so let's stay another twenty four hours and see what happens.' They all agreed.

'OK, the water runs out tomorrow anyway,' agreed Steve. 'But only one of us kips at any one time.' They all nodded. Les slipped his gonk bag over his head and was asleep before it stopped moving.

At about ten o'clock in the morning the people in the house started to move about and via small snippets of overheard conversation they picked up the name of the UDR hit they were going to make. Later they, or more accurately Les, got a fantastic picture of the top terrorist posing along with some of his acolytes with some automatic weapons. That underlined for Steve the fact that they had no idea that they, members of the local Enhanced Fertilizer Firework Club, were being watched.

'Just got a signal from the Argyles in code on the other side of the farm,' said Eddie taking off the headset. 'It seems that just after they turned off the tractors three guys came out the front of the house and deposited a long black bag into the boot of the blue Cortina. They suspect it was a body.'

For Steve the penny dropped.

'The bastards killed someone or nicked a carpet – I'd bet they slotted someone. That's what the fuckers were doing upstairs. We know from the logs that they did not kidnap or have someone there against their will, so it must have been one of their own, nasty, eh?'

'Well let's hope they do that several hundred times and we can all sod off home,' observed Les.

It seemed the OIRA thugs were in no rush to leave but Steve and crew were. They had all the pictures they needed and some serious intelligence about a potential hit. They had got names and matched them to faces and cars. By any measure this was a success. But they now had to recover their kit and depart.

Steve held a short briefing, but the plan was simple: dismantle the hide and remove any evidence that they had been there, and then do a close recce to get their kit back. First, they would establish an RV about fifty yards from the house; Steve and Les would go in and recover everything whilst Eddie and Kevin covered them. Pete would act as artillery again in the rear. Eddie would have the communications and his SLR and Kevin the Bren, so it made sense. The Tankies would be out of their hide and in extended line to the north of the building about two hundred yards out and the Argyles would do a similar extended line on the eastern side. This would minimise any possibility of them accidentally firing on each other if they had to use any weapons. If the bad guys did compromise the 'Tea Leafs' the life expectancy of said scumbags would be measured in seconds.

So, when it was well and truly dark Steve and team dismantled the hide and all evidence of their occupation until Les was satisfied. This meant that a team of university archaeologists could dig the site and swear nobody had ever been there for the last three hundred years or so. They then assisted each other with their camouflage until they became a part of the geography and then they moved 'ghostwalk' style back to the FRV. They cached their Bergens whilst Eddie and Kevin took up fire positions with all the heavy weaponry. The FRV was perfect as with the night sights most of the areas they needed to recover kit from could be seen.

The code words came in confirming that the other patrols were now in position. The whole house now had enough firepower facing it to demolish the building in minutes if someone was foolish enough to even look like they were going to use a weapon. HQNI signalled to confirm that the usual orders for opening fire had been suspended and this in fact meant that they could shoot first if they felt threatened.

The British Army has for many years in Ireland been accused by apologists of a policy of 'Shoot to Kill' and technically this is entirely true! If a British soldier shoots at you then he is trying to kill you, the British Army does not fire warning shots and neither do they try and maim or wound; if they pull the trigger they are aiming at the centre of the target and are intending to kill that target, it was nothing personal. That said, soldiers in Northern Ireland were heavily constrained and under orders to fire in self-defence only. Soldiers were obligated to act as per the guidance of the infamous yellow card but on occasion these were suspended, as in this case. Even so soldiers had to answer for their actions under all circumstances; it was still a hard decision whether or not to fire just because you saw an armed man. The person, even an armed man, would have to be a direct and imminent threat and in danger of shooting you. HQNI's signal just meant that if they saw an obvious threat from this house right now, considering the evidence already gained, then waiting for them to fire first was an unacceptable risk and not an invitation to waste a bunch of terrorists even if they have just potentially murdered someone. The people in the house, if they had known their current threat status at that moment, would most likely have taken it as a compliment and perhaps written a heart rending freedom song about it.

After a final viewing of the farmhouse and being sure no scumbags were about they moved out of the FRV leaving their Bergens, webbing and specialist kit cached and under watch by the Argyles and the Tankies. They left with only communications kit, weapons and ammunition. They settled into the agreed RV just behind the house about one hundred yards out. Pete set himself up and once convinced he was in a good covering position, stayed there just outside the house perimeter about one hundred yards out as artillery cover with his M16 and M79 whilst the rest moved in closer.

The four stopped by the farm perimeter and split up. Eddie and Kevin stayed put as close support whilst Les and Steve went into the farm complex itself to get their kit back. Eddie, via the radio, was informed by the Tankies that they thought they could see a guy acting like a sentry. He was coming their way, so Eddie signalled Kevin to alert Steve and Les. Kevin had perfected a low key noise that sounded like a small animal snuffling about that would not be out of place in the countryside. Steve and Les picked up on the signal just in time and merged into the hedge behind the kitchen whilst he walked past. He was carrying an AK47 and by the look of him knew how to use it. He ambled past unaware that two squaddies were no more than a few feet away from him, heavily camouflaged to look like the surrounding countryside, and at a whim he could have been dead in a fraction of a second.

Suddenly a car was heard coming closer and the Argyles warned Eddie that it was coming towards the farm. Steve and Les saw this as well and they merged again into the surroundings as the front door of the house opened and out came about five occupants who greeted the passengers of the car as they got out. Steve nodded to Les at the group that had just arrived seeing that the new visitors had a guy with them who looked of Middle Eastern origin.

'Shit,' whispered Steve.

'What?' asked Les.

'The new player's a camel jockey,' responded Steve in a whisper. 'We need a happy snap before we go.'

They were at the side of the house near a window that was placed near the bottom of the stairs.

'Go tell Eddie to go back to the RV and get the UGS Recorder going then get a camera and bring it back here. I've got an idea.'

'What leave you here?'

'Yep! Meanwhile I'm gonna replace this microphone. Tell Eddie to get back here as quick as he can with that camera.'

Les disappeared into the darkness and Steve crawled around the front of the house, a huge risk with the sentry walking about, scratched out an air brick and slipped a microphone into the hole. He then replaced the brick and dirtied it up a bit. He was satisfied that if they had to leave this then the baddies in the house would not find it for a long time to come. He then crawled back around the side of the house and met Les who was waiting for him.

'Got the camera?'

'Yep, what's the deal?'

Another message came courtesy of the Tankies and they paused and became a part of the hedge whilst the sentry walked past again, and once he'd moved on Steve continued.

'I bet the rag head will want to go upstairs for a piss or a shit eventually because that's the only toilet with a sink. If memory serves and he is a Muslim, he'll need a sink.' Steve was a mine of such normally useless information about religion, but right now that knowledge was priceless.

They waited about an hour, during which time the sentry seemed to lose interest and he went indoors. Eventually the chap from the Middle East appeared in the doorway through the well-lit window. Steve had been waiting with the camera poised all that time and he simply took a picture.

'Right, let's fuck off,' stated Les.

'No, we'll wait for him to come back down.'

The Argyles passed on a warning to Eddie that a different sentry was coming around again. Kevin made a noise that was barely audible but enough to convey the danger to Steve and Les. They knew that if this sentry started farting in church the Argyles' sniper would take him out so no need for Les and Steve to worry. The Argyles' sniper, a man known as 'Dismal' by his friends due to his lack of hilarity at social functions, was an uncannily good shot. If Dismal stated the sentry would be dead if he made a threatening move then Steve and Les knew that to be fact.

Again, the sentry walked past unconcerned about the twenty people watching his every movement through scopes of various types. Just after he sallied around the front corner of the house the Middle East gent appeared by the window and Steve loomed out of the hedgerow and took another happy snap. He trusted that Eddie had set up the UGS and was recording anything being said.

'I just realised we're leaving that mic behind! I bleedin' signed for that, the Colour will have my bollocks!' whispered Les, but Steve seemed unconcerned that shortly Les may suffer 'death by testicle' at the hands of the maleficent colour sergeant back at base, and simply moved off.

They slowly and silently 'ghostwalked' away and RV'd with Eddie and Kevin and then they made their way across the field to Pete. Pete challenged them and again asked the usual embarrassing questions regarding Steve's penis size. The answers convinced him all was well and let them in. Steve and Les rested a few moments and asked Eddie if he'd gotten anything from the UGS.

'It's still recording. I left it on in my Bergen with a trailing antenna. It will probably keep receiving signals until we're about two miles away in this ground,' Eddie replied matter-of-factly.

Steve smiled broadly.

'That's fucking excellent work, Eddie. Let's move out.'

They crawled a short distance and then carefully got up. They all moved up to the FRV and collected their Bergens and Eddie sent the code word stating they were now out of contact and all the patrols silently left the area as noiselessly as they arrived. It had been a classic operation.

The box body vans picked them up at the agreed locations and a welcome urn of tea was waiting for them inside. CSM Bruce, along with some Black Watch guys acting as security, was also in the van as he was paranoid that all his boys should come back safely. The box body they were in moved away then picked up the Tankies and then headed for camp.

'Bloody well-done, boys, an excellent op, the OC is extremely pleased as you'll find out,' said the CSM, but he was wasting his breath as they were all asleep. Two hours later they got back to camp, and they cleaned and handed in their weapons. Then they all had an intelligence debrief and after rewriting all the logs they handed them in along with all the photos. This all took several hours but thankfully the rest of the kit could wait whilst they, weary from fatigue, fell onto their beds still fully clothed for a few hours' sleep. In the afternoon, washed and cleaned, they were debriefed by the OC who confirmed to them that the contents of the vehicle boot was indeed a body, and the driver and passenger were currently being interviewed by the RUC as to why they had a still warm cadaver in their vehicle. The UDR guy had been warned and his entire unit put on high alert. The OC went on to state that it was possible that some friends from Hereford may be able to ambush a few well-armed chaps en route to the planned murder and if possible capture or kill them. The photos had already been developed and the quality from all patrols was excellent. A Middle Eastern chap with known terrorist links for arms supply was also answering uncomfortable questions regarding his activities in N. Ireland with MI5 at Musgrave Airport. Names and car registrations were all in the bag. The local Bad Boys Brigade would be having a hard time understanding how all the soldiers in the Province suddenly knew who they all are. With a flourish he finished off,

'The brigadier was most impressed and has asked if you'd join him for a small celebratory drink in the classroom tonight after you've finished your admin followed by well-earned rest and some good grub, shall we say 7.30pm?'

They all had another final MI5 and Intelligence Corp debrief and then they were free to all go away, shower again, eat and lose the compo. They cleaned their kit and handed it in. The Colour Sergeant was not very keen to bill Les for the microphone they left behind but his boss, the QM was. The OC found out what had happened from the CSM, a replacement was somehow procured in a way that only colour sergeants throughout the Army always can and the matter was quietly dropped. At 7.30pm the commandant met them for a drink. They envisioned wine and G&T; they were wrong, although the brigadier stayed until 10pm the beer didn't run out until four in the morning.

UK, Oswestry - December 1972 – Drill, Tea & Doughnuts

'Right you pissing useless load of sorry twats, that's the worst fucking turnout I've ever seen in my twenty-one years of exemplary military service,' screamed Sgt Williams - who was in his element. Dressed immaculately as a Drill Sergeant he had just finished inspecting his platoon of thirty-two Junior Infantrymen, all about fifteen years old, and had found them all lacking.

'Your boots are filthy... FUCKING FILTHY! You should be ashamed to put them on your feet. I also expect to see real creases in your trousers. I could get better creases than that by rubbing my bare arse against a ship's fucking sail at sea in a force 10 storm.'

It was a wet and freezing December morning and Templar Platoon, Z (Training) Company, were on the lower square of Buller Barracks in Oswestry and it was being mercilessly swept by a bone numbing cold easterly wind. It was just gone 9am and they were on their first lesson of the day: Drill! Sgt Williams' favourite trick was to get the Junior Soldiers to throw away the tea and doughnuts, the cookhouse habitually delivered for NAAFI break at 10am, if the drill was not up to standard, which usually was the case. However, Junior Soldiers were encouraged to use their initiative at all times. So, they had pinched an unsupervised tea urn from the cookhouse and had simultaneously cleaned out and lined a dustbin very particularly. When Sgt Williams checked he would always find an empty urn and a dustbin full of doughnuts. He would then nip off for his own NAAFI break thinking that a lesson had been taught. Meanwhile the Junior Soldiers, who were little more than boys, would get out the real urn and retrieve the doughnuts. This arrangement went on satisfactorily for about two weeks.

It was usual for the sergeant, always halfway through each drill lesson, to nip off for a few minutes to use the amenities. He had, earlier in his career, been attached to the Australian Special Air Service during their chapter of the Vietnam War. During his tour, he had been sprayed with a Russian 9mm sub machine gun. The flak jacket he was wearing took the main hits and saved his life but as he turned to avoid the gunfire five of the rounds went into his bottom cheeks. For that he earned the unfortunate nickname 'six arseholes' which after a while got shortened to just 'SA'. Unfortunately, shortly after being shot infection set in to his wounds and complications had left him with a slight bladder problem. Back on the square they were given the order to dispose of their NAAFI break and, once confirmed, they were fallen out and left to their own devices for their thirty-minute break whilst Sg. Williams went and had his own short siesta. Within minutes they were all enjoying the tea and doughnuts and basking in their ingenuity. The NAAFI break came to an end and they dutifully marched back onto the square under the watchful eye of Sgt Williams. They halted and turned to face him.

'That was absolute shite, you wankers and, I might add, sorry excuses for junior leaders,' he shouted at them. He paused and then continued in a lower tone, 'And if you think your pathetic tea and doughnut stunt is beyond the ken of man then you think again my young lions.' He looked triumphant as their faces fell, knowing their tea and doughnuts ruse had come to an end. He went on, 'My dicky bladder also owes you a debt of gratitude. As you were supposed to throw your tea away I took the opportunity to piss in your full urn daily to save me a short walk these last couple of days.'

It was another three weeks before he thought they had earned the right to tea and doughnuts after drill, but in the meantime, he knew this time around they'd not touch it.

After the twenty six weeks of basic training was completed he watched all his boys, now immaculate in their own No.2 dress, pass off the square without fault in front of family and friends. After the parade he addressed them and, amongst the swearing and profanity that is the infantryman's vocabulary, he used genuinely moving words like pride, duty, honour and comradeship whilst almost succeeding to hold back his emotions and the tears of pride in his 'Young Lions'.

Chapter 4

The Cattle Market

Ballykinler, N.I., November 1976

All British Army anti-terrorist operations in the Province went into limbo at about eight o'clock every Thursday night. The reason for this was deceptively simple as *Top of the Pops* was on. To underline the importance of the evening, in Ballykinler specifically, it was also the night that the local weekly 'Cattle Market' was held. This was the reference to the disco that was also held on that same night in the NAAFI All Ranks Bar. Terrorists throughout County Down of whatever persuasion, undoubtedly knew this and it was probably the reason why very few arrests were made when weapons, or whatever nasty stuff, were in transit as it was probably accomplished at this time on this particular night of the week. The bad guys would move them on a Thursday night whilst the highly trained squaddies were ogling Pans People and storing images for the masturbatory event of the week later on that night. That was dependent on how they got on at the 'Cattle Market' of course, where a possible shag at odds of about ten million to one were potentially on offer. But hope springs eternal…

It always amazed Eddie that girls used to actually turn up at the 'Cattle Market' every Thursday. Local girls were transported in by bus for hairy arsed Tommies to look on in awe as a reminder as to what girls looked like 'done up'. Eddie was sure that this was a ruse used by the MOD so that after an eighteen-month tour of Northern Ireland soldiers on leave knew, more or less, what they were supposed to try and screw rather than grab eighty-year-old women from the local *Derby & Joan*. Thus, headlines such as 'Drunk Squaddie Screws Pensioner's Poodle in Love Nest' were avoided – well mostly!

Eddie wasn't into pop music that much, in fact he preferred opera and classical. He'd kept this a secret from the other lads as he knew it would become something he'd be teased mercilessly about plus no one would ever think of bending over anywhere near him ever again, especially in the shower. However, he was as partial to long stocking covered legs and the odd glimpse of panty elastic as the next man, even if it was like viewing a new kind of moving image on a postage stamp in the TV room at the NAAFI. The telly was shared between 200 or so guys and usually Eddie was somewhere near the back. In addition, even if you did like the music you'd not be able to appreciate it much above the din of said 200 soldiers. All would be suggesting at the top of their voice what they'd like to do with whatever Pans People had inside those panties, in particular the opaque bit where all the action usually happened. This specific night would be no exception and Kevin had told Eddie enthusiastically that he'd decided to get over to the NAAFI early to get a good seat in the TV room. Kevin couldn't quite work out the purpose of knickers, apart from being kept as a permanent trophy or reminder of a girl's scent; they just represented a sort of barrier to get across when the opportunity presented itself. As most all hoped it would tonight.

They all showered and spruced themselves up. Then, all dressed in baggy Oxford trousers with a high waistband, platform shoes and flamboyant shirts with long collars rounded at the corners, they departed for the NAAFI. Even though he was in the height of fashion Eddie felt somewhat ridiculous dressing up more or less as the others did but that was the way of things. They all sauntered over to the NAAFI looking like a small flotilla of yachts with spinnakers deployed. If the wind had blown in any serious way they could have ended up looking like a fashionable Red Devils' parachute display going sideways over Ballykinler at great speed. In the event the goddess of weather stayed her hand and they all arrived safely. The NAAFI was already packed but this was for the other much anticipated event of the evening just before the News – *The Magic Roundabout*! This programme, along with *Sesame Street*, had a very special place in the hearts of soldiers and no doubt most servicemen of all arms had a soft spot for these kiddies' shows. Why? God alone knows. Eddie could recall some months earlier being at a battle camp in Sennybridge in Wales with close to 300 soldiers all dressed in full battle order, cam cream on their faces, rifles, bayonets, heavy machine guns, mortars and anti-tank weapons. Men representing the entire complement of an infantry battalion's impressive life-depriving tools, sat, some on their large packs leaning on their weapons, totally immersed as *Sesame Street* played out in its entirety on a Saturday morning. They loved it! Perhaps it represents the generally miserable and mostly deprived childhoods that a large minority of soldiers experience and largely join the Army to get away from. It's as if in that short period of time, although dressed and equipped to deliver unthinkable destruction, most would experience at least a small dose of a childhood that they perhaps should have enjoyed as a child.

With a huge cheer *The Magic Roundabout* came onto the television. Eddie was sure that some of the Black Watch weaved fantasies around Florence of the unsavoury kind. For that matter, Eddie chuckled to himself, whilst looking around the room; Dougal could have had a life changing experience if he exposed the wrong part of his anatomy to a kilted soldier.

Magic Roundabout ended, and the News came on. Angela Rippon, hair beautifully set with eyebrows high and well-shaped, came on and started to relay the events of the day which started with a story about HMS Glasgow getting damaged in a fire at a shipyard. Some distinctly Scottish voices were heard to suggest they were lucky it hadn't been nicked completely as it was being fixed in Newcastle-upon-Tyne.

Angela Rippon was considered by some soldiers to represent posh totty and weaved fantasies about her. It was suspected that officers had more extravagant ones about her possibly involving whips and dominant themes. Barbara Edwards followed with the weather and informed everybody that the next day would be as hot as today was. One of the jocks unkindly suggested that she'd be no good at giving blow jobs as her nose was too big. He immediately regretted it as a wave of insults suggesting that it was his dick that was challenged in length, surged through the seated mass. *Nationwide* came on, but Sue Lawley was noticeably missing so the men sauntered away towards the bar for a refill whilst asking mates to look after their seats. Recharged they would reclaim their places to get the best possible view of the box to watch *Top of the Pops*.

Eventually the favourite program of the week burst onto the television and on this occasion Tony Blackburn dominated the show dressed in a flowery outfit that gave the impression of a hippie who had escaped from long term psychiatric care in California. With distinctly stiff coiffured long hair he was the absolute opposite of the soldiers present. They screamed and shouted obscenities at the man who was doing a good impression of getting in the way of the more visual type of entertainment they had waited all week for. The program eventually dished up the goods and Pans People did a couple of sessions of prancing about the screen looking sultry and available. The Bay City Rollers sang last as they were number one in the chart, the lead singer Lesley McEwen was berated by his obvious lack of respect for Tartan. Another Scots voice was heard to ask why the tart on the screen sounded like a bloke. Everyone laughed. Then it was over.

The noise calmed down and many went to the bar for the beginning of the 'Cattle Market'. The local girls who were bussed in to make the poor squaddies feel that HM Government actually cared for their sexual well-being had arrived. However, as there were usually about 200 soldiers on camp at any one time and at best they'd get about 20 girls to volunteer to come along, you might have guessed not many soldier's sexual well-being would be satisfied that night.

It might have been thought that the type of girl willing to be bussed into an Army camp for a disco with squaddies at a ratio of ten to one might be of the more sluttish variety. Although there were a couple of bikes that did pop along most of the girls were in fact quite the good girl sort and perhaps even thought they were doing their duty in dancing with soldiers a long way from their loved ones. The majority though, were girls who just wanted to get out of the six counties and go anywhere else; marrying a soldier was a good mechanism to achieve it. That said it didn't mean that they perhaps did not love the soldier they would eventually marry and use to leave the Province. Many ex-soldiers who met their loved one in Northern Ireland were still happily married many years later. The bulk though are probably divorced, especially if they went to Germany afterwards as that posting had a knack for splitting soldiers from their wives anyway regardless of where they met.

It was a local DJ who had the contract for providing the requisite music for the 'Cattle Market' and obviously the Army didn't like to pay top dollar for the entertainment. Therefore, the DJ was of almost pensionable age with a questionable taste in music, especially pop music. It was generally understood that during the rest of the week he did charitable work at a variety of local rest homes where he was able to mingle with people of a similar disposition and that his day job was undertaking or painting white lines in the middle of the road. When working alongside pensioners a benefit that he gained was that most of his customers would have been deaf anyway, a problem most soldiers also had curiously enough, especially their left ear. This was due to the fact that whilst shooting on the range they were supposed to use ear plugs to protect their ears. In reality these were lost about three minutes after issue as they came in a container the size of a Vic tube. Once lost, the Army expected you to pay to replace them. So, soldiers just went deaf on one side instead. Bizarrely it was the crack of the rifle next to you on the range that caused the damage and not your own which, although scientifically accurate, was considered weird by the serving soldier.

As usual the geriatric DJ started the evening off with 1950s Rock and Roll music to get everyone in the mood, or so he'd claim. In fact, this was not a bad strategy as for some unfathomable reason Scottish soldiers, not all but a fair amount, were absolutely besotted with this sort of stuff. This had to be some form of gene problem and seemed to be very prevalent in the Dundee area where the Black Watch recruited many of its men from. Eddie and the rest took up their customary place alongside the dance floor but not too far from the bar and weighed up their chances of getting a girl to join them for the high hard one later. In general their chances were crap, as far as the local girls were concerned they were just another squaddie as they were not allowed, due to obvious security reasons, to mention the NIPG to impress any attractive and potential shag.

The DJ put the Disco Duck song on and Kevin was noticed humming along and was ribbed mercilessly after he confided to Les that he might buy it. At this point one of the young ladies present walked purposefully across to Eddie and asked him if he wanted to dance. Eddie immediately looked over his shoulder to see who she was asking. Kevin conspiratorially nudged him in the ribs.

'She's asking you, ya stupid twat,' he whispered in his ear.

Eddie paused for a moment and wondered if he had been set up. He allowed her to take him by the hand and they went off and he attempted to dance. Eddie was awful at these things. He never knew what to say and always came across as very serious when trying to talk to girls. Eddie had a problem here, he was not a homosexual or anything, but he always had a problem communicating with girls. He had been to a succession of boys' schools that were Roman Catholic, only had boys for mates as a kid and joined the Army at fifteen. He had lost his virginity to a Hong Kong prostitute on his short posting to the colony prior to Northern Ireland. She didn't speak any English and his Cantonese wasn't much up to scratch outside of asking for a pint and telling a cab where the barracks were. It was a quiet, tacky and not quite so enjoyable experience as he had imagined it would be. So here he was having been asked by a girl for a dance not knowing what to say and all his mates watching.

He needn't have been so worried; she could talk for Britain at the Olympics and gain a gold medal. He danced the whole evening with her pausing every now and then whilst he quickly darted off to get her a drink, scared that some other smart talking squaddie would muscle in. She squeezed out of him almost every last fact about his life, interests, wants, aspirations and of course a few free drinks. Eddie was on a cloud, not only did she actually talk to him; she was very passable indeed, with long flowing auburn hair, a pretty enough face, decent figure and a very nice pair of pins. She was well dressed and displayed some class when walking, talking and dancing. Eddie was immediately besotted and by the end of the first dance hopelessly in love.

Eventually the evening did come to a close and without his feet touching the ground he escorted her to the bus, which for some reason always dropped them off and picked them up from just outside the camp gates. There was also a chip van just outside the camp gates. She gestured to the chip van and he started to look for change. She motioned that it was not chips she was interested in and they went behind the van and much to his amazement and delight found himself snogging quite deeply and being allowed to 'feel' his way about a bit. He was definitely in love now.

The bus driver sounded his horn and they had to break off, it was time for her to go. He kissed her deeply and she said she'd be back the week after for the next disco. He watched his vision climb on the bus and she waved to him. He, along with a few others who were lucky that night, watched the bus disappear around the bend and then they were gone, at least for another week anyway. Eddie turned and started to walk back to his block. He crossed the road outside of the cookhouse and was just rounding the side of the band block when THUMP, something heavy hit him on the back of the head. He went down hard and he could feel himself being kicked about by at least four guys. Eddie rolled into a ball best he could, but he had already taken one kick full in the face and was now taking kicks all over his body.

'That'll teach ya, ya Englis basta for takin our giwrls,' he heard in the mêlée.

Suddenly and thankfully, for a change, the Regimental Police arrived and broke it up grabbing three of the perpetrators. They must have been too engrossed to see the RPs coming. They were all taken back to the Guardroom and Eddie was unceremoniously thrown into a cell. He curled up on the wooden shelf that acted as a bed with no mattress and lost consciousness. A few hours later he found himself being dragged up by the RPs. He thought he was being taken to the MO and was surprised to find that they had marched him around to the Regimental Sergeant Major's Office of the Black Watch. It was Friday morning.

He was still in his civvies and covered in dried blood; he could barely stand straight from the pain in his body but tried anyway to stand to attention. The RSM looked him up and down in some disgust. CSM Bruce was sitting in the corner.

'Well that will teach you to pick on one of our soldiers, eh? Serves you bloody right.' Eddie could not believe what he was hearing. The RSM went on.

'We know what camaraderie means in the Black Watch, lad, it's just as well his mates turned up and stopped you, eh?' At that the RSM really looked at Eddie and paused for a moment.

'Lift ya shirt, lad.' Eddie lifted it and the RSM could see how many bruises there were.

'Provo Sergeant!' the RSM called and immediately the small wiry anthropological oddity was in the room.

'I want this man examined by a doctor and I want to know why nobody has examined his wounds until now. Also, send in the RPs who arrested this man, I want a word with them.'

Eddie noted that the RSM didn't have to draw diagrams or hold up pictures for the Provo to understand what the RSM wanted. His worth went up a bit in Eddie's opinion. Eddie was driven down to the MRS[25] and a doctor examined him. The doctor gave him some *Aspirin* and had him showered and placed into a bed.

A while later the CSM came down and visited him.

'Nothing broken, lad, but you took a very severe beating. The RPs who arrested you have stated that the men they found you with claim that they were helping you and that they found you in this condition. The RPs say they did not see any of them kicking you or anything. The RPs also mentioned that they didn't take any names as they believed nothing wrong had been done by the Black Watch soldiers. Why did they pick on you?'

Eddie's face was a mess, but he was able to mumble.

'It was over a local girl. Seems one liked me, and they didn't want that, so they beat me up.'

---

[25] Medical Reception Station – Small Medical Centre in an Army Camp.

'Would you recognise any of them?'

'Probably two of them at least, possibly three, sir,' Eddie said, coughing a little.

'Good, then you can point them out to the RSM and we'll deal with them. I'll be back later,' said the CSM closing the conversation, but Eddie wasn't having any of it.

'Er, with respect no, sir, I will not point them out. We don't do that in our regiment.' Eddie looked the CSM in the face and he knew what that look meant.

'I'm not having you going on your own vendetta, lad. They might beat you up again. Leave it to me and the proper process for these things.' The CSM shook his head, paused and then left. As he walked back to the RSM's office he understood where Eddie was coming from and, although he'd never admit it, agreed with him. After all, he'd also been a private soldier himself a few lifetimes ago.

Eddie was out of the MRS the next day, all his wounds were quite superficial and being fit helped the repair process. His face though still had two black eyes and his nose was very swollen. Kevin laughed like a drain when he saw him and asked if she crossed her legs whilst he was going down on her. Eddie just grunted in disgust, and it was then that he realised that he didn't actually know the girl's name as he never asked.

Kevin looked him up and down, shook his head and said,

'I'm gonna read the fortune of the twats who did this to you. Just point them out and let me go at the cowardly bastards!' He spat out the last bit and Eddie knew that certain members of the Black Watch were going to have a very bad hair day soon if they met Kevin.

The following morning, a Sunday, the RSM paraded all troops who were in camp the night of the 'Cattle Market' on the main square. Eddie, accompanied by the RSM, was made to go along all ranks and point out who had done the deed. Eddie paused and looked very closely, one at a time, at the three whom he did recognise but continued onto the end. However, he indicated to the RSM that he did not recognise anybody. The RSM was not fooled but accepted it and dismissed all the soldiers.

Neither Eddie nor the rest saw those three again. The RSM had obviously had them posted to Outer Mongolia or perhaps worse but a potentially serious situation was defused. The men of the Black Watch noted that Eddie didn't tell on the guys who had done it, and although they had been moved they were not in any trouble. So honour was preserved and no more was said.

Unfortunately, the girl Eddie had fallen in love with never did show up again at the 'Cattle Market'. He persuaded himself that she must have met a major celebrity or perhaps a passing multi-millionaire, fell in love and lived happily ever after. For that he hoped she'd burn in Hell for eternity, or even longer.

The training and selection continued for another two 'Cattle Markets' during which time the group's members did in-depth helicopter training, did a week with the Royal Marines on their Cold Weather Survival Course plus a few days working with the SAS elite Mountain Troop as they'd be working in the Province over the winter. They did a lot of work at night learning how to work even more closely together, almost without needing to think, to know instinctively what the others were just about to do. For example, the others in his group realised instinctively that Eddie would almost always fall over at night when he had to cross a fence, and it was soon discovered that at night he was almost blind. This was soon sorted out by a visit to an optician where a new set of glasses were obtained, and he immediately stopped falling on his arse every time he met a barbed wire fence.

They worked on their webbing and camouflage using old clothes, sandbags and army green towels. Their webbing took time to get together as they had to know intimately where everything was in their pouches. Camera parts, batteries, magazines, smoke grenades, everything! First aid kits were owned by all and had been added to by the medics at the MRS. By the time they had finished they could probably equip a minor field hospital between themselves.

Pete and Eddie had spent three days at the A&E at Musgrave Park Hospital where they were expected to help, as medical assistants, with the goriest of incidents to pick up hints as to how such patients are treated initially to keep them breathing. The doctors and nurses sensed they were from some form of special unit and gave them all sorts of information and tips on how to keep people alive, especially when they have big holes in them.

Camera skills were honed to perfection and taking photos with 1000mm lenses became routine. How exposure worked, ASA, depth of field and how different types of film could be used to get the required results were subjects that were all mastered.

The runs still happened every day and, as a result, they were at the highest level of physical fitness. Even Eddie could run twenty miles in full kit and barely get out of breath. CSM Bruce was promoted to warrant officer first class and he celebrated his promotion in style with his boys. At the height of the evening WOI Bruce introduced the OC who informed them that on the morrow they had finished their selection training and would become operational. Pete was RTU'd immediately that same night as the backup. Eddie was relieved, but Pete cried like a baby.

UK, Exeter - May 1973 – Don't Forget to Lift the Seat!

Eddie and all the other Junior Infantrymen in his platoon had been on a hard exercise for three weeks at Oakhampton Camp. Afterwards, it had taken two days to get the chalk out of their webbing, kit, ears and in some cases from under their foreskin. They had been doing a defence exercise, which meant digging trenches, and just like family BBQs, digging trenches always brings rain. The heavens opened and for fifteen days they felt that the whole of the English Channel had fallen on their heads. Therefore, although only just under seventeen years old they felt it was OK to go for a few illegal drinks at the 'Hour Glass' pub in Exeter. The owner knew they were under age but at that time it was more accepted, almost a tradition and anyway he needed the business.

Eddie and a couple of friends trooped in and ordered a few drinks and the evening wended its merry way along. There were just a few old boys in the pub making their pensions go a bit further as the 'Hour Glass' was not the most expensive of places; rather the opposite and the décor matched the prices. After a couple of rounds some bravado surfaced and Tony, a friend, challenged Eddie to a drinking competition. The drink of choice was Vodka and lime. They both started off well and were matching each other drink for drink. After a few Eddie started to feel queasy and found that if he closed his eyes the room would start to spin at an alarming rate. He carried on and after a few more although matching Tony's appetite, he suddenly felt a serious need to get to the toilet and throw up. He got up from his chair and found walking was not exactly easy and kept hitting the wall. He hit the doorframe with a withering jolt but managed to ricochet down the short corridor and bounced along it until he ended up in the toilet proper. He could feel the entire contents of his stomach making its way up his neck and clenched his teeth to prevent him pebble dashing the urinal wall. He threw himself at the left cubicle and just as he entered managed a spectacular multicoloured yawn directed at the toilet. This was immediately followed by a second ejaculation of bodily content that no doubt still had bits of old compo mixed majestically with his last half digested Army supper and beer, interspersed with lager and splashes of Vodka and lime.

'Fuck me, I'm sorry,' he said to the old chap who was sitting on the toilet at the time now liberally covered with the contents of Eddie's stomach. Especially in the lower area where his trousers would normally have been had they not

been round his ankles at the time acting as a stop for anything that missed his lower body. Eddie promptly blacked out, although no one ever knew if it was from embarrassment, the alcohol or the sudden and severe beating from the walking stick he suffered.

Chapter 5

Soiled Vests and Tattered Underpants

County Londonderry, N.I., November 1976

The two box vans lurched over the sleeping policemen and drove into Fort George in Londonderry. It had taken almost two hours to drive from Ballykinler and for the whole journey they had to all sit on the floor with all their kit. Steve leapt out and told them to park and then to join him in the briefing room. Immediately they found they had a problem parking up. As they were just about to attend a briefing by the Commander Land Forces they felt it was justifiable that they could park literally anywhere they wanted to. Eddie pointed to some ATO[26] vehicles and suggested that they got them to move so they could park. Les got the driver to pull up just behind them and Eddie jumped out and ran up to the heavily armoured transit van and tapped on the window. Eddie could see there was a guy in the vehicle and from his cap badge he could see he was a signaller. The Scaly[27] was laid back, beret over his eyes and making a good impression of someone who was fast asleep. Eddie knocked again but the Scaly remained inert. As the door and windows were armoured Eddie felt it was OK to thump the door with his rifle – very hard. The signaller stirred a bit but was not waking up. Eddie again thumped the door this time generating enough noise to embarrass any self-respecting firework manufacturer. The figure lifted his beret slightly and with tortured and bloodshot eyes viewed the offender with undisguised disgust. Eddie thumped the door again and gestured to the Scaly to wind down the window. This the signaller did with such speed that a snail with a limp would have considered the man almost stationary. Slowly the window wound down and Eddie was

---

[26] Ammunition Technical Officer – Very brave people who deal with terrorist bombs.
[27] Royal Signals personnel were nicknamed Scalybacks or Scalies.

assaulted by the fetid air that rushed out reminding him of hangovers, stale breath, and old cigarette smoke, coupled a flatulent smell that would make any self-respecting cabbage enthusiast green with envy.

'What the fuck do you want?' half whispered the signaller managing, without effort; to convey the impression that he already hated Eddie with a passion.

'Er, can you move your vehicle as we have a briefing with the CLF and need to park up?'

'No! Now piss off!' The window started to crawl upwards again slowly but surely.

'But... but we need the...' Eddie's voice trailed off as he knew it would do no good. Defeated he walked back to the vehicle and told Les what had happened.

'Gus! Get the fuck over there and use your sensitive, physically persuasive yet diplomatic technique, to get Scaly arsehole over there to move his bleedin' vehicle.'

Kevin wandered over and after ten minutes or so was seen to enter into an animated discussion with the signaller over the subject of moving his vehicle. Kevin was soon back and suggested to Les, in a matter of fact kind of way that perhaps they should find somewhere else to park and without ceremony got into the back of the vehicle. Both Eddie and Les noticed that Kevin was definitely not holding any body parts and there were no signs of blood anywhere.

'Well fuck a donkey, there's a turn up,' said Les to no one in particular as their box van drove off past the ATO vehicles. The absence of the Scaly was now noted and meant he was probably off somewhere else contaminating all and sundry elsewhere.

'So what happened with the Scaly, Gus?' shouted Eddie innocently towards the back of the van.

'Not much, that turd of a Scalyback shoved a blow back automatic shotgun up my nose and suggested I fucked off before he decorated Fort George with the contents of my bogey filled nose and anything else that I may also have sitting just behind it. He looked like he meant it, so I took his advice, the man's obviously a bigger nutter than I am.'

They eventually found some parked up RAOC[28] guys who Kevin scared off

---

[28] Royal Army Ordnance Corp (or Rag And Oil Company) – Corp that handled logistics for the Army.

with a glare and a half-muttered insult. The briefing took place as planned and the job turned out to be a search of a barn that the Intelligence community suspected of being a bomb factory. However, it was thought that the place was booby trapped and if a full search with warrants etc. was attempted the place would be blown sky high and all the evidence with it. Along with the people who were carrying warrants and search kit of course! Basically, the place was to be infiltrated, made safe and then, when the cavalry appeared, the place wouldn't disappear from the face of the Earth. Arrests would be made, and judicial retribution would take its full course.

The presence of the ATO at the briefing made it plain that the bomb disposal team parked outside with the demonic Signaller were going to be part and parcel of the operation. The role of the NIPG was to get the ATO and his team near enough and then into the building stealthily to allow them to make the place safe. Steve rolled his eyes and pondered whether or not he'd prefer burial or cremation, if they found enough of him for either option that is. He mentioned that this was not their role, but the OC pointed out that this was urgent, and they were the only ones available. The remainder of both teams were briefed together by Steve and the ATO officer – he had captain's pips, but he introduced himself as Stan and was immediately popular with the guys.

All through the briefing Signaller Smale, as his name turned out to be, lurked darkly on the periphery of the proceedings whilst covering all present with an invisible coating of goblin breath and arse odour – it was as if he'd spent his entire life sitting in a sewer living on compo whilst smoking endless supplies of *Camel* cigarettes. What the guys were not aware of was the fact that the grimy signaller and the entire ATO team had been crawling through culverts most of the night checking for devices. Most had been full of cow dung and other stuff that smelt even worse; this explained why he was tired, not entirely in a good mood and stank to high heaven. All this was to make sure the route to the target was clear. After the briefing they all, including Stan who removed his captain's pips, drifted over to the NAAFI All Ranks Bar where Smale joined them and demonstrated his celebrated ability to get absolutely diabolically drunk. The booze flowed freely, and all present did the best they could to wipe out the thought that in just under eight hours' time some of them might be doing a passable impression of Smithfield Meat Market after a very busy morning.

At 4.30am Eddie woke with a hangover that felt like someone was leaping about inside his head in diver's boots wailing a tuneless song whilst a six-year-old accompanied him playing a drum.

Shit! he thought. *Never should have had that eighth pint.* He got out of his green maggot and stumbled over to the ablutions for the customary morning slash. At one of the sinks was a cheerful and bouncy Smale fully showered and now obviously revelling in a refreshing morning shave. He glanced at Eddie via the mirror.

'What a fucking lovely day, good morning!' beamed Smale indulging himself in the obvious discomfort that Eddie was suffering at that moment.

'I'm just off for a fucking huuuuugge breakfast, fried bread, greasy eggs, fried bacon the whole effing kit and caboodle, wanna join me?'

Eddie aimed his body at the nearest cubicle fell to his knees and quite colourfully threw up at the thought. Smale gave encouragement.

'Don't worry, I'm happy to wait for you… then again I may just go for the kippers, you know, bags of butter. Fucking excellent!' He licked his lips. Eddie threw up again and pondered if there was some clause in the Geneva Convention that was supposed to stop this kind of abuse.

After breakfast, they all met near the vehicles for a final briefing. Amazingly Smale had brought along a mug of steaming tea and offered Eddie some. Eddie accepted; it was great, bit sweet but lovely all the same.

'Thanks!' said Eddie with genuine gratitude.

'No probs, mate. Thanks for the beers last night – I was brasack I'm afraid.' He turned away and started to listen to Stan whilst Eddie felt he'd just glimpsed the part of the Devil when he was still just an Archangel with a poor attitude. He gratefully sipped at the tea.

Stan waited until he was sure all were paying attention.

'Right then,' he began, his Aberdeen accent made him sound quite posh. 'We're gonna be in a very dodgy situation in about thirty minutes as we have to get in fast and make sure the place isn't booby trapped before the search team swoop in. This means securing the area and checking for command wires. Smale here will do a check for radio controlled devices just as we get in.' He made it sound so simple.

'However, if it is a bomb factory they'll probably want it to blow sky high before we get any evidence. We'll need to know if they have got anyone on watch, a sentry or something. If there is then you have to nab him. If it looks like he's gonna press a button or something just shoot the bastard, OK?' They all nodded, Kevin especially.

'If you don't manage to do that then we will all hear a very large bang and then we will immediately spread ourselves over a very large area and await the police who will pick up our remains and place them into a communal plastic bag and you'll all get to spend eternity sharing a very small, but intimate space, with Signaller Smales' bollocks and other body parts that do not bear description – I'm sure you all get the message.'

They all did and as if to underline the remark Smale scratched his testicles vigorously. The briefing then went into some detail and all and sundry were shown aerial photos of the immediate area, plus mug shots of the suspected purveyors of homemade bombs and local mischief makers with Republican leanings. But the basic plan was to sneak up and sneak in.

The vehicles all rolled out of Fort George with the NIPG box vans a sensible lead ahead, so they were not associated with the small convoy. When they were about a mile away from the farm the resident battalion's vehicles peeled off and took up their positions at the various junctions around the farm. They were told to keep the engine noises down as Land Rovers were quite distinctive.

The ATO's armoured transit vans pulled up behind the NIPG vehicles and everyone silently debussed. Smale, Stan and the ATO team were surprised to see eight bushes climbing out of the NIPG vehicles. They all had their ghillie smocks and camouflaged hats on. Serious amounts of old sandbags, army shirts and other green and brown materials had to be ripped up and attached to the jackets, hats and other paraphernalia they carried. Their rifles and other weapons were covered in camouflage DPM materials and paints. At that, Steve gave Stan a slight nod as the patrols 'ghostwalked' into the hedge line and literally disappeared.

'I don't think I'll quite take the piss as much in the future. I'd hate them to effing sneak up on me,' commented Smale with a tinge of admiration.

'Yeah! I'm glad I'm standing here and not guarding that fucking barn right now!' Stan said still trying to see if he could see any of them.

The two NIPG teams had spread around the farm and were going to come in from separate directions at right angles to each other. Once secured they'd send the password and the ATO also would sneak in and start to clear the area.

The farm, as usual and as expected, had a farmhouse. This was an old rambling affair that had certainly seen better days. Tiles were missing and some of the gutters were hanging down leaving rust stains tarnishing the red brick walls. A few windows had cardboard in them where replacing the glass must have been too pricey. There were no lights on in the building and as far as they could see, if there was anyone in there, they were asleep. The barn was on the corner of the farm, it was huge and largely made from corrugated steel. In front of it was a large apron of concrete that was cracked and broken in many places. Beyond the concrete and just to the side of the house was a milking parlour. Steve's patrol was going to come in between the milking parlour and the barn.

'Steve?' whispered Les.

'What?'

'I can't smell any shit?' noted Les. Steve thought that was a blessing

'That's because that Smale git is downwind – you twat!' whispered Steve.

'No... fucking listen – it's a farm with no smell of shit? How many pissing farms have you been to in this toilet of a province that don't smell of shit, eh?' Steve thought for a moment.

'This whole fucking country usually smells of shit, so what's the point?'

Les sighed and went on.

'The whole fucking point is that this can't be a farm 'cause it doesn't smell of shit – so what else are they doing 'ere then?' Les rested his case.

'I thought the briefing said they were making bombs and not milk, potatoes or cow shit for that matter. So, fucking Sherlock, let's move on, eh?'

Les was a bit deflated but the team knew what he was getting at, more likelihood they were going to meet some dickhead with co-op mix than a cow. They fanned out and hugged the front of the milking parlour and covered each other as they moved silently across the concrete one at a time. They reached the side of the barn with no incident. A light rain started that sounded off the corrugated iron with a very low metallic hum.

'Piss and shit it would effing rain,' whispered Kevin. They were all in the lee of the barn except Kevin who was on the corner as he had the Bren. They were well into the shadow of the barn and that was a godsend.

A light suddenly came on downstairs in the house. They all froze and merged more into the shadows. A door opened and out came a small, but wiry older man wearing just underpants and a vest that had not seen a sink in several years. He stretched, yawned, looked up, and cursing the rain, walked a few paces along the building where he opened another door, and very soon the familiar sound of water tinkling into water was heard across the farm. Steve's team saw Mark's group, one of the Black Watch patrols moving alongside the house. They had also seen the guy and two of his team had set up either side of the toilet door, one with a silenced SMG levelled at head height and the other with what appeared to be a gag. The man pulled the chain and walked out still adjusting himself when the SMG was pushed firmly onto the side of his head. The man opened his mouth in surprise and the other team member stuffed a gag in his mouth and wrapped a hessian sack around his head then placed quickly plasti-cuffs on him. The two of them walked him silently to the rear of the milking parlour for a little chat on who else might be about, the SMG now pointed markedly at his genital area. The other two members of Mark's patrol joined Steve by simply crossing over the apron.

'Jeez, it's fucking quiet,' whispered Mark in a deep highland accent.

'Good,' said Steve, 'any big bangs right now would really piss me off.' Mark smiled grimly in response, his teeth showing through the cam cream.

Mark whispered to his last team member to go and see what the others had managed to get out of the man they had nabbed. After a few minutes, he returned and gave the details in his thick Glaswegian accent.

'He says there's nobody else in the house. He says he knows nought about any bombs etc.'

'OK!' said Mark and then looked at Steve. 'Your guys are going to check the barn aren't they? We'll stop anyone leaving the building, if we hear any noise we'll pop into their living room for a cuppa and a bun, OK?'

Steve wasn't impressed with the results of the interrogation of the man in the fifty year old Y-fronts.

'Are you sure he fucking well understood the questions, ya Scots twat?'

'Aye, he did take a bit a prompting but nought that a few days in decent medical care won't put right, though he stinks worse than a Chinaman's shithouse.'

Steve indicated to the others that the barn needed to be checked to see if it was booby trapped. The evening before Stan had given them some advice on finding booby traps his best line of advice was 'not to touch any damn thing at all – just look'. Steve sighed, infantrymen hated booby traps.

They moved around to the front of the building and found the barn door half open. They checked it for trip wires or any other wires for that matter, but found none. They moved into the barn and found the place completely empty. No cows, nothing. Just the odd bale of hay and a strewn floor so deep in dust and crap you could leave footprints in it. They checked the building and decided there was nothing there. Steve got onto the radio.

'Hello 2 this is Charlie 21 – Grass Moon over.' 2 responded likewise and that meant the area was clear and that ATO could come in and formally clear the building. The remaining NIPG members got into all round defence whilst keeping a watchful eye on the house. Stan turned up in a few minutes. The patrol was spread about the barn looking out through holes and gaps covering themselves just in case a swarm of Irishmen clad in soiled vests and underpants should come screaming over the horizon.

'Hi, it's only me,' said Stan as he wandered in.

He paused near the door and scanned the barn. Smale walked in just behind him and they conferred for a moment or two. Stan attracted Steve's attention by clicking his fingers softly.

'OK listen – I want all of you to leave the barn by walking clockwise around the walls from where you are now following your original footsteps. Got it? Be quick please.'

They all, quietly but without hanging about, did as they were told and then went outside. Stan went back inside and started to examine the floor very carefully. After a few moments he went back to Smale who was waiting patiently. He started to put on his helmet.

'What the fuck's happening?' said Steve to Stan.

'I think the place is wired – only need the helmet as it's got the radio in it – rest of the suit will be a waste of time if this goes up.'

'If what goes up? There's fuck all in there.'

'Smale has detected a radio-controlled device near here and I doubt it's some little boy playing with his plane right now. I suspect there is a pressure sensitive plate here as Smale points out that is turned on and off by radio – apart from you guys there are no other footprints in here. If any of you had stood on it – whoom! No more shagging... ever!'

'What the fu...?' Steve was speechless.

'You were supposed to secure the barn and look but not go into it without us remember? Intelligence has picked up information that indicates there is a rather serious lab below the floor protected by a booby trapped flap with a radio device in the house... if they hit the tit right now we're all dead men.'

Steve went green and gagged a bit – when he spat it out it was his breakfast. Stan went on,

'I suggest you guys make sure that no one in that house can hit a button whilst I sort this end out, eh?' Steve nodded. Steve told his guys what had just happened and they all went various shades of white except this was hidden by the cam cream. Mark and Steve conversed about what was the best plan of action to stop them all becoming part of a large barn shaped crater in the next few minutes.

'No one seems to have missed the vest over there, perhaps we can persuade him to assist us again,' said Mark. One of Mark's guys pointed out that as he could barely walk at the moment it might be a little hard to arrange.

'It's fucking amazing what you can get done with the proper motivation, eh?' said Mark, a little too light-heartedly as he sneaked away for another chat. The ATO went into the barn whilst 'The Pope' and team went into the house, very carefully indeed. It was like a deserted building with bare floorboards and cracked walls with huge amounts of dust and the odd piece of broken furniture about the place. It was Les that cottoned on first.

'Stand still,' he commanded, albeit whispered.

Steve was just about to walk up the stairs but respect for Les and his skills made him obey the order, but he was keen to know why.

'What's the fucking problem, Leather? I'm fucking wet and I need some breakfast, a shag and a good kip so can we just get on with it please?'

'Eh? I may be wrong but there are no other footprints in this room – just like the barn.' Les stated this coolly almost academically.

'OK, but Adonis in the vest came out of the house and he didn't appear to be in any way worried about this place, did he?' appealed Steve.

'Agreed, but he came out of the kitchen... not the living room! I am convinced there is nothing upstairs... don't stand on the staircase – if you do I think we'll all suddenly become a small yet important part of the local history here and our parents and loved ones will hear about it on News at Ten tonight... get my drift?' They did.

Eddie was the first to make the next connection.

'Then the ugly fuck in the Y-fronts told that bullshit story to get us to come in here then?'

'Looks like that, but in all honesty, he looks too thick to understand a plot like this,' Steve said it more matter-of-factly than he felt at that point.

'OK, so what do we do now then?' Les sounded impatient to get out and the rest felt the same way. Steve looked around at the rest of them.

'Do we all agree that we think there is no one else in this house right now but just a pile of perhaps co-op mix ready to blow our balls to kingdom come?' They all nodded.

'OK then let's get the fuck out - Eddie, once we are out, get clear of these buildings and get on the radio, tell the search team to come in carefully but to stay about one hundred yards out until Stan gives the all clear. Let's all slowly leave the building as Elvis has definitely done a bunk.' They left without mishap.

Outside the barn Smale was feeding cable into the ATO and listening to what he was saying over some earphones. Eddie found himself standing next to Smale whilst Steve briefed Stan on the house and the fact that it was probably just a big firework waiting to go off. Smale slipped a small flask to Eddie who opened it and took a quick swig of Brandy. Eddie offered it open back to Smale. Smale shook his head, closed it, put it away and said,

'I keep it for other poor buggers who have just seen ghosts – and you, you poor bugger, look like you've just seen one,' he whispered, his teeth shining in the morning light betraying a slight grin. Dawn was starting to creep across the morning, casting long shadows. Eddie nodded his thanks and moved on.

Later, over a brew, Stan explained that there was no lab underneath the barn just a very big bomb and the house was wired as well, but was designed to go up at the same time as the barn device was triggered and vice versa. He hinted that the guy who did it knew his business and it took Stan several hours to make the place safe for the search teams to discover what he already knew, that the place was designed to go bang in a big way with as many of Her Majesty's servants in it as possible. The intelligence about the place was a definite IRA 'come-on' and the Army had fallen for it. However, due to good luck nobody got hurt. The guy in the underpants was only supposed to nip in every now and then and stay only in the kitchen, then to turn on prearranged lights and such like to make the place look lived in. He had gotten a bit the worse for wear the previous evening and fell asleep in the house. He denied he knew anything about the bombs etc. The story he gave was one he was told by the people who were paying him to check out the house and the lights etc. It was most likely true as the man was little more than a tramp. The Republican movement had no qualms about using him as a decoy. The man had little more than his life, and that was crap! They were willing to relieve him of even that.

The search team did their thing after ATO had secured the area but found nothing of note except lots of Co-op mix. Afterwards everyone went back to the barracks and decided that getting drunk was probably the right thing to do. So once back at Ballykinler, and after the usual post operation debriefs, weapons and kit cleaning, shit, shave shower and shampoo, they decided to go to Newcastle for a night out. Newcastle wasn't that far as the crow flies, but they'd have to follow the A2 all over the place to get there. They showered and put on their most fashionable clothes and, due to the fact they all had to carry a pistol, a jacket was mandatory. Once ready they all tumbled into Steve's recently acquired Fiat 127, booked out at the Guardroom and rushed, as fast as that inept Italian technology would take them, to Newcastle, a small seaside town just below Ballykinler. It took about thirty minutes or so to get there and they parked up just off the promenade and found a likely looking pub. It was packed as it was a Friday night after all. Live music was in full swing and everyone appeared to be having a great time. They slowly weaved their way to the bar and ordered some drinks.

'You in the Army?' the barmaid asked. It was a common enough question and they were all used to it. Les responded first.

'No, we're Roman Catholic nuns on our day off,' he said seriously.

'I thought that was it, just couldn't quite put my finger on it,' she shouted over the din.

'I'll be happy to let you put your finger or any other part of your anatomy on it at any time actually.'

'It's tempting but as you're a nun and all that we'd best not, I don't want a reputation for hanging around with the tegs.'

'Okay I understand; would it be better if we were indeed squaddies?'

'Not a lot but it's better than being a nun I suppose,' she admitted, then smiled.

Eddie and the others could see that Les was smitten by the barmaid so left him to it and sauntered over to the live band to see if any more talent was about. There was lots of it but most of it was already anchored to a local guy as was the norm in these small towns. They were looked at with a mixture of admiration, disgust and fear. The various Loyalist factions had differing views on the presence of the Army and some were downright aggressive. However, they all knew that squaddies with jackets on usually meant they were 'carrying' and that meant no confrontations although the odd sideways insult was often sneaked out.

Newcastle was a Protestant stronghold and soldiers were generally very safe there. But Steve kept a watchful eye on his boys just to make sure. As he'd be driving later he had decided to stay relatively sober. Kevin and Eddie managed to find a table and were listening to the live band. A mixture of local traditional Irish and pop music was pumped out and as usual the quality of both the playing and singing was excellent. It was curious that traditional Irish songs were played in amongst the nationalist and pop music ones. Eddie, whose entire family, except him and his sister, were all Irish Catholics and born in Dublin, had an advantage over most soldiers in understanding the importance of Irish music and the meanings behind the tunes and he was intrigued by the mixture. It was almost as if the Protestants were admitting their Irish status by proxy of the band and music. He looked about the room but doubted if anyone had really noticed the irony of it all.

They wondered about Les, but on checking it seemed that Les had got himself a girlfriend so the evening was not a complete waste of time. They all managed to slip in a few more drinks and it was suspected that Les also managed to slip something in as well allowing for the time he was absent. Tiredness, however, caught up with them and eventually they made their way back to camp. Unfortunately, they got back to the camp five minutes past midnight and the Provo Sergeant was waiting for them with undisguised glee. Soldiers were supposed to be booked back into camp before midnight or they were in trouble. The Fiat had managed the sleeping policemen without falling apart but the noises it made meant it was threatening to. They parked outside the Guardroom and they all trooped in to sign back into camp. Not only were they late but it appeared to the Cro-Magnon man in the Provost uniform that they had probably had more than the regulation two pints as well. The Provo Sergeant immediately called them to attention and started to dress them down about drinking and being late. However, they couldn't quite understand all the grunts and noises he was making but they got the message and they all said, 'Yes, Sergeant,' when he paused as it seemed sensible to say something. They all took Steve's lead as he was the sober one plus he was their boss. Steve said nothing except 'Yes,' when his name was called out from the booking in and out sheet. The remainder did the same. They then left the Guardroom suspecting that something was up but not quite sure what.

They all got back in the car and agreed to forget the whole thing. Meanwhile the monkey in the No.2 Dress uniform was writing up four charge sheets for being drunk and booking into camp late. As an aside it is said that if you get an infinite number of chimpanzees typing on an infinite number of type writers for infinity then they will produce a bible or some such work by chance. Well it didn't take the Provost Sergeant quite that long but it did take him a few hours. But a large number of new AF252 Charge Sheet books would need to be ordered by the RQMS at Battalion HQ to fill the sudden void created.

UK, Southampton, February 1976 – What Dress Sense?

Eddie felt great! He'd just had a few buckets of the old amber gargle with a few mates and was now off to see his girlfriend hoping for a deep, satisfying shag. This would take all his powers of persuasion as he was sure that she was still a virgin. At least he was sure she was one when he left to go to Hong Kong just over a year and a half earlier. He had just arrived back in the UK from a posting to Hong Kong and was on disembarkation leave prior to his regiment's posting to Ballykinler in Northern Ireland. His free time in honkers was mainly taken up by excursions into Wan Chai to drink too much San Miguel beer and listen to ancient wrinkly Chinese guys whose only words of English were 'you want rovery giwl, velly yung, rong time, row plice?'

He was back now and walking along Brinton Road, at the end of St. Mary's Street to the bus stop where he could catch the number 5 bus to Sholing in Southampton. In Hong Kong, the fashion was for very colourful clothes, extremely baggy trousers with an enormous waistband and flowery shirts with very long pointed collars. He was currently wearing a tailor-made Kermit green silk jacket with big bright yellow buttons. He had also taken advantage of the cheap tailoring facilities to have a full-length leather coat made for him. At the time, due to excess of alcohol, a huge fur collar seemed an entirely reasonable thing to add. His shoes had such high platforms that he was in serious threat of breaking something if he fell over. He was rolling along thinking he was looking like a rather attractive version of something out of the Shaft movies. He was, but without the dress sense, style and was certainly lacking in the easy cool of the genre. It was a certainty that heterosexual men wouldn't bend down anywhere near him and it was doubtful that gay men would be seen dead near him either. His civvie mates that he just had a beer with did give him a double take but, after a while, realised that it was still in fact the same old Eddie it was just that he had been kidnapped by aliens, brainwashed and dressed up like an eccentric pimp without him knowing it.

'He'll get better,' they all agreed. Eddie was oblivious to this and felt that he was at the height of fashion in the place, and of course he was – but that place was eight thousand miles away somewhere east of Suez and not gritty, dirty Southampton. He was walking towards the bus stop but between him and his target was Nichols Road. This junction had the old corner barriers that looked like scaffolding and followed the kerb on each side of the road. The reason was to stop people crossing the road at the junction and damaging cars by bending the front of unsuspecting vehicles with their grossly negligent bodies. The idea was to follow the barrier and cross the road at a safer spot further around the corner. But Eddie was a fit young soldier at the peak of his physical prime and could not be bothered to follow the implied advice of Southampton City Council. He placed his left hand on the top bar and propelled himself feet first over the obstacle.

Unfortunately, his rather oversize platform shoes of diver's boots proportions caught the top bar and Eddie unceremoniously rolled over the bar and cluttered down the other side managing to land face first in the gutter. It was the five inches of water that his face and body found themselves in that made Eddie realise he had not noticed that it had in fact rained whilst he was in the Kingsland Arms imbibing. The excess of cloth caused by the baggy clothes he was wearing managed to soak up almost the whole puddle by the time he had recovered and stood up again. Eddie sheepishly brushed himself off best he could and strode across the road and, in a gesture to make amends, launched himself at the barrier on the far side. Eddie's face hit the floor hard as exactly the same thing happened again. He lay on the floor for a few minutes hoping that perhaps the gods would smile upon him and make him disappear from view and perhaps, in their mercy, just allow him to spend an eternity in purgatory for him to recover from the embarrassment, but unfortunately that never happened.

Slowly and painfully he stood up. He tasted blood and realised that he had a nose bleed and some of the blood had splashed on his now muddy and wet flowery shirt. He sniffed a few times to stop the flow of blood and walked the last thirty or so yards to the bus stop all the while feeling the curious stares of the twenty or so people already waiting for the bus, who had watched the entire performance as they were looking up the road waiting for the same bus that he was going to catch. Eddie tried to stand amongst the other pedestrians who slowly but surely moved away from him thinking that he was a tramp that had found a stock pile of clothes from a deranged male with the taste for Liberace, but was not quite as restrained. Eddie didn't get a shag either, in fact he didn't even get into the house. Next day his girlfriend took him shopping.

Chapter 6

A Day at the Races

December 1976

'Where the fuck is Santa Claus when you need him, eh?' Les' whispered comment punctured the silence but failed to stop the heavy snow falling all about them.

'Shut up, Leather,' came a fervent whispered response from Steve.

'Well,' continued Les ignoring Steve's command, 'you'd think the old bastard would give us good guys a readymade effing hide for Christmas just so we didn't have to dig one out again.'

'Don't be a twat, Les,' interjected Kevin dismissively, 'where the fuck would Rudolph land the pissing sleigh and anyway none of us 'ave got a fucking carrot for 'im.'

Eddie stopped digging and looked up. 'I dunno, I think Steve's nose right now could be mistaken for a carrot or has someone stuck their dick in his face?'

'If you bastards don't shut up I'll fucking charge the lot of you now shut it and dig, this has to be finished before first light and it's a tough fucker.'

'The Pope' was right, the ground was rock hard, but the problem was more the case that they'd had to put the hide at the edge of a greyhound track in the Belfast suburb of Lambeg, close to Lisburn town. This was very much a Loyalist stronghold and it was suspected that the local UFF[29] scumbags were using the track to hide weapons and other nasty stuff away from the prying eyes of the proper authorities. In their wisdom those same proper authorities had got Steve and team in to see if they could catch said scumbags red-handed. They had two patrols covering them but due to the fact that the 'Tea Leafs'

---

[29] Ulster Freedom Fighters – A very nasty extremist Unionist terrorist group.

were inside the stadium and the others were outside it was impossible for the others to see directly if they got into any trouble.

'Kermit, test the radio please, do a radio check,' Steve ordered.

'I've tested it ten times already, Steve it's OK, we're in touch,' Eddie whispered, pausing a moment from his labours, exasperation evident in his voice.

'Do me a favour and test it again – Gus get in that hole and take over.'

Kevin was keen to get in there as he was freezing, it had to be about minus eight degrees and a chance to warm up was welcome.

They were digging the hide literally at the edge of the track under the eaves of the standing rail and retaining fence that kept the punters off the track. They already knew where the arms cache was, as an electrician doing some work there had stumbled across it and informed the ever present proper authorities. All Steve and team knew was that their hide had to be able to see the electrical switch boxes that serviced the floodlights as the arms cache was immediately below it. The fact was it was a false electrical cabinet hence the electrician noticing the problem. Said electrician was now on an all-expenses paid holiday hosted by the Government in a safe house in Putney, South London. His wife and family were not pleased with the arrangements or the notice period to move.

The Intelligence Section from Lisburn HQNI had good info that the local QM of the UFF was suspected of being responsible for the placement of the weapons there, but it was thought he was going to move it out very soon as he had gotten wind that it may have been compromised. Pictures of nasty people and possible arrests were all on the cards.

Steve had made sure that they were well armed and had borrowed a second M79 from another group and Les had left his sniper rifle behind and had swapped it for another Bren. They were also carrying twice the ammo that they usually carried as the tab in was relatively short at only just over a mile. If they got bumped by a bunch of armed enthusiastic members of any illegal organisations in the next few days they were sure they'd be able to persuade them to go away, and quickly. The team busied themselves finalising the hide. It was easy with the snow, but they had to be sure that if the weather changed suddenly then the hide must still be invisible if the snow melts. All of a sudden, Les declared the hide was good enough. Good enough meant that it was totally invisible to the human eye and only barely noticeable if someone got close enough to poke Kevin in the eye with a two-inch stick. Of course, if some would-be assailant did get that close, Kevin would have already stuffed a bayonet up said assailant's arse and would most likely be waving it about like a kiddie with a balloon, smiling and enjoying himself immensely.

They slid into the hide and got as comfortable as they could. It was estimated they'd be in there for about five days and nights. As ordered they had all avoided curry in the last few days as shit bags were the order of the day. Cold food and no hot brew as the heat already generated by them was possibly enough to melt the snow above them – cooking would definitely do it. In addition, the smells of cooking and tea would be a bit odd mingled amongst the dog shit and gravel. They closed up the hide behind them and Eddie and Kevin went to sleep covered in their gonk bags but not actually in them with rifles ready to hand. The Brens had been set up as immediate protection with the M79s placed next to each Bren. If some stupid politically motivated and inspired member of any illegal organisation decided to bump Steve and team they'd get a very nasty, probably their last, Christmas present.

Nothing of any note, except for greyhound racing of course, happened for the next five days and Steve decided that they'd had enough of this. They were freezing, almost out of food and water and their Bergens were getting a bit too full of their personal outpourings for the area to remain unnoticed for much longer. In addition, they had no idea how the outside of their hide was bearing up to the rigours of greyhound racing. Eddie was sure that a certain greyhound was on to them as he kept looking directly in the hide and took every opportunity to piss on it. A side effect was that one end of the trench smelt strongly of dog's urine as did the kit there. Could be a big problem if a greyhound suddenly started digging them up.

On the last evening at about midnight, when all was quiet, they exited the hide and started to clear the area, so it was back to exactly the same state before they moved it. This was completed by about two o'clock in the morning. Morale was low as they had spent a lot of time and effort there with no results. The snow had melted in certain areas but as the whole place was covered in patchy and slushy snow it was doubtful anybody had noticed the hide. They tooled up and started to patrol out of the track when a vehicle was heard arriving and started parking up just outside. They heard voices and the Tankie team told Eddie over the radio that four men were walking towards the race track entrance. Steve's team hid in the spectators' stand just behind the front facing fence and watched the men arrive through the wooden slots. They all agreed that these guys were probably not looking for advance purchases of entry tickets. This suspicion was strengthened by the fact that one of the gentlemen appeared to have keys to get in.

'What in the name of Beelzebub's underpants do these twats want?' whispered Kevin to no one in particular.

'I think they're kinky buggers who like the smell of two-day old dog shit,' giggled Les whilst lining up the second Bren on the first person to walk through the gate.

Eddie got Steve's attention by tugging on his combat trousers.

'Steve!'

'Stop pulling my trousers down, Eddie are you randy or something?'

'No, Brigade has just sent a signal. If target B is there we have to arrest them. They want pictures of them opening the cache and we are to catch them red-handed.'

'What... we are to engage them after they have gotten their weapons out? They fucking crazy or something?'

'That's what they want... sorry!'

'Leather is target B there?'

Les looked at the four with his NITECH.

'Yep! Definitely, can't miss that ugly bastard.'

As they were debating the four men were walking towards the electric cabinets concerned.

'Gus, you go over to the right there and take up a right flank position with the Bren. If they as much as poke their dick in our direction I want them dead.' Kevin moved off in that direction, he didn't have to say anything he knew what to do.

'Kermit, tell the two patrols to get out of their hides and put two guys on each entrance of this place, but tell them to be discreet. You stay here with the radio and that M79. We are gonna go way over there to the left side and take some piccies. Then we are gonna tell them to all stand still. If they start shooting fire the M79 and Kevin and Les will peg the fuckers with the Bren, but only if they start shooting, OK? Tell the other teams and Brigade what the plan is. Send it in clear as I doubt they have any radio kit with them. Finally, tell and don't ask HQ, that we are not on the yellow card for this.'

'Yes, Boss,' replied Eddie and busied himself with the radio.

'So, the plan is to just tell them to stand still?' said Les looking a bit concerned.

'Yep, that's about it, and we will walk over and tell them all to lie down until the cavalry arrive.'

'Steve?' whispered Eddie.

'What?'

'Said cavalry is en route, be here in fifteen minutes.'

'Thanks, Kermit, Leather, let's move.' They both silently sneaked away along the stand until they were about forty yards from the baddies and at right angles to Kevin's position with the Bren. They watched as Les was busy taking snaps as the baddies opened up the cache. Once they had opened it and peered inside Steve, staying in cover, shouted,

'STAND STILL! You're all under arrest. You're surrounded by heavily armed soldiers if you move you'll be fucking dead ever so quickly.' None of them moved.

'Lay down on the ground arms and legs spread, move very slowly.' Slowly they all obeyed.

Steve and Les hard targeted over to them whilst Kevin and Eddie provided cover. They could now hear Land Rovers approaching at great speed. Eddie and Kevin came out of cover so the goons on the ground could see that there was serious firepower available.

Steve was very surprised to hear one of the terrorists giggling like a little girl. Two others were smiling broadly. Steve walked over to the cache and saw that there was absolutely nothing in it. It was emptier than a condom machine in a Vatican public toilet.

The *Land Rovers* arrived and Steve and the others handed over the suspected Unionist terrorists to the local battalion and wondered what it was all about. They were all cold and grim as it seemed they had wasted five days there for no reason. They got their kit together and tabbed out to the pickup point to meet the box vans. As usual WOI Bruce was there with a hot tea urn.

The trip back to Anderson Town Police Station was a miserable one. After cleaning their weapons and handing them in and having sorted out and cleaned the specialist kit, they had a hot meal and then realised that they needed a drink and quite badly. It was almost 3am in the morning so Steve and team then went over to the UDR bar for some light refreshment, unsurprisingly it was still open. They hadn't showered or washed for five days whilst living in a hole in the ground shitting in bags with a dog pissing on them. This did generate an air about them that was less than pleasant. The UDR bar was not big. They ordered some drinks and walked over to a corner to enjoy them. A UDR sergeant, who had probably had one over the eight walked over to them and suggested they left as they needed a wash. Steve quietly stated that they were all going to have just two pints and then they'd leave. The sergeant became quite insistent until Steve suggested that if he had a problem he should get his Orderly Officer to kick them out. The sergeant did exactly that and after ten minutes or so a young and harried looking subaltern marched forcefully up to them and demanded they leave immediately. Steve took a sip from his glass and pointed to the phone on the bar.

'Do me a favour, sir, pick up that phone and ask for the Commander Northern Ireland Land Forces, when you get through tell him we're in the bar for two beers and if he says we should leave we will.' He then ignored the officer and carried on drinking.

'Stand to attention when you address me, Corporal, I am an officer and you will do what I say.'

'I can't be arsed, sir, I'm too tired,' came the reply from Steve. Frankly the others in his section were amazed at 'The Pope' and his outburst but they stuck by him and all ignored the officer and carried on drinking.

At that point Major Twigge walked into the bar went over to the far corner and gestured that the officer and 'The Pope' should come over and have a word. Both did. The major said a few words to both and then the major and the lieutenant left together, while Steve ambled back over to his crew. He sat down and took a sip of beer. The entire UDR bar was watching them and it was deathly silent. Les was first to speak.

'So, what happened, Boss?'

'Oh, the major told the sprog that if he could not recognise a Special Forces group who had been on a long and dangerous operation and still found it hard to let them have two beers then he should not be in the Army.' Steve took another sip. Les persisted.

'Did he say anything else?'

'Oh yes! He mentioned that if I was ever that cheeky to an officer again he would stuff an M79 up my arse and pull the trigger prior to busting me to something well below a private soldier.'

'D'ya think he meant it?'

'Nah! There is no way he'd bust me, and he knows that, but if pushed I think he would stuff an M79 up my arse, and he just might pull the trigger.'

'Yep!' agreed Kevin raising his pint.

Next day they took part in a debriefing from the local Intelligence people. They suspected that the weapons had been lifted probably by the local Republicans who probably found out about the cache from the same electrician source that they had. It was a lucky break that the UDA had no idea that the electrician had also become an informer. If he had it would have been very likely that they would have been ambushed. Seems he was less than discreet about the hide to all and sundry. The Intelligence guys also let them know that it wasn't a complete washout as Target B had been carrying an illegal pistol plus he had some interesting documents with him. They said he'd probably only get three months for that, but it's better than nothing.

Meanwhile MI5 were having a ball with a certain electrician and who he had links with in the local UDA cell and other small details such as how did he know them. Eddie and team were informed at about the same time that their presence in Lambeg was not yet over as the Intelligence community thought it would be a good idea to do some sneaky beaky work on the people who were with the big man and to see who their friends might be. It was suspected that it might be possible to identify the members of the local UFF ASU by doing this.

They worked with the Intelligence guys for the remainder of the day helping to develop the pictures they had taken and working out a basic strategy as to how to get more information on these bad guys. It was about 6pm by the time they had done all this, and it had definitely been a long day. The Intelligence captain from the local unit they had been working with dismissed them and said that he'd be in touch with their commander to agree the next steps. Exhaustion had overtaken them and without any delay they all went to bed and slept soundly.

Next day, all the Section Commanders of the NIPG turned up for their briefing with the Intelligence Section. Now rested, fed, showered and squeaky clean they felt ready for anything. They knocked on the door and walked into the room. Their own major was already in the room along with the Company Commander and the Intelligence Officer of the local unit stationed there. In addition, so was the officer from the Intelligence cell attached from the Army Intelligence Corp, it was the same lieutenant that they had met in the bar the previous evening. He didn't seem to be impressed and had a face like a bulldog that had just licked piss of a thistle. Just the kind of situation 'The Pope' enjoyed and an opportunity to toy mercilessly with an officer. The lieutenant started off asking if anyone knew why they were here. 'The Pope' shyly put his hand up as he felt he could answer that. The officer gestured for him to go ahead.

'Well, sir, the principal issues at stake are the constitutional status of Northern Ireland and the relationship between the mainly Protestant Unionist and mainly Catholic Nationalist communities in Northern Ireland. This has both political and military, or paramilitary, dimensions. Its participants include politicians and political activists on both sides, Republican and Loyalist paramilitaries. From 1608, British settlers, known as planters, were given land confiscated from the native Irish in the Plantation of Ulster. Coupled with Protestant immigration to 'unplanted' areas of Ulster, particularly Antrim and Down, this resulted in conflict between the native Catholics and the 'planters'. This led to two bloody ethno-religious conflicts in 1641 to 1653 and 1689 to 1691, each of which resulted in Protestant victories. British Protestant political dominance in Ireland was ensured by the passage of the penal laws, which curtailed the religious, legal and political rights of anyone who did not conform to the state church—the Anglican Church of Ireland. As the penal laws broke down in the latter part of the eighteenth...' Steve paused mid-sentence as the young officer had been fiercely gesturing for him to stop for about fifteen seconds and he felt he could not get away with ignoring him any longer.

'What the hell are you going on about, Corporal?' he asked in exasperation. Steve looked quizzically at him.

'You asked if anybody knew why we were here,' he said innocently and then continued. 'As I was saying, in the eighteenth century the...' The officer stopped him again.

'I meant why we were here at Anderson Town Police Station today.'

'Well how would we know that, it's supposed to be a secret isn't it?' said Steve with a hint of irritation. The OC of the NIPG almost burst out laughing but he saw what was happening and decided to nip it in the bud.

'Gentlemen let's get down to the matter at hand and a little less of the history lesson, although in all honesty I think you might want to get your fellas together later and give them the benefit of your knowledge, most of them think they are here to kill Micks and impregnate as many of the local female population as possible.'

'The Pope' having made his point listened in to the remainder of the briefing only to inform the officer that he had his map grid references all wrong. This was at the end of the briefing and Steve was able to read out all 8 grids from memory and provided the approximate correct ones without the aid of a map. The young lieutenant went beetroot with embarrassment. The major made a mental note of talking to Steve later again about why he was not an officer himself.

In short, the big idea was to see if they could get enough intelligence from the local area to see if they could pinpoint who had been using the greyhound track as an arms cache and therefore hard information as to who the local baddies really were. They had few things to go on with the exception as to who actually owned the place. They had SOCO go over the area, but no other evidence of any importance was forthcoming. They did however, have the details of the four baddies they had picked up. So, the idea was to spend some time looking at these guys in some depth. The usual type of operation would take place on the four targets.

Steve's group and the Tankies were paired up again and were given one of the targets to watch. This time it was a semi-detached house in the middle of Anderson Town, so hides might be difficult to arrange. Steve and Pete the two commanders of the patrols, nipped off and thought about this over a few coffees.

'I can't believe this, someone's pulling our leg,' stated Pete looking at the file that the Intelligence guys had handed to him.

'What's the problem, Pete?' said Steve trying to look at the folder.

'Would you believe it, but this bloke lives in a road called Murphy Crescent! That's got to be a pigging joke?'

'I dunno, Pete, sounds like the ideal address.'

'For fuck's sake, Steve, remember that this bloke would love to kiss the Queen's arse, he's a Unionist, a paid-up flute and drum player, he probably wears orange underpants!' Steve laughed at the irony of it.

It was decided that they'd dig in Steve's patrol, as they were best at sneaky beaky stuff, close to the target's house on the edge of St. Patrick School's rather expansive playing fields. As this was during the Christmas holidays for kids then the roof of the school was chosen as a very good cover position. Pete's patrol would break into the school and live on the roof. They'd be able to see for miles up there, so it should be a good place to watch the suspected bad guy from.

They went at it with a will packing their Bergens with food, water, ammunition, film, observation kit, radios, batteries plus kit to build a hide, until their Bergens weighed in between a hundred and a hundred and fifty pounds each. Add to that their webbing, an additional weapon to carry plus their ghillie suits and they were all carrying a huge amount of weight. They were busy checking each other's equipment, testing technical stuff like radios, UGS, NITECH and the IWS[30], looking at the ground using stereoscopic techniques to check the terrain, testing cameras and lenses, and test firing weapons. The list was endless. After a while Steve reviewed their progress and muttered thoughtfully to himself the bit of Shakespeare he loved the most.

'And gentlemen in England now abed, shall think themselves accursed they were not here and hold their manhood's cheap...'

'What was that, Steve?' asked Kevin.

'It's nothing, just a line from a bloke called Shakespeare about three hundred years ago, for a moment there it seemed appropriate.' He shrugged his shoulders like he was a bit embarrassed and then pulled on his webbing, grabbed his Bergen and swung the deadweight onto his shoulders and lastly picked up his weapon. They, like him, were all ready to go.

'Right, let's do this,' Steve said to no one in particular and they all strode out under their weight to meet whatever the fates had in store for them on this task.

It was two o'clock in the morning when the box van stopped near the back of the school playing fields. Mess Tins, the driver, gave the all clear and the door opened and both patrols slipped out the back and almost immediately they were over the fence and into the playing fields. They got down in all round defence and the vehicle, as quietly as possible, drove away up the road. Without any noise, they listened and observed the local area. The nearest houses were on a local estate near the back of the school about fifty yards away. After about twenty minutes listening and observing from the frozen ground a signal was given and both patrols got up. After a brief nod between themselves the Tankies patrolled away to the school main building where they were going to spend the next few nights.

Steve's team slowly made their way to the edge of the field close to the road. It was bitter cold, their breath creating huge clouds in front of them. The effort of carrying about one hundred or so pounds of weight was exhausting, so their breathing was heavy and their breath warm. They were in luck in that

---

[30] Image Intensification Weapon Sight – a large and heavy technical item that was placed on a weapon – a green image using light available could be generated and could be used to engage targets in the dark, also known as a 'starlight scope'.

there was absolutely no moon, so it was almost pitch black in the playing field. The nearby street lights gave a ghostly sheen over bushes and trees with associated long shadows. Dogs barked occasionally and now and then they'd see a light go on in a bedroom or toilet window.

High above in the starlit dark sky Steve saw a passenger jet flying west, its presence betrayed only by white and red strobes and a low roar. He momentarily wondered where it was going and wished that he too was going somewhere else right now.

The Tankies had quickly arrived at the school and, using their new-found lock picking skills, were soon inside. They decided that two of them would work on the roof whilst two would stay in a classroom overlooking the playing fields. They all agreed that it was so perishing cold that it was the best option. They felt a bit sorry for Steve's patrol as his team would not be having that option, they'd be outside all the time. They had soon set themselves up and were observing the required address through drainage gaps in the flat roof.

Steve and his patrol were going to dig in and build a hide but as they got closer to the house they discovered a natural dip in the ground that was covered in dead foliage. The fence was crisscrossed with now defunct ferns awaiting the early warmth of spring. The nice bit about this spot was they would not have to dig a hole, it was a readymade hide. In addition, it was also slightly lower than they had seen in the aerial photos. In fact, it was a God send as they could actually see in the lower windows even though they were at a slightly lower angle than was perfect.

'This will do, guys. Get stuck in and make us disappear.' They all agreed and after discreetly checking the local area they did just that and literally disappeared.

Eddie and Kevin were asleep almost immediately whilst Steve and Les set up the techy kit and pondered if they could risk using UGS on the subject property as they were close knit houses, but they were semidetached. It was 4am and they knew they could not risk it at the moment as soon people would be leaving for work.

About half an hour later they were rewarded for their restraint by seeing that the milkman was an early bird and was diligently doing his thing in the freezing cold. He was wearing fingerless mittens and an absurd red scarf and a Santa hat. It was then that they were reminded that Christmas was almost upon them, perhaps they could get a good Christmas present this year by bagging a murderous terrorist bastard and get him a new job as a walking masturbatory toy in Brixton or Wandsworth.

At about 8.30am the Tankies warned them that a 4-man Army Brick was meandering down the same road that the target house was in. Eddie and Kevin woke the others and they 'stood to'. Eddie used the radio to inform their HQ to get onto the resident unit to tell the patrol immediately that some friendlies were in the area. The problem was that if one of the soldiers saw them they may think it was an ambush and start shooting, and a 'Blue on Blue' would happen. Unfortunately, if they did start shooting then Steve and his team would have no option but to shoot them dead in self-defence. That was why the whole area they were in was out of bounds to troops but obviously someone had not passed the message along.

The patrol was almost level with them when the Section Commander got a message over his radio, he raised his hand and they all got into a variety of fire positions in all round defence. The commander listened intently to his radio for a few moments and acknowledged the message. He reached into his combat trouser packet and pulled out a memo book and consulted it. This corporal, who was probably only about twenty-two years old, folded up his memo pad put it away and rubbed his head.

'Listen in,' he shouted loudly but without looking at his men, he didn't have to.

'I want you to all remember the yellow card and obey it to the letter if something happens or if you see something suspicious, got it? Right, Deano and Phensic, I want you two to make your weapons safe right now whilst Billy and I cover you.' They all cast a weird look at their boss but if they were given such an order they knew there was probably a good reason for it. The command 'Make Safe' referred to fully unloading a rifle and refitting a full magazine but not cocking it. In that way, you knew there was no bullet in the chamber and that the weapon was in a safe condition. Once the two members of his patrol had finished he instructed that the last one and himself should do the same. The Section Commander then went around his whole team and whispered something in their ear.

None of this was lost on Steve and crew and they got the message. The patrol commander knew of their presence somewhere but wanted them to know that right now they did not want to be thought of as a threat as their weapons were 'safe'. If they saw a man right now with a gun covered in rags and stuff, they knew it was a friendly so neither would they fire or acknowledge sightings. It was a small stroke of genius and Steve and team relaxed a bit. The Brick Commander nodded at his team and slowly they all meandered up the road continuing their patrol.

'Eddie, get on the radio and tell the boss to send a bloody big well done to that Brick Commander – that was a class act.'

It was just as well as it offset the almighty bollocking he did get for not checking with Intelligence before he took out his patrol. It might also have given them a slight edge as the more hardened terrorists knew that no patrols in an area usually meant that some form of special op was in progress, so a patrol wandering down the street would have made the local baddy probably a bit more relaxed.

'Our scumbag has just woken up by the looks of it,' announced Les on seeing the bedroom curtains being pulled back by what appeared to be the target they were studying. The 1000mm lens captured a few snaps but it was unlikely they'd be of any use. They were rewarded shortly afterwards by the target himself, freshly washed and shaved, walking up the road past them barely twenty feet away.

'Well I don't think we need any more of him. Christ, we have such good piccies now I think we could sell them to him for his album.' Les was pleased and his voice betrayed it.

'OK, good stuff but let's work out how we are gonna get some interesting stuff over the next few days, we need to get some UGS in there.'

It had become cloudy with a light wind. It was colder than ever but now with wind chill. Steve's face was red from the cold. Kevin found that the water in his Bergen water bottles had almost become ice. With no cooking heat the only thing that could be done was to put the water bottle inside your jacket so that your body heat thawed it out, even in the cold you had to drink! After a while a sparse snow was billowing across the fields, it was barely there but unhurriedly everything started to turn white. They removed their ghillie suits and got out their waterproofs and turned them inside out. The inside of these jackets was white, so they had a simple but effective camouflage as the snow slowly built up. They had some cold food and did their best to follow routine.

That night they inserted the UGS devices without incident, but they wished they had done it the previous evening, because putting them in place without leaving footprints in the snow made the work protracted and strenuous. Job done they went back to the hide to listen in. For the next two days, they got nothing of note except some photos of some visitors who perhaps may be fellow terrorists or people with an interest in helping their political ambitions. Of course, they could have just been friends or relatives and completely innocent. The UGS devices listened in to everything said but there was nothing of note only the usual sort of stuff that a family of four would discuss with each other or friends. It was almost as if the targets knew they were being watched and listened in on, they just had no idea how it was done.

On the fourth morning, the man came out of his house as usual at exactly 9am and started to cheerfully and unsuspectingly walk up the road. As he passed them they took some photos of him but just observed him once he had passed as his back was of zero interest. A vehicle came down the road behind him and although the team noted it they did not pay any attention to it. The vehicle slowed as it got level with their target and the passenger fired a couple of bursts from an automatic weapon. The range was literally point blank and Eddie and team didn't need a doctor or anyone to state that the baddie was dead almost instantly. Kevin lined up the Bren to take out the car, but Steve stopped him.

'Stop, do not fire,' he said deliberately and quietly whilst placing his hand gently on Kevin's shoulder, but he was talking to the whole team. Kevin was surprised but obeyed the order.

'Why, Steve, they just blew him away?' complained Kevin.

'That will not bring him back to life and in all honesty, I doubt we'd hit the vehicle hard enough to stop it now. If we miss the target everyone will know we are here because of the noise and they will think we did it anyway. If we do get them the bloody flute players will still think we set it up, plus we will have to answer questions as to why we did not stop it in the first place. That said they probably did the world a favour taking him out. So, we are gonna lay low until the whole thing is finished.'

'Steve, I got a load of pictures of that vehicle and I think we can recognise the shooter but not the driver. Need to get these piccies back to those green bereted bastards so they can have some fun of their own.'

Steve and team did lay low. They radioed what had happened back to their HQ and outlined their decision. HQNI agreed and told them to stay put and out of sight. The Army arrived and cordoned off the area, the police then arrived and processed the scene and eventually the dead man was loaded into an ambulance and slowly everything returned to normal. There was an unexpected bonus. It was obvious that they would have to get the UGS out in the early hours next morning as they had planned to leave that night so they had to wait.

In the afternoon after the police had finished interviewing the widow, friends and relatives arrived to comfort the family. The widow was not very happy and over the next few hours berated and screamed obscenities at the people who had involved her husband in the nefarious activities that he had taken part in. It was almost as if she was purging his history from her mind to try and justify her role in all that misery. She was very angry and over the next several hours gave out names, situations and information in her grief that would have taken months of painstaking intelligence gathering to get hold of.

Eddie and the guys wrote everything down and used up all of the recording time of the UGS. Whilst she was crying herself to sleep Steve and Les retrieved the UGS kit and they slowly moved out. They liaised with the Tankie patrol and RV'd with the box vans. CSM Bruce was there with the usual urn of tea. They had a mug full each to warm up and, as usual, almost immediately fell asleep.

The next morning having cleaned up they attended a debrief with the lieutenant of UDR bar fame. His attitude was completely different, it seemed he now fully appreciated the fact that they had been out in the freezing cold and under risk had managed to get a photo of a scumbag actually pulling the trigger. The photo was so clear that you could see the expression of sheer malice on the man's face as he was shooting. Another bonus was even if it was only the back of the driver's head they could see, it was so clear that they knew who he was as even from the back he was so distinctive. The young officer was full of gratitude for the pictures and the information from the victim's widow. The operation was considered to be a success even if Eddie and the guys knew it really was not. They all packed up their kit, albeit miserably, and got into the box vans for their return to Ballykinler. Just as they were climbing aboard Les said with feeling,

'When we get back I'm gonna have a good shit, shave, shower and a shampoo, a kick arse meal, then a few beers and a damn good shag... then I'm gonna take this fucking webbing off!'

Northern Ireland - March 1976 – Such a Waste!

The stolen car had been left to 'soak' for a few weeks on the Kilrea Road. The road was closed off by the RUC, so no one could go near it. If it was a 'come-on' and was indeed equipped with an IED the batteries or whatever may just give up or the damn thing may explode in the interim thus removing any risk that it might kill someone. So it was left for a while to itself. After several weeks nothing happened so ATO was tasked to examine the car and see if it was in fact a huge firework engineered by a fertilizer lover with a keen interest in electronics and politics. FELIX, after a very close and intricate examination declared that the vehicle was clear and that no bomb was in the car. It was released and the RUC were told they could take it away whenever they pleased for their SOCO to get any dabs or evidence they needed to secure a possible arrest of the idiot who nicked it and abandoned it in the first place – probably for a joy ride. The RUC backed up a Land Rover to it and Eddie assisted by loaning one of the tow cables to the RUC from the radio vehicle he was working from.

'Titch' a private in Y Company, offered to steer the vehicle for the RUC but was overruled by a very young policeman. 'Titch' was not wearing gloves and could leave additional fingerprints in the car and would cause a bit more work to be done by forensics. Eddie was standing at the rear of the RUC Land Rover watching the situation unfold and saw the policemen get into the car and adjust the seat etc. Titch, in an effort to assist, guided the RUC Land Rover as it took up the slack on the stolen vehicle. The vehicle had moved about six inches when the explosion happened. The stolen car was blown almost twenty feet vertically into the air and about thirty feet into the field next to the road. It was completely blown apart. Eddie, Titch and the others although standing literally next to the vehicle were all, apart from the odd scratch and sudden deafness, unharmed. Later it was determined that the bombers had dug into the bank by the side of the road and had placed the bomb immediately where the vehicle would be and left, leaving a plunger that was hidden by a plate or something similar. They then hid the hole very well indeed and left it for several weeks for the grass etc. to grow over the hole. They then stole a car and placed it over the bomb as planned with a wheel over the plunger thus completely hiding it.

Eddie, Titch and the others had to wait for SOCO to secure the area for evidence and were then asked if they would assist in gathering up the remains of the young policeman. He had been twenty-four years old when he died and had been a policeman for about eighteen months. Eddie and Titch along with about twenty others, policemen and soldiers, went about the gruesome business and recovered a fair amount of the young man's remains. They were treated with solemn dignity and many of the older policemen could not hold back the grief and tears rolled silently yet brazenly down their cheeks as they continued to search for as much of their fallen colleague as they could find. Their quiet determination was noted by the soldiers who grimly helped.

Much later both Eddie and Titch accompanied the Commanding Officer to attend a memorial service held to honour the young victim. They met the grieving family and his widow whom he had married just under six months prior. Many hundreds paid their respects to a young man whose promising career was cut short by someone who felt it was acceptable to try to change opinion using violence.

Eddie was moved to tears as he heard the speeches and saw and felt the raw emotion that accompanies such a waste of young potential. Almost immediately afterwards Eddie went on a long-awaited leave and spent three weeks at home in the bosom of his family and more importantly, occasionally in his girlfriend's.

By contrast, Titch a few days later witnessed the aftermath of another explosion in a fish and chip shop in Derry that killed two very young children. Thereafter he fought a personal battle with alcoholism and depression, thus becoming another unheralded victim of the incidents he had witnessed. So strong are the bonds that hold soldiers together that even thirty years on Titch, when he feels his 'black dog' coming on does not seek out this family or professional help. He reaches out for an old comrade, who without fuss or judgment, helps with the tears and with no shame hugs Titch until the demons go.

Chapter 7

The Problem with Routine...

The Maze - December 1976

The Land Rovers approached the Maze Prison's entrance at breakneck speed and, almost reluctantly, stopped at the steel gates. It was a weird experience sitting in the back as the vehicles were fitted with infrared headlights, so the beams could only be seen by wearing special optics. Eddie and the others were spread across both vehicles, courtesy of 2 Para, but were not blessed with the required goggles so they were sitting in an almost pitch-black vehicle wondering how fast they were going. This was designed to counter the local bogeymen's tactics of blowing up as many of the Paras as they could by using culvert bombs and IEDs at the side of the road.

It was worrying travelling with Paras as PIRA had a definite grudge against them and took delight in topping as many of them as they could. They had decided not to wear the parachute cap badge and had opted for the Royal Corps of Transport just in case they did become the subject of a Republican sniper with a thing about maroon coloured berets – anyway none of them had qualified on the Pegasus course and therefore had not earned the privilege of wearing the coveted maroon beret and wings and they were sure that the Parashites, as they were affectionately known, would all moan like buggers if they ever found out.

Driving down country lanes at breakneck speed in almost complete darkness was akin to floating in a kind of Land Rover based continuum of Hell with only the very dim dashboard dials giving off a little light. Travel sickness was a must. Abruptly to the passengers it seemed that they had suddenly stopped in the middle of nothing as on this particular night it was very dark indeed. Eddie glanced out the front of the vehicle, relieved at the break and potential removal of the constant feeling of nausea and saw the indistinct lights of a compound and realised they had arrived at their destination.

The Maze was a prison, about nine miles from Belfast, holding inmates who were considered to be hard line terrorists of whatever persuasion. Around it had grown up a collection of huts and buildings that could compete with the best that any refugee camp anywhere in the world could produce. The gates were constructed out of a steel frame and corrugated iron and were about twenty foot high. Slowly they opened and in they drove like alcoholics attacking a brewery. The Paras, of whom none seemed to be over nineteen years old, explained that this was probably the most dangerous part of any patrol as they had to go in and out here. The NIPG lads gasped in awe at them and made it clear that as poor drivers they were glad to be in the hands of such experienced and war hardened veterans whilst also giggling under their breath. They debussed and, as they were unexpected, waited whilst Steve went off and did his duty to get them a decent meal and somewhere to kip down. A harried and worried looking RQMS came rushing up to them with Steve in tow.

'Where in a rat's ball bag are you twats from? Fucking Bethlehem or somewhere?' the RQ said in exasperation. They all felt very welcome at this approach and Kevin was spotted looking at his bayonet and a potential ceremonial disembowelling seemed to be on the cards.

'You'll have to wait in the cookhouse whilst I try to arrange some accommodation for you. It's over there.' He pointed to what appeared to be a collection of travellers' huts, but they were not as well maintained. Les, talking to no one in particular indicated that he was unhappy in that he had to eat before the usual wash, shave, massage by exotic women and a generally satisfying wank.

The RQMS glanced across the camp and mentally assigned a billet in the most flea and rat-infested area that he could find. Grabbing all their kit they ambled over to the cookhouse and walked in. They left their kit near the door and walked over to the hot plate. There was nothing there to eat. This was not surprising as it was after 10 at night.

'Oi! Anyone about?' shouted Les, his voice echoing through the building like a lonely sad note.

'What the fuck do you want?' came a disappointed and dislocated voice from somewhere in the back of the kitchen.

'A damn good shag?' questioned Kevin hopefully.

'What! You a bandsman then?' responded the remote voice at the back.

Before Kevin could respond with a suitable expletive the voice owner appeared from the dark of the kitchen in his underpants and vest but still resplendent in his chef's hat. He was obviously pissed as he was holding a half empty bottle of *Jack Daniels*. Steve could see that this might get awkward and it was nothing to do with the alcohol or the fact that he was pissed and only in his shreddies. He was wearing a wrist band showing he was a warrant officer 1st class, so he was a demigod in the non-commissioned officer world.

Steve intervened.

'Well actually, sir we have been on a five-day operation in open country and we're starving. We just want something to eat.'

'Not a shag then?' said the WO1 cocking his head to one side and taking a quick swig from the bottle.

'I think we'd rather eat first...' Steve's voice tailed away worried that he was being given an offer he'd rather refuse.

'Just as well,' slurred the cook, 'shagging is all done in the officers' mess apparently. Any of you lot officers?' he asked raising an eyebrow.

'No, sir,' stated Steve.

'Thank fuck for that. I've just realised I'm only wearing my shorts cellular and vest... no offence meant, lads, but I was in my bag in the office back there with only Jack here and a couple of back issues for mates.' He paused.

'If you're hungry just help yourself, fridge over there has got steak and eggs and stuff... just take what you want and cook it over there on the hotplate... Any objection if I slip back to the bag before I fall down?'

'You go ahead, sir – no problems, we'll be as quiet as we can.'

'So will I,' said the WO1 with a wink and turned away back to his office to reacquaint himself with whatever pornographic image he was associated with before being rudely interrupted.

They all fell onto the fridge ripping it open. The fridge was incredible. It was full of all sorts of lovely grub, steaks, joints, prawns, you name it, and it was in there.

'No wonder their all fat fuckers,' said Kevin.

Steve grabbed a tray of steaks and sent Les off to find some garlic salt. Eddie got some frozen chips out and filled a pan full of vegetable oil. Within twenty minutes they were all sitting down to steak, egg and chips, with some onions and tomatoes thrown in for good measure. Apart from the sound of knives scraping across plates not a sound was made. It was lovely. Once they'd all finished they sat back for a moment and quietly savoured the feeling.

'God... urgh!' came from the small office at the back.

'Sounds like Cooky has been bashing some meat of his own, eh?' said Les. They all giggled like little boys at a midnight dorm feast. They washed up the plates, cutlery and dixies and put them away.

'Right let's see if we can get a beer at the NAAFI and if we're really lucky we might get a shag at the officers' mess, so come on,' announced Steve.

'I knew you were fucking bandsmen!' announced a disembodied voice from the back.

They all laughed, got all their kit and sauntered into the night leaving the chef to his love of porn and hate of bandsmen.

They were halfway to the NAAFI when the RQ caught up with them.

'OK, got somewhere for you to sleep. Follow me,' he commanded.

They trooped off behind him. Eventually they came to a hut and the RQ ushered them all inside.

'Sorry it's a bit rough but we're quite full tonight.'

Eddie looked over the room. In the Army if accommodation is referred to as 'a bit rough' then the word understatement is at its optimum. A 'bit rough' means you automatically catch the entire range of Hepatitis from A to Z plus Syphilis and Gonorrhoea just by looking in the window. They all reluctantly picked a bed space and put their kit around it. Kevin was suspicious that the RQ may have painted a red cross on the door as he left.

'Let's use our maggots to sleep in tonight, guys... now the bar I think!'

The NAAFI at the Maze was, like most things in Northern Ireland, nondescript and had seen better days.

'What a dump,' said Eddie as they went in.

The bar was crowded with Paras and they were all in varied states of inebriation. Steve's guys were still wearing the RCT cap badges and they were a bit worried that this would provoke some humorous comments from the Paras. However, from the moment they walked in the men of B Company, 2 Para took them to their hearts, drank with them, shared jokes and generally enjoyed their company. This small group of NIPG operatives had a great time. This belied the generally felt opinion that the Paras were arrogant, it also subsequently turned out that they also had guts as well.

Next morning Kevin was first up. This wasn't particularly unusual, but it was particularly unusual for him to sprint to the wash house. Eddie then noted that Les, who was normally up by now having shaved, done a ten mile run and had probably either shagged three nuns or as a minimum had at least had a gratifying wank, was still in his bag. Not only was he still in there but he looked like death itself. At this point Steve rolled over and popped his head out of his green maggot and puked openly onto the floor.

'God,' pleaded Steve as he slowly disappeared back into his bag.

Eddie immediately discounted the possibility that they had been the subject of a biological or chemical warfare attack by the local chapter of the United Ireland Society. This was mainly prompted by the fact that Kevin had been holding the anal area of his underpants whilst racing towards the bog. Kevin would never have done that if chemical agents were in the air. He'd have far rather just shit in his gonk bag. After a few minutes Kevin walked slowly back into the room.

'Did ya make it?' Eddie asked helpfully.

Kevin looked at him mournfully.

'Nah, had to jump into a bush, only fucking bush for miles by the look of it and a very small bush at that. Beethoven didn't make it either.'

Eddie nodded in sympathy; he knew how attached Kevin was to his underpants. He had them for years and they all had names, but nobody understood why they were named after famous composers.

Kevin continued, 'Whilst I was shittin' through the eye of a needle that fucking cook came over and asked me if I was an effing bandsman... man's a nutter.'

Kevin suddenly looked alarmed and was gone. Eddie pitied the bush.

It was obvious that with the exception of Eddie, they'd all eaten something that did not agree with them. It had probably been the eggs as Eddie had not had any of them. Eventually they got over it but the only bush in the entire Maze Prison area unexpectedly died. Late in the afternoon they cleaned the room best they could for handover back to the RQ but there was no hiding the fetid smell of puke, urine and diarrhoea. The RQ came over and declared the room OK and was pleased to see that the room had improved in cleanliness and thanked them for their efforts. He billeted them down with the Paras as he had found some spare bed spaces over there.

As far as the Paras were concerned these new RCT guys were just gonna sit in the *Saracen*[31] armoured vehicles and take photos of guys in cars that they asked the Paras to stop at the VCPs[32] that they had set up. Their officer was in

---

[31] A six-wheeled armoured personnel carrier.
[32] Vehicle Check Point.

on the secret, so he knew the RCT guys were in fact NIPG. He had been practicing his guys in doing VCPs in *Saracens* for the last three days. The two *Saracen* armoured vehicles left the Maze and raced to the spot where the VCP was to be set up.

It started the moment the first *Saracen* stopped. The driver was ratcheting on the handbrake and the door was just opening when CRUMP! The 13-ton vehicle suddenly rolled violently over onto one side, the blast ripping off two wheels rocking slowly until it finally came to rest. The armoured vehicle protected those inside from the worst of the blast but most of them had at least bruises and a nose or ear bleed from the concussion. The vehicle commander was screaming as he was trapped. All of them were disorientated but they very quickly realised that they all had to get out. Somehow, they struggled to their feet and the Paras' Platoon Sergeant was first out the now sideways on door. He was instantly hit in the chest by a bullet. The high velocity round went straight through the gap of his open flak jacket and was stopped as it exited his back by that same flak jacket. Blood gushed out of his mouth and nose as the force of the bullet pushed the contents of the lung it had hit inwards. He slammed into Les and both fell to the floor blood already forming a pool under the victim. They all rushed for the exit as bullets pinged off the overturned vehicle and they could hear the crack and thump [33] of high velocity rounds going overhead as they ran for cover. The NIPG guys felt particularly vulnerable as they did not wear flak jackets. Eddie threw himself behind a stone wall and tried to gather his senses. It was pandemonium!

He cocked his rifle and peered over the wall. It came to him as a shock that he could see someone firing at him from behind a similar wall to his own about seventy yards or so away. It was strange almost surreal. He took aim with his SLR and fired straight at the other guy's head. When the smoke cleared he was still there firing. He had missed but no doubt given him something to think about. He concentrated on shooting at the terrorist and fired about 18 bullets at him and they all missed. As soon as it had begun it was all over. They had gone, the firing stopped and the Para lieutenant shouted for them to 'Stop and make safe!' Eddie looked at his weapon and wondered why he hadn't put a hole in the terrorist's head a few times. He noticed that his scope had been hit by something and was slightly skewed and he guessed it was probably hit a glancing blow when the vehicle rolled over. He paled and almost threw up.

---

[33] Crack and thump refers to the bullet breaking the sound barrier as it passes over head (Crack) and the thump is the sound of the gun firing reaching the hearer.

Very quickly it was decided by the officer that the NIPG team would join his sections to try and hot pursuit the ambushers whilst other units were drafted in to flood the area. The Para radio operator had had the coolness to send a word-perfect contact report and to instigate a rat trap operation even though he was almost upside down in the vehicle and unable to get out. He was mentioned in dispatches for his calmness during an ambush where some 200 bullets were fired at them. In addition to a dead sergeant another Para had been seriously injured, and two more had slight injuries where bullets had grazed them. The *Saracen* vehicle commander had lost three of his fingers when the vehicle overturned. His career was over – tough luck at twenty-six.

It took a while for Eddie to realise that he was half deaf, his left ear was ringing but he could hear nothing on that side. He was suffering from shock and too much adrenalin. He quite openly burst into tears before being told to 'shut the fuck' up by Kevin. There was little wrong with him physically except the kind of shock that anyone gets from being in what was similar to a serious car crash and gets away with it when others die. The NIPG team broke out their arsenal of weapons, much to the surprise of the Paras, from their Bergens and started off after the terrorists. Les spotted a blood trail.

'Looks like we got one of the bastards anyway!' he shouted without stopping.

'Let's hope it's nothing fucking trivial, eh?' shouted back Kevin.

Eddie felt embarrassed by this earlier outburst and wasn't looking forward to having the piss taken out of him later by the others. The trail of blood stopped when they came to a small road. It was obvious that a van had been waiting for them. It was doubtful they'd get the sods that did this. They walked back to the ambush site.

The NAAFI that night was not so much fun. The soldiers talked, commiserated and remembered their absent friend. Eddie need not have worried as his outburst was never mentioned and never would be probably because they all felt the same urge at that moment. It was soon noted that the young officer had used the same location on three previous occasions to host a VCP and that routine was exactly what the IRA needed for their ambush.

The scene was cordoned off and the RUC and SIB came along with the RMP and examined the scene of the crime. Pictures were taken and statements given. Eventually the NIPG could leave as the whole operation had been cancelled. The ubiquitous box vans with the genuine RCT drivers picked them up and after an uneventful journey got them back to Ballykinler just before the

NAAFI bar closed. They got out of the vans and unloaded all their paraphernalia and weapons. On the way to the armoury, loaded down with their weapons, Bergens and webbing, Les decided to nonchalantly address them all.

'After I've handed my weapon in I'm gonna have a shit, shave, shower and shampoo, a good meal, a few beers then a fantastic damn hard shag… then I'm gonna take these fucking boots off.'

Northern Ireland - April 1977. Road Tax?

Les' motorbike was great, and he loved it. It was a 50cc CZ and represented the pinnacle of Czech engineering. That was because it looked like a 250cc bike with a huge headlight, chrome and everything plus it was two shades of brown. He'd got it cheap as well at fifty sobs and a free helmet to boot. The speedo didn't work but that was OK as the seller said that if he did get close to fifty miles an hour he'd know, as the helmet would start to wobble on his head as it did not have any lining – probably why it was free. Les wasn't worried as he'd only bought it to visit his girlfriend in Ballynahinch just fifteen miles away so that he could shag her more often.

The ignition key was a bit weird; it looked like the plug you inserted into a stereo that sat on the end of the cable that headphones were attached to. He lost that almost immediately but found that a small screwdriver worked equally as well. But on occasion the ignition would fail because the screwdriver wasn't quite in properly. After a few trips, he also found out that the electrics were not quite as sound as he thought but if the bike started to jump and hop due to engine problems a hefty kick with the heel at the electrics box sorted that problem. Insurance? Who needed insurance just to nip along the road a couple of miles for a nifty poke and of course that meant no road tax as well, but nobody in Northern Ireland had road tax anyway – surely the authorities were far more intent on catching the baddies rather than mere motoring offences?

This night Les (or more accurately his penis), decided that he needed to see the girlfriend as a matter of urgency. It was freezing so he wrapped up warm and jumped onto his steed. After a bit of fiddling about trying to get the screwdriver to start the bike he was off in a roar surrounded by a cloud of fumes. A few minutes later he was following a lorry going about forty-nine miles an hour, he knew that as his helmet was only in a mild wobble. His penis sent him a message saying that if he could get another two miles an hour out of the bike and therefore arrive earlier he'd be shagging even quicker. Les, who did everything his penis told him to, hit the indicator and pulled out level with the truck. His bike, in comparison to the truck, was going about one mile per hour faster and was therefore overtaking the truck about as fast as an asthmatic, rheumatoid, one legged man with gout. He pulled his throttle as far back as possible and almost reached the magic fifty miles an hour; he knew that as the helmet was wobbling all over his head. He was now almost halfway along the truck when he lost speed suddenly. He cursed and started to kick the electrics box with his heel, a surge of speed answered and again the helmet started to wobble. He slowly crept up the side of the truck and again the bike slowed down. He wrestled with the screwdriver and again the bike, now almost at the end of the truck, found a new surge of life and pulled forward. Almost immediately again the bike lost power, his helmet stopped wobbling again, but a swift kick and he was again level with the back of the truck.

The truck driver was watching his progress and giving encouragement, by now they were definitely on nodding terms. Les decided to give it one last go so he pulled back on the throttle and again the bike lurched forward gaining an extra two miles an hour.

He crept along the truck as they both veered along the country lanes. Again and again the bike slowed for a moment and feverishly Les fiddled and kicked until the helmet was in full wobble again. Eventually he finally got level with the cab and the driver winked at him. The road went downhill slightly and Les took advantage, the helmet was indicating fifty-five miles an hour and was wobbling hard. With a triumphant grin Les eventually pulled in front of the truck just in time for his engine to seize up. His rear wheel locked and so out of control he veered off the road into a hedge.

The truck driver showed his appreciation of the entertainment by hooting his horn and drove on. Les, after checking his body and finding only minimal cuts and bruises and relieved to still be the owner of a functional erection, was wrestling his bike out of the bush when up pulled an RUC Land Rover. The policemen got out and surveyed the scene.

'Can we see your licence and insurance please?' The copper paused.

'And oh! Where's your tax disc?' he said looking at the bent front forks. Les noted the bastard smirked as he said it.

Chapter 8

Pubs and Priests

January 1977

The *Scout* helicopter rattled and thundered as it landed, its rotors whirling at full tilt. The doors had been removed and they were going out 'eagle' fashion. The pilot gave the thumbs up and all four of them approached the helicopter quickly in the usual crouched position. It was a curious matter that anything to do with helicopters was always done 'at the double', even if the helicopter was in the middle of Ballykinler Camp. It was almost as if the damn thing might fly away before anyone was on board. With the packs loaded in the middle of the helicopter and with Steve and Kevin on one side and Eddie and Les on the other, weapons in hand, feet firmly placed on the skids the pilot applied even more power. The din increased to deafening and the helicopter lifted off, turned a little and then flew off into the dark night sky like an angry dragon fly. The pilot, as usual in the Army, was experienced and very much a professional. Even though it was night he flew just above tree top height somehow managing to avoid little things like power pylons, church spires and even the odd tall tree, almost by a sixth sense.

Sitting on the edge of the helicopter deck whilst flying along in excess of 200mph in the dark was scary and exhilarating at the same time. Especially as every now and then the helicopter would lurch up and a power cable would zip under the skids at an alarmingly close distance. There were no lights except a dim green glow from the pilot's controls and every now and then a short burst of a small torch as the pilot checked his position and bearings. Steve who had a headset on and who could commune with the pilot shouted as loud as he could,

'STAND BY, STAND BY!'

It was almost lost in the noise but all of them knew that the drop off point was coming and that they should prepare to debus. It was important to be sure that the helicopter had actually touched the ground before leaping off clutching your Bergen and gat. This could be quite fatal if done from a couple of hundred feet up. The odd squaddie has been known to step off a helicopter thinking they were a few feet off the ground in mist when in fact they were a couple of hundred feet up and in cloud.

They felt the *Scout* touch the ground but they all looked down instinctively to make sure Mother Earth was indeed ready to accept them. They grabbed all their Monkeys and Parrots and in a split second they were off. The helicopter was already noisily lifting into the darkness, and within a few moments the racket was replaced by a low drone slowly fading away to silence. They were in all round defence their entire armoury ready to spit defiance should a group of unruly Irishmen of whatever persuasion decide they were worth tangling with. After waiting twenty minutes it seemed that they were not at this time a high priority on the IRA list of things to do, so at the signal from Steve they silently got up and moved away.

Shaking out into a loose formation at a distance between each other where they are not too close but could still see each other in the dark, they started to move. They walked relatively slowly looking around for tell-tale signs that they were expected. Wires, newly dug earth or even sweetie wrappers could mean a booby trap. Every now and then at a given signal from Steve they'd all get down in all round defence on their belt buckle and listen. Heads tilted slightly to one side with mouths open just a little bit to aid hearing. They'd listen for about twenty minutes. Steve and Les had starlight scopes and would also scan to see if any members of the local Irish bomb making and maiming society were taking any interest in them. Then at a sensed rather than seen signal they'd move off again silently almost wraith-like. Their understanding of each other and senses that they used to communicate were closer than any family member, it was almost telepathic.

This job was slightly different from the others as there was to be no close mutual support. It was considered that the risk of compromise was too high if more than one patrol was in the area. The target was a pub that was thought to be used by the higher echelons of the Republican hierarchy for meetings and things, although for some reason overhead projectors and whiteboards with team building events didn't spring immediately to mind.

It was almost 1am when they arrived at the final RV about one hundred yards from the pub. They had traversed two miles in about one hour and that was punishing, but Steve was pleased with progress. They needed to be in the hide and totally part of the landscape by 5am; not a lot of time. The pub itself was set back from the road and appeared to be a converted farmhouse with a selection of outbuildings. A gravel car park was on one side that was fairly large. The entrance to the pub was on the side of the building facing the car park and consisted of a large black door with a small lobby that seemed out of keeping with the building. There was a promising piece of scrub with a few bushes almost opposite the pub entrance about fifteen yards from the edge of the car park. The ground rose a little here, so it would be an ideal spot to get some happy snaps of the local dignitaries if they should arrive. However, Steve knew as did the others that if they were compromised they'd have their arses seriously out on a limb.

Kevin and Les sneaked forward and did a full recce of the site; this took about an hour as Les was very thorough. So much so that Eddie was tempted to ask him how many insects they'd be living with for the next five days, he'd probably know the exact number. Les, on their return confirmed the best place was the bushes by the car park but also its drawbacks; if they were seen it was a death trap if somebody wanted to do something about it. Steve got them all into a huddle and they very quietly discussed it. They all agreed that it was the best option and they'd go for it. But it was also decided that they'd make sure they had their best set of cutlery out in case unexpected guests came along.

There was a half-moon, so they could use hand signals to communicate. In complete silence and highly tactically they moved into the bushes. They dug a four foot deep hole in the ground and then camouflaged it with the clods of earth and attached scrub. A mixture of this and their scrim nets finished the job. They were sure they were invisible to all but the closest of examinations. For five days and nights they would be there in that hole and they would have to eat, shit and sleep there. No cooking or smoking from then on, totally silent mode and all their bodily effluent would have to go into a bag and be kept with them. Very difficult in an area where swinging a cat would most certainly mean getting a rifle barrel shoved firmly up your arse with a few apt suggestions as to where you could stuff said cat.

The cameras with NITECH ready were set up so that piccies could be taken of any bad guys or even any attractive women for that matter.

The first few days were extremely quiet and the four of them had to wonder how the place made a living. But on the Wednesday night the place was alive with people and the car park was almost full. One guy came within fifteen feet or so and had a leisurely piss. Just as well he stopped there as Kevin would have shoved the M79 where the sun didn't shine and then pull the trigger if he'd come any closer. Steve, Les and the cameras had been busy all night taking pictures of all comers. However, all of them recognised some of the revellers as hoods from a well-known terrorist organisation with a penchant for topping taxi drivers. Thursday and Friday nights were the same, with the added bonus of a well-known PIRA spokesman testing the suspension of his brand-new Cortina in the car park after receiving a satisfying blow job by the side door. Steve was put off buying one as he noticed that at least one window had to be wound down so his partner could open her legs wide enough in the back.

'Christ in a sack! Can't have much legroom in the back,' he said to Les who was going blind at the time watching the whole thing on NITECH.

'Yeah, but at least it gets them into the back, eh?' Les said licking his lips.

By 2am on the Friday morning the car park was empty and the pub had closed down. There were one or two lights on in the building and Steve put it down to a few having a lock in or perhaps there was a conference going on. From the people count in versus the people count out it seemed that five people were still in the building. But as all was quiet and nothing could be seen it was decided to go to night routine so that by twos they could get some much-needed sleep. Eddie and Kevin opted for the first watch.

Apart from the odd car passing on the main road absolutely nothing out of the ordinary happened. At 4am they woke Steve and Les so they could take over. They pulled their bags over them for a bit of warmth and both dropped off immediately into a deep sleep where they sat leaving Steve and Les to it.

'Stand to, stand to,' Les whispered into Eddie's ear and Eddie woke not initially realising he was in a hole somewhere. He shook the sleep from his head and rubbed his eyes with one hand. Meanwhile Les was waking up Kevin, as usual Kevin was awake and alert in seconds not needing another nudge.

'What the fuck's happening?' whispered Eddie to Les.

'Probably nothing but the same Austin has gone by four times and slowed down. Plus, two guys did a slow walk around the car park, best be on the safe side, eh?'

'Too fucking right, mate!' Eddie whispered back and checked his SLR was ready. He then broke radio silence and asked for a radio check – all worked OK. Steve silently handed the M79 to Eddie.

Crack, thump. Crack, thump. High velocity rounds coming from the pub started to impact the area around them and fly over their heads. A white Transit van reversed at speed from behind the pub and turned in the road so that its rear doors were facing their position. At the exact same moment, the Austin came from the other direction and turned so that its headlights had lit up their position like a fairground. The Transit van doors were just being flung open, and there were no prizes for guessing that an M60 machine gun was probably inside it.

Steve was rapid in his sizing up of the situation and the months of training in the NIPG plus his many years of experience as a soldier had better show their worth, or they'd be on the news that morning.

Steve shouted at the top of his voice,

'Les, car fucking headlights, take them out. Kevin, the pub windows, kill those bastards! Eddie, lose those cunts in the van. FIRE!'

The LMG started firing raking each window with a vicious hail of fire. The headlights went out almost immediately courtesy of Les and the Transit van lurched into the air twice as M79 self-propelled grenades went straight inside and blew up in the van. There was pause as the terrorists started to work out that this was not just a local army observation post thing. With such a full-frontal type attack Steve was convinced that these IRA types had already arranged a nice surprise for them if they now took the obvious route out behind.

The two guys from the car were now laying down and firing at their position, and AK47 high velocity bullets were tearing through the trees and bushes around them. Eddie coolly noted that they had obviously left their sight setting too high as the rounds were going over the top of the hide. Kevin gave them the odd burst.

A man, his face a mess, stumbled out of the back of the Transit. Eddie couldn't believe that anyone had survived in there; he must have been in a real state, so Les put him out of his misery with a single round to the head. Fire started to come from the pub again, it sounded like M16s.

Steve screamed out his orders, 'We're bugging out, were gonna cross the car park and go behind the pub.'

'You sure, Boss? Fuck, they'll pick us off like flies!' screamed Les.

'Better than walking into a full ambush behind us!' shouted Steve to all of them.

'Right, Les, Kevin I don't want anyone alive on that road in ten seconds' time, Eddie, how many M79 grenades you got?'

'Four!'

'Use all of them - two into the car and I want that pub fucking demolished. Standby… Standby... NOOOW!'

They broke out of the hide and knelt. The car was blown onto its side by a grenade; the two gunmen got up to move and were instantly dead as Les had them. Next second the car then blew up as the next grenade hit the base of the fuel tank. The concussion would have killed anyone else near the vehicle anyway. Kevin started to rake the pub and Eddie lit the place up as the M79 was used to fire the last two grenades into it.

'Move!' screamed Steve. They pepper potted across two by two firing as they went, and all four crossed the car park to the rear right of the pub. They took up defensive positions but for the moment they were out of the line of fire.

'EDDIE!' bellowed Steve.

'WHAT, BOSS?' Eddie screamed back.

'I HOPE YOU'VE FUCKING TOLD SOMEONE ABOUT ALL THIS ON THAT FUCKING THING YOU CARRY ABOUT.'

'Yeah, but they're a bit busy right now working out how to respond as they think it may be a 'come-on'. There will be a helicopter along at the agreed RV as planned. The boss does not want us about when the cavalry arrive as there are too many questions to answer. He wants us to bug out now.'

'You are fucking joking, aren't you?' shouted Les in surprise. 'What about all that mutual support shit we're supposed to get?'

'Yeah, I know, but Brigade Intelligence thinks this is a 'come-on' and they will use a mine somewhere to take out a good number of us and they don't want to risk a chopper full of squaddies.'

'Well four at least, eh?' said Kevin almost smiling. 'Jezzas!' he shouted as a bullet hit his Bergen spinning him around.

Steve realised that the ambush behind them had realised they were not going to take the bait and they were now taking fire from the position they used to be in on the other side of the car park. Steve's thinking was definitely in good form today. It was well into sunrise now, so the advantage of darkness was gone but they had no M79 grenades left.

'Les, Kevin! Make those fuckers think twice about shooting at us.' Les was already sizing up a victim in his L2 sight. Kevin was really pissed at getting a hole in his Bergen and was giving the PIRA members opposite the impression they were fighting an Infantry Company.

'Kevin, slow down a bit we need the ammo. Les, how many of them would you say?'

'Nine perhaps ten? But nine I'm sure of,' he shouted, and then pulling his trigger he corrected himself. 'No! Eight perhaps nine now I'd say!'

'Bleedin' smartarse!' shouted Kevin over the din of his LMG. 'Eddie, I need your Bren mags. Now!'

Steve thought for a moment. He had three options. Stay and fight as terrorists usually only hang around for a short period of time and then bug out. On this occasion, he was worried about the come-on issue, so they may have planned to stay awhile knowing that the cavalry won't be coming immediately. Two was to turn and run; using fire and manoeuvre to make his way back to the RV and wait for the helicopter. That meant a lot of exposing their backs and only having half their fire power facing the enemy at any one time. The last option was to do a full-frontal assault. One of them was almost certain to be killed, perhaps all of them. But they would not be expecting it and surprise was a very, very effective weapon.

'Eddie, empty your Bergen except your radio and put all the specialist kit from the others into it. Eddie you'll be carrying the Bergen on this as we practiced.' At this remark the others knew what was coming. He went on, 'Give all your mags to Kevin, Les sling your sniper rifle and get your M16 out. Bergens will be left here with only personal kit, shit and food in them. Spread the photo cassettes amongst all of us, except Eddie. Kevin, you know the drill on this?'

Kevin looked directly at Eddie at this point, Eddie looked back and slightly nodded, he knew what that meant. Kevin looked unconcerned but also nodded knowing that if Eddie fell injured or shot, and there was a prospect he may get captured, then he was to fire a burst into the Bergen to destroy all the specialist kit and to kill Eddie. They all had their targets if it came to that but more to the point it meant that they'd rather be shot than captured. The local PIRA had a bad habit of using electric drills during interrogation sessions on the knees, then they just killed you anyway. If you were injured it may as well be a mate that takes you out.

'You've all got a smoke grenade each. When I give the word throw them as far across the car park as possible, slightly up near the road to allow for wind. Everyone ready?' A bullet ripped a hole in his combat jacket as he stopped speaking. They all knew it was time to go.

They spread out in a line as far apart as they could manage. Eddie and Kevin were together and Steve and Les would work as the other team. They would be doing this from the kneeling position because although it had a greater exposure risk it was faster, and you had better vision.

'SMOKE!' Steve shouted and all three followed in unison. Eddie got up ungainly and hobbled forward a couple of yards. Kev's LMG was blasting the edge of the car park forty yards away – Eddie knelt brought his weapon up, started firing and shouted,

'GO!'

Eddie was shooting into the bushes in front of him. The SLR gave a mighty kick when it fired and you knew you were shooting the damn thing. He saw a flash then smoke and felt a bullet zip past him but he concentrated on the smoke and fired about ten rounds into the spot.

'GO!' he heard Kevin shout and he was again up and running breathlessly; the Bergen weighed a ton. He ran another ten yards or so and noted he was almost halfway across. He was too scared to hear any bullets or commands he just got down started to fire and shouted, 'GO!' at the top of his voice. He fired and fired into the area where he thought he could see the enemy, a face appeared and he fired at it then it was gone. He felt something hit his Bergen. He sensed Kevin go by, he was firing his LMG on the move from the hip.

Kevin shouted, 'GO!' and Eddie was up firing as he ran. Kevin knelt and screamed, 'GO!'

Eddie, the weight of his Bergen forgotten as the adrenalin really kicked in, got up and ran. He didn't know it at the time, but he was also screaming his head off, as were all the others. Suddenly a searing pain hit him in the foot and he tumbled. He landed face down smashing his nose and chin; blood filled his mouth and spurted from his nose. For a moment, he thought he'd been shot in the neck. He started to get his rifle into some sort of firing position, but blood was also getting in his eyes he must have cut his head somehow. His foot was all pain and he wondered what was up with it. He then realised Kevin's orders and he suddenly heard the LMG fire a long burst right next to him. He closed his eyes and said, 'Fuck,' to himself a few times before he realised that Kevin was using him as a firing position and had the LMG on his Bergen and was firing hard into the edge of the car park.

'If you don't get up I'm gonna fucking shoot you!' he screamed between bursts. Eddie knew his foot was injured.

'I've been shot in the foot and perhaps the head. I'm not sure I can fucking move.'

'Well at least fire your fucking gat then whilst I have a look.'

Eddie fired into the general direction he was supposed to whilst Kevin looked at his foot.

'Just a fucking scratch, mate – I've licked more blood than that off a tart's tampon!'

Kevin fired another couple of bursts for good effect.

'NOW GET THE FUCK UP!'

Eddie hobbled to his feet; Les and Steve had made the edge of the car park and had personally scared off the remaining terrorists that they found there. The six or so left alive near them had decided to leg it.

Steve and Les started to give fire support to Eddie and Kevin. Kevin helped Eddie with one arm whilst shooting the LMG with the other. Eddie also kept his SLR firing and the two of them hobbled onto the grass and then thankfully down into a bush. The two terrorists who were left in front of them also decided to run away and Kevin fired after them but by some twist of fate luck was with them that day and he missed. They counted two dead bodies in the grass. Steve didn't stop there.

'Reload; let's get the fuck out of here.'

All of them with Eddie being helped by Kevin and Les jogged and hobbled across the scrub into some welcome woodland about one hundred yards beyond the pub compound.

They got into all round defence and looked out above their weapon sights to see if there were any immediate threats to deal with. Steve shouted,

'EDDIE, AMMO AND STATUS?'

'SLIGHT INJURY TO RIGHT FOOT, TWO 7.62 MAGS, FORTY ROUNDS. ONE MAG 9MM. RADIO WORKING AND CONTACT REPORT SENT!'

'LES, AMMO AND STATUS?'

And so it went around the three of them. They were a bit low on ammo and apart from Eddie's foot they were all OK. Les was despatched to examine Eddie's foot and he declared him fit. Kevin was sent to get the remainder of the Bergens.

'It's a 9mm round by the look of it, went through his boot and has ripped off most of his little toe,' said Les matter-of-factly to Steve.

'He'll be tap dancing in two or three days, he's OK... it's painful but he'll live. Want I should give him something for the pain?' Les asked already suspecting what the answer would be.

'No, we need everyone on high alert, Les. Don't need Eddie out on a trip right now. Give him a few of your compo sweets.' Eddie heard this and was not impressed but he knew the reasons why. His foot was bloody sore and he was in great pain. Almost not much bleeding though which was a blessing.

Kevin having just got back with the Bergens looked over at Eddie and in just above a whisper said,

'Cheer up, Eddie! You may have lost a toe but you're gonna get a new pair of boots ya lucky bastard!' Kevin grinned.

'Fuck off!' said Eddie but even with the pain he had to laugh. It wasn't the joke it was the adrenalin leaving and the relief all coming in. They all had a short fit of the giggles due to Kevin's remark. Steve, however, cut them off after a while and they silently slid off to the RV for the chopper. It wasn't far away and they'd wait there whilst the police and the rest of the Army tried to hot pursuit the bad guys around the countryside. HQNI wanted them out of the way and debriefed before the awkward questions started, after all there was a lot of broken and damaged vehicles, about four or five dead men lying about the place not to mention a half-demolished pub.

It had started to drizzle, nothing heavy but persistent, the kind of rain that gets into everything and they were indeed quickly soaked to the skin. The PUP[34] was about half a mile away, but they had up to an hour to wait. They could hear a helicopter and police sirens in the distance. Eddie was in some pain with his foot, but Steve would not relent in giving him some relief with drugs and Eddie was in agreement, it was more his face that was hurting, he'd find out later that he had a broken nose, concussion and lost the top section of his little toe.

They plodded on in the rain towards Derrylin, a small village south of their target area; eventually it started to slowly appear out of the murk. On the edge of the village was a church, surprisingly large for such a small place but not that old, perhaps Victorian. As it was extremely unlikely that a fervent Republican had given up the opportunity of a nice Sunday morning's lay in after the strains of a busy Saturday night in the pub. Les suggested they get out of the rain and shelter in the lee of the church as there was no porch. After all, it was a Catholic church so they might as well get something out of the locals – even if it was only shelter. They all agreed that it was worth the risk. However, their professionalism had not entirely departed so after quickly setting a snap

---

[34] Pick Up Point

ambush in case they were being followed, they then checked the immediate area around the church and then thankfully got in out of the rain and took their packs off.

They were standing near the door in the lee of the wind. Kevin immediately lit up a ciggy and leaned back on the door only for it to open suddenly and he fell on his arse in the vestibule of the church. His shout of 'Fuck!' as he fell was obviously missed by the Choir Invisible as he was thankfully spared the customary lightning strike.

'What stupid bastard left that pissing door open? Place is full of thieving fucking Micks,' he shouted as he regained his composure and slowly got to his feet. Again, no retribution from God in a form of punishment by weather.

None of them could say a word as they were apoplectic and unable to speak. Kevin momentarily considered shooting all of them, so the matter could be forgotten and expunged from the memory of man, but realising that he would have found it funny as well, he relaxed and smiled deciding he would piss in everyone's locker later to get his own back. He wandered into the church and was gob smacked by the beauty of it. The smell of the place confirmed its religious importance with a heavy mixture of stale frankincense and old wood. Mesmerised he wandered further in and was struck by the morning sunrise bursting through the leaded windows, blues and reds illuminating the inside of the church contrasting the darkness. The light reflected off the cream coloured plastered walls and lit up the altar with its white cloth and golden tabernacle. The light striking off the eight ornate matching candlestick holders was kaleidoscopic and mysterious. He amazed himself with his own reaction of respect and awe. That's when Kevin saw the organ, a full 40 stop organ. He looked up behind him and saw the familiar outline of the huge bass pipes partially hidden in the balcony above the entrance. He walked over and touched the leather seat.

'Fuck it!' he half whispered to himself and sat on the seat. He lifted the cover and revealed the ivory coloured keys. He breathed deeply and just looked at the keyboard and after a moment pushed one. Nothing happened and for a moment he was confused until he realised that it was switched off. He sighed, looked for the switch, found it and pushed it down. After a short pause a small red light showed that the organ was ready. He took a deep breath and depressed a key. Instantly a deep sonorous tone filled the church. Eddie and the others reached instinctively for their rifles before realising the noise was inside the church. They ran in as Kevin hit a few more notes in no particular order. Steve was scared shitless that something was happening and was trying to get to grips with the plot. He saw Kevin at the keyboard and sighed.

'Kevin! For fuck's sake get down from there.' The shouted whisper sounded like he was telling off a little boy for farting or something similar. This seemed a bit pointless considering that Kevin had woken half of the Province already. He raised his voice. 'Kevin! Leave it alone.'

'I'm just getting the key won't be a moment,' said Kevin ignoring his Section Commander and pushing a few more notes.

'Key? What the fuck's he on about, what fucking key? Shitting door key? What in the name of St. Peter's frigging jock strap is he talking about?' shouted Steve.

'Get down from there or I swear I'll fucking shoot you.' Steve considered raising his rifle to underline his point, but he knew that shooting Kevin would mean a board of enquiry, endless paperwork and still ending up doing porridge and using up shed loads of KY jelly at the same time.

Kevin paused and looked at his boss for a moment. Steve was surprised to see that this was a different Kevin, gone the glance that made your blood run cold. Kevin looked away and placed both hands on the keyboard and a miracle happened. The organ somehow started to play, not just play, not chopsticks or something childlike, but really play; something sublime and beautiful like only an organ can. The notes danced around the church as if guided by an angel. This was perfection witnessed by the stationary soldiers', mouths agape taking in this apparition. The music soared and swooped like a lark on the morning wind, sometimes deep and enigmatic and then light almost diaphanous. Kevin's arms were moving with a sort of controlled chaos, like a calculating demon in the house of God. Suddenly as quickly as it started the music stopped. The church was silent except for the heavy breathing of Kevin sitting at the keyboard.

'That was beautiful,' said a voice at the back of the church.

'Fucking Jesus!' said Steve spinning round bringing up his rifle at the same time.

A priest in full vestments was standing there.

'Not very apt,' rebuked the priest glancing disapprovingly at the guns. Steve lowered his rifle and apologised, the priest could see he meant it and nodded his head in a sort of acceptance, almost forgiveness. He went on nodding at Kevin.

'So where do Her Majesty's soldiers learn to play Tannhäuser so well then?'

'Orphanage,' spat Kevin quietly, in a tone that told the Father the matter was closed.

They all trooped out under the watchful eye of the priest who was wondering how he'd explain the blood from Eddie's foot on the floor. Again, Steve apologised for bringing weapons in.

'That's alright, son, stop worrying about it, it's the heart that has evil in it not a lump of steel, now go in peace before the 7 o'clock service starts, or I'll really have a lot of explaining to do here. Bless you all!' The priest was still definitely looking disapprovingly at the blood trail left by Eddie's foot.

Kevin stomped out and joined the rest outside and Eddie couldn't help himself.

'Bugger me Gus, that was fantastic where did you learn to do that?'

'As I said, at the orphanage – and if any of you tell anyone fucking else you'll not be writing many Christmas cards ever again.' The cold glance was back – they knew Kevin meant it.

The rain beckoned and they all slowly walked out into the weather fading away until they were a part of it along with their weapons, webbing and Bergens. As if in a final statement a bolt of lightning lit up the sky and a deep thunder resonated across the fields. The thunder echoed away, Eddie mused whilst peering into the rain just as the expected *Puma* helicopter thundered into earshot.

'Hmm... God's pissed, must have been kipping and missed the whole thing,' he chuckled and limped on towards the LZ.

Kevin, face soaked by the rain, watched the helicopter land and with the LMG in one hand, his Bergen in the other and after helping Eddie on board, he scrambled onto the helicopter along with the others. As he manoeuvred himself in he was deep in thought.

Yep, I'll do it tonight when they're all drunk, I'll piss in their lockers. No... No, in fact I think I'll shit in their boots. He smiled in anticipation. With that the helicopter rose into the sky, turned and tilted towards Lisburn and a million questions about what happened.

Northern Ireland, May 1976 – Some Light Entertainment!

The Operations Room was Eddie's responsibility. It was in Masonic Camp in Londonderry and he, as a corporal now, took this responsibility seriously. His regiment was on a four-month 'Op Banner' tour of Northern Ireland and their turf was East Londonderry City Centre. Southampton FC, by a miracle, had somehow made it to the FA Cup and, as the regiment was mostly from Hampshire, the guys wanted to watch the match. One of the officers had graciously offered to stand in for a soldier in one of the sangars[35] so a Tom could watch the footy. This subaltern was into rugby himself and so had no need to watch that 'soccer rubbish'.

Eddie was a stickler for procedure and even if this chap was an officer he would get the proper briefings etc. and he must be made to understand what was expected. This particular sangar overlooked the Rossville flats and it was well known that one of the windows, on occasion, hosted a rather well bestowed young lady who would entertain gents in her room with the curtains open. Not only was she entertaining but she would also wear very interesting and exotic clothes that usually entailed stockings and high heels. She also evidently enjoyed her hobby and went at it with gusto and enthusiasm. So that this would not be missed a powerful scope had been set up perfectly to ensure that if any entertainment was on offer it would not go unnoticed. If the scope was moved it would be on pain of death as it was difficult to find the correct window again.

Curiously this sanger had a more savoury smell than the others and there were no trophies for deducing the reason why. This was duly explained to the officer who very openly stated that this was a disgusting thing to do and he would have none of it. However, it was suggested to him that if sexual athletics were going on it was his duty to explain in graphic language what was happening over the intercom. The officer flatly refused to cooperate but agreed that he would at least leave the scope alone and he would not touch it. He left the Ops Room and took up his position in the sangar. Eddie would, every ten or so minutes, ask the officer over the intercom if the girl was up to anything yet. The officer would bluster down the phone how disgusting they all were and that it was below his rank and standing as an officer and a gentleman to indulge in

---

[35] Lookout/Sentry Post, usually at the corners on the camp high up. Made of concrete it had viewing slots at various points around it.

such behaviour. Eddie, however, kept asking every so often throughout his tour of duty in the sangar and received the same response each time. This young lieutenant obviously had high ideals and was not to be moved on them.

The officer's two-hour stag[36] eventually came to an end and in the meantime Southampton, by the virtue of a phenomenon nobody could explain, had won the FA cup. In celebration, much noise was coming from the crowded Char Wallah[37] hut where the TV was. The officer went back to the Ops Room and filled in his report all the while being probed as to what the young lady was doing during his shift. He dutifully ignored all such requests. Once done he left the Operations Room and passing the Company Commander smartly saluted and for a brief moment explained about the sangar and the scope etc. The Company Commander took his points on board and agreed that the scope should perhaps be removed to protect this young lady's privacy. The subaltern then went into the crowded and noisy TV Room to buy a burger and a drink from the Char Wallah. On his grand entry, all soldiers in there momentarily stopped reliving the great match and looked at the officer, and immediately a huge cheer went up, so loud that it startled many a terrorist miles away. The officer stood there bemused by such behaviour until he caught his image in the mirror above the Char Wallah's counter. There, surrounding his right eye was a huge ring of black polish.

'Oh bugger!' was all he could muster, before laughing out loud himself.

---

[36] Stag or Stagging on was slang for sentry duty of one sort or another.
[37] Indian/Pakistani, usually Muslim, who would sell tea, coffee and burgers from a small hut – Brave men.

Chapter 9

Stop 2 Echo

February 1977

The box van was stationary by the side of the A1 just outside Newtown, a small built up area just prior to the border with the South. The vehicle was made to look like it was broken down and looked even more miserable due to a heavy rain that moved over the landscape draping all with a heavy skirt of mist and accompanying puddles. The odd car swished past splashing the van with another coat of filthy water. Each time a car went by the box body swayed slightly and the incumbents felt rather than heard the splash from the passing vehicle on the side.

'What a fucking stupid job,' exploded Eddie looking suspiciously at the cup of tea he had just extracted from the flask. It was so strong it appeared stationary in the mug like a deep brown slime. He took a mouthful and agreed with himself that it tasted as foul as it looked.

'We're sitting ducks for any pissing Paddy with a grudge.' He gestured at the road and continued, 'We've even given them a fucking great getaway route – any daft shit could just drive by and take us out.'

Kevin grinned whilst cleaning the barrel of the Bren.

'Be better breakfasting with the Devil than doing this shitty job.'

'Shut the fuck up here comes another one,' cautioned Steve. They all went quiet as Les called out the registration number and Eddie passed it over the radio. As the car passed the vehicle swayed with a thud as a wave of water hit the van again.

It was about ten o'clock in the morning and they had already registered about two hundred cars since they started at seven. The job was to register all the cars going out of the Province and in the afternoon, they'd check the registrations of the vehicles coming back. They were in direct contact with the ladies at DVLC in Swansea and if the response in the afternoon was 'stop 2 echo', they'd radio that on to the Gloucesters and they'd stop and search it. The idea was that some terrorists were crossing the border in the morning and coming back with their shopping in the afternoon comprising M16, Semtex and bullets, type shopping. The whole group were doing this at various points along the border.

The work was very boring though. In the vehicle, they were tooled up and wearing combats. Only the RCT driver was in civvies.

Kevin had a thought.

'Hey, Mess Tins, if we get a flat your gonna have to go out and do the repair yourself, mate, on your tod, alone, if you get my drift.'

'So fucking what, better than being in here with you four dipsticks, eh?' the driver replied. Kevin continued,

'Anyway, how did you get that silly nickname?

Mess Tins looked uncomfortable for a moment and then admitted,

'When I joined up I thought the mess tins I was issued with were for shitting in. I was effing surprised when they said we cooked in them, difficult to explain as I'd already had a crap.'

They all burst out laughing just as a car hit the front of their vehicle crushing the cab. The car, in a cacophony of screeching steel with the engine screaming, tore off the front left quarter of the van before spinning off onto its side and then into a tree. The impact knocked everyone off their seats and onto the floor. Kevin and Eddie banged their heads on the side of the van. Les was OK, as was Steve. Mess Tins, the driver, had disappeared from sight. It felt to Eddie like it all happened in slow motion, but it was all over in an instant. Steve was the first to react.

'Where's Mess Tins?' he screamed.

'Bollocks if I know!' shouted back Les.

'What in the name of Beelzebub's ball sack happened?' said a groggy Kevin rubbing his head.

'Perhaps you farted and blew off the front of the van?' Steve said sarcastically. He continued,

'What do you think happened, eh? A fucking car hit us, that's what happened, now get out and find out what the fuck's going on and don't forget your gats either.' They all rushed out of the damaged van and saw that a Ford Consul had hit them and was now part of a tree on its side, smoke and steam pouring out of the engine area.

'Kermit and Gus, go and check that car and help the stupid git that hit us. Les use your scope and look about, see if we're being set up or something – you watch out for us. I'm gonna try and find out where Mess Tins went.'

Eddie and Kevin ran over to where the car had ended up and looked in through the broken windscreen. The driver was a complete mess with half his head splayed over the dashboard. He was as dead as anyone could get. In the back Kevin saw two unconscious children.

'Kermit! Christ, there are kids in the back,' Kevin screamed.

'Shit!' was all Eddie could say as he tried to climb up onto the side of the vehicle which was now up in the air.

'Kermit!' Kevin shouted and Eddie paused. 'Getting in through the back window will be easier.'

Eddie nodded in acknowledgement whilst Kevin smashed the rear windscreen with the butt of his Bren. He reached in and pulled out the first person he got his hands to. It was a young girl about five years old. He roughly passed her to Eddie and then he climbed half into the vehicle. The smoke was stinging his eyes and he was wondering if the fuel tank was going to go up at any moment. His groping hands found a leg and without ceremony he pulled it until he found he was dragging a young boy of about seven years old out through the remains of the rear window. The boy was coughing and spluttering, a good sign that he was OK. He pulled the boy out fully and dragged him to one side and shook him to get his attention.

'How many were there in the car?' he asked. It was obvious that the boy was in severe shock; he shook him again and asked the same question. The boy seemed to understand, spluttered and said,

'Mr. Leary and me sis, are they OK? He offered us a lift to school.' The boy started to cry and Kevin tried to stand him up. It was then that he noticed the boy had severe bleeding just above his knee. It was definitely arterial bleeding.

'Oh fuck! Kermit get your arse over here NOW!' he shouted.

'Sorry, you deal with it, Gus, I've got a problem here with the little girl, she's stopped breathing.'

Kevin pulled out his first field dressing whilst trying to remember the First Aid he knew. He put it over the wound and tied it off. He laid the boy down and lifted the leg high, so it was above the boy's body, but it was still bleeding heavily. He pushed down hard on the gash and felt that the bone was just under the skin, the poor kid had broken his thigh bone.

'Bollocks,' was all he could say. Les joined him and took over having checked out the local area. Almost immediately he could hear Eddie sending a radio report requesting assistance.

'What about the girl, Kermit?' Eddie didn't respond and Les knew by the look on his face that the girl was probably dead.

'Let's try and keep this one going, eh?' suggested Kevin. The boy had lost consciousness when Les started to look at the leg whilst feeling his pulse; it was weak. Les rummaged about in his webbing and pulled out some medical items. He pulled off the blood soaked first field dressing, the bleeding was very heavy. He poured the entire contents of his water bottle over the wound and saw bone poking out of the surface. It looked like a major artery had been broken.

'Gus, put his leg onto your shoulder and get ready to hold these forceps when I tell you to.' Kevin did as he was told and immediately got splashed with blood over his face and neck. Les was right, an artery had been cut.

Les pushed his fingers into the wound and managed to pull the wound open and to grab the artery with the forceps using his other hand. He locked the forceps and then passed them to Kevin.

'Don't let go of that OK?'

Kevin nodded whilst Les started to close up part of the wound with dressings his hands covered in blood; Kevin was holding the leg up on his shoulder. He looked at Eddie and was about to say something when Mess Tins and Steve appeared. Mess Tins had what appeared to be a broken arm and the way he was being assisted some snapped ribs into the bargain. Mess Tins smiled at them at exactly the same moment the car exploded.

The first thing Eddie felt was water running down his leg and it seemed that he was pissing himself, but for a few moments he couldn't move. He opened his eyes and slowly gained consciousness. Wherever he was it was very noisy and vibrating like hell. As reality became more acute around him he realised that he was in a *Puma* helicopter and it was flying somewhere. Why couldn't he move? Almost snail like he peered about and then realised he was strapped down and a medic was stitching up a gash in his leg.

'See you've joined us then!' the medic shouted above the din. He was a small bald chap with a Welsh accent; he was quite effeminate and obviously as bent as a nine-bob note. But as most infantrymen will agree the bent ones always made the best medics and they didn't lack guts either. If you had a serious injury in combat a gay accent was comforting – there was a bigger chance you'd survive.

'Don't worry just a few cuts and bruises but you seem to have a head injury and we need to check for concussion, so relax.'

Eddie closed his eyes and remembered the car. He looked at the medic and began to speak. The medic saw the expression on Eddie's face and put his fingers to his lips.

'Shush now, boy! Your mates are all OK, except the ugly one here.' He gestured and strapped into a seat nearby was Mess Tins still holding his now strapped up arm.

'Your muckers have all gone back to Ballykinler as there is nothing the local MRS there can't handle, but the car occupants... well.' He paused. 'The girl died at the scene, sorry but we got there too late – your mate Gus took it very badly. There was nothing you or he could have done, she would have died anyway. Boy was picked up by a local ambulance seems you two saved his life, even when the fuel tank exploded those forceps stayed on – a good job boy!'

Eddie laid back and remembered the little girl. He tried not to cry but tears welled up and flowed down his cheek. The medic had seen it all before, shock often did this; it was the adrenalin and coming down off it. On this occasion he was wrong as Eddie thought, regardless of what the medic claimed that a little girl died because he did not think to get a message out immediately. He sobbed until the medication he was given robbed him of consciousness.

The *Puma* landed at Musgrave Hospital and when stable the pilot gave the stretcher bearers the thumbs up and they rushed around to the helicopter door and skilfully and quickly extracted the injured and then with a well-practiced gentleness they rushed them into the A&E department.

They checked him over and saw that whatever part of the exploding car hit Eddie it had definitely given him a nasty concussion, so they felt it best to get him into a bed and monitor him just to make sure he didn't cone or suffer any number of the other myriad of complications that head injuries can generate. It was decided that he should be kept in overnight and he regained consciousness in a hospital bed between crisp clean sheets with his head nestling on a nice white fluffy pillow.

After twenty four hours, they sent him back to Ballykinler. He had enjoyed himself in Musgrave Hospital. Crisp linen, good food and real women in the guise of nurses. He felt like faking a psychiatric disorder, loss of memory or something, but had heard nasty tales of Netley Hospital or wherever they sent soldiers that had gone bonkers – plus he couldn't remember any of them coming back to the regiment either... best not to risk it. When he got back to Ballykinler he was welcomed by the usual banter.

'Did you fuck any nurses, Eddie?' Les shouted bluntly as he entered the block.

'Did your pink pogo stick get any exercise?' asked Kevin.

'I think I may have missed one or two, but I'm surprised I can walk after all the shagging I've been doing,' lied Eddie blatantly.

'Ya lying bastard, Eddie!' Kevin screamed.

'OK you got me, but I did manage to nick some soiled nurses' knickers from the laundry whilst I was there, don't ask me how!' retorted Eddie with a knowing look. Kev's eyes lit up.

'Did you bring any back?' he said hopefully.

'Here ya go.' He handed over a plastic bag with what appeared to be things made of white cloth inside. Kevin was on it like a shot.

Eddie shook his head and said to Gus,

'Best to leave them in the bag, Gus and sniff them whilst there still in there.' Kevin saw the sense in that and gingerly opened the bag and put his nose in and took a huge sniff. Eddie took a few paces nearer the door and then said,

'Well, Kevin, how do Steve's underpants smell then?' Kevin immediately looked up in disgust, but Eddie had scarpered. He looked at the underpants and made a mental note to remove Eddie's spleen with a compo tin opener whilst he slept that night.

They were all called to a debrief where it was revealed that the car slid on the wet road purely by accident. The explosion was the petrol tank going up and they were lucky there were no further injuries. However, it turned out that they had been double lucky as the driver was a well-known local player who had been using kids as a screen to transport explosives. There were no explosives in the car at that time, but it was thought he was off to pick some up.

Due to the explosion and the trauma of seeing a child die the patrol was given a long weekend's R&R effective immediately. It was 4pm on a Thursday – Eddie was sure that by the same time tomorrow he'd be deep into something warm, wet, furry and smelling of fish!

Bay of Biscay, LSL Sir Galahad, April 1979 – Echoes of D-Day!

The 'Landing Ship Logistics' had been rolling across the Bay of Biscay for three days en route to Portugal and it wasn't the easiest of crossings. Being a landing ship, the Sir Galahad had a flat bottom and was not best suited to sea swells. Therefore, most of B Company were running from their accommodation to lean over the side and would attempt to shoot seagulls with the contents of their stomachs for most of the day.

Portugal had been going through political changes since the Carnation Revolution in 1974 and had reached out to its oldest ally for assistance. This was to help with training its army so that it could become a proper member of NATO and not just an acolyte as it had been.

Pete's company had been chosen to spearhead the new diplomacy between Britain and its oldest ally. The ship's radio operator approached Pete who was now a corporal running B Company's Signals detachment and handed him a very long decoded signal from Admiralty. He took it and read it and ran headlong into the officers' quarters where the OC, a tall and gangly ex-SAS man by the unremarkable name of Jones, read the signal quietly to himself before bursting out loud with,

'FUCKING HELL! We've orders to invade Portugal, we are to invade and make contact with anti-fascist forces to assist them with reinstalling the democratic government as there has been a coup. We are to hold until reinforcements arrive from the UK.'

He was absolutely gob smacked.

The signal gave grid references and contact names and ominously the fact that to link up with friendly forces B Company would have to fight through two enemy infantry regiments. The OC in good SAS style wasted no time. Ammunition was brought up and all soldiers were made to test fire and zero their weapons over the side.

Suddenly the captain of the Sir Galahad insisted that they stopped firing for a while and soon after this a black submarine appeared about fifty yards from the Sir Galahad. The crew waved from the conning tower and the two vessels sent cryptic messages to each other with their signal lamps.

Slowly and surely the black shape started to sink again, and the Hunter Killer sub was gone. The pace of the mission stepped up as the troops could see that Her Majesty's Armed Forces meant business if they were using a *submarine. Meanwhile vehicles were being checked, the 81mm mortars were check fired into the sea, and anti-tank weapons were also test fired at wooden boxes thrown over the end of the ship. The OC fully briefed the entire Company, witnessed blindly by the Chinese crew members, on the political history of Portugal, the current situation, their mission and the likelihood that many would not make it due to the fact that B Company would have to fight through to friendly forces. They were short on ammunition and food but drops by the RAF had been planned at strategic points along the route for re-supply. At the end of the briefing the captain of the ship came down and stood next to the OC and announced that he had a message from the Commander UK Land Forces to the Officer Commanding B Company. He paused and coughed to clear his throat prior to reading it aloud. Everywhere there was silence except for the heartbeat of the ship's engines shuddering through the ship, everyone expected one of those sombre Nelson inspired 'hope you're happy to die for your country' type messages. He began,*

'To the officer commanding and men of B Company, LSL Sir Galahad, Biscay. From Commander-in-Chief UK Land Forces, Admiralty. Priority: Immediate.

Barry, remember Lai Chi Cock, Hong Kong 1976? April fool! Regards John.'

The OC stood there stunned for a while then shook his head and said,

'The bastard got me back and good,' and burst out laughing. He looked at the captain quizzically.

'What about the submarine, how did he do that?'

'They had no idea they just popped up and asked us if we'd be a target for some torpedo exercises they wanted to do. Just coincidence.' He shrugged.

What had actually happened at Lai Chi Cock nobody ever found out.

Chapter 10

Rest & Recuperation

March 1977

During R&R Kevin was never sure where to go as everyone from his past was associated with the orphanage. The others all offered to spend the break with him and for him to go to their house or girlfriends or whatever, they'd be OK about it they all said, almost as one. But Kevin knew that the guys wanted to get home to some serious banging with whomever they called partners and didn't really want him kicking about trying to screw the girlfriend's mother, sister, brothers, dogs, guinea pigs or whatever. So, although grateful for the offers, he declined. They split up from Kevin at Birmingham New Street. Kevin said he was going to meet a girl he knew, it wasn't true, but it gave him a way out. Eddie was going to see his girlfriend in Southampton, Les was going to London to meet the barmaid he met in Newcastle and Steve was going to Winchester to see his family. They, apart from Kevin, stayed on the train and slowly got legless all the way to London Euston, it was dirty but it had a buffet car that smelt like a pub, so they stayed and played *David Bowie* and *Thin Lizzy* loudly not really giving a shit who they might upset.

Kevin felt a kind of relief when they had gone. He was now free to be himself. Birmingham New Street was as impersonal as ever. A concrete maze designed by a mad whirling dervish on uppers. He got a bit lost and found himself in the immense concourse where people were making efforts to ignore the seething mass of humanity around them that was ebbing and flowing through the labyrinth. He paused and wondered where he should go. A tramp sitting against the wall touched his leg and startled Kevin. He looked down and saw a mess of filth wrapped up in a coat that was threadbare and stained, a head poked up out of the fetid pile with grey hair that was speckled black and brown with God knew what.

'Got a few bob, mate, jus' for a cuppa?' the stinking pile asked. Eddie was about to tell him where to go when he noticed pinned on the coat a worn and rusty British Legion badge leaning drunkenly on his collar. Kevin looked closer and saw he was wearing a old KF shirt, probably the one he left the Army with. Kevin leaned down to speak to him and got the full impact of the grimy choking smell.

'What mob were you in then, Grandad?' People passing glanced at him as though he was mad and then they were gone.

'Eh?' He paused to recall his past, and coughed. 'I was a "Farmer's boy", lad, D and Ds,' he croaked. Kevin smiled, he had a few mates in the Devon and Dorsets and it was a good regiment. Sometimes called the Armoured Farmers! Kevin reached into his wallet and slipped the old fella a fiver. The old boy couldn't believe his eyes, Kevin didn't mind he was flush and he needed the karma.

'You should have joined the Hampshire's, mate, you'd be begging in a much better station like Winchester if you had,' suggested Kevin.

'Hampshire's? Fucking cardboard cavaliers! They took over from us in Malaya in '68, what a shower, but we all had a few laughs though.' He chuckled. Kevin was sure that just for a moment he saw a snapshot of the proud man he once was in amongst the muck and shit of a wrecked life. Then it was gone, and the pile of rotting clothes was shuffling off to whatever Hell he inhabited to get enough meths, or whatever, to thrust himself thankfully into the oblivion he called relief.

Kevin went back to pondering his next move. Oswestry popped into his head. *No! That place was boring to the point of suicide*, he recalled his Junior Leader days there as a boy soldier. He'd rather spend the weekend with the tramp he just met. Lichfield? He liked Lichfield as he did his basic training there. *No! Place will be full of bloody squaddies again*, he thought. He dug deeper and glancing across the concourse he noticed a sign advertising York Minster.

'That's it! Never been there.' He said to himself.

He bought the required ticket and trundled off to York. He loved cathedrals and history. He could immerse himself in that, have a few beers some nice food and if a bit of fanny came his way then all the better. He was off...

There are a lot of tourists in York normally, but not so much in March. So he was a bit surprised when four B&Bs refused him and said they were full. He was convinced they had something against soldiers. After a while though, he came to a likely looking place. Not too posh and not too bad either. He strode up the steps of the Victorian pile and knocked on the black painted door. Whilst waiting for the door to be answered he admired the brass fittings. They were glorious, a brass doorknocker that had a bust of Shakespeare, a massive letter box all ornate with flowers and swirls, door plates and knobs. It was beautifully looked after and shone radiantly. It reminded him of a doctor's surgery. *Can't be bad*, he thought. The door opened.

'Hello, can I help?'

The voice emanated from an elegant lady in her late thirties, tall, extremely well turned out with a generous figure. But, as Kevin noted with appreciation, all the right curves were still in all the right places. It looked to Kevin like she was just about to go out or something as she was dressed up. Kevin eventually took his eyes off the fun bits and looked her in the face. She was quite lovely even if she was a bit older.

'I hope so I'm looking for lodgings. I am a soldier on R&R from Northern Ireland and would like to spend a few days looking at York.' He wondered what she must have looked like when she was a teenager.

Bloody stunner I bet, he thought.

She paused.

'Well at this time you'll be pushed to find somewhere as most are closed, in this case we are just about to decorate so we are also in fact closed.'

Kevin tried not to look too disappointed. A room and potentially classy shag had just evaporated before his eyes.

'Thanks, sorry for bothering you I'll try and find somewhere else.' Kevin turned and started to walk down the steps. The lady looked at his retreating back and called to him.

'Wait,' she said, and Kevin turned on the bottom step looking up at her.

'R&R? Did you say you're in the Army?'

'Yes. Home from Ulster, been there for almost a year.' Eddie tried to look manly yet dejected to inspire some sympathy.

'How long are you thinking of staying for?'

Kevin looked back over his shoulder,

'Four nights and not a moment longer, that's all they gave me.' She paused and cocked her head sideways.

'Cash in advance?' she asked.

'Sure, how much?'

'Forty pounds and that includes breakfast, the best breakfast in York actually.'

That was steep, and Kevin wondered if for that amount she was included in the price but he kept his thoughts to himself. He walked back up the stairs and put his large pack down and reached out his hand.

'You got a deal. Call me Kevin.'

'Mrs. Jackson.' There was an emphasis on the Mrs. that suggested she might have read his mind in that way that all women can when it comes to male requirements. That said, with men it can't be difficult, after all. Men on the other hand find women a complete and utter mystery. It's like playing poker with a statue.

'Come in and I'll show you your room, but we'll have to be quick as I'm just nipping out.'

'I thought so,' said Kevin, adding as an afterthought, 'you look radiant.' Kevin had seen that line used in an old film with Cary Grant, it never failed to impress.

Kevin noticed that she blushed ever so slightly; she raised her eyebrows a bit and said,

'Thanks, bloody fibber. Come on,' and she flounced up the stairs to show him his room. She showed him in, passed him a set of keys and excused herself. She had to go.

His room was quite large with a big bed and a variety of different types of cupboards and sideboards. It was clean if a bit feminine. It spooked him a little as he was used to spending his time in Army barracks that had almost zero in the way of humane accoutrements. He tried the bed; it was soft with squeaky springs. He burst out laughing imagining how many times rhythmic springy noises had rung out in that room. He showered and changed into very casual, jeans, a loose woollen top and some slip-on shoes. It was freezing in York, so he had put on a shirt underneath as well. Kevin had never owned a coat and decided that he really didn't intend to ever own one either. Waste of good beer money. He picked up the keys she had given him and walked downstairs. He realised that she had already left so he slipped out the door to discover York. He walked down the road acknowledging the cold by sliding his hands into his back pockets.

York was wonderful and full of surprises. But it was early in the season and most of it was shut. He persuaded himself that it was time for a sit down and a jar, not a difficult job. He selected a pub, mainly because it had a guy dressed up as a Roman soldier outside. Kevin knew his history and any pub that needed a Roman soldier as a bouncer must be a seriously fun kind of place. He sauntered in and bought a pint, sat down and then engaged in his favourite pastime of people watching.

People were always interesting. People were weird. People were better than the telly. Of course, people from different parts of the world, let alone the country, were currently in the bar engaging in downing the amber gargle and who knew what would transpire! However, it was early days and at 8pm he didn't exactly expect much. He ordered a meal, pie and chips. It was alright but lacked the vigour that Army cooks would have spent ruining it in creative and imaginative ways.

He relaxed and surveyed the scene, especially the availability of the species that were of the feminine variety. Another pint followed another as he realised that it was actually quite hard to find a single female in a pub these days. They all seemed to be in packs or with boyfriends. He had another drink as it seemed a good idea. He was surprised to note, considering how much he had drunk, that it was only half nine by the pub clock. He considered that perhaps he'd gotten a bit soft in the NIPG in the drinking department. He ambled up to the bar to check his hypothesis. Why was it that barmen never ever see you? He had contemplated wearing an orange wig to pubs so that he'd not be considered to be the invisible man. He had a definite theory that this was down to his diminutive size. He was pondering whether or not to grab the barman by the hair or perhaps his ears to attract a little attention to his alcohol-free plight when someone shouted in his left ear.

'KEVIN! It's you isn't it?'

He braced himself expecting a fight or something, but nothing violent immediately happened; it seemed that this bloke was going to wait for an answer. Kevin pondered for a moment whether or not he should try and get the barman's attention and ignore the interruption, or to actually find out what was going on. It sort of dawned on him that he was actually in York, not the NAAFI at Ballykinler and, as he didn't actually know anyone here, it was probably worth finding out if the person bugging him actually knew him or, as most likely, it was a mere error in identification. He turned and looked at the cause of his minor irritation.

'Fuck me! It is you, Kevin. How are you man?'

Kevin looked up at a mountain of a bloke. He was a least 6' 4" or so. But that wasn't all he was 'built'. His huge muscles were painfully obvious as he was wearing a vest to show off his charms to greatest effect. He was looking into the face of an Olympian, possibly Hercules himself.

....and he knows me? thought Kevin and quickly added to his alcohol fuddled thinking that he hoped he was friendly and not some cuckolded husband whom he had unfortunately bumped into on what must have been the last day of his mortal life.

'You must remember me, you bastard! Come on think about it.' The word bastard made him think a bit more and he was tempted to stick a glass in his face just in case it was a hostile gesture. But the chap seemed genuinely pleased to see him, so he decided not to. In any case it would probably only annoy this mountain of muscle and gristle and would therefore mean a longer and more painful, lingering death.

'Ha! It's me. It's Michael, Michael Windows. Remember?'

Michael Windows? He instantly recalled Michael. Michael was a wimpish kid about four years his junior whom he used to do dreadful things to for fun. Beating him up was a normal kind of thing to do... he sort of asked for it. Kevin looked at him just to be sure.

Christ... it is him! Kevin admitted to himself and then realised that the man was now a close copy to a grizzly bear but without the body hair. Kevin wondered if he held a grudge.

'Fuck a duck, Michael; you're the last guy I expected to see today. How are things?' he managed.

'Terrific, Kevin. I'm married now with three kids and a thriving electronics business, how are you?' He paused, 'Can I get you a drink?'

'Be my guest, fucking barman seems to be ignoring me anyway.'

Kevin thought he saw Michael raise an eyebrow perhaps a millimetre or two by which time two barmen plus a barmaid he hadn't noticed before all tried to serve him in quick succession. His suspicions were confirmed: he was too small!

'What ya drinking, Kevin?'

'Lager and lime please, Michael.'

The drinks were served, and Kevin was convinced the barmaid hung about just in case the six foot odd pile of skin and muscle wanted some peanuts, crisps, his testicles scratched or something else as equally trivial. He considered his situation and thought that at least he'd have no problem getting drinks for the rest of the evening.

Michael was one of the kids in the orphanage with Kevin. Quite a few years younger though. It was considered to be quite normal to treat the younger ones as a kind of slave labour. Make them get things, fetch and carry type of stuff. Although on occasion bullying and other nastiness would raise its head. Kevin racked his brains and wondered if he'd done any of the nastier stuff with Cro-Magnon man next to him. Nothing apart from the usual sprang to mind, although even that might leave a revenge ethic deep enough for him to look carefully at his life expectancy over the next few hours. Michael, however, was sweetness and light itself. He spoke with great affection of his memories of Kevin and the others at the orphanage. How they had looked out for each other and taken care of each other. Kevin bought him a pint and they continued reminiscing. The memories flooded in like a wave.

Two hours later the bar staff were tentatively giving them both hints that the pub was closing. Kevin still had a pint to finish and Michael still had the remnants of a Vodka and Coke in front of him. Kevin gave the staff 'the look' and they decided to clean up around them. They were both quite drunk but not exactly legless. They had talked about their respective lives and discovered much. Michael recalled Kevin leaving at fifteen to join the Army. Kevin was very surprised to discover that many of the kids really missed him. Kevin's memories were different but apparently the younger ones had the distinct impression that he very much looked after them. Michael's story was one of success; he had worked his way through school and earned a sponsorship to go to university. From there he started his own business in fitting car radio cassette players. This was now a strong business with three workshops going full out.

They finished their drinks and ambled out into the chilly night air. Michael placed his arm onto Kevin's shoulder and turned him around.

'You're coming home with me to meet the family. Julie the wife has heard a lot about you. She'll be bloody pleased to meet you!' Michael beamed.

'Eh? Not in our current condition,' cautioned Kevin, surprisingly balanced. He went on, 'I think it best that you give me your address and I pop along tomorrow, when we're both a bit more sober, eh?' Kevin cocked his head and looked up at Michael.

'Good thinking, Kevin! Wife might be a bit pissed bringing a mate home this late, even if it is you. Look, tell you what, come over fairly early on Sunday, eleven or so. Spend the day with us. A good old Sunday lunch and all that. How does that sound?'

'Better get some beers in.' Kevin's smile beamed across his face.

He walked Michael to a taxi rank and almost immediately a taxi came and carried him off home. Kevin had to wait another half hour for the next one.

I'm gonna get him to put some money on a horse for me before I go, thought Kevin when a taxi finally turned up. *Be a dead cert!*

The taxi dropped him off and he negotiated the stone steps successfully. It didn't seem to matter how much alcohol he would consume in an evening, a taxi journey seemed to always make you drunk. He could probably save a fortune by just getting a taxi to and from the pub without touching a drop. He got to the top of the steps and paused for a moment and sat down. Suddenly and without warning tears welled up in his eyes, and his shoulders started to jerk uncontrollably. He was crying, sobbing like a baby, huge surges of emotion welled up in him. He didn't understand what was happening and it wasn't the first time either. He tried to stop but couldn't. The ambush at the pub in Ireland, the car incident and the dead little girl and the other events took their toll. Meeting Michael had triggered a huge well of feelings. He wept with his head in his hands, tears welling up squeezed themselves between his fingers, running down his hands. His face was soaking wet.

'What's up, love?' a voice in front of him said. He looked up; it was Mrs. Jackson back from her night out. He tried to speak but couldn't, only blubbing noises would come out. She was closer now, next to him.

'Christ, Kevin, what's the matter?' Her voice was concerned but also had an edge to it that suggested she thought he might have had a few too many.

'Nothing, just happens now and then, comes over me,' Kevin managed to stammer out.

She sat next to him; put her arm on his shoulder.

'What comes over you?' Her voice cared but betrayed that she was feeling the cold air.

'Orphanage, Army and all the shit they put us through. Just gets a bit too much now and then.'

His body shuddered with the emotion.

'Come in, I think you need a coffee.'

She helped him up and opened the door.

Kevin woke up; it took a moment for him to remember where he was. The room was dark, and he was still fully dressed minus his shoes. He sat up and looked about, he couldn't recall going to bed. His head was a little worse for the alcohol but not quite a hangover, just felt out of sorts a bit. He looked at his watch; it was 8.30 in the morning. He lay back down again and tried to get some shut eye. Whilst struggling to go to sleep bits of the previous evening started to slip into his mind, the pub, Roman soldier, Michael and of course breaking down on the steps. He remembered that she'd helped him in the door but after that it was a blank, nothing... bugger all. He hoped he'd behaved himself. Then he realised that he was too drunk to have managed anything and he was quite upset at the time, plus he was still in the B&B and not a cell. So it could not have been that bad. He pondered Mrs. Jackson for a while and wondered where her husband was. It was obvious she was married and was not backward in making sure he had understood that.

Oh well, I'll find out in good time, he thought.

He couldn't sleep and was gagging for a tea. He got up and had a wash down and after realising that his breath was able to kill nuclear resistant cockroaches a thousand miles away he cleaned his teeth. Dressed and refreshed he ambled downstairs. Mrs. Jackson was sitting in the lounge. She looked him up and down to see if he was now sober.

'You're earlier than I expected. Breakfast?' she enquired. Kevin thought better of that.

'Perhaps just a cup of tea, Mrs. J.'

She went into the kitchen and banged about for a while and returned with two cups of tea, one for each of them.

They sat in silence for a while whilst Kevin had a few sips. He could feel her examining him with her eyes.

'What was last night all about then, Kevin? You were very upset.' She looked concerned.

'I thought I told you last night. I was an orphan and the Army kind of screws you up a bit.'

'How screws you up? What do you mean?'

Kevin was uncomfortable talking to her but she continued to look at him her eyes demanding an answer.

'Erm... OK, I work with a crew that does kind of secret stuff. Not really dangerous stuff, but the other day we got ambushed and were all very nearly killed. In fact, one guy working with us was killed plus we saw a little girl die. I think I am a little bit in shock. You know like after a car crash?'

'And that makes you cry?' she looked questioningly at him and went on. 'You mentioned that you're an orphan, does that upset you as well?'

Kevin really felt on the defensive as no one had really ever questioned him about his feelings before, including himself.

'Not always but I met, right out of the blue, a kid that I was actually in the orphanage with last night in the pub. I think both things got the better of me.'

'And the booze of course couldn't have helped!' She gave him the feeling that the matter was not over but for the moment she was going to drop it.

'Sorry about last night,' Kevin started, 'I trust Mr. Jackson was not too happy about my performance. I'll be happy to apologise to him.'

She looked at him with a slight grin.

'OK, if you insist. He is over there on the sideboard in the wooden cask with the brass bands on. He's not much of a conversationalist.' She pointed to a casket about a foot high, very ornate with brass fittings. Kevin followed her gaze and the penny dropped. Mr. Jackson was brown bread.

'Oh sorry! I didn't mean…'

She cut him off by putting her fingertip onto his lips.

'No offence taken so don't worry and before you ask he died about eighteen months ago of cancer.'

'I'm sorry, please accept my con…'

Again, she placed her finger on his lips.

'Stop that. I'm over it now so don't worry.'

So Kevin didn't, and he went back to his tea.

When she touched his lips, he could smell her fingers. They smelt like flowers or if he knew what flowers actually smelt like then that would have been it. Anyway they smelt nice.

Mrs. Jackson left the room and he was free to ponder what he wanted to do today. It was Saturday and he recalled that he was going to spend Sunday with Michael so he had no idea what he would do today. After thinking about it for a while he had a vague plan and it was to see the cathedral. He would play it by ear from there.

'What are you planning to do today?' called out Mrs. Jackson from the kitchen, it was almost as if she had read his mind.

Kevin stopped on the stairs and walked down and stood in the hall looking into the kitchen at the end.

'I have no idea. Thought I'd just look about the place until I found a nice place to take you to dinner to say sorry about last night.' Kevin thought, *In for a penny in for a pound.*

Mrs. Jackson was bending over looking in the oven; she froze and looked sideways at him. It was obvious she was blushing. She paused and looked back at what she was doing regaining her composure.

'You'd be a long time finding somewhere good enough to make up for that.' She stood up laughing.

'I've another appointment tonight but why don't we meet at the *Olde Starre* pub at about one and you can stand me lunch. If you're very good, I'll give you a guided tour of the cathedral.' Kevin needed no second chance.

'Done, I'll see you at one.'

Kevin leapt upstairs and shaved, showered and shampooed until he felt he was clean enough to impress. Then, dressed in jeans and little more than a T shirt for a top he went out to sample some of the delights of York. Once outside he did, for a moment, feel that it might be a bit on the chilly side, then shrugged and wandered off down the road to find something to do until lunchtime. If he had bothered to check the weather forecast, he would have known that it was just above zero. A light mist had settled over York and the old buildings slowly appeared to him like ships in a fog. He walked about looking at plaques and architecture. He looked at the Art Gallery, something he loved doing. He enjoyed looking at pictures to try and see what the artist was saying rather than just take a scene in at face value. He discovered that if you looked long enough you would see clues. For example, an artist may have thought the patron he was painting was mean and tight with money. There would be something in the picture hinting at that, very subtle. He remembered seeing a painting of a Dutch family very austere with the women in black and white dresses. However, the artist had painted it in such a way and with subtle clues that it told the viewer that of the six children only two belonged to the father. He felt sorry for the wife who had to view this everyday wondering if her husband would ever notice the clues, perhaps he did.

Kevin got to the rendezvous fifteen minutes early and got a good table. He went up to the bar and ordered a pint and went back, sat down and waited for Mrs. Jackson to arrive. He looked about the room taking in the sights. It was an old pub and from the smells he was sure they did a lovely roast. In the corner were a couple of punk rockers, with rainbow dyed hair and a mass of chains. They were seemingly out of place in such an old-world pub. He winced inwardly as *Brotherhood of Man* started playing *Save your kisses for me* via the jukebox.

Kevin was beginning to think he had been stood up by her until quarter past the hour when Mrs. Jackson came through the door. She looked about the bar and Kevin stood up and waved. She smiled back and started to walk across to him. Kevin was mesmerised by her. She was simply dressed in a white blouse and a black skirt with her coat hung loosely around her shoulders. He was quick to note that the blouse was of the type that showed off a glimpse of bra now and then if the angle was right. He thought he'd better sit down before his appreciation started to show a bit too much. She reached him and sat next to him on the bench-like seat.

'Don't worry, Kevin – if anyone asks you can tell them I'm your mum.' She smiled at him betraying a little embarrassment in sitting with a twenty-three-year-old in a pub.

'They'd never believe it, I'm far too ugly and too old to be your son plus I know that every bloke in this bar wishes he was me right now.'

'Why?'

'Because I'm sitting with the loveliest woman in York at the moment that's why, now what do you want to drink?'

'I'll have a gin and orange please.'

'No problem,' he said as he passed her the menu and asked her to choose for him as well whilst he got the drinks.

They had the roast, him the beef and she had the chicken. It was lovely and he was amazed that that was how beef really tasted. Somehow the Army made all meat taste the same it was just the texture that distinguished one from the other types. They spoke for ages and he discovered that she was a seamstress and that she could play the piano. She had a stall in a market in York and sold little keepsakes that she made on her sewing machine at home. She also did repairs and on occasion made the odd dress. With the B&B she made enough to get by but that was about all. Her husband had not been insured so he left nothing but the endowment on the mortgage but at least that meant the house was hers free of debt. She also confided in him that she was thirty-nine and far too old to be seen out with a mere boy.

'So, you're a woman of substance Mrs Ja... What is your first name, if you don't mind?' asked Kevin.

'It's Jenny.'

'Nice name.'

'So if you're fed and watered let me show you the Minster.' She got up and he followed savouring her perfume as he walked behind leaving Johnny Mathis singing forlornly, and out of place, about Christmas on the jukebox.

The cathedral was beautiful. It smelt of history and frankincense. The place was huge and largely quiet with the exception of footfalls and a few whispered conversations. Figures of stone lay sternly about the place, witnessing the passing of the brief lives around them as they themselves waited cold, mute and unseeing for their own eternity to end. Jenny had been born and bred in York and knew the Minster like the back of her delicate and tapered hand. She explained everything to Kevin who tried to take it in but found himself looking at her in a kind of daze. Normally Kevin would relish being given such a tour but on this occasion he was being distracted. He thought it was just lust but in fact Kevin, for the first time in his young life had fallen hopelessly and deeply in love. Kevin did not know this yet as he had never been in love before. It was just a pleasant feeling and he was enjoying it, she could have been showing him around the local Marks & Spencer's as far as he was concerned. Kevin was confused by all this but happy at the same time. Eventually the tour came to a close and as all the pubs were shut during the afternoon there was not a lot to do. Mrs. J. hinted that if he behaved she did have a bottle of *Blue Nun* wine at home lingering in the fridge that they could open. Kevin, much against her wishes, insisted on a taxi and they went home.

Kevin woke up and as usual was a bit disorientated. He opened his eyes and he saw Jenny was asleep next to him. He could smell the fragrance from her hair and he raised himself onto one elbow and just looked at her. She was lovely in the tranquillity of sleep and in his eyes her beauty shone through. Her eyes opened and she looked up at him. She snuggled closer and said,

'I've not done that since Colin died, it was nice thank you.'

Kevin reached down and hugged her.

'Well, let's not wait any longer then, me just being a mere boy I need the practice.' She giggled and accepted him again… and again.

Sunday morning arrived and Kevin had remembered that he was going to see Michael that day. He didn't want to leave Jenny but she was not keen to go.

'They'll laugh at us, dear. You go don't worry. Just try to get back quickly.' Kevin could see she wasn't going to bend on this matter.

'OK, but I'll be back soon.'

He was off to see Michael in a taxi more for expedience than comfort. In addition he had no idea where Michael lived so this was the best bet. The taxi dropped him off by a semi-detached house in a council housing estate. The house was obviously in some need of repair. An old Ford Prefect was abandoned in the front garden. He walked down the broken path and knocked on the door, its paint was flaking and the pane of glass in the small window was cracked. He could see they used to have a bell on the door but all that was there now was the old bare wire green with neglect.

'Christ! Perhaps Michael is not as well off as he thought he was or is this the wrong gaff?' muttered Kevin to himself.

A large figure moved towards the door from behind the cracked misted glass. The door opened in stages as it was stiff, stuck due to moisture but eventually Michael's beaming face appeared, his body filling up the entire hallway. There was a burst of noise from kids playing and screaming from further inside the house.

'Kevin, good to see you, c'mon in.'

Kevin followed Michael down the corridor. It was filthy with toys everywhere and the carpet was hard and black down the middle but brown with a 1960's era flower pattern near the edges. He followed Michael into the kitchen. There was a baby on the floor playing on a blanket that can only be described as a danger to human health. The other two children were squabbling over a toy or something in the corner; they looked about three or four years old. Kevin did a bit of arithmetic and worked out that Michael must have been just about sixteen when he had the first one – if indeed they were his. He looked across the kitchen and there was a blonde girl, chubby with heavy black eyebrows and an earring through the side of her nose. She had a cigarette stuck to her top lip that hung there almost as if by some form of black magic. A quick recalculation and he worked out that she could not have been more than thirteen when she had the first one.

'Julie, meet my old mate Kevin, he's a soldier but he was a good mate when I was in the orphanage.' She looked across at Kevin, took out the cigarette then nodded and grunted at the same time. After that she acknowledged his presence by replacing the cigarette back into her mouth and she then totally ignored him. Kevin responded by saying,

'Hi, pleasure to meet you.' to the top of her head as she had bent down to slap the two squabbling kids. She used language that almost made Kevin blush with its obscenity; the kids ignored her and kept belting one another.

'Beer?' said Michael his smile beaming all over his face.

'Er, yeah, please yes.'

'Glass?'

Kevin looked into the sink at the black water with a scum writhing on top.

'No, out of the tin is fine.'

A gold tin of Carlsberg Special Brew was duly passed across. Kevin was completely mystified as to what was going on. He was half expecting everyone to burst out laughing and take off the costumes. But this was real; Kevin wanted to get to the bottom of this.

'So how is the business going you said the other night that it's going well and the three shops are going strong. What is it you do as I am completely non-technical but it's something to do with cars isn't it? At this Julie sniggered and glanced at Michael and said something to herself that sounded like 'kinnell'.

'Well I was so surprised to see you that I may have been a bit over the top if you know what I mean?' He looked humiliated especially with Julie smirking and swearing under her breath.

'Do it all the time myself, Michael so don't worry about it,' Kevin said dismissively but he was desperate to change the subject.

'So what's for lunch then?'

A silence descended over the kitchen as Julie looked at Michael with daggers. She mumbled something that sounded like 'uckfroth' around her cigarette and simply left the room. The baby had picked something up off the floor and was sucking it. It looked like a burnt roast potato that had been there for about six months. Kevin looked at the children and wondered if they'd be better off in an orphanage. He drained the last of his *Special Brew*.

'Thanks for the drink, mate but I think I'd best be going, Julie doesn't seem too keen.'

'Yes she's a bit out of sorts at the moment I think it's that time of the month, if you get my drift?'

From upstairs loud music started to blast from one of the rooms and Johnny Rotten screamed down *God Save The Queen.*

Kevin was aghast and needed to get out. He felt soiled, dirty and it was hard to make a soldier feel that way especially considering some of the places that Kevin had served in.

He moved towards the door, the two children were still shouting over another toy and the baby had fallen asleep, despite the music. Kevin thought that perhaps the baby has just died from poisoning but decided that it was probably best if it had.

He got to the front door with Michael behind him.

'Kevin, how about a pint tonight?' He sounded almost desperate.

'Yeah, no sweat. The pub where we met the other night at say 9 o'clock, sound OK?'

'Great, Kevin, see you there.'

Kevin was back out on the garden path and he could hear Michael swearing as he was trying to get the door to shut.

Kevin reached the road with relief and walked away down the short hill knowing that whatever happened he wasn't going to be at that pub that night.

He caught a bus to the town centre and picked up a cab back to the B&B. He let himself in with the key. Jenny met him in the hall.

'That was quick, I thought you'd be gone all day and a bit into tonight.' Kevin explained what happened and walked into the lounge. A man was sitting there obviously at home drinking what looked like a large whiskey. He was very middle-aged.

'Hi,' he called out, 'you must be Kevin,' and he put out his hand.

'Jenny has told me all about you.' Kevin doubted she did tell all but Kevin suddenly felt very jealous. Kevin limply took his hand and shook it.

'I'm Kenny, Jenny's older brother. Just popped over for a chat with my younger sis to see how she is doing.' Kevin lightened up a bit and hoped that his jealousy had not shown through. But it had as he'd find out later.

Kenny eventually left but not until he had bored Kevin to death. Kenny was a lay preacher or something with the Christ the Scientist movement and was very much into God. Kenny had tried and failed to get Kevin to convert but Kevin outfoxed him. Kevin had been brought up by god fearing Catholic monks in the orphanage where worship was a daily chore so he was in no way interested in finding God. Jenny rolled her eyes and muttered something before using the excuse to make tea to escape from the issue. He left him thinking up a new approach with his glass of whiskey whilst he sneaked into the kitchen to be with Jenny.

'Were you jealous when you saw Kenny in the lounge? Be honest now,' she looked at him over her nose expecting an answer.

'Well a bit perhaps but it's good he told me he was your brother quickly though as I was just about to disembowel him with my dog tags.' They both laughed and sneakily kissed in the kitchen.

'Will he be leaving soon?' Kevin asked with that hopeful look in his eye.

'He was just about to when you arrived and gave him the opportunity to be a bloody missionary.

"This whole deal could be just a honeytrap to make me convert to the big man in the sky.'

'Perhaps I could persuade you later on when you're tired?' with her eyes looking upwards and not Kevin noted, in humility.

Kevin decided it was time for Kenny to go as the afternoon was ticking away. He bundled Kenny firmly but politely out the door and needed no hints to know that Jenny was upstairs. They went out in the early evening as Kevin had insisted that he take her out to dinner, on his last night, somewhere special. She folded and allowed him to indulge and she suggested a nice place. Jenny had a phone so he was able to book a table. That was a first and he wasn't quite sure what to do. But he managed it alright but the disembodied voice at the other end stated that a tie and jacket were required. The only tie and jacket that Kevin had was his No. 2 dress and that was currently in Ballykelly going mouldy. He informed Jenny and she glanced at him.

'You're about the same size as Colin, I'll get some clothes out for you.' She was nonplussed by it all. Kevin didn't mind either he was entirely comfortable wearing a dead man's clothes whilst at the same time screwing his widow to the bed. She duly appeared with a jacket that fitted OK and a tie. It went quite well with his own clothes, so he felt okay. Two hours later and with Jenny looking gorgeous they sauntered out to the taxi for the short ride to the *D'Manor Restaurant*.

Kevin was an expert in restaurants but the problem was they tended to be Indian ones where culture and good manners were not the norm. He was used to a good ruby after a skin full in the local hostelry. *D'Manor* was a posh French affair in a beautiful historic building. They were ushered in and the waiter initially took them to a table that looked like an afterthought. It gave Kevin the impression that it was bolted to the wall and was flipped up when they got busy. He felt that it was not the kind of table he thought a soldier with his lady should be sitting at. He gestured to the waiter that he wanted a word; Kevin discreetly slipped a note into his top jacket pocket and suggested that he'd appreciate another table. Another table was duly found and Kevin waited whilst his lady was seated before sitting down himself. The waiter brought menus and a wine list and asked if they wanted a drink. He automatically ordered a pint of lager and she had a gin and orange. After about ten minutes or so they were ready to order but no waiter was in evidence. Kevin and Jenny's glasses were both empty. Kevin tried to attract attention discreetly but was not successful. He was starting to get a bit embarrassed and a little annoyed. Jenny said it didn't matter but Kevin was definitely getting more than a bit annoyed. A waiter was passing when Kevin hissed a quiet,

'Oi! We're ready to order.'

The waiter stopped and looking a bit miffed took their order, steak for him and lamb cutlets for her and they both ordered a prawn cocktail as a starter. This included another round of drinks and a bottle of the house red. Kevin waited another twenty minutes and nothing appeared. So again, he attracted a waiter's attention and reminded them that they owed him a round of drinks. The food turned up ten minutes later with the lager and the gin but no wine. The food order was wrong as they had given Jenny the sea bass and his steak was burnt to a crisp. He sent it all back dismissing Jenny's comments that it was okay and suggesting that it was normal to provide the main course before the starters anyway. Kevin finished his lager and ordered another. The starters arrived and he sent them back as they had provided pate on toast and he ordered prawn cocktail. The manager came over and explained that they had run out of prawns. Kevin explained that this was not mentioned at the time and perhaps they should train their staff considering the amount they charged. Kevin then went over the list of problems they had suffered since arriving. The manager defensively suggested that the problems were because they were full tonight and they were lucky to actually get in. Kevin exploded.

'Lucky to get in? Fucking lucky to get in? I've had better service at the worst shittiest cookhouse in the Army than you give here. Is it something to do with being French?'

'Oh, you're a squaddie, I should have known. I don't know why you guys bo…' That was as far as he got as Kevin had blatted him in the head with the flower vase from the table. He went down heavily onto the floor and another two waiters waded in to constrain Kevin. Almost immediately they were spread out unconscious, one across the table they were sitting at and the other was spread eagled and face down in the main course on the next table. He looked apologetically over at Jenny.

'Sorry! Think we had better get our coats, eh?'

He held her hand and they walked towards the door. The police burst through the door and the doorman pointed at Kevin.

'That's the bastard!' The policemen looked at Kevin and rushed towards him. Kevin gently pushed Jenny away. Kevin was eventually overpowered but it took five policemen to do it. Two of whom had to go to hospital afterwards for minor wounds.

It was the next morning, Monday when Kevin woke up in the cell. The custody sergeant unusually brought him along to the station canteen for breakfast. The police, once the whole story had been explained placed most of the blame onto the restaurant manager but that was natural justice and the state wanted its own version. They had to charge him and, as he was due to leave to go back to his duty station that day, he was going to go before the magistrate that morning.

He was taken to the Magistrate's Court and was first on. Jenny was sitting in the public area and looked very worried. The situation was explained by the police, plus the fact that he was on R&R from a combat tour of N. Ireland and that stress may have played a part in his behaviour. Kevin pleaded guilty but the three magistrates leniently stated he had no case to answer and largely blamed the restaurant manager for intimidating a soldier who was on R&R. The clerk to the court agreed with their findings and the brief that represented the Crown Prosecution Service seemed not to want to challenge those findings. Kevin expressed his gratitude to the court officials and thanked the policemen for their help and for their kind words. He was very conscious of the fact that he injured two of them and that they never actually mentioned that in court. If they had done so he might have gone to prison for a short spell and that would have meant the end of his Army career as well. He did note that a couple of the coppers had Army campaign medal ribbons and that probably helped a lot. He shook them all warmly by the hand, left the court, grabbed a taxi and they went home to Jenny's. They had a cup of tea and they spent the rest of the morning and early afternoon in bed. He packed his bags gave her a long kiss and jumped into a taxi for the train station. He couldn't wait to come back again and he wasn't at the end of her street yet. She waited until the taxi turned at the end of the road and then sadly went back indoors back to her normal life again.

The letter arrived two days after he got back. The CSM threw the letter to him across the room.

'I took the liberty of smelling the envelope, laddie. That's a woman of class ya lucky bastard.' The warrant officer 1st class smiled at Kevin conspiratorially.

Kevin laughed, picked up and opened the letter, it was from Jenny but he knew that already as he never normally got letters from anyone. He read it quickly, it was a short letter. His mates watched as his face fell. Crestfallen he stood there in shock as the contents hit home.

'Fuck, Kevin, what's happened?' burst out Les. Kevin said nothing but thought to himself.

'Usual shit, it'll never work, age difference, blah bloody blah.' He paused, and the old Kevin resurfaced hiding the pain. He ripped up the letter and threw it on the floor. 'She says my cock's too big and it has to end.' He thrust his hips forward in a familiar gesture.

They all laughed, it was more out of sympathy but it cleared the air. That night Kevin went quietly to the NAAFI and pulled over a chair and sat facing the wall all night except when getting a drink and he did that a lot. His friends were with him more to ensure nobody bothered him or took the piss. That would be bad… very bad!

West Germany, Münster - April 1979. Jumbulance?

Eddie and the tracked AFV 436[38] that he and his Signals Detachment were in had broken down whilst on the way back to camp after an exercise. The REME[39] recovery, after an hour or so of swearing and banging about, had fixed them up enough to at least move along under tow and they were now en route in a fusion of noise, exhaust fumes and flashing amber lights. Eddie, now a corporal, and a Company Signals Detachment Commander spotted a white coach broken down at the side of the road. Getting closer he read the word 'Jumbulance' on the back and sides. The fact that it had UK number plates also attracted his attention. They were just passing it when he spotted two of what appeared to be nurses in front of the vehicle, complete with uniforms, black tights and instant erotic thoughts. On the Intercom, he told Czech the driver to pull over in front and signalled to the REME guys to tow them in front of the bus. They had also spotted the skirts and were quick to follow the intent. They all dismounted and in a show of bravado, Eddie asked the girls what the issue was. It appeared that they were basically a big charity ambulance taking some terminally ill kids and their parents for a jaunt round Europe for two weeks and they had broken down. The REME guys had already diagnosed the issue and said they could fix it but it would take a day or two due to getting the spares. The lady doctor who was in charge agreed but was concerned as to where they would stay. She was also concerned that a bunch of guys in a broken-down vehicle were making claims contrary to her understanding of their current predicament. The doctor was informed that accommodation had already been taken care of as their predicament had been radioed ahead. The CO had been informed and a complete block was already at their disposal as the lads had volunteered to kip down elsewhere for as long as required.

The coach was towed back to camp and the kids were ferried to the accommodation. The MO[40] and his team helped out as did the other 650 guys in the regiment. The soldiers made it plain that if it had been required they'd have carried the bus physically to wherever it had to go. Sentries were posted

---

[38] An AFV 436 is an AF 432 armoured personnel carrier converted into a Radio Command Post.
[39] The Royal Electrical and Mechanical Engineers: better known as 'Rough Engineering Made Easy'.
[40] Medical Officer.

around the block to ensure privacy and, as it was getting late, meals and goodies were delivered from the cookhouse so they could have a decent meal before going to bed. The next day the regiment took over and had decided, with the doctor's blessing, that the kids deserved some special fun. Military training was cancelled and children, parents and nurses alike were spirited away to all manner of activities like shooting and driving a variety of armoured vehicles. Word had spread and after a few hours the Tankies in the next camp were allowing eight-year-old's to drive 56-ton Chieftain tanks and six wheeled amphibious Stalwart lorries about the place. The Army Air Corp were flying helicopters about with children in and it was rumoured that the RAF at Gutersloh were sneaking them to the airfield to fly them about in their training Harrier that had two seats; this had miraculously appeared from RAF Wittering somehow overnight.

More than once a Tornado high-speed jet had flown over looking remarkably like someone was being given a lift. That night the kids were royally entertained by an impromptu show that at some point involved each of their young guests being the centre of attention. Sweets and goodies flowed like water. The next day was similar and it was rumoured that the nurses had suggested that the repair should take a bit longer just to make sure it was a good fix. All in all, the kids were there for a full three days. Every night the children would require washing and cleaning to remove the cam cream, mud, gun oil, dirt, aviation fumes and diesel but no matter how much they were washed the memories were indelible. The regiment's band of wives were all mobilised to help look after the children for the night to give the parents a break and an opportunity for a few nights off in Münster.

On the final morning after a fun filled and lavish breakfast the coach was declared fit and was parked next to the block to accept its charges. The nurses wished fond farewells to the squaddies some who, no doubt, had a few rides of their own. In fine British Army tradition ropes were attached to the coach and the vehicle was pulled to the gate by the muscle of the 'Poor Bloody Infantryman'. Soldiers were waving like grieving grandparents seeing young children leaving home for the first time; many had tears dripping down their faces. These were hard men living and working in a brutal regime, trained killers who were expected to take life without a moment's thought if asked by their country to do so. Such men, due to the burden of the potential of what they may have to do and what they may have to face have huge reservoirs of compassion and have a magnificent capacity to link that with fun. Such men feel no shame in showing their emotions if only to their fellow comrades in arms where trust and respect is paramount.

The children probably did not forget their experiences there for the rest of their tragically short lives. Eddie, for the rest of his life, always looked back on this incident with a huge sense of pride, knowing that if the bus had broken down outside any other establishment, factory, business or whatever, even the headquarters of the AA itself, the kids would probably have been ignored and left to fend for themselves. Such is the magnanimity and generosity of the military psyche.

Chapter 11

Voyeurs & Dogging

April 1977

The insertion was a classic piece of infantry work. Camouflaged up wearing ghillie suits they moved in like ghosts albeit at a God-awful hour in the morning. Two patrols mutually supporting each other. They dug their hides and disappeared into nature. However, this one was different. They were watching the edge of a public car park in a park on the edge of Londonderry with a narrow road that was little more than an alley that cars would negotiate until they got to the small car park at the end. This was where a lot of action of the 'getting your rocks off' variety happened, and the Army Intelligence guys had gotten a tip off that someone very special was going there regularly and duly 'getting their rocks off'. So, it might be possible to get a few piccies of that and it might turn out to be of use. They were going to become sexual voyeurs and they all thought it was great fun!

The routine was that during the day they stayed in the hides completely closed down so that no one would see them. They required minimal observation for the purposes of self-protection with as much sleep as humanly possible. Cold food only so no smells. At night, they'd sneak into the trees and bushes around the car park and observe the vehicles, so they could see what was going on. If a player was up to something, then a few happy snaps would be taken. Les was not a happy man as he'd gotten a case of Delhi belly and couldn't wait until nightfall to open his bowels. When in the hide if you got caught short you'd have to get a mucker to hold a plastic bag for you to go in. Of course, if you were in a hide for a long time it was inevitable, but on this job they could crap in the bushes at night as they were patrolling, but not during the day – except Les.

''old the fucking bag against me arse; I don't want any blow back going into me strides.' Les' whisper was urgent as this was a man in dire need.

'I'm holding the fucking bag as close as I can so just get on with it for fuck's sake.'

Kevin was kneeling behind the squatting Les holding a plastic bag to catch his outpourings, his head turned away slightly. Not a pleasant task. Kevin spoke up.

'Les, what was that Indian restaurant you went to with the bird again? You're shitting through the eye of a needle and the stink is giving my nose blisters.' He gestured to Steve to hold his nose for him.

'Got a mind to take this bag and suffocate the fucking owner with it when we get back,' Kevin said quietly.

'You're bloody welcome to it, mate, want to keep it in your large pack until we get back?' Les suggested.

'No, you can keep it. It is yours, after all.'

A stream of brown liquid splashed unceremoniously into the bag splashing Kev's fingers. After about five squirts Les declared he was done and Kevin sealed the bag by the simple expedient of knotting the top a few times after expelling the air from it. Of course, the odour was strong and they all grumbled.

'Breathe deep, boys, it will go sooner that way,' suggested Les with a triumphant smile. Steve spoke up,

'Christ in a hat, Leather, that's bad. Listen, no more curries before operations. That's a fucking order and I'll stick anyone's head in their own crap bag if that order is ignored. Got it?' They all mumbled in agreement.

Eventually the smell passed which was just as well as Steve thought it might give the game away if anyone had come too close. Dog shit doesn't have quite the same odour as a squaddie's outpouring after too much beer and a curry. At that point, Les looked uncomfortable and glanced at Kevin who, with a gesture of defeat, got out another plastic bag.

'Please do remind me not to lick my fingers until after I have had a fucking good shower and have been rubbed down with emery cloth, OK?' pleaded Kevin but Les ignored him, he had other things on his mind.

At 11pm, which coincided with the pubs closing times, they checked their weapons and made sure their cameras were all working. Eddie did a radio check. All was OK, so they sneaked out of the hide to become voyeurs covered by the silky blackness of the night, assisted of course by cam cream, DPM and camouflage suits. The smart piece about it all was that they were using infrared lights and associated film. This meant that the punters who were being photographed had no idea. In fact, someone could be riding the big high one in the dark and a member of the patrol would be standing almost next to them using an infrared search light, so to anybody who had infrared glasses or lenses that could convert IR it looked like they were doing their most intimate things in broad daylight and out in the open.

They were all amazed that most of the action in the car park was male on male and totally illegal as homosexuality was certainly not very well accepted in Northern Ireland. This gave the Intelligence Services quite an edge if they caught a player humping with a member of the same sex. It was a distinct opportunity to blackmail them with exposure that could go as far as being stuffed in a gaol for several months. However, the threat of exposure that they were 'queer' to the remaining members of their terrorist acolytes was more than enough to blackmail them. Eddie was unmoved by homosexuality and accepted it as a fact of life.

It was a Saturday and the patrol had been in situ for three nights already, but they had not yet seen the main subject of interest that the Intelligence guys had suggested would be active. Tonight, was the most likely time he'd be showing up. They decided to just keep an eye out for this well-known terrorist commander who'd recently been given high rank in the organisation that he was a part of. Unfortunately, although they knew he was a murdering toerag, there was no evidence to arrest him, let alone convict. Eddie and Kevin had secreted themselves alongside the access road and were radioing in the registration numbers of the vehicles to get the owner's details as they arrived. Les and Steve were waiting on the edge of the car park itself. Kevin would indicate the right car had arrived by pointing an IR searchlight into the sky. Several cars arrived and each slowly drove up the lane and once near the car park would turn off their lights and quietly reverse their car into a parking spot. The gravel crunched as the cars moved about slowly as the drivers occasionally moved their vehicle to try and get a better slot in the car park.

After two hours, the car park was almost full and occupants were flashing headlights and signalling and occasionally a male couple would disappear into the woods, much to the obvious disgust of Steve. Whilst Steve was mumbling curses of damnation onto all people who 'pushed shit uphill without a wheelbarrow' as he so graciously put it, Les nudged him in the ribs and gestured towards the road where a beam of invisible IR light was now pointing upwards into the sky. The VIP they were expecting had arrived. Almost immediately the car slowly came into view and the driver switched off his headlights. Les shone his IR searchlight right into the vehicle which was only about twenty yards away. There in the driver's seat was said scumbag and sitting next to him was what can only be described as a young teenage boy of between sixteen and eighteen years old. Steve was already clicking away with the camera with a long lens with an IR conversion kit. Unaware of all this attention the driver did the usual and drove his car to the most secluded spot he could find and backed it in. The occupants had parked their car quite close to another one but the people in that car were unable to object as one had his eyes closed and the other's mouth was full and was looking down. However, the other side of the car was parked next to the bushes.

'He likes his meat young, doesn't he?' commented Les in a whisper to Steve.

'Man's a pervert, should be taken out and shot,' retorted Steve.

Steve, covered by Les and his M16, took almost one hundred and fifty photos of the bad guy, who surprisingly, appeared to be the less dominant member of the pair and seemed to enjoy taking what would be seen to be the more feminine role in a series of sexual acrobatic acts that can be accommodated in the front and back of a stationary vehicle. Les was amazed at the younger man's energy and the older man's flexibility.

Eventually the show came to a close and both adjusted themselves back to a semblance of normality and as slowly as they entered, the vehicle negotiated its way through the other vehicles that were having their suspension tested and, once they were on the link road, he turned on his headlights and was gone. What Eddie and the others did not know was that the vehicle was going to be stopped and the driver and fellow occupant put through a normal VCP check just to document officially the fact that both were together in the same vehicle at the same time close to the park concerned. It would probably help with the blackmail later but the Secret Services may prefer the curiously apt phrase 'turned'.

Eddie and Kevin slowly appeared out of the darkness invisible to all but Steve and Les. They moved as a team into the back of the small copse and huddled in all round defence for a discussion.

'OK, we got all we need on the dirty bastard, we go back to the hide tidy up and leave in the early morning. Eddie, when we get back to the hide check with Sunray that we have permission to bug out.'

Eddie nodded in the darkness and Steve saw his teeth bobbing up and down in the darkness. Slowly they patrolled back to the hide. When close they did the usual snap ambush and, once clear, they did a quick recce of the hide just to make sure nobody had left any presents from personalities who might be keen to screw them in a different way than to what they had been recently witness to. The bosses agreed that the mission was accomplished and that they should come in. This would be accomplished by the simple expedient of picking them up from the road that bordered the park at 4am, back to camp and sleep.

Later on Les woke up and felt they would all benefit from listening to a bit of music. Suddenly Freddie Mercury started screaming from the Queen album and *A Night at the Opera* reverberated around the room at full volume. Initially nobody moved but after a while they all slowly surfaced and started to get on with things. The music was barely noticed.

West Germany, Münster – March 1980. Hair of the Dog!

The green and black matt painted Chieftain tank from 4 RTR[41], an immense machine weighing 56 tons, began to slow down as the brazen red and white automatic railway barriers lowered themselves in a small suburb on the south side of Munster, a town in the area of Westphalia in West Germany. The tinny bell was going ten to the dozen whilst the traffic lights were flashing alternately on and off like some demonic set of red winking eyes. The great machine's engine coughed and spluttered as it was used to brake the mass of steel hammering along Mondstraße. The tracks screeched and complained but eventually the steel behemoth came first to a halt and then rocked slowly backwards and forwards on its suspension.

A horse with a lady rider was at the barrier and the tank had spooked it so it started to jump about a bit and almost dislodged the rider in charge of it. A long suffering local pensioner who was out walking his dog was upset by this and decided to give the driver of the tank a piece of his mind for driving so recklessly. He tied off his dog and standing square in front of the tank started to shout his point of view at the driver. The tank's turret was facing backwards so the driver was barely visible under the turret's back overhang. As the train trundled by the German pensioner was just getting into the swing of it and in his guttural national language started to spout a new chapter describing how bad it was living with main battle tanks running past your house every day.

The driver, wearing helmet and goggles, didn't understand a word of German but appeared to be listening patiently to the old man. The train eventually passed by and amongst the usual din of bells and whirring the barriers once again rose to resemble four gaily painted flag poles, albeit ones that wobbled a bit. The German had not noticed that the barrier had now gone up so engrossed was he in the flow of Germanic abuse towards the poor driver who, after all, was only doing his job.

The German paused when he noticed the driver's head was bobbing up and down and appeared to be gesturing upwards. The tall pensioner with the neat grey hair then realised that the train had passed, and that traffic was now flowing over the crossing but on the other side. The German, however, glanced up towards the area where the driver's head clad in a green helmet seemed to

---

[41] 4th Royal Tank Regiment based in Münster.

be gesturing. Hanging high up on the now vertical quivering barrier was his poor dog that he had tied up earlier before his tirade, swinging forlornly and slowly getting strangled to death. The tank driver moved his tank slowly forward and the commander climbed out of his cupola and rescued the German's canine companion and reverently handed the dog down to him. He thankfully grabbed his pet and whispered a barely heard and rather ungracious, 'Danke.'

Then the 4 RTR Tank Commander remounted the tank. Inside the tank the commander spoke over the intercom.

'What was all that about, Tinker?' he said, aiming his question at the driver.

'Eh, buggered if I know but wasn't that Captain Smithers' horny wife on the horse?' came the reply.

'Yeah, nice arse and it's rumoured she'll ride anything after enough gin and tonics, but she never could ride a bloody horse. She's a pissing menace.'

At that the engine revved up and in a whirl of noise and screeching tracks the tank lurched off to terrorise the rest of the town on its way to Waterloo Barracks.

The old German stood immobile and embarrassed, watching as the orange flashing warning light slowly and noisily disappeared around the bend, and he quietly said to himself,

'Scheiße, wo wir gingen falsch in den Krieg?'* and shuffled off to the nearest Bierstube to soften the pain.

* 'Shit, where did we go wrong in the war?'

Chapter 12

Field Fury

May 1977

'It's going to be a long tab in as the geography about there is quite flat, something like five clicks I'd say. In addition, the Met looks like shit and it's gonna piss down for a few days.' That's how the captain finished the briefing on their latest caper that they were about to embark upon. In a nutshell, the Army had been given intelligence that a farm was being used either as a large arms cache or as a transit point for weapons and potentially explosives as well. It was down to the NIPG to find out.

'Another fucking long walk!' complained Les as they walked out of the briefing room. 'Surely they could let us have one small insignificant chopper for a few hours?'

'It's your bloody fault, Les, you're so bleeding noisy that they can't afford to have you and a fucking helicopter in the same place at the same time,' quipped Kevin.

'And fuck you too,' stated Les. He continued with a smirk, 'Although, as we're not going in until tomorrow I think I'll go an' see Miriam tonight and get me a good shag before we go in. I'll just go get a shower and look my loveliest and then leave you guys to an evening of personal masturbatory exuberance – have fun!'

Les had recently met a girl at a bar in Newcastle and it was very obvious that he was head over heels in love. If not that then it was certainly lust. The rest of the guys went on to Newcastle for a few beers in the local pubs. They were all armed with a 9mm Browning discreetly hidden away. They all still felt a bit like James Bond but without the tuxedo. They were only really allowed to have two pints but as Steve was driving they decided that a few more would be OK as Steve was staying sober.

That evening the local girls took absolutely no interest in them so eventually they went back to camp dejected and finished the night off in the NAAFI bar. Les had arrived back just in the nick of time as all had to be in camp by midnight. In the back of all their minds was the thought that on the morrow they'd be back in action and at risk again.

The morning came and they readied their kit, got their stores, did a number of rehearsals, and studied the ground so they'd know it blindfolded at night wearing a diver's helmet and boots. After a short sleep in the late afternoon they loaded up the vans and off they went to Newry to watch a farmhouse again. It was just getting dark when the vans arrived and then discreetly dropped the patrols off around the area. Steve's team on this occasion was mutually supporting one of the Black Watch team's that had been given the job of close observation. So, for this task they were bodyguards at a distance of about one hundred yards. They found the spot that they had seen using the aerial photos and confirmed via radio that this was going to be the spot they'd use. After the customary snap ambush and recce they moved in and used the night to blend their hide into the countryside. By the morning you'd literally have to be standing on top of them before you saw anything. Their job was to make sure that nobody sneaked up on the close observation crew and rumbled them or worse attacked them. Although Steve and the crew could not see them they knew exactly where they were. The scene around the countryside was perfectly calm and it was hard to believe that four patrols were dug in and watching everything around them very carefully indeed.

The Intelligence Officer was right about the weather, it tipped down with rain relentlessly for three days and nights. Everything in the hole was sopping wet. But monitoring the situation was critical and they kept at it. At least they could have hot food in their hides as they were so far from the target, but the Black Watch guys would be having cold food and no brews, just water. Les was as happy as a pig in shit as he loved this sort of thing.

'Fucking great this,' he stated to no one in particular.

'Leather, you're a nutter and no mistake,' said Kevin in disgust looking decidedly dejected and curious as to why Les was not pissed off missing his regular nightly shag. From the lack of movement at the house it must have been the case that they had picked a time when the occupants must have gone away for their annual two-week holiday to the Costas or wherever they went for a dose of sun.

On the third day the Black Watch guys reported over the radio that they had observed someone near the house. It was 6am when the tractor started and drove into the field behind the Black Watch crew, the far corner of which Steve and crew were in. It looked like he was spreading something about and it probably wasn't very nice as they could smell it from two hundred yards away. The farmer kept coming and going like this for the next two days doing his job. It seemed that no baddies were ever gonna come near the place.

On the fourth day the farmer started as usual doing whatever farmers did on a tractor. But on this occasion the tractor stopped immediately alongside the Black Watch hide and the farmer got off the tractor and slowly walked along the edge of the field checking the fence. Suddenly he pulled out a pistol and started shooting into the Black Watch hide. After firing four rounds or so he rushed back to the tractor and tried to drive away. Eddie and Kevin who were on stag were amazed that there was apparently no reaction from the Black Watch patrol. Kevin woke up Les and pointing towards the farmer said simply,

'Take that fucker out! He just blew away a few of the Black Watch guys.' Les was up in a second with his L98 ready to go. Just as he was sizing up his shot Steve said quietly,

'Try not to kill him I'd be keen to know how he knew they were there.'

Les adjusted his aim and fired one shot and the farmer flew off the tractor as the high velocity 7.62mm round hit him just above the right bum cheek half removing it and most of his right kidney along with it. The tractor continued on a bit and was eventually stopped by a tree. The farmer was lying lifeless where he had been shot off the tractor. Steve looked despairingly at Les.

'You've killed him, you twit, Christ! All that fucking paperwork and questioning – not to mention Brixton,' whinged Steve.

'No I haven't, I shot him in the right arse cheek, he is probably concussed but he won't be going anywhere fast. Plus, he'll have a hard job shitting properly on a toilet for the rest of his life.'

By now three of the Black Watch patrol were out of their hide and pulling out one of their people who was obviously injured. Eddie spoke to them over the radio and learnt that one of them had been shot in the face by the farmer.

Steve told Eddie to tell them to look after their guy and Eddie was to order a CASEVAC by helicopter immediately. In return HQNI told Eddie to tell the other two patrols to stay hidden in case it was a 'come-on' and more baddies were about. Steve decided that they'd use the farmhouse as base until the box vans and helicopter arrived.

The farmer, now half-conscious, was dragged unceremoniously into the farmhouse, where his wife was almost catatonic with rage that soldiers should shoot her husband for ploughing a field. She was sat in a chair and plasticuffed to it to keep her out of mischief. Almost immediately afterwards the Black Watch carried in their casualty and laid him onto the sofa in the living room. He had been shot in the cheek with the bullet coming out below the jaw bone under his chin. It was a serious wound but it did not break the jaw bone, but he had lost a few teeth. Luckily the round had missed all the important bits.

'Les give that farmer some first aid but get Kevin to ask him some serious questions as to what happened.'

Les started to patch him up. Kevin started to question the almost unconscious farmer who probably thought he was already dead and was in Hell with Beelzebub himself asking the questions. Eddie pulled out a few pots and pans and started to get some scoff going for all and a good brew.

From what they could ascertain from the half dead farmer he saw a group of dodgy looking characters watching him from the wood line and the more he saw them the more he thought they were going to try and kill him. He habitually carried his father's old Second World War revolver whilst working on the farm for purely self-defence purposes. He had never taken any sides in the Republican/Nationalist controversy and largely had ignored it all and some locals didn't like that and found it suspicious. In the past he had received death threats so carrying the gun seemed a sensible thing to do. It appeared that he saw a face looking out of the wood line and as he got closer to the wood line he pretended to check the fence and shot at the face in self-defence and then tried to get to the farmhouse to call the police by which time Les had shot him.

Eddie nudged Steve and gestured towards the fireplace in the living room. On the mantelpiece was his father's full set of medals from the Second World War. Campaign stars for North Africa, Italy and Germany adorned the shelf along with the medals the farmer they had just shot had earned in his day. Medals for campaign service, the Reserve Medal, plus a few others he didn't recognise. They'd shot a WW2 army veteran's son who himself had also served in Korea and Aden.

'Fucking Black Watch were lucky he hadn't fired a gun in a while, we got a regular Audie bleeding Murphy here,' observed Eddie with respect.

The helicopter arrived first and the farmer and the Black Watch guy that had been shot were strapped in for the short flight to hospital. He was unconscious, but they were convinced he'd make it. By the time the local police and the Army arrived Steve's team had discovered that these people were apparently in no way associated with any terrorist group but were just trying to scratch a living out of a very small farm. Steve was of the opinion that the local Intelligence cell had some serious questions to answer.

They left whilst the wife was being questioned by the police and got back into the box vans and departed. After about twenty minutes they arrived back in Newry and they were all immediately debriefed. It appeared that two of the Black Watch team on stag at the time of the shooting had been asleep. That was an unforgiveable offence and if found guilty twenty-eight days in pokey was the penalty. Of course, getting killed or injured along with your entire team was the other option as they had discovered. All that said, these kinds of operations were absolutely exhausting and falling asleep was a constant threat. If asked to answer honestly almost all soldiers will admit that at some time or another they had fallen asleep on stag – they just hadn't been caught.

It appeared that the Intelligence cell had gotten the wrong address and kicked into place an entire operation against an innocent ex-war veteran with an exemplary military record. He had been mentioned in despatches twice for gallantry in the field.

The operation was a complete washout so they climbed onto the box vans and made their way from Newry to Ballykinler to lick their wounds and to get ready for the next operation. However, for such a breakdown of military discipline retribution had to take its course so the Brick Commander of the team that were shot at by the farmer was busted to lance corporal and the guy that fell asleep with the victim received the customary twenty-eight days in gaol. The NIPG boss felt that although the guy who got shot had received a serious lesson in why you should not sleep on stag by the permanent removal of most of the teeth on the left side of his head with serious scarring on both sides of his face where the bullet had entered and left his head, he should still suffer something in the form of punishment. He was sentenced to seven days in gaol 'after his wounds be healed'.

It was at the same time that the OC of the NIPG was dealing with the miscreants that fell asleep, that the charges from the Regimental Provost Sergeant against 'The Pope' and team regarding getting into camp late and being drunk came to light. They were duly commanded to appear to answer for their crimes in front of the OC immediately after the Black Watch contingent.

They had no idea that charges had been brought in the first place so when WO1 Bruce ordered them to appear at the NIPG office as defaulters they were very surprised. Once in the office block and in the corridor outside the OC's office they were, as per custom, ordered to remove their belts and headdress and were marched by the warrant officer into the OC's office to answer for their alleged crimes.

The OC was brief and to the point.

'You have all been charged under section 69 of the Army Act 1955 of behaviour prejudice to military discipline and good order in that on the 14th February 1977 at Abercorn Barracks Guardroom you did book in late at 00:05 hours and that you were inebriated. Do you understand the charges?' The OC looked up at them and then directly at Steve expecting a reply.

'Yes, sir! We understand the charges, but we protest in that we were not made aware at the time of the offence that we were actually being charged with any misdemeanours, sir,' responded Steve very matter of fact. The other three got very worried. In the military you very rarely, if ever, protested at a charge. You just took it on the nose and got on with whatever punishment they had in store for you. Defending yourself was unheard of as it was futile. However, most squaddies were not 'The Pope' and that was what they were really worried about at that exact moment. Steve continued,

'Before we plead, sir we'd like to hear the evidence of the charges against us please.'

'Your protest is noted, Corporal and as to the evidence then certainly, by all means,' agreed the OC and the Provost Sergeant was wheeled in to state what had happened. He spoke for five minutes but the OC had to stop him after every second sentence and ask WO1 Bruce to clarify what he had said. But basically, the Provo had accused them of coming in late and being drunk. The OC enquired as to whether or not they would like to challenge the evidence. All of them shook their heads except Steve who articulated that he did wish to challenge the evidence.

'Please proceed,' said the OC looking a tad concerned at the warrant officer. Steve leaned slightly forward and looked directly at the Provo Sergeant.

'Provo Sergeant you state we were late. What time source were you using?'

The Provo answered, via WO1 Bruce, that he used the Guardroom clock.

'When was it last calibrated to an accurate time source such as the talking clock, Provo Sergeant and if it was can you produce the log book or a reputable record of it being so checked please?'

The Provo Sergeant was flustered and stated that the Guardroom clock was always accurate and that was just a known thing. Steve addressed the OC directly.

'Sir, we are being charged with being late and as far as I can determine there is neither mechanism nor a record of whether or not the clock was accurate at the time. It may have been five or ten minutes' fast, sir.'

The Provo Sergeant butted in stating that they could check it now and prove it was accurate. Steve was light years ahead of him.

'Sir. The question is, was it accurate at the time of the offence and not now. By the Lord Chancellor's rules of Evidence, it is for the Provost Sergeant to prove that his Guardroom clock was accurate at that time and not for us to prove that our watches were right. As far as we can recall we came into camp about five minutes early and we were not late. So, if the Provo Sergeant can produce any evidence that the clock is checked regularly and that it is noted somewhere then fair enough. If not, then he must accept the fact that my watch may have been more accurate than his clock.'

The OC looked at the Provost Sergeant.

'Well do you check your clock and do you have evidence of that?'

The Provost explained in his own guttural way that the answer was a negative. The OC picked up his red pen and struck a line across the charge sheet.

'OK, well we'll drop that one. Corporal how about the inebriation charges, although I have a feeling that you may have an explanation here as well.' The OC looked expectantly at the young corporal.

'Yes, sir, if we could hear the evidence or see any evidence of drunkenness then we can answer to the charges.'

The OC said nothing but moved his head so that he was looking at the Provo Sergeant and in truth, was feeling a little sorry for him.

'Well, Provo, please give your evidence.'

Again, the Provo Sergeant tried to explain that when they arrived at the Guardroom they were drunk and that he had charged them as appropriate. However, the OC was not fully aware of these facts until Warrant Office Bruce translated it for him. He moved his head again until he was looking directly at the corporal in a heightened sense of expectancy as to what the answer would be. He was going to enjoy this!

'Well, Corporal, your response?'

'Well, sir! I'd just like to ask the Provost Sergeant on what pretext he places his assumption that we were drunk. Is he medically qualified? Has he done any professional training in when people are drunk or not. He did not breathalyse us nor did he take blood and have it checked. As far as we are concerned the only evidence he has is hearsay. In other words, it's his word against ours, sir. You cannot find a person guilty without concrete evidence that an offence has been committed. I personally remained completely sober as I was driving back that night as the nominated driver, so I can one hundred per cent state that I was sober, so if he made that mistake with me then he probably made the same mistaken assumption with the others. This seems to me, sir, to be a case of discrimination similar to the one that happened when Kermit, sorry Private McGee, got beaten up, sir. Unless evidence to support these empty accusations can be brought forward, I put forward that we have no case to answer and hence whether we enter a plea of Guilty or Not Guilty is an irrelevance.'

The OC was impressed and could not argue against the points raised.

'Well, Provo Sergeant, do you have any such qualifications or any such evidence to produce?'

The Provo Sergeant answered in the negative and the OC asked him to leave the room but to wait outside.

After he had left the OC stood up and addressed them.

'I am convinced you were probably a few minutes late and I suspect, with the exception of you, Corporal, you were all probably over the top in the alcohol department. However, as you are aware I am a stickler for fairness and your Brick Commander did a sterling job here in refuting the official charges. But justice has not been done and that must be our main goal. I expect to see a cheque on my desk in the next twenty-four hours made out to the Soldiers, Sailors and Airmen's Families Association for £10. Or I will RTU all of you tomorrow because, be you innocent or guilty, I can do that anyway. Is that going to happen?' He raised an eyebrow in question at them.

Steve looked along the row of them and then at the OC and smiled.

'Oh yes, sir, a donation to such a worthy cause would be our pleasure and our privilege.'

At that the OC ripped up the charge sheets and threw them in the bin.

'March them out, Sergeant Major and get that dipstick of a Provo Sergeant in here as I want a word with him.'

'Yes, sir!'

In a moment they were out of the office and blinking in the bright light of the day. They could hear but not understand the OC's voice reverberating against the walls of his office whilst he was having a little chat with the Provo, without tea and biscuits.

'Well fuck a badger's hairy arsehole, Steve, how in the hell did you manage that?' burst out Kevin still in shock that they had not been fined or thrown into the corner shop.

'Well my father is a lawyer and some of it rubs off I suppose.'

'You're a regular Perry Mason. We owe you a few beers tonight, Steve!'

At that Warrant Officer 1st Class Bruce arrived and suggested to 'The Pope' in his usual discreet but forceful style that the OC wanted a word with him asap and that he should move his arse in a style more suited to a greyhound in getting said arse to his office.

'What does he want to see me about now, sir?' enquired Steve.

'I imagine he wants to know why you're not interested in attending AOSB[42] as soon as you possibly can.'

'Oh bugger!' said Steve in a kind of defeated tone as he started to make his way over to the OC's office.

---

[42] Army Officer Selection Board.

West Germany, River Weser area, September 1980.
Broken Biscuit Company

Exercise 'Spearpoint' had been going on for three weeks now and Eddie's Signals Detachment were all exhausted. Therefore, the opportunity to spend a few nights in a German farmer's barn was too good to miss. They manoeuvred the Company Commander's Rover Group into the barn and busied themselves setting up the radio kit and remote aerials, so they could operate from their vehicles whilst hidden inside the barn. It felt like they had been on this exercise for an eternity so none of them needed to be told to get their heads down. Eddie bravely opted for first stag and the others slipped off to whatever part of the barn they had grabbed for their very own and crashed out. All except Jim, a very bright and unusually well-educated private soldier who had recently joined Eddie's team. He decided that he'd like to look about a bit as being a city boy he had never been this close to a working farm before.

After about an hour he returned with his arms and pockets miraculously full of custard creams, chocolate digestives and other lovely biscuits. With cups of tea added the Command Post was suddenly lively with all and sundry enjoying the fresh rations. Jim was vague about where he got them from but was sure more could be obtained. He was as good as his word and over the next twenty-four hours more of these treats were magically conjured up.

Eddie, who understood how nefarious soldiers could be, decided to find out where they were coming from and so followed him to the spot where he had gone to get these much-enjoyed biscuits. It was inside the very modern pig sty where Eddie found Jim, who was in amongst the pigs jostling for room as the biscuits cascaded down a chute for the pigs. Jim fought his way to the front and using his combat jacket scooped up a huge amount of biscuits, much to the pigs' disgust. Far from being put off by the idea of stealing biscuits from pigs, Eddie thought this was great and helped Jim to remove the colourful capsules and tablets mixed with the biscuits. He promised to assist Jim on the next run. So, a few hours later there they were in amongst the pigs with lots of pushing and shoving with obscenities being screamed out, and that was just the pigs. Eddie and Jim were holding their own when bang on time the delectable custard creams and chocolate digestives started tumbling down the chute mimicking Moses' biblical nectar in the desert. They battled with the condemned porkers to get out of the sty and eventually, if a little weary from

~ 183 ~

the effort, stumbled back to the Command Post. They were surprised on their return to see the Company Commander and most of the others feasting on roast meat, potatoes, all sorts of vegetables and in the corner, were a few cases of German Beer.

'I want a word with you two, come over here,' summoned the Company Commander whilst chewing on a huge piece of roast pork. He was a major and his nickname was 'The Duke', and he had it for a good reason.

'Are you stealing those biscuits?' he enquired bluntly.

'No, sir,' responded Private Lisle almost too quickly. 'I can assure you we are earning them.'

The Company Commander looked at Eddie for confirmation. Eddie just sort of half nodded in agreement and mumbled something unintelligible as it was obvious the Company Commander had information that they were currently unaware of.

'The Duke' continued,

'We just had the farmer here speaking to us.' Eddie's well evolved sense of danger suddenly jumped into action and, as a consequence, his face started to redden in embarrassment. The OC went on,

'He tells us that two squaddies in combat dress have been fighting the pigs in desperation for food looking like they were starving. He was so concerned that he spent the bounty he was given for allowing us to stay in the barn on all sorts of lovely grub, plus he supplemented it with fare from his own farm which his loving wife cooked up for us.' He suddenly looked sternly at Jim and Eddie.

'Were you fighting the pigs and stealing pig swill?' The Company Commander cocked his head to one side accusingly and awaited the answer with an eyebrow raised.

By now Eddie was so red he looked like he was about to burst. Lisle kept his cool and with a straight face said,

'No, sir! I admit we took the custard creams but we left the swill alone so I can only assume there is another unit near here stealing the swill, sir!' He paused and looked at Eddie for back up.

Eddie took the hint and added,

'Sir, Battalion HQ is not far perhaps the Provo and his RPs are hungry and may have been venturing outside of their compound!' The Company Commander paused and then laughed out loud but took a moment to point out that the porkers, going forward, were to be left alone and for the next twenty-four hours Eddie and Jim were only allowed to eat biscuits.

That night the farmer passed Eddie, and Eddie noticed that the farmer looked more knackered than they were, and they had been on manoeuvres for three weeks. He nudged Wharton who, by virtue of his German mother, spoke fluent Deutsche albeit with a Berlin accent. Eddie called out to him,

'Hey, Wart! Do me a favour and ask the boxhead[43] farmer why is he so knackered.'

Wart obliged, and both had a good five minute interaction during which time Eddie had absolutely no idea what was being said. Eventually Wart stopped babbling in German and explained to Eddie that the farmer had a horse that was just about to have a foal, but he didn't think that the birth was going to be a simple one. The farmer had spent an absolute fortune having her mate with some super stud horse, so he wanted to make sure he was aware early enough so that he could get a vet if he needed to, very quickly. So, he checked on the horse every hour and couldn't sleep. He had been doing this for three days. Eddie suddenly and with great relief saw an opportunity to redeem himself.

'Wart ask him where the horse is and to brief us on what to look for when the time comes. We'll remote the Company HQ into there and we can watch the horse for him whilst he gets some sleep.'

Wart duly explained this. Initially the farmer appeared sceptical but after a few moments he could not fault the logic. The farmer, via Wharton, briefed Eddie on what the early stages would look like. He said if it started, to come to the house and to bang on the door like Hell. Eddie and his detachment moved their kit into the stable and operated from there and, like a bunch of DPM[44] wearing midwives, watched the horse. The farmer gratefully went to bed.

Nine hours later Jim was dispatched to wake him up as labour appeared to have started. The farmer was even more surprised to find a Scorpion tank outside his house and vet already in attendance. 'The Duke' had used his many contacts to get one dispatched from the Life Guards, a unit that has a huge amount of experience with horses. The foal was delivered safely and, as it turned out, it did require the skills of a very experienced vet to avoid disaster. For the second time that week the farmer stuffed food and beer down the throats of all whilst the pretend battle against Warsaw Pact Forces waged around them.

In a deep gesture of gratitude, he named the new foal 'Minden'. This was

---

[43] General squaddie nickname for German nationals referring to the WW2 German steel helmet.
[44] Disruptive Pattern Material – The name of the camouflage material used in combat clothing.

the primary Battle Honour of the regiment that Eddie was in. Curiously, many years later Eddie was amazed to see that a horse called 'Minden' was running in the 3.15 at Newmarket one day. He placed a good chunk of his meagre resources onto it and it romped home second to last. Seems that in a funny kind of way Eddie paid for the custard creams after all!

Chapter 13

The Dog of War

Newry - June 1977

It was just breaking dusk in the wood at the edge of the Annaghmare Road near Newry. The *Scout* helicopter abruptly reared up, rattling even more than usual in defiance of gravity and landed rapidly. A maelstrom of dust and grass was thrown up by the rotors as it landed in the middle of a clearing in a wood that was not much bigger than the radius of the rotors. Flying tactical meant it had no lights on so the pilot had to judge from experience when the *Scout* would actually touch down and the heavy mist was not helping much.

The patrol was sitting on the edge of the helicopter compartment with their feet on the skids. The moment this thing touched down they'd be gone. Of course, if the helicopter hit too hard they'd all have dislocated spines and probably be good for naff all for ever more. The knack was making sure you waited until you were sure the helicopter was on the ground. Many a guy had fallen a very long way by jumping off the helicopter when it had merely hit some turbulence. The pilot had skilfully touched the ground like a knife buttering bread so they were not actually sure they were down for a few moments but Les jumped off first and as he did not plummet out of sight and was not particularly gifted in the miracle department, the rest of them were convinced it was OK to get off. They all grabbed their Bergens and dashed out into the semi-darkness and assumed an all-round defensive position.

The moment their arses had departed the chopper, it lifted off, turned a bit, and was gone. Once the noise had died away the night silence crowded in on them and they waited for about twenty minutes to ensure that no curious eyes were waiting for them to move. On this trip, they were alone with no back up so they had to be extremely cautious. Steve gave a sharp but quiet tap on his rifle and they all stood up and moved away north from the LZ. The darkness had descended fully now and with a light mist coupled with their blackened faces and wearing sniper camouflage they would have scared someone half to death if they bumped into them and that is exactly what happened. An elderly gentleman was out walking his dog. They heard him coming along the road that they were paralleling in the field next to it. There was no way he could see them, but at that moment the little dog had managed to break away from him and dashed under a five-bar gate in the fence. Before they knew what was happening they had this little rat dog barking and snapping at their heels. It seemed to like Kevin the most as it was his heels he was nipping the most. Kevin managed to keep quiet and just kept trying to kill the little thing with a mixture of his DMS boots and swings of his Bren butt. They heard the old guy calling out for his dog and hoped that he'd coax the dog back to him before Kevin managed to kill it or send it in the direction of the helicopter that had just dropped them off. They remained as still as possible, but the dog was still very interested in them. The owner eventually opened the gate and came over looking for his dog. Unfortunately, he came too close and Les suddenly loomed out of the darkness and the mist and put the barrel of his L98 against the head of this poor man. He almost died of fright and was convinced that they were going to kill him.

'On yer knees,' whispered Les in a very convincing Belfast accent. 'NOW! Do it NOW, or I'll blow yer fucking head off.' The old chap knelt down and did as he was told. Kevin had the dog held down by the simple expedient of having his boot pressed down onto the dog's neck. Steve went over and whispered to Eddie that he needed to know if they should continue with the mission or abort as they had been compromised. Eddie got onto the radio and asked HQ what they should do. They were told that due to the importance of their task, plus no post operational compromise risks, they should do their best to continue if they could. If necessary, take their guest along with them. Steve told Kevin to finish off the dog, but the dog had already expired under Kevin's boot – Kevin seemed curiously untouched by the dog's demise. Les put plasticuffs on the gent and they carried on to the hide with him in tow. The idea was to make sure that the guest believed that they were terrorists and not the British Army. So he was not to hear them speak at all unless it was Les with his rather good impression.

The old chap asked about his dog but got no reply from any of them, but it was obvious that the dog had already become the latest victim in the grim toll of death in the Province. Strangely, the visitor, like Kevin, did not seem too upset with the news. With one of them watching their guest and one of them on guard, it left two to dig out the hide on the side of the railway embankment. They were to dig in and stay there for three days to try and photograph some OIRA whom they had excellent intelligence were going to uncover some weapons nearby. If they could get some pictures of them red-handed on film, then that would be very useful for their masters of deception whom they handed the pictures to after each mission.

When the hide was almost completed Steve instructed Kevin and Eddie to do a sweep around the back of the hide before they actually occupied it – just to make sure they had not been compromised and some of their OIRA friends were not forming up ready to storm the four of them sometime later in the morning. Kevin and Eddie left their kit with Les and Steve and, with their M16 lightweight assault rifle and SLR respectively, started their sweep. Their location was on the side of the embankment that led to an old stone railway bridge over a road. Just before it went over the road the railway branched off into two lines. Between these two lines was a re-entrant used by gypsies but at this time had no actual gypsies using it, but it was obvious that until recently some itinerant families had been there. They had just got to the part where the two railway lines join up when Kevin gave a cry and disappeared down the embankment having lost his footing. Kevin then gave out a second sound of abject misery mingled with disgust and scrambled up the embankment to Eddie. Before he got ten feet from him Eddie could smell Kevin getting closer.

'What the fuck is that smell, Kevin?'

'Bastard gypsies! I just found their fucking toilet. Gimme a hand, mate!'

Eddie saw his hand come at him through the mist and he examined it to see if it had anything on it that might have come out of a gypsy's arse at some time in the near past. It seemed clean so he helped him up. Kevin was covered in shit and God knows what from about the waist down and he was still calling every gypsy that had ever lived bastards of every shape and description.

'Where's your gat Kevin?' asked Eddie. Kevin's face collapsed as he realised that in his rush to get out of the gypsies' man-made nightmare he'd left his rifle down there.

'Fuck it. Do you think the Army would miss just one fucking M16?' he asked.

'Probably not, but Sarn't Major Bruce will tear you a new arsehole and bury you here face down for eternity if you don't get it back,' Eddie pointed out.

Kevin looked down the embankment and with a sense of utter dejection slowly and carefully started to move down the hill. He slowly disappeared into the mist and soon after gave a pitiful cry and Eddie heard him again slide down the embankment and stop with a wet sounding thud.

After a short silent pause a barely muttered, 'Fuck it,' was all Eddie heard. After a while Kevin reappeared with rifle in tow, he was quiet. Not a good sign!

Eddie suggested that he should perhaps rub his body on the clean, dew laden grass, and get most of the shit and stuff off himself. Kevin looked at him like a man who had found a lifebelt just after the *Titanic* had disappeared and the band had definitely stopped playing. He threw himself down and jiggled himself about like a speeded up camouflaged slug. He jumped up.

'Better?' he asked.

Eddie looked at him and nodded. Kevin seemed happier and he picked up his weapon and they both started to wander back to the hide. Eddie glanced at his back and thought it best not to mention the sanitary towel stuck there. He was sure the others would have the common decency not to mention it either.

They finished their sweep and having discovered no fiendish plots to ambush them, they went back to the hide.

'What's that fucking smell?' erupted Les forgetting to use his best Belfast twang. Les glanced at the old chap and was convinced that in his misery he didn't notice that his captor had changed country of origin; in any case he probably had guessed they were the British Army. Kevin slid up to the hide and slipped inside followed closely by Eddie.

'Christ in a sack! What the fuck is that, Gus? You shit yourself or summat?' whispered Steve.

'I fell over in an effing gypsies' bog up there.' He pointed in the general direction of where they had come from.

'Is the old fucker a gypsy? Ask him. If he is, I'll shoot the fucking bastard right now and bury him with his rat dog. In the meantime, breathe more deeply and the smell will go quicker!' Kevin whispered between clenched teeth but the intensity of the feeling behind definitely came across.

'Leather, ask the old fella where he comes from,' ordered Steve.

Steve asked him, and it turned out that he was in fact from Kilrea. He was an ex-taxi driver who had retired about five years earlier.

'So not a gypsy then?' whispered Kevin obviously disappointed.

'No,' replied Les looking closely at Kevin's back.

Eddie saw the glance and shook his head and waved his hand suggesting that Les perhaps should not mention the item stuck to Kevin's back just at the present moment. Les took the advice and kept mum. They fell into the routine of the hide but with their guest they all had to do an extra shift to guard him. During his stag Les got him to empty his pockets and found out a bit more about who he was, something they should have done hours ago. Steve then realised that they should forward this info to HQ. He was convinced that with all the kit they had plus how they worked the old chap would be in no doubt that he was a guest of Tommy Atkins.

Several hours after ringing in the info on their guest they got a signal back. Eddie was amazed and immediately informed Steve that their guest was a well-known player whose credentials went a long way back. He was never charged but he was suspected of being involved in several murders, one of which was an off duty UDR soldier in Dungannon quite recently.

'What? That old fucker, who looks like butter wouldn't melt in his mouth, is a Fenian hit man? Bollocks!' whispered Kevin.

Steve swore loudly completely destroying the 'we're terrorists – honest!' cover plan.

'Fucking arsehole, I should have bleeding guessed it, all of you stand to, NOW!' He reached over and pulled the old guy up by his jacket.

'You're the fucking sentry for the stash we're here to watch aren't you, ya fucking little shit of a weasel? AREN'T YOU?' Almost immediately his Browning 9mm hi-power pistol was being forced under the chin of the old bloke. He said nothing, just looked at Steve with seriously hate-filled eyes. Steve put his face up very close to the guy.

'What's the fucking plan if you go missing, arse wipe?' The man responded with silent defiance.

'Kevin, have a chat with badger's arse here and see what you can get out of him – I'm not worried about his survival, we can bury him in the fucking hole we're living in with the dog. I wasn't keen to mention it earlier, but I am sure with that surname he must be related to Fenian gypsies somewhere along the line!' He made sure the man heard him and Kevin's face veritably lit up.

'No problem, Boss!' Kevin pulled the man over to his side of the trench by the simple expedient of pulling him by his hair and started to whisper agitatedly into his ear. It was noticeable that Kevin had borrowed Les' *Remington* blow-back shotgun and had that stuffed under the man's chin.

Ten or so minutes later Kevin informed Steve of the whole arrangement that was in place for guarding the weapons hide. It seemed that all over the place around the cache of arms, that thin black cotton had been strung. Once or twice a day he would amble over with his dog and see if any had been broken. If they were damaged, he would watch the cache from the far hill and see what happened. It seems that they turned up just as he was checking. If he did not return within a few hours his mates would assume that he had been arrested or something near the cache, and would wait until further orders from their Belfast Brigade Commander.

'How did you get him to talk, Kevin?' muttered Steve out of curiosity.

'I said I'd suffocate him in the plastic bag we've all been shitting in for the last twenty-four hours, and showed him I meant business by undoing it and opening it right under his nose.'

'Think he is telling the truth?'

'No, I think he is so full of shit that the bag would make no difference to him. He also says that the dog was his wife's and he hated the little shit, so he thanked us for doing him a favour.'

'He's a nasty little bugger. OK Kevin, thanks.' He turned to the rest of them. 'Kit on we're bugging out in the next five minutes. We'll leave the hole here in case we need it for cover later.'

They were ready in three.

'You!' Steve pointed to the OIRA man, 'Fuck off. If I see you again I'm gonna kill you, now get the fuck out of here before I get my mucker to pour that bag of shit on you for a going away present – go on, PISS OFF!'

The man needed no encouragement and scampered away, his clothes filthy from the dirt in the hide, glancing back every now and then expecting to be shot or something. Steve led the guys off in the exact opposite direction.

'Eddie, get on that radio and tell the boss we're moving location. Ask him to get a chopper to fly over and land somewhere and then to fly away again as if we had been picked up.'

Eddie sent the message and got a positive acknowledgement about the helicopter with the orders that they were also to actually get on it and come in now that they had been compromised.

'Eddie, tell those fuckers that we're staying but not to watch the hide. I think if we get near to the local town we are going to see some serious players tonight who will be coming down for a chinwag about their cache with that dead dog shagger we just met – get some nice piccies.'

Eddie passed it on and the order to end the mission was rescinded. It was now early evening and would be dark soon. They decided to lay an ambush to see if they were being followed. They broke track and waited for twenty minutes. Nobody came along. Steve moved them another couple of hundred yards and they set up an ambush again to be sure. In addition, after breaking track, he took them well back along their route to make sure they were not being followed. They got into their ambush positions and decided to wait for thirty minutes this time. The precaution was a good one as after about ten minutes the OIRA guy, still filthy from the trench, appeared along the track and was spotted by Les about one hundred yards away from them. It was obvious that he wasn't easily scared. He had been following them and was no doubt briefed on some of the tactics that patrols did. He knew the local area and probably had been watching them all along. It was obvious that he had lost them now as he would never have walked anywhere near the ambush position.

At that moment the noise of a helicopter came into earshot. The old man stopped looked in the direction of the helicopter and listened. It landed about a thousand yards away from where they were, paused and then took off again. Steve saw Eddie was doing his thing on the radio and indicated that they were all to remain hidden and to do nothing until he had gone away. The old OIRA man started off again but this time with a will. When he was almost out of sight Steve informed them all that they were going to follow the old guy now as it was obvious he had not been able to tell anyone yet about what had happened plus he thought they had been picked up and had flown away. It was a risk but they all agreed.

Keeping well-hidden they followed him through the wood and through some fields until he got back to his home just on the outskirts of the town of Newry. It was a small terraced house that was about one hundred and fifty yards from another wood line on the edge of a copse. Steve was very pleased. It was obvious that they were now in the clear and had a good prospect of some interesting intelligence being gathered.

'Good work with the radio, Eddie, that helicopter really did the trick, getting it to land where you did was brilliant, well done.' Eddie nodded his thanks for the recognition but kept it to himself that he was actually just changing frequencies when the helicopter arrived and had nothing at all to do with him where it landed. They waited until nightfall in the hedgerow closest to the target's house. Steve told them the plan.

'We need to know what the fuck is happening in that house. So, Eddie and Kevin. Immediately it gets a bit darker you're going to get some UGS around that house. If his goldfish so much as farts, I want to know about it, OK? Les and I will choose a hide location and set it up – we will be watching you and covering you so don't worry about that. If anyone so much as glances at you in a threatening way Les here will take their head off.'

Eddie and Kevin got out some detectors and then adjusted their personal camouflage until they were literally invisible. Les had contacted Lisburn and they were informed that the rules governing opening fire had been suspended and they could cock weapons. Quietly they did. They were also informed that two other patrols of the NIPG were now in the area and also giving them cover – and that explained the helicopter. The grid references of their hides were provided and Steve, along with his team, breathed a small sigh of relief.

'C'mon, Gus let's go steal some knickers,' whispered Eddie.

'No point, it seems every tart in this country has naff panties, really boring ones, barely worth the effort, but I'll come along anyway just for the fun of it.'

In a moment they were gone and Les, even though he knew they were there, had difficulties seeing them. They'd have to be quick as in two hours or so it would be dawn. Over his shoulder he could hear Steve breathing hard whilst digging out a hide.

It took a while to crawl the one hundred and fifty yards to the target. This was a typical terraced house two up and two down kind of affair and from the look of it not very well maintained. It was a drab yellow with guttering missing here and there with the tell-tale smears of green moss showing the careless attitude of the owners. Eddie and Kevin could hear the various noises of the night whilst they were assessing the place, a dog barking, the odd car driving nearby, a dustbin lid clattering to the ground. It started to rain, just a light rain that blew in and out, it was barely there at all. A half-moon shone through scudding clouds that caused frantic shadows on the buildings around them. It was like a psychedelic slide show in black and white.

Eddie leaned close to Kevin and whispered,

'I think we can leave the UGS almost on the window sill, these things haven't seen a lick of paint or maintenance for years and neither have the windows. I don't think they have been cleaned since Hitler was a corporal.'

Kevin just smiled back and nodded, his camouflaged face lit up momentarily by the half-moon showing between the flitting clouds. They placed and hid them away best they could and managed to get back to the hide without discovery just before dawn. As expected the suspected pensioner terrorist stayed in bed and had a good lay in and roused himself at about 10am. His wife though was up at about 8am and could be heard banging about with pots and pans, cooking and doing whatever housewives do for aging murderers.

With the UGS in place they could hear everything. When he did get up the first thing she asked about was the dog. He fobbed her off and lied saying that the damn thing had legged it again and it would find its own way back again as normal. From the way she spoke they could detect that she cared far more for the dog than she did for him. They had relayed this back to their masters via the HF radio. They were informed in code that MI5 had taken a keen interest and that two operatives are watching the house as well.

MFI, as that particular segment of HM's Secret Intelligence Service was known to the common squaddie, never took part in ops, they always used someone else. They did not like to get their hands dirty. This probably meant that they had asked 14 to look at the place as well. The main reason was that this small cog in the Irish terrorist machine would almost certainly have to go and report what happened but the GPO records showed that no telephone existed in the house. The NIPG could not follow him so it made sense as 14 could.

Eddie, Steve, Les and Kevin continued listening and taking photos whenever the opportunity presented itself. His wife did a lot of toing and froing and so did he but nobody of any interest came anywhere near the house. The NIPG were getting fed up after the third day especially when they were told that two patrols who had taken over from them observing the hide had arrested two players who had opened the cache and started to empty it. It seemed the OIRA were keen to get their kit out of the cache as it appeared that both of them had no idea that the hide had been compromised and was most likely still being watched. They were small fry in the organisation and not really much more than kids and the top scumbags in their freedom organisation had intentionally fed them to the Green machine to satisfy their curiosity and to confirm it had been compromised. They'd get about eighteen months as a walking sex toy and a criminal record for the rest of their lives but that was the risk.

They were informed that they were to retrieve the UGS that night and to leave their position in the early hours of the morning. They acknowledged the request as they could see that it was going nowhere at their end. However, until they had retrieved the UGS they'd continue looking and listening.

'Christ, he is absolutely rat arsed,' said Kevin to Eddie. The old man had returned home from the pub and it was 11pm, he had come home a bit early. They were listening in and both of them could hear that she was asking him about the dog and what had happened. He explained again that it had run away and he had no idea what had happened to it. In any case he hated the damn thing and he made that plain. It went quiet for a short while and all they could hear was him trying to open a bottle of something and her footsteps. Suddenly there were three 'whang' type sounds that were very loud followed by a single thud and her saying very quietly,

'Lying bastard.' Then silence apart from her footsteps.

They woke up Steve and Les whilst they watched her go next door to the neighbour's house. Then nothing until an ambulance arrived followed by a police car. They watched over the next three hours as the ambulance men took out a shrouded body on a stretcher and her away in a police car whilst other police arrived wearing white coveralls, who removed things from inside the house.

'Well fuck a badger's hairy arse, she's gone and topped the old bastard,' Les said to nobody in particular and all in general. He was voicing what they already knew.

Once everything had settled down they retrieved the UGS and RV'd with the box vans and the other patrols. Once back in camp they cleaned everything, had a huge breakfast and then slept until about 4pm. On waking they were summoned to the OC's office where two men in suits were already drinking coffee and eating biscuits. The OC addressed them.

'You may have felt that this op was a failure but the info you sent in about the dog was superb. Certain chaps approached the target's wife and informed her about what had happened to the dog, but intentionally left out your role in that unfortunate episode. They left it that the old boy had got pissed off and killed the poor little thing. The results were impressive.' The major glanced across at the taller of the two suits and he took over.

'Yes, after that little chat she told us everything she knew about that evil little bastard and his mates. She has been on the edge of his world for thirty odd years and surprisingly she knew a great deal about what was going on. This info will set the OIRA back about ten years and put about six of them off the street for many, many years. It was your quick thinking that kicked this all off, and we just wanted to show our gratitude.'

Steve interrupted.

'Shame she'll be doing life for doing us a favour though, seems a tad unfair.'

'We did not expect her to beat him to death with a frying pan, seems quite apt though in a funny kind of way. But no, she won't be doing time. She is currently being debriefed and yes there will be a short trial and she will be found guilty and sent to prison to ponder the errors of her ways. After about twenty-four hours though, she will have a new identity and a nice new place to live somewhere near Milton Keynes or wherever. We have even promised her a nice new puppy.' The spook looked genuinely pleased. The OC had the last word.

'Just to emphasise how grateful these guys are they have used a part of their not so insignificant budget to buy you guys a drink, a big drink! It's in the QM's store at the moment. I think it will take the lot of you about two days to get through it – so you'd better start now as you're off again a few days after that.'

They rushed to the QM's store and moved the huge pile of beer cans into the classroom. Other patrols sauntered in and grabbed a tube, a music system appeared and shortly afterwards the *Eagles* started to rock about life in the fast lane. The beer kept going until 3am… not that any of them remembered that!

West Germany, – December 1980 – Grab a Shovel!

A foot of snow covered Lunenburg Heath and if you weren't a part of the scenery, as Kevin was, it was probably a beautiful sight. Kevin, now Platoon Sergeant of 3 Platoon had just received a new Platoon Commander. Kevin thought the new officer wasn't a bad lad, a bit green but the new boy was intent on letting all and sundry know who the boss was. They were currently on exercise with 4 Royal Tank Regiment who had decided to go out to play with their Chieftain tanks. It was about 2am and one thing Tankies do not like is operating at night, so they harbour up in woods and suchlike. Kevin's platoon was dug in around the Chieftains in the infantry support role. The new Rupert[45] had rubbed Kevin up the wrong way several times since joining but Kevin bided his time and was waiting for the exact moment to teach him a lesson and to wreak a little revenge on the young subaltern.

'erm... Sergeant, may I ask an awkward question?' queried the sprog officer.

'Certainly, feel free, sir,' responded Kevin in his best 'I'm just a thick sergeant' voice.

The officer paused for a moment trying to select the right words. 'I'm in need of some relief in the bowels department. I know some of the lads may try to er... ambush me in some way for a prank. How do I avoid that?'

Kevin immediately had a brilliant solution.

'Well, sir, if I was you I wouldn't go in the woods at all as that's just an invitation for them to play a trick on you. I'd go about one hundred yards out into the middle of that field. It's dark and nobody's going to see you. Take a shovel and starlight scope along and have a quick shifty all around you before you squat, if you get my meaning, sir?'

'A brilliant idea, Sergeant, many thanks.' The lieutenant grabbed a shovel, a scope and was off in quite a hurry, he'd obviously been waiting a good while. Spoon, the platoon signaller looked disappointed once he had gone and asked,

'Sarn't, why are you spoiling our bloody fun? We were looking forward to shovelling his own shit back into his Bergen, no way we're gonna catch him out now.'

Kevin watched the officer walk into the open field using the other starlight

---

[45] Rupert was slang for a new officer fresh from Sandhurst

scope and he watched as the lieutenant found a promising spot and dug a hole about one hundred and fifty yards into the field. Just as the officer reached to undo his trousers Kevin said to Spoon,

'Give me the radio, Spoon.' The handset was dutifully handed over and Kevin pushed the button and spoke into it. 'Hello, Tango Two One this is India One Three, over.'

'Tango Two One send, over,' came a crisp reply from the tank troop commander over the ether.

'India One Three; our forward positions have spotted an enemy recce patrol observing your call signs with night viewing equipment. They are one hundred and fifty yards to the front of your position. It is possible they may call in a strike. Your position has been compromised. Over.'

'Tango Two One, roger, out to you. Hello, Charlie Charlie Tango Two One this is Tango Two One, move now to... wait... wait... Pepper Dwarf. Move now, now, now, out.'

'You bastard, Gus,' said Spoon smiling.

Suddenly four engines each giving eight hundred and fifty brake horse power suddenly burst into life and revved up whilst four one million candlepower main armament searchlights abruptly came on in chorus. They swept the field until they found a young squatting officer using a night scope and illuminated him brighter than a thousand daylights. Instantly a complete Sabre Troop of four Chieftain main battle tanks burst noisily and powerfully out of the woods and swept across the field firing blank machine gun ammo. The steel monsters rushed past either side of the unfortunate Lieutenant and the commander of the second tank threw a thunderflash at him for good measure.

The officer, in shock, half stumbled and half ran back to his platoon with his trousers still halfway down his leg, his body covered in effluent from tanks literally splashing through his outpourings.

'Sergeant, what the fuck's happening, has the enemy been seen?' The officer paused and realised that the entire platoon had just watched, with some humour, what had happened and then he spotted the radio handset held by Kevin. He put 2 and 2 together. He said just one thing.

'You bastard!' He paused for a few moments and then burst out laughing. It was at that moment 3 Platoon were relieved that they had the beginnings of a commander who at least had a sense of humour.

Chapter 14

Where There's Muck...

July 1977

Fort George in Londonderry hadn't changed much in the four months since they had been there last, it was still a dump. The Group were in Derry to get some much-needed intelligence on a local dignitary who was allegedly a high-ranking member of an illegal organisation, namely PIRA and more recently the INLA[46] who had a particularly hard line approach to politics. These people were of the opinion that killing the opposition to your political aims was far better than persuasion and boring old voting. The unit responsible for that part of Derry, including the Creggan, Rossville Flats plus the famous Free Derry Wall area, and currently on a four-month Op Banner tour, was the RGJ[47] with B Company occupying Fort George itself along with battalion HQ. This famous regiment had an enviable reputation as a reliable unit coupled with no lack of courage and fortitude. However, that didn't mean that you didn't take every opportunity to poke fun or call them crap whenever you met any of them. This 'The Pope' and crew did and of course they did exactly the same back, it was expected.

All of the NIPG were now wearing the cap badge of the RCT again so the sudden occupation of Fort George must have given the impression that there was a sudden surge of vehicles coming along, for over thirty drivers to suddenly turn up.

Earlier in the box vans as they approached the camp, Eddie noticed through the windscreen that the advertising hoarding across from the camp gates still had the ad from a local butcher proclaiming 'You Can't Beat Meat'

---

[46] Irish Nationalist Liberation Army.
[47] The Royal Green Jackets

to which some wag had added underneath, 'you can after four months in this place'.

'It's still there. I'm amazed that nobody's removed it,' observed Eddie.

'It's still there because it announces the British Army as just a bunch of wankers. It's probably protected as a national monument to futility,' commented 'The Pope' wryly.

'Is that why the taigs have so many bleeding children then?' asked Kevin who had just woken up. Steve rolled his eyes.

'Futility, you prick, not fertility! Where were you when the brains were handed out, Gus?'

'In the other queue getting a sense of humour and manners.'

'Sorry, Kevin, I'm knackered and need some kip,' apologised Steve.

'Don't we all!' stated Eddie ending the conversation as the box van lurched over the sleeping policemen and through the high corrugated gates into the camp.

They had removed all their kit from the vans raising a few eyebrows from the local 'stubble hoppers' as the infantry was called by most other corps. RCT drivers don't usually have cammed up rifles and weird camouflaged outfits and webbing to match. The locals assumed correctly, that the RCT front was just that and that the new visitors were in fact the SAS, something the NIPG guys were not going to try and change and would enjoy living in the reflected glory.

A colour sergeant appeared and without fuss allocated them all somewhere to live and sleep. It was crowded, and it was obvious that up until a couple of hours ago this was living accommodation for some poor beggars who were now shacked up somewhere else.

WOI Bruce addressed the colour sergeant in his soft highland accent.

'Please do extend our gratitude to the boys who were inconvenienced here, we'll see if we can get a few beers down their necks whilst here to demonstrate our thanks.'

'Your OC has already arranged that, a couple of cases of beer have already been delivered and are in the process of being dispatched at the moment, the boys *were* impressed.'

The colour left them and they all started to busy themselves settling in. They had a briefing to attend in just over an hour and the rumour was that they'd be out on ops very soon after that. In short order they were in and sorted and most were having a nap when WOI Bruce woke them up and they all trotted off to the briefing room.

The Intelligence Officers were there alongside some new faces that all had red staff officer tabs on the collars. The NIPG OC came into the room accompanied by a tall guy in civvies. The OC addressed them first.

'Welcome everyone, this operation that we are about to brief you on is very, very sensitive indeed. You are not to discuss any aspect of this operation with anybody outside of this room.' That got everyone's attention and he underlined it by pausing and scanning the room. He introduced the tall civvie next to him as just John. It was obvious that John was a member of some sneaky beaky crew probably 14 out at Ballykelly or MI5 itself and that John wasn't his real name. His real name was probably something like Timothy or Charles with one of those double-barrelled surnames. These 14 people were frankly crazy and very brave, but bonkers all the same. They considered it to be a challenge to integrate and infiltrate the very organisations that the British Army were fighting namely PIRA, OIRA and all the other acronyms with either Republican or Loyalist leanings. Their work was dangerous and evoked huge respect from anyone who understood what they did.

He gave the team more of a picture rather than a briefing of what was happening in Derry at that time regarding the status of PIRA and the INLA. They had been involved in some quite nasty murders, bombings and shootings of late, and it was rumoured that a concerted effort by both was about to be perpetrated against the Army in Derry to raise the body count in favour of the *Doc Marten* boot wearing fraternity rather than the good guys in the DMS ones. To do this the local bad guys would need to get weapons and explosives into the city and store them somewhere. It so happened that the Intelligence community had a good idea where it was going to be stored but not when or by whom. Therefore, they needed these places to be watched and when the scumbags delivered the stuff they would arrange for all to be arrested and the weapons confiscated to the delight of all and justice would be allowed to take its natural course, or so it was hoped.

Unfortunately, the safe house that the PIRA people were allegedly going to use was a terraced house between a betting shop and a corner house just next to the river and observing this place consistently for about two weeks was going to be a big challenge. The people in the adjoining properties were clean as far as the Internal Security and Armed Forces were concerned so moving them out would be suspicious and none of them had or were planning to go on holiday as far as the authorities were aware. The OC stepped up after John had finished.

'So this is how we're going to do it...'

The briefing lasted three hours and every single aspect about the operation was gone into in huge depth. Logistics, rations, signals, orders for opening fire, the local baddies and other personalities were discussed.

It was 5am when they crashed through the door of the terraced house on Carlisle Street just up from the Presbyterian church. RGJ soldiers immediately rushed upstairs and made sure they had entered every room and quickly ascertained that every person in the house was accounted for and had a rifle pointed at them. This was incredibly easy as it was known that only one person lived in the house and he was quite an old chap who used to be a major political activist in the mid-fifties. He was not actively involved now apart from hurling abuse at soldiers at every possible opportunity and although he might hate the British he was never, as far as MI5 knew, into terrorism. This was one of those activist opportunities and he was making the most of it. He was standing plasticuffed in just his pyjama bottoms, his tackle almost hanging out. His pyjamas were filthy as were the sheets on his bed. It was a close approximation to most of the house as it was disgusting and dishevelled almost everywhere. It was explained to him that they had intelligence to suggest that his dwelling was being used to store illicit arms and that a search was to be done. He suggested in colourful language what they could do with their intelligence as he was led downstairs into the living room whilst a Royal Engineer search team undertook a look-see. The chances that a small but not insignificant find comprising an old, but serviceable, Second World War rifle and some matching ammunition was definitely on the cards. Just the right sort of set up for an opportunity sniper shot at a passing patrol. The chance of a find such as this was excellent today as the Argyle and Sutherlands NIPG Brick had been in the previous night and had planted the weapon and the ammo.

'Even a fucking Slapper search team should find this,' they had laughingly whispered referring to the nickname that the RE Sappers enjoyed. They hid the weapon under the sofa and they agreed that the ammunition had best be left in a kitchen cupboard, as that was also easy to find. Justice would be done when later it would become obvious that the occupant had no idea the stuff was there and it had probably been placed by an ASU unit in preparation for a hit. The old chap would be free to go home having witnessed how even-handed British justice was. He was not what they wanted; they wanted his house for two weeks and had to work out a wheeze to get rid of the occupant. The search teams finished and eventually everybody left except Eddie and crew who now sneaked out of the bathroom that they had slowly but secretly occupied during the operation. The search commander knew about the insertion, but the rest of his team had no idea – this was on a need to know basis and they didn't need to know. Eddie and his mates were going to be cooped up in this house for the next two weeks.

At Lisburn five days earlier, the Intelligence Officer had explained in great depth that the tactical change in PIRA into small non-linked units of just a few terrorists had made intelligence collection very difficult. However, they were sure that the occupant of the house next door to the one they were currently in was probably the commander of a clutch of ASUs and it would be good if they could monitor what he says indoors for a while as it may give them some info on when the arms etc., were going to be delivered. The plan was to get them into the house next door and work their way along via the attic until they were in the house of the target. They would then deliver a number of UGS and then sit in the next house and listen in to what was being said. If they could photograph people going in and out then even better.

So now here they were in this grotty house ready to eavesdrop on a terrorist scumbag. They took photos all over the house, as they'd have to make sure it was in exactly the same level of filth as when they had moved in. They were extremely careful not to be seen in the house, as in this part of Derry if it got out that there was a small group of soldiers in a house alone, it was probable that they would not make it until the next morning.

Eddie had a thought and said,

'What if his daughter or someone comes along to clean up or feed him or something? What we gonna do, she might have a key.'

'I suppose she also washes his pyjamas and underpants, eh? He has no regular visitors, 14 have been watching the place for a few weeks, and if they say he has no visiting friends then I believe them.' Steve said this flatly whilst pointing towards the fetid underpants littering the bedroom floor.

As mentioned 14 were a reference to the loonies who were a part of 14 Intelligence based in Aldergrove Airport but with a detachment in Ballykelly. These people were linked very closely to the SAS and MI5 etc. and were serious Bad Asses. These extremely brave and resourceful soldiers both male and female lived and communed amongst the nastiest of the extremists, if they said something about the locals it was hard earned and worth listening to.

They did a quick recce of the house and decided that they would occupy the main bedroom as that was also where the loft hatch was. Once they had done the UGS one of them would monitor the systems and the other would man the Bren in the hallway looking obliquely down the stairs. If anyone came into the house from any direction they would hear them from the hall. A length of communication string was laid out between the sentry post and the UGS monitoring spot. Two tugs meant a problem and three to stand down. One tug would be ignored as it would be possible to accidentally pull it. The M79 was put away in a Bergen as in these close quarter conditions if fired it would probably kill them as well. It was agreed that they could have brews but no hot food as the smell might be left behind and they'd be compromised. They'd also have to use shit bags as the sound of a toilet flushing occasionally in an empty house would also give away the game.

Until 2am, when they were going to insert the UGS, the team took it in turns to do sentry, sleep and dig out the bricks in the walls in the attic between the house they were in and the target house. They didn't need much of a hole but they had to be careful with noise plus they'd have to put back the bricks each time in case someone looked in the loft. Of course, you would see the loose bricks if you looked closely but in a darkened loft they'd most likely get away with it. Everything had to be done extremely slowly and quietly. It would be only too simple for an IRA gunman to be below them and shoot upwards into the ceiling and kill one or perhaps all of them. The problem with this type of work is that you'd not know that you'd been compromised until they were shooting at you, not a nice situation to be in. Their back up was sitting in two *Humber* one ton vehicles, better known as Pigs, with their engines running about five minutes away in Masonic Camp. Five minutes was not a long time but it could mean eternity.

The PIRA character concerned in the next house was a well-known hard man in the Creggan who would later become a prominent politician in whose mouth butter wouldn't melt. But at this time, he was as close to being scum as you could get. A distinct bastard who was associated with more than a few murders of soldiers, RUC and UDR not to mention a few taxi drivers. He was also suspected to have been involved in a number of terrorist operations in UK and Germany. Certainly a busy bunny that loved his hobby and British and Army Intelligence were hoping he would talk in his sleep or something.

At almost 2am Eddie woke Steve up to tell him they were through to the target via the attics. Ropes had been strung along the route so that they didn't have to run the risk of slipping on the rafters and allowing a sodding great British Army DMS boot with associated puttees and DPM combat trousers to go crashing through any ceilings, as that might be a bit of a giveaway! The plan was for Les and Kevin to actually enter the house whilst all were asleep and place movement and listening UGS in certain places around the house. Les would do the planting and Kevin was his bodyguard. Eddie would stay in the safe house with the radio whilst Steve covered them in the attic with some serious weapons in case they got into any real bother downstairs. Les was to have a pistol and Kevin would have the *Remington* semi-automatic shotgun just in case he needed to persuade anyone to leave them alone. If they were compromised they were to scarper out the front door and make like burglars. There was no chance they'd run into any passing squaddies who would take interest in two guys all dressed in DPM wearing balaclavas of which one was carrying a shotgun, as local intelligence had placed this area out of bounds to patrols.

They were all ready and after listening for a while to see if anybody was up, Les and Kevin shimmied down the rope and waited for a moment both kneeling one legged on the floor. They slowly sneaked downstairs like black ghosts and started their sneaky work. They were placing an audio bug under the sofa when Les looked at the sofa and in the darkness picked out the shape of a very small child. The small child's eyes were wide open and looking directly at them. Kevin placed his hand quickly over the child's mouth just before she screamed. It was a little girl of about three or four but she did not seem exactly terrified of them. Kevin whispered in her ear.

'What is a nice little girl like you doing out of bed? Speak quietly now.'

'I leep down dairs cause of noisies upastared,' she muttered very quietly. Kevin had a stroke of brilliance whilst also making a mental note that they needed to be a bit quieter in the attic.

'OK so what's your name?'

'Aine.' Kevin knew immediately this was the target's eldest daughter

'Right, well you know who Father Christmas is don't you?' She nodded. Kevin gestured that Les should carry on.

'Well we help him, and we are checking the chimneys to see if they are OK... Now promise you won't tell anybody and we'll tell Santa to bring you a special present. OK?'

The child smiles and nodded quickly, and Kevin said she should go back to sleep, much to their amazement she did and very quickly.

'Jeez that was fucking close,' whispered Les in relief.

'Don't swear or Santa will stop Sandra shagging your worthless body this Christmas.' Kevin saw the white teeth as Les smiled back and mouthed a silent, 'Fuck off!'

They finished downstairs and silently placing their feet at the edge of each step to stop creaks they got to the top of the stairs. A rope ladder crept down to them and slowly each of them climbed up and out of the hall into the attic. Just as they were closing the attic lid a little voice on the top stair said quietly,

'Bye.' She had followed them upstairs. Kevin waved back and the lid was closed.

Steve was livid.

'Who the fuck was that?' he asked in an agitated whisper. 'Fanny fucking Hall?'

'It's OK, Steve she thinks we're Santa's little helpers,' said Kevin trying to calm Steve down.

'I should have sent a bunch of fucking drunken dwarfs wearing pissing diver's boots,' said Steve despairingly.

'It's OK she is too young to understand what's happening,' contributed Les not fully convinced.

They agreed that they had not been entirely compromised but they did a good job of the attic wall as daddy might be dispatched to prove there were none of Santa's elves hiding up in the attic once the story got out. But it wasn't lost on Kevin that two men in balaclavas had not been that scary to the little girl, perhaps she had seen a lot of men in balaclavas in her young life already.

They went back to the safe house and got into the routine two on two off staggered shifts. At about 6am they started to hear the familiar noises of a family waking up. As they listened they could hear the little girl recounting her story to her mother. They were pleased to hear that her mummy was equally convinced that she imagined that her daughter saw two of Santa's little helpers overnight.

The day moved along with them guarding themselves and listening to the antics of the children. The next day came and not much more happened to report in on. Definitely there were no murderous plots or grand schemes. All day they had not heard from the father at all. Just the mother and family doing typical mother and family type stuff. They moved into night routine and started staging on two on and two off. Eddie and Kevin got the first stag until one in the morning. They were listening and could hear dogs barking and at one time a couple was arguing in the street. Another man was singing a sad song out of tune until someone told him to 'shut the fuck up!'

Slowly but surely the sounds of the local streets became less and eventually became quiet. The creaking of the house unnerved them a bit as the temperature changes made the house stretch and contract. It was just as they were waking up Eddie and Les and handing over that they all heard the slight smack as one of the windows downstairs was smashed. They all grabbed their weapons and stood to. They heard the door open and a few whispered voices were conversing in a heated way, but Eddie and the others could not hear what they were actually saying but they worked out quickly enough that they were just a bunch of kids doing a burglary whilst the real owner of the house was away being entertained by Her Majesty's Intelligence community. They started to look about downstairs and they could hear them emptying drawers and stuff.

'How do you want to handle this?' asked Kevin. 'They're gonna be up here soon and we'd be noticeable I think.' Steve could be seen in the dark thinking about the situation.

'I think we'll just scare them off, they're probably Catholics and Catholics are into the supernatural so let's give 'em a bit of a spook. If it doesn't work we can always just arrest them and call off the whole thing, not our fault.'

Kevin leaned near the door and started a low wailing noise that was barely audible. Slowly he increased the volume. Then Les joined in and started to make more unworldly sounds. Downstairs they could hear the kids stop and listen then they talked a bit sounding worried and then legged it out of the house. Eddie and the others allowed themselves a quiet chortle. However, with the child and these kids Steve was not of a mind to stay in the house as two compromises in one mission was more than enough to spell danger.

Eddie got onto the radio and gave the code word stating that they had been compromised without any immediate danger and that they would be using the pre-planned arrangements to bug out. They untidied the place and made sure it was exactly the same as they had found it minus some evidence of a minor burglary. HQ instructed them not to retrieve the UGS but to leave them in situ. They cleaned themselves up and put berets on resplendent with RGJ cap badges. They exited the house via the back door and patrolled back to Masonic Camp like a normal foot patrol except they had Bergens and weird weapons. But at 5am on a cold morning with a light rain it was unlikely that anybody would notice.

They arrived at Masonic and persuaded the gate RGJ sentry to let them in, it wasn't hard as not many locals tend to amble up dressed in DPM, armed with M16s, a sniper rifle, SLR and a Bren gun weighed down with huge Bergens. The company based in the camp fussed about and gave them a hot breakfast that they'd never forget and almost drowned them in a sea of tea. They were very grateful and wolfed it all down.

A bit later two Land Rovers turned up for them, so they wished the RGJ Company a fond farewell and they were taken to Fort George. Once there the NIPG OC debriefed them in his usual informal but efficient manner and commiserated on their bad luck. They cleaned their weapons and sorted out their kit, all of them were tired but they couldn't sleep so they decided to have a look around the camp.

It was about 11am by now and even though they'd already had a mega breakfast, they still fancied some tea and a burger just for a change of diet. So, they sauntered over to a small dilapidated caravan that was, as usual, being assaulted by a variety of squaddies not actually hungry but bored with the usual fare supplied by the cookhouse. The Char Wallahs as they were called, were unsung heroes who spent months, or even years working in their small hut or caravans making beef burgers, sandwiches and tea for soldiers who barely regarded them as human beings. Most of them were from Pakistan or Bangladesh and therefore Muslim. More than once squaddies would throw bacon or pork sausages at them or, even worse, turn their caravan upside down, usually when the poor man was using his toilet. The soldiers found it hilarious but for the poor bloody Char Wallah it was no fun at all.

They all got their tea and burger and sat about outside silently enjoying the moment. Suddenly a loud bang came from just outside the camp wall followed by two more in quick succession and an even bigger one a few moments later but from what felt like much further away. All of them had, without thinking, immediately leapt behind or under whatever cover they could find and Kevin had found himself hiding under the Char Wallah's caravan with six other guys. The Char Wallah himself was still inside working as though nothing had happened, he'd been there years and it was just routine now. When they were sure it had stopped they all crawled out from whatever cover they had found.

'What in the name of Beelzebub's Y-fronts was that all about?' shouted Kevin whilst trying to rebuild his burger without all the dust, cigarette ends and crap picked up whilst he was under the toilet block.

'Fucked if I know,' said Eddie flicking a myriad of ancient bits of discarded burger off his body.

'It was a mortar attack I think,' said Les whilst watching the standby section of the RGJ jumping into two Pigs[48] and scream out the gates.

It later turned out that some local terrorists had decided to attack with a homemade mortar from the back of a truck. The bigger explosion was the last two mortar tubes blowing up simultaneously on the truck itself. Unfortunately, it missed the culprits as they had already bravely legged it thus allowing two civilians, who were seriously injured, to innocently walk past it at precisely the wrong moment. For all that the terrorists fortunately missed the camp entirely.

It seemed that the burger and tea accompanied by all the excitement was enough to tempt the 'Tea Leafs' to amble back to their temporary cardboard box walled area and grab some sleep.

They awoke a few hours later and sorted out their kit for the upcoming operation. Once all their kit was ready they all staggered back into the Char Wallah's and ordered a couple of cans of Tennents lager and, after commenting on the more pertinent points on the various pictures on the can of the teenage models that Tennents thought would sell more lager, they proceeded to consume the contents. The 'only two pints' law that existed was broken within twenty minutes and Kevin was well on his way to his sixth can when the OC came in and ordered them to bed. He was concerned that this op was going to be a lot trickier than the usual fare and he wanted his people ready. Without any murmur of discontent all of them realised why and quietly went to their gonk bags.

Next morning the OC called a briefing at 10:00 hrs and WO1 Bruce made doubly sure amongst threats to life and limb that all were present, correct and listening. The OC had hung some maps on the wall and they were all handed some photos of the interesting parties in the area. He cleared his throat and began.

'Well as all of you are no doubt aware the OP in the target's house was interrupted by two bits of bad luck so it was considered compromised and it was thought best to bug out. A decision I fully support.' He took a mouthful of water, then glanced around the room and continued.

'So, the UGS are in place and they should be OK for another week or two but in a built-up area the range is only a couple of hundred yards and we need to know what's going on in that Fenian bastard's house! This is what we are

---

[48] An armoured 4 wheeled vehicle built by Humber. Referred to as a 1 Ton Humber. It was a 'Pig' to drive hence the nickname.

gonna do about it. Right listen in. Situation: friendly forces...' His crisp Sandhurst accent carried on and the troops all listened intently to his orders.

In short there was an old Salvation Army hall in Carlisle Road literally facing the target's house which was near the bottom of Hawkin Street. It could be well defended and had a good field of vision. It had been arranged just a day or two earlier that members of the UK Health and Safety National Asbestos Action Team had inspected the place and found white asbestos lining in the ceilings. The building had to be closed immediately whilst remedial work was done. Amazingly this Government agency had funding for listed buildings and so the work could start almost immediately, if not sooner. Kev confided to the others that this might be the flaw in the plan as usually it would take 'fucking forever and a day' for a Government organisation to do anything! The ceiling would have to be sealed and a lick of paint could give that impression. So, the God-fearing members of the Salvation Army were going to have their ceiling painted absolutely free.

The OC was enjoying explaining that they would all be coming and going in protective suits with masks and that nobody else was going to go in there unless they wanted asbestosis in a couple of years' time. Of course, there was no asbestos anyway, nobody had really checked, so nobody really knew. The UKHSNAAT was a fiction carried out by some 'Slappers' from the Royal Engineers. There was also a pub on the corner opposite and a small bookies next door to that.

They did not want the locals to get wind of anything, so the area was not placed out of bounds but patrols from the local unit in Masonic Camp were informed about the operation, but not every detail.

The next day they donned white protective suits with bright yellow masks and matching protective foot gear and they loaded up two vans which had magically transformed into UKHSNAAT vehicles which had been painted white as well.

'Nothing quite like fucking turning up discreetly, eh?' commented Kev whilst loading an UGS console onto the van disguised as a cardboard box full of paint tins.

'Fucking right, I might as well have "Shoot me" written all over me!' moaned Les looking in disgust at his bright yellow boots. "I feel like a fucking fisherman in a gas attack!' he continued.

'A fucking idiot who couldn't normally hit a cow's arse with a banjo could take us all out with a fucking popgun we stand out that much,' agreed Eddie.

Steve and the others laughed but they all got the drift, if they get into a firefight dressed like this they were going to stand out somewhat. The plan was to get out of the white and yellow stuff once in the building. But if the baddies got a whiff of what was happening they'd be sitting ducks walking from a van into the building.

It took about seven visits with the vans to get the guys and the kit into the building. It was an old one storey Victorian hall with parquet flooring and arched ceilings. Some offices had been built on the inside, originally meant to be temporary but looked about fifty years old. The place smelt old and slightly damp, neglect creeping up on a place that was slowly rotting away.

The Sappers made the place look like a building site on the outside and sealed off the windows so no nosey parker with a vendetta complex could see in. The building had a small kitchen and the OC had agreed that hot drinks were allowed plus they could cook food as long as they left the place as bad as they found it.

By 5pm they had moved in. Two patrols would work inside the building and another would linger about outside in civilianised patrol vehicles. Two members of 14 were going to drop into the pub and betting shop just to listen in and see if any interesting conversation was to be had.

Eddie's patrol had been given the CPC task, so they were in civvies. They had been growing their hair slightly longer than your usual squaddie since joining so by now they had enough hair to pass a sideways glance without attracting attention. Everyday they'd go to Ballykelly and pick up a different CPC vehicle. It was considered to be a bit silly to drive the same one all the time. Especially if four grown men were in the damn thing all the time. On the fourth day of the operation they were issued with an Austin Princess. This specimen was particularly bad and whomever the Army had bought it from must have breathed a huge sigh of relief, especially if they actually paid real money for it! The CPC's were up armoured and had steel plates in the doors and floors with bullet proof toughened glass all around. Unfortunately, the additional weight made the car a bit underpowered and 0 to 60 could be measured in minutes, and going uphill was just embarrassing.

'What a piece of crap!' said Les in disgust as he dropped into second gear to negotiate a very small slope. 'I hope the buggers at the top of the tree are not seriously thinking that we are going to chase anyone in this are they? We'd all be faster and more comfortable sharing a unicycle.'

'And safer,' added Eddie who was convinced the brakes were not up to stopping it if they ever decided to go down a hill. 'This thing deserves to be shot and finally put out of its misery.'

Every time Les changed gear the exhaust gave off a belch of black smoke so to anyone in the distance it must have looked like a tribe of asthmatic Red Indians giving off smoke signals whilst on the move, albeit slowly.

"I'm fucking sure that MT twat was fibbing to us when he said the temperature gauge was just stuck in the red, I'm sure this thing is about to blow all our balls off at any moment – that needle's pushing against the side of the dial like a mongrel shagging Twiggy's leg.'

They all tensed as the aging Princess started to go down Carlisle Road, which had enough gradient for the car to pick up speed. Les was terrified the brakes would fail and they would all end up in the Foyle River at the end of the road. Assuming of course they made it across the roundabout in front of the bridge and were not squashed by a surprise articulated truck. He changed down a couple of gears giving off the usual smoke signals to any Apaches nearby. This was the fifth time they'd done the loop and they were sure the locals had opened a book and were betting to see if they made it safely down the hill on each occasion they attempted it.

The two patrols inside the Salvation Army hall had sorted themselves out for the five days or so they were going to be in there. Compared to a hole in the ground this was paradise. They took turns to guard the place and operate the equipment. They were in touch via radio to Ballykinler and HQNI at Lisburn and the UGS hardware was performing well in the target's house. However, they were a bit worried they might have to take up playing brass instruments and gathering at points in the town centre to play *Onward Christian Soldiers* if they stayed too long. All was going well except for the selection of CPC vehicles that were only fit to take part in clowns' acts in circuses.

After another two days of using decrepit vehicles the 'Tea Leafs' were well and truly fed up driving around trying to look like they were doing something useful. They were always wondering if the car they were in would blow up or try to jump into the river after a long and terrifying free-fall down a steep hill. The OC noted that they were probably in the car for too long and decided to change things a bit so the locals would not get suspicious. Because Kevin and Les had the longest hair, plus as Kevin's mastery of the sport of kings was legendary, it was decided that they would infiltrate the bookies for an afternoon dressed in civvies looking like a couple of unemployed lazy gits, they'd fit right in. Lazy gits with pistols of course but lazy gits all the same. Something the OC felt they could easily achieve without too much effort. Their job was to just listen in and see if anyone had noticed that the Salvation Army centre across the road had suddenly become an Army base of sorts.

Steve and Eddie were given a more traditional task of working with the local Roulement Battalion and to help man the permanent VCP at the bridge end of Carlisle Road. This meant full uniform and flak jacket carrying an SLR and basically being an almost stationary target for a terrorist with sniping for a hobby. Steve was an expert in recognising the 'players' so he could, for a day or two, report if any known baddies were driving or walking along Carlisle Road with a possible intent to get up to some mischief. Eddie was along to operate the radio should Steve need to tell the guys in the Salvation hall if any problems were possibly coming their way.

The operation was going well and the UGS microphones were picking up good intel on what the top brass of PIRA were intending to get up to in the next few weeks especially during the Queen's visit. The OC was getting suspicious as it was just going too well.

After another day and with no apparent interest from the Derry Brigade Homemade Explosives Association, it was obvious that the locals had no idea what was happening. Les and Kevin went into the betting office for an hour or so to bet on the gee gees and to listen in. After about twenty minutes a scruffy middle-aged man, who had obviously had one over the eight, suddenly decided that he should get some winnings without having to complete the risky business of placing a bet. He pulled out a pistol and whilst waving it about started shouting that everyone, meaning all four of them in the betting shop, and that included the lady behind the glass counter, had better,

'GET ON THE FECKIN' FLOOR OR GET FECKIN' SHOT.' Les looked at Kevin, who seemed just about to disarm the assailant and place said pistol up his arse and pull the trigger, indicating that they should lie down as ordered. Kevin grudgingly got down and lay on the floor mentally noting that if he got killed by that twat with the gun he'd make sure that Les never ever forgot it!

Next the highly organised master criminal ordered the betting shop teller to, 'HAND OVER ALL THE FECKIN' MONEY, YA BITCH!' The teller responded by grabbing the £15.14 that was on the premises out of the till. She slipped it under the glass whilst looking at the assailant with undisguised disgust.

'Brian Slevin, don't you ever call me a bitch again, I'll be tellin' Sean about this caper and he won't be happy, now get out, ya bastard!'

The robber turned and ran out the door and, wobbling due to an excess of alcohol, ran into Hawkin Street still holding the pistol. About forty yards away up the hill a four-man Army Brick was meandering down the road. They couldn't believe their eyes, a man holding a pistol in broad daylight and in the street, what a target, they couldn't miss. The target that was armed with the pistol would be lucky to hit the light bulb on the street lamp over his head let alone four heavily armed squaddies with high velocity rifles fifty yards away. They on the other hand couldn't miss from that range! But unfortunately, the niceties of the yellow card had to be adhered to, so the Brick Commander shouted,

'STAND STILL! DROP YOUR WEAPON! WE ARE ARMED SOLDIERS!'

The man looked up the road and visibly, perhaps actually, shit himself. The gun clattered to the ground as he immediately dropped it. The four squaddies up the road sighed audibly in disappointment as the gunman took their advice. The now ex-gunman, turned down the road and began to leg it. The Brick Commander and his three section members followed suit and charged down the hill. At this point Kevin and Les rushed out of the betting shop to see four fully armed soldiers running after the tipsy gunman, as they turned right down Carlisle Road as well. Kevin and Les decided to follow after them so also started to run down the hill. The gunman, realising that perhaps his days of running and doing other such sport-like activities were perhaps behind him, decided that the best thing to do was to run towards the river and jump in it as a desperate bid to get away from justice. He drunkenly reasoned that the four fully armed soldiers would not be able to swim after him in flak jackets, as they'd drown - he was right!

As they all ran down the hill Steve and Eddie saw them coming down the hill. Steve initially wondered why Kev and Les were chasing a four-man Brick down the hill but then noticed the older chap, complete with red face, running in front.

Steve decided to act, raised his rifle and shouted,

'STOP, STAND STILL!' The man being chased by the four hairy arsed squaddies declined this invitation and instead took a sudden hard left and disappeared down an alleyway towards the river. The soldiers all screeched to a halt and turning down the alley decided to follow him. Seconds later Kevin and Les also scooted down the alleyway. As Kevin and Les cleared the alleyway they could see the man was just mounting the wall that indicated the river's edge. He jumped off the wall and disappeared from view. The four soldiers rushed up to the wall and looked over it and into the river. They paused for a few moments and, ignoring the potential threats from terrorists and scumbags, started to fall about laughing almost with tears in their eyes. Kevin and Les, now sensibly walking so as not to get shot by the soldiers, walked up to the wall and peered over it and immediately burst into laughter. The gunman was up to his waist in mud with one armed pierced by the rusted handle of an old discarded pram. Luckily, he had missed an upturned old bike by inches. Unfortunately for the robber the tide was now out and the River Foyle had become a rubbish-strewn mud flat.

The RUC and an ambulance were called and the robber, amongst much unwelcome mirth, was eventually soggily extracted and arrested. It turned out that the gun he had was a toy he'd borrowed from his son that morning.

Things calmed down and Kevin and Les went back to the bookies to find out that Kevin had won a small fortune on an accumulator but unfortunately due to the robbery no funds were available and for the second time in an afternoon the bookies teller received less than complimentary comments.

After this much welcomed interlude the operation was carefully wound up and the NIPG left the Salvation Army hall with a newly painted ceiling courtesy of the Royal Engineers but they'd never know that.

The operation was a success by all measures. It was discovered that the master scumbag in the house under surveillance indeed had a plan to store weapons and other paraphernalia designed to deprive innocent lives. Due to the level of detail obtained eight of his minions were arrested and put away for a significant amount of time due to being caught red-handed, apparently by chance, doing something very illegal. A few large arms dumps were 'discovered' accidentally thus removing the Derry Republicans Brigade's ability to be nasty to anyone for a long, long time. However, the main scumbag himself was not arrested nor even charged with littering… strange!

In the CPC on the way back to Ballykelly Les announced,

'When we get back I'm gonna have a shit, shave and shampoo, a fucking good meal, a beer or two and a damn good shag… and then I'm gonna take these fucking civvies off!'

Falklands, Wireless Ridge, May 1982 – 'Blue on Blue'

Les was rocked by the impacts even though he was over four hundred yards away. The 105mm L118 guns of 97 Battery were bang on target. As he watched the rounds hit home he could feel the blast on his face. Out on his own near Mount Tumbledown, on the wrong side near Wireless Ridge, he was in his element. His mission was to bring accurate fire down onto the enemy but if the Argies saw him he'd definitely be very dead, very quickly. He was bringing fire down onto the HQ of the 5th Marines Regiment to soften them up prior to a night attack. He was always amazed that artillery could come in this accurately even though the gunners couldn't see the target.

The walk up to his current position was hellish and certainly as hard as anything he had to do during his selection for 'The Regiment'. He'd been in it about eighteen months and was still considered to be a sprog. He'd managed to do a few courses but in comparison to the others he was a mere beginner. He keyed Morse code into the radio and then sent it off, the PRC 320 was a state of the Art HF radio and he'd used one before in the NIPG. However, this one had Morse store and forward. He would enter the message into the machine and then when he was ready it would squirt it at high speed across the ether to whoever was supposed to receive it. Since doing this job he had to admit that he had a preference for Navy fire missions and he had just been working with HMS Ambuscade and they were so accurate it was scary.

He waited for the rounds to hit home from the latest fire mission he had sent to 97 Battery. He was using a new secret system that they had deployed using UGS as a base for the electronics. Basically, it could work out where the enemy was where you were and send the correct co-ordinates.

All of a sudden, he was being blown about like a rag doll, explosions all around him. Huge chunks of earth were flying high, and the blast hit his body and winded him. He could feel the superheated air blowing past. He hugged the ground whilst the deafening and deadly barrage blew up around him. He felt puny and completely beyond help. He tried to push himself into the ground, he just wanted to live. Then it was silent. He was dead still and then he surprised himself by breathing in. He had held his breath all the while as artillery explosions that close tend to push the air out of your lungs. At least he was alive. He checked himself all over. Nothing, not a scratch. His head cleared a bit and he wondered what had happened. Those were British artillery shells! What went wrong as they almost killed him? He switched to voice on the radio as he felt that this was worth the risk. The other end said that they had received a properly formatted fire control order and they followed it. He looked at the UGS display and immediately realised that the system had switched the grids. He was looking at a software bug that almost killed him. He radioed that in and a quick process was thrashed out that made sure they would confirm the info before pulling the trigger.

He guided the shells in again and again until they had seriously impacted the Argentine Marines' ability to fight a war. Night came and Les hid away whilst the battle for Tumbledown was fought. He heard the gunfire plainly. A few hours later the battle was over and he trusted the Scots Guards had indeed triumphed. He laid back and looked up at the stars. In the stillness he started to hear other noises. It was crying and wailing and was coming from the 5th Marines direction. For hours he heard the poor sods crying to God and their mamas, their weeping and screams of pain would not cease. He found that he could drown it out by pulling the sleeping bag down over his head, but after a while the sounds of misery would creep in.

He fell into a sleep and after a short while was wakened by the noises of footfalls and jangling kit. He slowly moved until he could see through his hide and saw British soldiers about fifty yards away. He stored his kit and stood up surprising four Scots Guards not twenty feet away. He went over and greeted them, and they were amazed but sort of realised the unit he was from. They exchanged news and Les, after a while, shouldered his Bergen and started to walk back to Mount Kent. The Scots Guards watched him walk away.

'Nice bloke,' one of them said and then they immediately forgot him. The six footers adjusted their kit and moved on into Port Stanley and became a little part of history.

Chapter 15

Tea and Buns

Coleraine - July 1977

They were all woken up early and rushed over to Lisburn for a briefing without any breakfast.

'Get on the fucking vans and stop your effing whinging,' said Sergeant Major Bruce in his best caring voice, 'I'll have a good layout ready for you when ya get back after the briefing. In the meantime, eat as many fucking biscuits as you can get in.'

The vans all pulled away as one and within the hour they were in the HQNI briefing room again quaffing coffee and eating biccies. The top brass was very much in evidence as the commanders from both 39 and 8 Brigade were present as was God himself in the persona of Commander Land Forces Northern Ireland, a bespectacled gent whose quiet and polite manner hid a very determined man. His briefing was quick and to the point. Basically, the Irish Government had just changed and now a guy called Jack Lynch was the Taoiseach heading up what was their version of the Labour Party. Kevin whispered to Steve as he was master of all knowledge,

'What's the fucking T shag, that some Irish Druid or something?'

'It's what the Irish call their President, it's pronounced Tee Shook.' Steve noted the sudden silence and the fact that all the big bosses in the room were looking intently at him. 'Sorry, sirs!' said Steve.

The general continued and pointed out that Jack Lynch was the guy in 1969 who hinted that the Irish Army should not stand idly by and allow the British and the Northern Irish to massacre Catholics. It also coincided with the Queen's Jubilee and the fact that she would be visiting Northern Ireland as part of the celebrations. When and where was a closely guarded secret, but the IRA had already stated that they were going to make her Jubilee visit a memorable one. The general ended his bit by saying that for the next two months they were going to close down the Republican terrorist movement and if one of them so much as picked his nose he wanted to know about it.

Both the other commanders also spoke a bit but largely said the same as he had. Then after they had walked the room giving crumbs of praise to the troops they were gone and it was left to the Intelligence Officer to give the detail on what they were going to do. Kevin was into his twentieth biscuit and was so full of coffee his bladder was causing him breathing problems. The plan was similar to most of the others they had received. Go in at night, hide, watch baddies and get piccies, then sneak away again. However, Steve's patrol was given a more difficult task for their target. The Intelligence major explained.

'The guy you're watching has never even been arrested so we do not have his fingerprints or any good pictures. Now we know he has been a bad boy and we'd like to see if we have any matches so that we can put him away before Her Maj visits. He is the area commander and it would be a big blow to OIRA if we nabbed him.'

He went on to point out that this punter was considered to be very dangerous indeed and could call up some pretty serious players at very short notice. So, they were advised to do their very best to not be seen.

Much later the van rattled away after it dropped off its four packages. It was a full moon and as it was June it was not going to get dark until about 9.00 pm and, as it would be light again at close to 4.30am, it did not leave much time for digging out a hide. It was a long tab in as well so they went at it with a will. There was a slight mist which would help, but the Bergens weighed in at ninety pounds plus and along with their webbing they were surprised they could actually move. The effort of merely carrying the weight without having to remain tactical and ready for a firefight at any moment would have been hard enough. Even so they crossed several fields of longish grass which the mist was making moist. Their boots were getting wet and this also meant they were leaving footprints. A trail that any half blind, half stupid excuse for a terrorist could follow, let alone one who had actually listened to their training in Afghanistan, Libya or wherever it was fashionable to do that these days.

Having crossed several hedgerows Steve got them into all round defence to listen to see if they were being followed. Grateful for the rest and sweating hard they listened and observed. It appeared that they were of no interest to anyone with murderous intent except for the fifteen or twenty cows that were right next to them and were following them. Cows are very curious and will follow well-armed and equipped soldiers across fields just for a bit of a break in their normally quite humdrum day.

'Bloody fucking stupid cows! I can't hear a fucking thing in this. The mass bands of the entire Guards Division slapping their dicks on endless bass drums could be following us and I would have no fucking idea,' exclaimed Les in disgust.

Steve decided to give it up and they moved on. Field after field came and went. Eventually Steve got them down again and gave them the signal for the final RV. They were about four hundred yards from the target and if they got bumped or compromised this is the spot where they would meet before bugging out pronto. They set off on their last segment and this time they were very, very tactical. Suddenly there was a loud cough and Steve almost jumped out of his skin. He spun around ready to dispatch the offender in a display of fire and wrath, but a cow looked back at him forlornly.

'Fucking cows again,' he whispered angrily, 'scared the piss and shit out of me.'

There is nothing a human being can teach a cow about moving quietly at night, plus a cow's cough is very similar to a human cough and when you're sneaking along thinking you're alone and a cow coughs just behind you, it can quite ruin your night. They got to about two hundred yards from the target house and it was time for Steve and Les to do the customary recce and find a suitable spot to go Paddy spotting from. Eddie and Kevin took up fire positions with their weapons and placed the M79 between them. If Steve and Les needed to bug out it would be hard for them to turn and fire so all the serious hardware stayed with the cover team.

After about an hour Steve and Les returned. They'd found a likely spot and it also meant hardly any digging at all. It was a sharp but natural drop in the ground at the intersection between three fields and it had a great view of the target house. They started the process of merging in with the background. Once done they could see that the hide was perfect. It was almost impossible to see unless you were standing literally on top of it. They slowly occupied it and got out their entire camera paraphernalia and their collection of varied bang sticks were made ready in case unwelcome visitors came prowling. Now well-rehearsed in the routine Eddie and Kevin nodded off and Steve and Les took first watch.

A couple of hours later and it was Steve and Les' turn again to watch the house. Eddie and Kevin, just prior to having some scoff and occupying their gonk bags, looked apologetically at Steve. Steve gestured as if to say 'what'? They pointed out through the slit towards the house and all they could see was cows' legs. All the cows in the field were gathered at their corner no doubt looking directly at their hide.

'How long have they been there?' Steve asked. Les was just stretching his legs and rubbing his face to remove the sleep.

'About an hour,' said Kevin, 'the farmer let them in and the first thing they did was gather at this corner and then started fucking looking at the hide.'

'What do you think, Les, think the farmer will rumble that there is something here?' Steve sounded worried knowing the fact that the farmer was a serious player and if compromised they'd be in deep shit.

'Do I look like a shagging cow psychiatrist or something? I've no idea. I suppose cows do tend to gather about the place and just look at stuff. I doubt the IRA has bred a secret super cow that seeks out observation posts. We'll be OK, but let's keep a good watch out just in case.' He paused and said, 'Eddie, best check the radio before you kip in case we need a taxi to get us the fuck out of here.'

Eddie and Kevin had a quick bite before going to kip whilst Steve and Les kept watch. Eddie remembered to check the radio link. It was good. After a while the cows moved a little and Steve and Les were able to see where the farmhouse was but only a part of it. But that bit of it was now shielded by the trailer of an articulated lorry. It was completely blocked.

'This is fucking ridiculous we've been here almost twelve hours and we haven't even seen the fucking house yet. How can we get these cows to move?'

'Dunno,' uttered Les defeated, 'we don't tend to 'ave cows in Brick Lane.' He paused and added, 'Well not four legged ones anyway,' and giggled impressed by his own humour. Steve ignored him and got onto the radio and informed HQ of the situation.

Eventually the cows moved on, but the articulated trailer stayed where it was covering the view of the buildings. Steve decided that a close recce was in order and on handover told the rest of his patrol that they'd be popping out that night to run a few errands down at the farm. Kevin and Eddie took over from them and they settled down to sleep. Eddie and Kevin had been stagging on for about an hour when they roughly woke up the boss and Les. He shook his head and looked up. They knew not to speak when woken up as it may be a situation where any noise may give them away.

'Eh, Steve we thought you'd best see this.'

'What?'

'Er, look across the field, there's a guy coming towards us.'

Steve looked through the slit and about eighty yards away there was a chap coming towards them. They did not recognise him as a baddie but were very surprised to see that he was carrying a very large wooden tray.

'Stand to,' whispered Steve. They didn't need telling. Kevin cocked the Bren and Steve loaded up the M79. Les readied the L42 and had the guy dead to rights via his scope, he'd be dead instantly if he tried anything. The man kept coming closer and closer. The other patrols radioed in and tried to alert Steve's team and they acknowledged they could see him.

'Is he alone?' Steve asked no one in particular as he walked closer.

'Seems to be,' whispered Les, 'no one else about.'

'Get your pistols out if he gets too close all this shit will be useless plus he may just walk past us.'

As he got closer the group could see that he had a tea pot and cups with a round of sandwiches on it with tea cakes. The man got to the fence line and put down the tray about ten feet from the hide.

'Hello, boyse, I know ya there so me wife thought you'd like some refreshment. Cuppa tea and some bacon butties seemed appropriate. I don't know what you're looking at, but the cows gave you away big time. The wife and I moved in about two weeks ago. I'm a sergeant in the UDR meself so I kinda know how you operate.' He smiled. They stayed silent but realised they had been seriously compromised.

How bloody embarrassing, thought Steve, *found out by a bunch of cows and a UDR man, a part time fucking soldier*. Steve whispered into Eddie's ear,

'Eddie get on that fucking squawk box and tell those twats back at base they have made a fucking big mistake, ask them to check the facts.' Eddie did as he was asked and after a couple of minutes grinned at Steve.

'We're looking at the wrong farm; they gave us the wrong details.'

Steve looked out the slit and said loudly to the UDR guy,

'We're gonna come out, if you move one bleeding iota you'll be plugged by a sniper not more than two hundred yards away to your front do you understand?'

'Yes, I do,' announced the UDR man quite nonplussed.

Steve's group answered by breaking out of the hide and pushing the guy to the ground and searching him very thoroughly.

'Now take the lid off that teapot,' Steve ordered. The farmer acquiesced, and steam duly rose from the hot tea inside.

'Eat a sandwich, not the top one the third down, that one.' Steve pointed to the third sandwich from the top. The UDR man twigged and did as he was told. It all looked pucker. Eddie grabbed a sarny and demolished it in one go.

'Bloody lovely grub.'

'So, who do you think we are?' asked the UDR man.

'Someone else, who do you think we are?' Steve asked curtly.

'The SAS of course,' the farmer said.

Steve thought for a moment.

'Sorry, please accept our apologies but we thought we were observing someone else, we got the wrong details. We had to check that you were clear, but we're not the SAS just the local regiment covering the ground.'

'I understand that,' he said and went on, 'we have to do that all the time.'

'Do what all the time?'

'Lie about what we're doing.' The UDR man sounded flabbergasted that he had to explain this to *them*.

'How did you know we weren't IRA or someone setting you up?'

'You were too good and around for too long, the bad guys aren't that patient, they'd have popped in, blown me away and be gone again,' he looked relieved, 'although initially I wasn't sure.'

Eddie nodded to Steve, Steve looked around and coming up the field was the farmer's wife. She was bringing more tea.

'Why the trailer?' asked Steve as an afterthought.

'I put adverts on it and park it near the road for my farm shop.'

As Steve and the crew knew they were being covered by three other patrols they felt safe to indulge in the farmer cum UDR man's hospitality. They finished their tea and gulped down the sandwiches. Over the radio came the order to bug out with an RV to join the box vans.

They tidied up the hide and got all their kit out and were about to fill in the hole when the farmer said he'd do that with his digger, take him a few minutes that's all.

Les suggested that perhaps they should be issued with a digger for this job.

'We'd have to carry the bloody thing if we did,' Eddie sadly announced. They all laughed even the UDR guy.

A few hours later they were back at Ballykinler their kit cleaned and weapons handed in so they all went to the cookhouse for a meal. When they returned each one of them had a fresh pint of milk on the locker next to their beds.

'Bastards!' was all Les could manage before they all burst out laughing.

Germany, Münster – October 1982. Mutually Assured Destruction!

Eddie's signals detachment were all in the Signals store drinking tea and, helpfully and skilfully, watching 'Czech' charge the Clansman radio batteries. 'Czech' was a tall chap whose real surname of Ciechoniak was impossible for the average squaddie to pronounce, spell or even mumble. Therefore, even if his family had come from Poland he had been christened 'Czech' by the green mafia and that was the end of it. Charging Clansman batteries was achieved using a large complicated looking green box that had a myriad of red, orange and green lights accompanied by lots of switches and sockets with what can only be described as a generous portion of spaghetti-like cabling coming out of it. The general idea was to attach the battery to a cable, trip the switch to start charging and eventually the complicated light array would go from red to green to indicate the process was completed and you had a charged battery. It was incredibly simple, but it gave the appearance that you needed a PhD just to get it out of the box.

At that point a young, new and very green second lieutenant by the name of Lieutenant Whent, uninvited and unexpected, invaded their womblike store as if lost.

'Sorry, chaps, sort of lost the Company Office, can you point me in the general direction?' His middle-class Surrey accent had an edge to it that conveyed contempt to anyone who had less than a couple of million quid in the bank.

Eddie and the others decided not to get up and stand to attention, as is customary at these times, as the sprog wasn't worthy of that honour just yet. Eddie paused for a moment and took a swig of tea. He responded in his best 'I'm just a thick squaddie' voice.

'Yes, sir! It happens a lot to newly commissioned officers for some obscure reason. It's behind the door you just walked past about ten feet away. It's the one with the sign that says, 'Company Office' in big red letters on a white background. If you still can't find it, come back and we'll draw a map for you complete with directions and hand drawn pictures, sir! Eh, was there anything else you required?' The sarcasm seemed to be lost on the young wart as he was watching the battery charger very keenly.

'Eh? No, Corporal but thanks anyway. Just as an aside, what is that thing for?' He said this whilst pointing in that limp way that public schoolboys

seem to master at an early age just after they get issued the chinless wonder look.

Before Eddie could demonstrate his technical skills to the officer in describing what a Charging Set, Mass, CSSU 6574 Clansman did, 'Czech' jumped in and very coolly and with immense authority on the subject stated,

'It's a Portable Encapsulated Nuclear Incoming Signal System, sir! It uses Doppler Shift radar technology to detect nuclear missiles equipped with sub 10 megaton devices and tells us to within a hundred yards whether or not it will impact close to our location.'

The others looked at 'Czech' with undisguised admiration and awe as they thought it was just a battery charger, and then they looked at the young officer whilst he digested the information. The officer then asked 'Czech' how they knew a missile was inbound. The others in Eddie's detachment were equally keen to hear how it worked and just like at Wimbledon during tennis they all swivelled their heads around until they faced 'Czech' again.

'Well, sir,' Czech began, 'when the lights show steady red it means that enemy missiles are within our tactical area of responsibility are fuelled and ready. This information is passed to the device by military NATO satellite technology. If the light goes green it means that a missile is inbound and that means we must send a FLASH message to all call signs instructing them to don NBC suits immediately. Flashing red means it will impact within one hundred yards of our location. That's it in a nutshell, sir!'

'Wow, that's impressive. Anyway, I'd best be off to see the OC as I think I'm a little late. Bye, chaps.' He half saluted in a slightly embarrassed way and left their bijou store en route to the Company Office next door. Once gone Eddie's little detachment fell about their store laughing until tears broke out.

Three months later they were on exercise at the Fulda Gap. This was a piece of ground that was strategically important should Warsaw Pact forces decide they fancied some 'Pommes frites mit Bratwurst' and started to pour over the Iron Curtain into West Germany. The Company Commander had called a briefing to inform his young Platoon Commanders what the plan was to stop the million or so Russian soldiers and accompanying T92 tanks using the meagre resources of BAOR[49], in particular the very meagre resources available to B Company. The Company Commander was mid-stream explaining his plan when suddenly one young officer screamed 'Incoming' and

---

[49] The British Army of the Rhine – the tiles of all British Forces in Germany

ran full pelt out of the HQ shelter leaving a bemused Company HQ staff and the remaining Platoon Commanders wondering what was happening, and why Lieutenant Whents' platoon were donning Noddy suits like they were going out of fashion.

About an hour later Eddie and 'Czech' were stood to attention in front of the Company Commander being asked to explain why they were in possession of a top secret Tactical Nuclear Detection Missile System Called PENISS when the remainder of the British Army thought it was just a plain battery charger. Furthermore, they were told to apologise to a certain intellectually challenged young officer regarding their behaviour and to explain to him the correct procedure on finding out that a Tactical Nuclear Missile was inbound to their location, which was typically, to bend over as far as physically possible and then attempt to kiss your own arse goodbye!

Chapter 16

Phone Box Vandalism

July 1977

Eddie looked up at an angry sky with black clouds scudding along in the wind. The moon, although full and bright, struggled to shine through. It was like a huge blue strobe light falteringly flashing on and off. The wind was strong and kept changing direction and the occasional smattering of light rain would pepper them as they edged along the wood line. The wind was blowing through the woods generating weird noises, like Irish banshees clattering about amongst the branches.

Steve stopped and gestured downwards with his hand, the signal was passed along and they stopped and got down in all round defence. They waited for about ten minutes listening to try and detect if anyone had any interest in them. It seems that at 3.30am they were not on anybody's social visit agenda. Steve pointed to the ground twice and then drew an imaginary circle around it indicating that this was the FRV for this op. The signal was duly passed along so they could familiarise themselves with the location. If they were bumped on the way in this would be the position they'd gather in after returning fire and fragmenting into different directions to confuse any ambusher. The rain continued, it was a light rain and fine, almost a mist. With the wind, the rain managed to get up their sleeves, into their jackets, into almost everything. They were not allowed to wear waterproof clothes as those made a loud rustling noise on walking and moving. Better to be quiet and wet than dry, noisy and dead.

They moved on and through a hedgerow and caught a glimpse of their next target. Through the rain the solitary payphone seemed quite sad with its single and not very effective light. As usual a few panes of glass were broken and the inside no doubt would smell of urine and God knows what else. Why anyone in their right mind at the GPO felt that a payphone was needed in such a God forsaken place was beyond the ken of the Intelligence Services. But what they did know was that regular calls were made from this call box to interesting numbers in the Republic of Ireland and North America. That was not illegal in itself, so it was determined that a few piccies of this nocturnal caller would be very useful, it might also be good to listen into what was being said without the whole of the GPO knowing that a wiretap had been officially placed onto it.

They decided that as they were only going to be there for two nights a full hide was not required especially as there was no other habitation for about five hundred yards in any direction. They saw a promising spot in the hedgerow. Steve and Les went and did a full recce and once everything possible about such a forlorn and lonely spot was known they occupied the hide. They made sure they were as close to invisible as possible, and then got out all their monkeys and parrots and placed them close to hand just in case a serial telephonist turned up with a love of co-op mix and AK47s. Eddie radioed in and informed the bosses that they were now in play. They knew that two other patrols were within three hundred yards of them no doubt with all their monkeys and parrots out as well.

Steve and Les, with Eddie and Kevin keeping watch, sneaked over to the telephone box in their best sneaky style and almost invisibly installed a UGS microphone. Eddie and Kevin never saw them from leaving until they were almost back at the hide. The dawn rose late and it was cold, the mist almost a light rain, was still blowing about and they were soaked to the skin. An easterly wind had started to blow gently but every time it blew it pushed freezing cold pins into their bodies. Steve had forbidden hot meals and even hot drinks as the steam, smoke and the smell may be enough to get them noticed by a passer-by, not that there would be many.

At about 9am Steve got them all stood to as a van had stopped by the phone box. It was a small yellow van and it was sporting the new blue British Telecom logo. A man got out and emptied the phone out, he was mumbling to himself but made it plain that he was impressed by the amount of cash in the phone, especially for such a fucking bogshite and dismal spot, as his opinion was overheard. Eddie almost burst out laughing in agreement even though he was drenched, cold and hungry.

For the rest of the day and the following night nothing happened. They carried on looking at the phone box up until about 9pm the next day when a dark blue car turned up and parked just across the road from it. The driver stayed inside but turned off the lights and waited. Les and Steve woke up the other two who had, surprisingly considering the weather, fallen asleep.

'Stand to, seems we have some business turning up.'

Eddie got the radio ready and Les started to get a good bead with a camera on the phone box and another on the car. Curiously the phone in the box started to ring and the man in the car got out and whilst pulling up his jacket cover in a vain attempt to stay a little bit dryer, went in and picked up the receiver. All they heard via the UGS was him saying yes and no and grunting in agreement. The call lasted about fifteen seconds and he ran across the road again and got back into the car and waited. Steve immediately saw the flaw in this operation... probably would have been a good idea to work out how to hear the other end of the conversation as well on a phone! After about ten minutes Kevin said to nobody in particular,

'What the fuck's he up to?'

As if in answer to the question a little red mini turned up and parked right next to the phone box. A buxom blonde in what can only be described as almost a skirt, very high heel shoes and a top so skimpy you could almost see what she had for dinner, got out and allowing her blouse to get quite wet, walked quite seductively into the phone box. They were all very awake now as the woman, who was quite mature but probably no older than forty, had an excellent body and certainly knew how to move in it.

The man from the other car slipped across the road and into the phone box and they both kissed and hugged intimately. Of course, with the UGS kit they could hear what was happening and it was obvious that the woman enjoyed getting the high hard one in public places and the guy was only too willing to oblige. The phone box due to the cold soon started to steam up and although they could hear what was going on the four could not actually see in the phone box hence it was probable that the two people inside the phone box also had limited visibility to what was going on outside.

'If she leaves her knickers behind they are mine,' claimed Kevin.

'Personally, I'd rather be playing with whatever is in those knickers,' stated Les and after a deep breath continued, 'he's a lucky bastard, I bet the husband has no bleedin' idea this is going on, eh?'

After about fifteen minutes or so it was plain from the sounds in the phone box that they were now 'well connected' so to speak. At this point in the proceedings a third car with no lights on came coasting down the lane and stopped very quietly about twenty yards from the phone box. A man got out and sneaked up to the phone box with what appeared to be two large straps.

'What did you say earlier, Leather? I bet that's the hubby and he's after revenge,' commented Kevin sagely.

'Well done, Sherlock are there any other dregs of knowledge that you'd like to share with us? Get his piccy you never know who he might be,' said Steve.

Without any preamble the new addition to the situation started to wrap the straps around the phone box and pulled on what appeared to be large buckles. The straps looked similar to the ones used by lorry drivers to secure loads. The two lovers had no idea that this was going on as was witnessed by the grunts and groans going on in the opaque glass box. When he was finished he walked away and disappeared up the road for about ten minutes. By this time, it was obvious that the two were by now beyond caring what was going on, especially the woman who was screaming out loud and using phrases that would put some famous female porno stars into a state of permanent embarrassment.

At that point the noise of a tractor was heard and it appeared moving along the road from the direction the man had gone in. It stopped in front of the phone box and the farmer arranged it so that the rear crane he had on the tractor was now facing the scene of the crime. Inside the phone box they had finished on a high and were now curious as to why something noisy had stopped outside plus they realised that they could not push the door open. All of a sudden the farmer attached a chain to an eye that he must have somehow fitted to the top of the phone box earlier and before anyone knew it he had ripped the phone box out of the ground and was happily driving off with it dangling from the crane at the back of his tractor. The phone box was swaying precariously from side to side. The woman started screaming, so did the man actually! As GPO red telephone boxes usually had a concrete floor they were surprised to see that the two were not left standing there, it became obvious that the farmer had put some form of floor in. He had planned this very particularly.

Les reacted immediately and realised that he had signed for the UGS kit on the phone box.

'He's taking my fucking UGS kit the bastard.'

'And a blonde tart into the bargain,' added Eddie laughing.

'OK, there's fuck all we can do here except get the kit back,' observed Steve.

'Let's go! Eddie get a message off and tell them what happened.'

'Righto, Boss,' exclaimed Eddie.

They moved off quickly in the direction of the now disappearing tractor following the noise whilst Eddie reported in over the radio. They were extremely fit so they could move fast especially now stealth was no longer that important. Steve had considered an IRA 'come-on' but felt that even they couldn't think up anything this entertaining.

They were trotting up the road when Eddie told Steve,

'OC wants us tested when we get back for hallucinatory drug abuse and the other patrols want to know what's happening as it sounds great fun and are asking do we need help?'

Steve laughed and replied,

'Tell them the 'Tea Leafs' need no assistance with a blonde and that we are just going to sort out the situation. Best add for them to get ready to leave as I think this op's done.'

After about ten minutes they caught up with the farmer and the stolen phone box. He was in a field and he had laid the box down in a prepared trench which was now half full of water. The phone box was about a third submerged and they could hear the woman's muffled screaming.

The tractor driver was now starting to use the front dozer blade on his tractor to push dirt in around the phone box. He was going to bury them alive!

Steve's group all moved into the field carefully as farmers were well known to have shotguns and the mood that this particular one was in right now meant he was possibly in the mood to use it. Steve shouted over to him.

'Oi! You got some of our kit in that phone box and we need to get it back, stop what you're doing please.' The fact that Steve and three others were pointing all manner of weapons at him made him pause for a moment and he turned off the tractor.

In the immediate silence he shook his head and said,

'Jesus! You mean you lot have been fucking her too? Well bollocks to it. You get her yourselves,' and with that he threw the key to the tractor away into the darkness.

Les was already on the phone box splashing about and cutting at the straps with his bayonet. Kevin helped him lift up the heavy phone box door, which luckily was facing upwards. Inside were two very wet adulterers the male half of which was still impotently holding the phone. Les apologised to the woman, leaned in and cut away the UGS microphone they had earlier secreted into the box. The man was obviously grateful that they had in fact saved their lives. Kevin caught full sight of the fact that she was not wearing her panties anymore; this meant him looking about for the item in some panic as his reputation was at stake.

Whilst this was all happening Steve had stopped the offended farmer walking away and was getting his details with Eddie radioing them over the ether to see if he was a player. It turned out that he was not, at least not a known one anyway.

The man who had just got out of the phone box was livid and stormed over to the farmer asking him, in no uncertain terms, why he had done it. It turned out that they were brothers. The farmer shouted back at him and denounced him, in every way he knew how, and wanted to know why he was having carnal relations with his wife. His brother was about to reply in kind when the words struck home.

'Your wife? That's not your fucking wife it's Jamie O'Shaughnessy's wife, Bridget! You prick!'

Mrs. O'Shaughnessy had by now managed to extricate herself from the phone box and to also extricate her knickers from Kevin, which was probably the more difficult of the two, and was now marching across the field somewhat wobbly in her heels, but marching all the same.

The farmer was confused.

'But the car! She was in Karmel's car, my wife's bloody car.'

Mrs. O'Shaughnessy filled in the gaps.

'Karmel comes over to my place and watches Coronation Street as you don't have a telly, you tight bastard! I then go out and shag your brother whilst Jamie's down the pub. I take your Karmel's car as I don't have one as Jamie is almost as tight as you are.' She paused but then continued with even more directed vitriol, 'And who are you to speak anyway, you screwed me just a few weeks ago, ya fucking hypocrite? Where were all your high and mighty morals then, eh?' She took off her shoe and started to hit him with it. The patrol felt sorry for him as it looked like a lethal weapon the heel was so long.

Steve and the others made their excuses and as discreetly as possible exited the field. They got no thanks for saving the two lovers but that was probably because all three of them were now engrossed in exchanging blows and insults of one sort or another.

'Should we not ask for the police as this was a definite attempted murder?' asked Les gesturing at the radio.

'I can't be arsed to get that involved and think of all that bleeding paperwork. It did us a favour though; no phone box to watch means no operation.' He paused and looked up. 'I'd loved to have seen his face if he had buried them when his wife turned up minus the car.'

They could see the box van through the light rain approaching up the hill so they paused and got down. Les called over to Kevin.

'I see she got her knickers back, Gus. I bet that was a blow?' Kevin reached into his breast zip-up packet and triumphantly held aloft a white rag.

'She got the flannelette from my cleaning kit and I got her panties, I'd like to see her trying to get into that stuff, wonder if she's noticed yet.' The other three all glanced at each other in panic and remembered Mrs. O'Shaughnessy and how she handled her high heel shoes.

'If she does notice I hope that pigging van gets here before she does,' muttered Eddie, looking fearfully up the hill for all of them.

UK, Chatham - August 1982. A Calculated Mistake!

It was Eddie's first day on the Education for Promotion course. This was a prerequisite to getting a third stripe, unless you were going to be the Regimental Provost Sergeant, in that case the ability to breathe, dress, wash and shave occasionally with the added skill of dragging knuckles along the ground was all that was needed. Eddie wanted to be a proper sergeant in Signals Platoon and that would need this qualification. He was doing the course at The Royal School of Military Engineering at Chatham, not unusual as he was at that time based in Dover. He was on the course with another guy from his own regiment called Steve. Steve was a well-known character in the regiment who could do stand-up comedy routines in the NAAFI and almost get the guys catatonic with laughter. He was a natural comedian. The course was being held in a large, draughty and barely furnished room that looked like it was an old Victorian accommodation block. The room was whitewashed and had parquet flooring and voices echoed slightly eerily.

The course teacher was a young female captain in the Royal Army Education Corp, and not a bad looking one at that. Good looks and the RAEC were usually mutually exclusive. In this case the whole officer selection process had gone awry and a good looking and shapely young lady was now trying to teach horny and generally sex starved infantrymen simple arithmetic and English.

The EPC was not difficult, but it did mean that the senior NCO corps of the modern British Army could all spell their name and get their age almost right when filling in forms etc. Eddie was not bad at math's but his mental arithmetic was rubbish, so his sister had lent him a calculator and this was allowed on the course. However, it was a model that she had used as a very small child in infant school. Every button was big, number shaped with a different colour for each one. It was designed for a five-year-old, but it worked and the arithmetic they were going to be doing was not far away from a five-year-old's level anyway. So, Eddie thought, 'What the hell, it will save me a few shillings', and took it along.

The captain walked around the classroom and introduced herself whilst giving a general outline of the course whilst all the squaddies watched the bouncy bits. Suddenly the captain spotted Eddie's calculator and picked it up.

'What's this, a baby toy?' she asked with her eyes wide in amazement.

'It's a calculator, Ma'am, I thought you being a teacher and an officer would know that,' he responded a little hurt by the childish inference on his calculator and by association, his manhood.

'But this is for a child, Corporal,' she chided as the calculator was at odds with the image of the heartless killing machine that Eddie should be representing. Steve, in a whisper all could hear, summoned the lady captain over to him and spoke conspiratorially into her ear.

'It's his sister's Ma'am and she's blind, she feels the numbers as she can't actually see them, thought you'd better be aware of that.'

Her face reacted like she had been stung by a scorpion and she reddened with embarrassment. She looked at Eddie like she had just accidentally killed his favourite pet rabbit.

'I am so, so sorry I wasn't aware your sister was blind, please accept my apologies.' She placed the calculator gingerly down in front of Eddie as if it might explode.

'I don't know why his sister bothers though,' quipped Steve to nobody in particular but loud enough so all could hear, 'she can't see the answers.'

Chapter 17

Pilot Error

July 1977

A few days later they were again clattering across the night sky eagle fashion in a *Scout* helicopter. This meant sitting on the floor with their feet out on the skids with weapons at the ready. They were flying tactical again which usually meant the pilot pulling tree branches out of the helicopter's undercarriage later. They suffered sudden ups and downs as the pilot tried to hug the ground as best as possible at the same time missing things like church spires, power cables and, at times, washing lines. Steve could well remember, before the NIPG, landing in a helicopter that had somehow managed to get a lady's bright red lacy bra entangled onto the end of the right skid, it was still a prized possession on the Sergeants' Mess wall of the helicopter squadron that won it.

They zoomed along seeing the lights of farms and small villages, car headlights moving along darkened lanes whipping past below them. The helicopter would occasionally bank and then tip forward onto a new heading whilst they all strained to listen to Steve and the pilot shouting over the noise through the intercom about the time left before drop off. The pilot, face and helmet partially lit up and looking unworldly in a light green glow from the instruments, was glancing almost unconcerned left and right as the world flashed by. They certainly felt alive!

The *Scout's* engines and rotors suddenly changed tone and the pilot landed the beast almost without a bump in the total darkness in a clearing that was probably close to an exact match to the diameter of the machine's rotors, possibly even a bit smaller. They offloaded their kit as quickly as possible and then in a flurry of noise and dust the helicopter was suddenly gone almost before they were all off. In the silence afterwards, they waited until they knew no one was about and then they skirted over to the nearest wood line. In all round defence Steve checked the map and his prismatic compass indicated the direction they needed to go in. It was a beautiful evening with a half moon and a gentle breeze; however, the odd scudding cloud told them there may be rain later. They moved in complete silence, slowly keeping about twenty yards to one side of the track. Every two hundred yards or so they'd stop and listen ready to dispense death and destruction to anyone foolish enough to rumble them. So far so good and after they had gone about two miles Steve ordered for them to stop and to get in all round defence.

Steve then informed them that they were, in fact, lost.

'Lost? What the fuck do you mean we're lost, Steve? It's not difficult to read a fucking map. What do we do now, call the fucking AA?' whispered Les.

'The pilot dropped us off at the wrong spot. This wood is too big we would be in the middle of a big field now if we were in the right place,' said Steve looking at the map for inspiration.

'Typical! Fucking fan jockey dropping us off at the wrong place. So where are we then?' asked Kevin.

'How in the name of a badger's arse would I know?' tempered Steve, 'I don't know where on the fucking map he actually really dropped us. Place look familiar to you, Kevin? Perhaps Les' girlfriend has shagged him near here, if any of you know where in Her Majesty's shithole of a province we are then tell me – otherwise shut the fuck up!'

In this situation, it was standard to keep going in one general direction until you could see enough to get an idea of where you were. Steve signalled for them all to move off. He had decided that they would continue going south until they came to something of note. The wood suddenly ended and they saw in front of them a huge field. They clambered over the fence and as usual Eddie fell headlong into the ditch on the other side.

'Fuck a bloody duck – Eddie shut the fuck up you're making enough noise to wake the bleedin' dead,' whispered Les.

'Well you carry all my frigging radio kit in the future then. You know I carry more effing weight than the rest of you lot put together.'

Steve butted in.

'Both of you shut up. Looks like there's a road up ahead.'

They followed the tree line down to where it met the road. The road was a B road – little more than a track.

'Which way?' asked Les.

'Buggered if I know,' said Steve. He paused, 'Let's keep going south.'

After about thirty minutes of walking along the track they came to a bigger road.

'Christ in a tent, Steve, don't you know where we are yet?'

Steve was getting worried – where had the pilot landed them? He could not see anything he recognised on the map near them.

They walked for about another two miles. Still no landmarks were recognisable on the map. Steve put his hand up and they all stopped.

He signalled and they all went up on the top of the right-hand bank and got into all round defence in the field alongside the road.

'Eddie – get on the radio and ask those stupid fuckers if the pilot would be so kind as to let us know where he dropped us, please!'

Eddie switched the radio on and after checking frequencies got through to their HQ straight away.

'So, what did they say?' asked Steve.

'They have just received a signal from the Fan Jockey Club; apparently they dropped us off at the wrong spot.'

Steve almost burst.

'Sherlock fucking Holmes, I already know that!'

'Calm down, Steve – they are just going to send us a grid of where he did drop us off.'

Eddie went back to the business of speaking weird stuff into the radio whilst Steve simmered in the dark.

Steve heard Eddie receiving a map ref in MAPCO a code used by signallers for map references.

'Steve! Here is the grid reference where he dropped us. They are saying that it is very near the bottom of the map.'

Steve looked quizzically at Eddie and then consulted the map with the grid they had.

'This grid is not actually on this map. From my reckoning it's about six miles south of the bottom of this map.'

'OK,' said Kevin, 'so we tab six miles north and we're back where we should be.'

'Er, not quite, Kevin. About two miles above the bottom of the map is the Irish border – plus we have walked about three miles so we are about eight or nine miles inside the Republic of Ireland without our passports. So, we are currently illegal immigrants who are armed to the teeth and the map doesn't tell me which way to go.'

'Guess we go back the way we came and keep heading that way.'

A blue flashing light, a long way off, could be seen heading in their general direction. They all saw it.

'It wouldn't be looking for us do you think?' asked Kevin.

'Nah, just a coincidence I imagine,' replied Steve, 'but we'll keep low until we get across the border again. Might be tough as it is light in about two hours – let's get tabbing!'

They moved off with a passion, a political incident was something they'd really not want to get into at this time. After about an hour it was obvious something was up as they'd seen four different blue lights flashing about the place and now they could hear some lorries, military type lorries. Les piped up.

'I think someone has bubbled us. I suppose the Irish Army hasn't got many *Scout* helicopters and I bet someone saw the fucking thing landing.'

'It's about one hour to sun up and we need a place to hide until dark, so get creative with the ideas, guys,' Steve half shouted to them. They were all exhausted as they must have walked something like fifteen miles overnight tactically, in full kit, with no food and with no sleep.

'There's a likely spot over there, Steve.' Kevin pointed to a piece of dead ground just twenty yards inside the rough wall of the field they were in. The grass was fairly long and apart from an aerial search someone could walk within fifteen feet and not see them if they were cammed up properly.

'Fucking ideal, well spotted, Kevin!'

They got down in all round defence whilst Les and Steve did a fast recce of the spot. Steve signalled for them to come in and they feverishly made themselves invisible.

'Listen, guys, serious field discipline OK. No hot food, no brews, no talking. Eddie get off a SITREP and tell them what we are doing. Staggered sentries two on two off, Les and I go first. We are not allowed to be taken prisoner by the Irish Army or the Garda because it's too fucking embarrassing, OK?'

They all nodded in unison and got into the routine. As the day progressed they could hear vehicles moving about but nobody came anywhere close to where they were. Also, there was no aerial activity either, it appeared the Irish Army's helicopter, if they had one, was being used somewhere else that day. The day passed uneventfully and they managed to get some scoff and some much needed sleep. Near dusk Steve let them have a hot brew and then gave them a warning order to get ready to move.

'Guys listen, I haven't heard any activity for the last couple of hours so either one of two things has happened. They know we're here and they have set up nearer the border knowing we have to go that way or they think we've fucked off home already and they have all gone away for a few Guinness's.' Steve paused.

'So what's the plan, Steve?' asked Les.

'OK, we're gonna go due west for a good couple of miles and go in near Dundalk, that means a heavy tab but less likelihood of being caught.'

'Sorry to ask, Steve, but what do we do if we look like we're gonna get caught?' It was always Les who asked the awkward questions.

'Good point actually. Let's get all the specialist kit into two Bergens and the other entire gunk into the other two. If it looks like we have no choice but to give up we drop a grenade into each and leg it for a bit. See if we can get away individually. Under no circumstances are we to engage with the Irish Army or the Garda in a fire fight.' Kevin looked crestfallen.

'What we just give up, no scrap?' he asked.

'I didn't exactly say that, Kevin but if it comes to it please do exactly as I say at the time, OK?' The OK signalled the end of the briefing.

'Right, Boss!' said Kevin quietly, almost as an afterthought.

They moved the kit around, recammed themselves up for night work and moved out silently. They were now fully alert moving silently through the night like armed wraiths. Every twenty minutes they'd stop and listen to see if they were being followed. After a few hours Steve halted them for a rest and informed them that they were now on the map again and he knew where they were.

'We're about two miles from the border. Dundalk is over there. We're going to stay this side of it and once parallel we will make for the border. Eddie send a grid in MAPCO so the arseholes who got us into this mess know where we are if we get caught.'

Eddie hunched over the radio for a while and did his magic.

'Seems we're an international incident at the moment. Irish Government knows something's up and have lodged a complaint at the British Consul in Dublin.'

Steve feared the worst.

'So someone is probably waiting for us up near the border, chaps, best get cracking. OK! Make sure you've got our very best cutlery on display guys, if we bump into someone I would like them to think it best to look the other way rather than challenge us, OK?'

They moved on through the woods and occasionally they could hear noises of people talking and laughing in the distance.

'Coppers!' whispered Kevin. 'I'd know that sound anywhere.' They moved on and after about two miles Les signalled rapidly for all to get down. They instantly got down and in all round defence. Nothing was said, if Les thought he heard something that was good enough.

After a minute or so they could hear footsteps moving through the wood, they were noisy, sloppy. An Irish Army patrol walked past them not twenty feet away, one of them was actually smoking a fag. It was most likely they thought that there was nobody out there and it was a fool's errand. Their passing was punctuated by a loud fart from one of them in the squad. The Irish lads all burst out laughing whilst their NCO scolded them and told them to be quiet, or words to that effect anyway.

Steve waited twenty minutes until he was sure they'd gone before he signalled they should move on again.

They got level with Dundalk at about 3am and now turned north. They were going to parallel Fork Hill Road and then break off across country towards Roskeagh and that should bring them into the Province. It was planned that they would stay about half a mile away from the road. They moved on, it was only about four miles to go before they were home and dry. They stopped again and listened. They could hear nothing, all was going to plan.

They got to within half a mile of the border when they had to cross a small road going east-west directly crossing their path. It was a very old road and over the years had created a deep cutting. They very tactically got into line abreast and climbed the fence as one. The idea was for them all to cross the road at the same time thus giving anyone interested only one opportunity to spot them rather than getting four chances. They tumbled down the high embankment, and reaching the road they all moved fast across it and started to climb the steep embankment on the other side.

'Excuse me,' a disembodied voice asked from out of nowhere. They all froze.

'Excuse me, are you the Brits we're looking for?' Two Garda walked out of the shadows.

They all looked around as one and looked at the two policemen. They automatically took up tactical fire positions in all round defence.

The two coppers were unimpressed and got closer and the taller one spoke again.

'What, has the cat got your tongue or something? Are you the people we're looking for?'

Steve was stunned, the two policemen were armed but neither had their weapons out, neither were they wearing body armour. 'The Pope' spoke up.

'I doubt it, Officer, we are tourists out for a walk but it was later than we thought and so are out later than we planned as we got a bit lost. But all is OK now so we're now off to our local B&B for some breakfast.' Steve said this in his most posh English accent. Kevin almost pissed himself.

'Are you now?' said the taller officer who was obviously in charge. 'And what's with all the weaponry then?'

'Well, we're enthusiasts, it's our hobby.'

'Well that's OK then,' the officer responded. 'I suggest you get away now off to the B&B or your breakfast will get cold. I think you'll find it's OK to use this road for the rest of the way now. There's a right turn up ahead that will take you all the way to your... er... B&B quicker. Those weapons look heavy but I am sure that's OK with you being enthusiasts and everything.' His soft Irish accent was lilting almost musical.

Steve was confused, was it some form of trap or something?

'Are you sure, Officer, I mean is it OK?' Steve stammered almost.

'Sure it is. Do you know how much effing paperwork we'll have to do if you fellas came quietly now, we'd be there forever. So, if you'd kindly disappear for your breakfast we'd be grateful plus we appreciate the overtime here.'

'Er... well many thanks, Officers. Bye.'

'Goodbye to ya now... an' God bless.' The two officers turned and slowly started to walk away. One lit up a cigarette.

They moved away and followed the road.

'Do you think soldiers cross the border a lot, Steve?' asked Les.

'They weren't exactly surprised, were they? Nice guys actually,' Steve added as an afterthought.

The box van met them with the customary urn of tea and WO1 Bruce to make sure his charges were well. He was intrigued by the attitude of the police and their hate of paperwork.

'It's the same the world over; I recall a similar incident on the Hong Kong border when I was there when...' Bruce started but he noticed the tea had been left alone and they were all asleep already, exhausted by the walk.

A few days later they were all sitting about in their room, loud music blaring from four different stereos. Steve was cleaning his boots and the others were generally sorting out their stuff when in walked WO1 Bruce.

'TURN THAT FUCKING RACKET OFF!'

They all leapt at their music machines and as one they turned them off. In the immediate silence the warrant officer quietly mentioned they had a visitor.

In walked a sergeant from the Army Air Corp complete with sky blue beret and resplendent in No.2 dress. He stood awkwardly in the middle of the room.

'Er... I was the umm... pilot who dropped you off in Ireland. I came over to apologise unreservedly. I'm very sorry.'

They all looked at him. Kevin, as usual only wearing underpants, moved over to him. He looked him up and down with undisguised disgust.

'You stupid cunt, do you know how far we had to effing walk?'

The pilot sergeant was embarrassed at being accosted by a private soldier wearing only his underpants, well he imagined they were underpants anyway.

Kevin smiled and put out his hand. The pilot took it.

'But at least you came and said sorry. That's a bloke for ya, well done. No harm done, mate, eh?' They laughed as Kevin broke the ice. The flight sergeant was flabbergasted.

They all came over and shook his hand and gave him absolution in the usual welter of swearing and insults as is the military way.

'Before I go I have a little something in the way of restitution from me and the other lads at 457 Squadron.'

With that he started to bring in four crates of beer with twenty-four cans in each. Not the small stubby ones but the nice long ones.

'Now that is what I call an apology,' stated Les.

Kevin was on the first crate like a demon, and grabbing two cans he immediately pulled the rings on both and, giving the pilot a can, toasted the Army Air Corp.

'Here's to the effing fan jockey club,' and took a huge mouthful. WO1 Bruce coolly sat down on one of the beds and grabbed one for himself. A few lads from the other patrols sauntered in sensing an opportunity. A party started, David Bowie started singing about life on Mars and they were off. The pilot was sent back several hours later almost comatose from alcohol in a Land Rover. Nothing was said. His colleagues in the squadron thought he'd come back with a broken nose as a minimum. That's what usually happened when they dropped the infantry off on the wrong side of the border!

Iraq, somewhere near Basra - May 1991. Winning the Fire fight!

C Company Commander heard the familiar crump of small arms fire followed by a slap of a bullet hitting flesh. 'The Pope', now a captain and the Company 2iC, lurched and was thrown as if an unseen hand had thrust him backwards. The major turned just in time to see the end of the small red explosion where the round hit Steve in the collar bone and was exiting out the back of his neck. Blood splashed across the company signaller as he was standing immediately behind Steve. Instantly the major returned fire with his SA80 in the direction of the sniper.

'STEVE'S DOWN!' he screamed. The Company Commander's bodyguard, a private by the name of Shearer, had his rifle up and was scanning with his TRILUX sight towards where the shots seemed to have come from but could not see the assailant. The major and Shearer alternately returned fire into the area where they suspected the sniper to be. With covering fire in place, the company medic looked at Steve with a measured eye and tried to forget that he was a close friend. Steve was bleeding badly from the back of his neck where the bullet had exited. He was coughing and spluttering uncontrollably with spasms every now and then.

'By the wound I think it was a 9mm round so the fucker's close, keep your eyes open it could be a set up!' the medic screamed out. The medic undid the top left-hand pocket of Steve's combat jacket and took out his first field dressing. They all kept one there so everybody knew where it was. The major and Shearer had stopped firing but neither had even glanced at Steve, their professionalism was needed now more than curiosity.

'Can the 2iC be moved?' the major shouted at the medic.

'I'm not sure, sir, I just don't fucking know!' The medic was scared and it showed.

'Then make a pissing decision on it, NOW!'

It was a low velocity round but the exit wound was near the spine. The medic saw that Steve was breathing unaided but his eyes were not responding to light. He was not happy about the location of the wound so close to the spine, so he made his decision.

'If we come under fire again I'll move him – if not we stay put. OK!'

'OK, you're the doc,' the OC responded as he attached a new full magazine to his rifle and scanned the area. The medic unpicked the M79 grenade launcher

from Steve's shoulder and threw it to Shearer with the bandolier of grenade rounds.

'Load up, Eddie!' he said quietly; he felt useless watching Steve gurgle and lurch every now and then. He was still bleeding badly but the dressing had staunched most of the flow. The medic was whispering in Steve's ear telling him to stay alive, to keep breathing, to fight it, to live! He'd never felt so useless in all his life. Suddenly three rounds whipped just above his head.

'HUNDRED, THREE QUARTERS RIGHT, CORNER HOUSE FUCKING TOP WINDOW, GUNMAN, RAPID!' Shearer screamed. More rounds came their way but Shearer's response was almost immediate and an M79 grenade rushed through the air straight into the window and exploded, closely followed by a second. The OC's rifle spat into the neighbouring windows whilst the medic moved Steve behind a low wall out of harm's way. The firing had stopped. The OC and Shearer took up fire positions behind the wall as well but not too close to each other, even a small grenade or explosive device would take them out if they were in a close group. In the immediate silence, they could hear approaching warrior AFVs. Help had almost arrived.

They operated on Steve for seven hours at the field hospital but they could not save him from becoming paralysed from the waist down and it was irreversible. The bullet had damaged the spine but the surgeon claimed that it was moving him without a neck brace that had done the damage; somehow and insensitively he had forgotten the bullet and that it was the bullet that had hit him first.

Steve regained consciousness a few days later and saw the medic privately after he was informed of the bad news. Steve told him it wasn't his fault just bad luck. All the guys comforted the medic and pointed out that if he had stayed where he was he would have been shot and most likely killed and not to feel bad about it. The medic knew all that but even ten years later sometimes when alone this one and other decisions he'd had to take would loom out of his memory, but the alcohol helped to keep his personal demons at bay.

Chapter 18

Surprise, Surprise!

Toomebridge - August 1977

The weather was hot and sticky and all of them were sweating profusely. The kit was heavy as usual with equipment, ammo, food and especially water. This was to be their last op and they were all extremely on edge as none of them wanted to pop it during their last gasp with the NIPG. In addition, it was a long tab into the hide area. This was an unusual insertion as they had to do a daylight move due to the distance involved. They were moving through a deep gorge somewhere in County Fermanagh, soon they'd stop and harbour up until dark when they would do the two mile tab into the final position.

Steve saw a likely looking spot about four hundred yards ahead. At the signal, they quietly broke track and did a loop behind their original path and hid in bushes to cover where they had just walked. Doing a snap ambush was SOP and it was useful to make sure you'd stay alive after you'd put yourself into the hide. They waited and listened to see if anyone was stupid enough to be following. Nobody appeared to be interested so Steve and Les left Eddie and Kevin at that spot. Steve indicated this was the FRV and off they went on a recce to see if the harbour area was safe and appropriate enough to hide from prying eyes during the day. After they left Kevin spoke quietly to Eddie.

'Fucking great! Last bleeding op and we have a huge tab in.'

Eddie lifted his hand for Kevin to be quiet as he was holding the headset of his radio up to his head and was obviously listening to a message.

'Zulu two one roger out,' Eddie whispered into the mouthpiece. Eddie got out his MAPCO kit and worked out the grid reference that he was sent. He looked at Kevin and rolled his eyes.

'Change of plan we have to go somewhere else and looking at the grid it's a hell of a walk.'

'What's the job?'

'Not sure but we have to rendezvous at an RV to pick up more ammo and night vision kit,' Eddie shrugged.

'More ammo? We have enough fucking ammo to invade Ireland between us.' He paused thoughtfully. 'I think some twat has come up with a right bloody nightmare for us this time.'

Eddie silently nodded. Eddie used his shaving mirror to attract Steve and within ten minutes or so Steve with Les covering his back both slipped into the RV. Eddie looked at Steve.

'Got a message on the blower whilst you were out. We have to change location and go to this grid plus we have to pick up additional ammo and night vision stuff.' He passed Steve the grid.

'Shit and crap that's a long fucking walk. When do they want us to RV?'

'Twenty-one hundred hours, and they said don't be late.'

Steve glanced at his watch it was now seventeen hundred hours so they had four hours to move tactically across six miles of farmland. It didn't seem far on the face of it but carrying one hundred and twenty-pound Bergens, webbing and weapons was no easy matter. Moving tactical requires staying out of sight which means following hedgerows and staying in the shadows, perhaps even crawling occasionally. It was a tough order.

'Prepare to move,' ordered Steve. They bustled and made sure all their kit was in order and then crawled away from the RV about ten yards in all directions.

Steve tapped his magazine quietly and they all got silently up and started to move alongside the track spaced about ten to fifteen yards apart. Moving tactically meant looking ahead and planning your route. Checking for booby traps, small wires, and even broken plants that meant others had been there before you. Moving tactical meant not making noise and staying hidden, using shadow and dead ground thus not providing a silhouette so someone can take a pot shot. They were used to this and did it almost automatically but not quite. If you became an automaton then that was very dangerous and you could get yourself killed with your entire patrol, so it had to be familiar but not routine. They didn't want to get sloppy as that could mean discovery and a potential ambush. If they were ambushed because they were sloppy there was also the embarrassment let alone the threat of death to contend. The other patrols would never let them live it down and nor would they.

Steve glanced around at his patrol and took a moment to watch. They were all good, *the bloody best,* he thought and hoped they'd all get through this last test. He shuddered suddenly as if someone had walked over his grave.

They arrived at the RV twenty minutes before they were due and again carried out a snap ambush. They found a nice piece of dead ground and they waited in all round defence until the radio told Eddie that they should send the commanders plus one in for a briefing. Suddenly from all around the RV soldiers silently got up and sneaked into the RV. All the patrols had been called together. Eddie was impressed as he had not seen anyone arrive.

In the RV the OC and CSM Bruce were cammed up and waiting for the patrols' commanders to arrive. Silently the commanders all sneaked into the small copse that they had commandeered for the briefing. It was OK to speak as they had serious all-round defence out as far as sound would go and they would get good notice if any unexpected visitors popped along. The OC got them in a small circle around a model that he had constructed for his briefing.

'Gentlemen, bloody well done I never saw any evidence that any of you had arrived and was bloody surprised to find you were all here. CSM Bruce and I thought we were all alone.' All the patrol commanders swelled slightly with pride as that was praise indeed coming from the small but wiry commander of the NIPG. He began his brief. It was a long one but in essence the local unit Intelligence team had good information that OIRA were going to attack a police station in Toomebridge in some force. The Galgorm Road Police Station to be exact. The attack was due to take place that night at about midnight. He also said they had details on their possible intended routes in and a group of about ten OIRA who would be going in by foot. The NIPG's part was to try and ambush the OIRA thugs before they even got into the town. The SAS were going to handle the operation in the town itself. Unfortunately, they did not know the exact route of these terrorists so the patrols were all given an ambush site to watch and if they saw said bad guys to engage and if required kill them. The OC warned them to be sure that they engaged armed terrorists and not groups of kids going into the woods for illicit drinking parties, devil worship, gang bangs or whatever they did in these parts for fun.

Steve's team plus one of the two Black Watch patrols were given a likely ambush spot. They picked up the extra ammo and additional night sights and sneaked back to their patrol. The Black Watch patrol agreed to meet them at an RV and once together they'd make up a fighting patrol and Steve would be the overall boss.

Steve's team bugged out and made it to the RV. They teamed up with the Black Watch and Steve briefed them and gave them their various jobs. Basically, the Black Watch guys would be the cut offs at either end of the ambush and Steve's team would cover the killing area. They all waited and listened to ensure they had not been followed and then they all glided into their positions like a well-oiled and quiet machine. Comms cord was set between the cut offs and the killing team. Arcs of fire issued and then the waiting began. It was tough doing ambushes as inevitably squaddies were very tired after all the work they had to do plus ambushes were almost always done late at night, just at the time when most people became sleepy and that's not a reference to that figment of Walt Disney's imagination either.

The big difference here was that if they did see a group of armed men walking by they were supposed to challenge them and only fire if they were, or threatened to be, fired upon. They had not been given permission to disregard the yellow card on this Op. It was a difficult dilemma to be in as shouting a challenge gave your position away. Steve decided that he'd rather give a correct challenge than spend ten years in Brixton for manslaughter. It was dark and they had night vision kit. If the paddies decided to fire back it was unlikely they would know where to shoot anyway. Steve decided to remind his team of the rules. He sneaked over to Les and whispered,

'OK, remember we do not have a get out of jail free card so I will give a challenge, pass that along.'

'What, those twats in Lisburn still have us on the yellow card? What do they think we're doing here playing crazy fucking golf or summat?'

'Yeah, I know but if someone does come along wearing an old balaclava carrying an M60 then we will have the drop on them, and they'll know that.'

'OK I'll tell Kevin but if any fucker even looks like he is gonna fire in my direction I'm gonna turn his head into mush.'

'But not until I've told them we're armed or we'll all go to Reading Prison and end up getting shagged like Oscar Wilde, but he enjoyed it, OK! I doubt you would nor would you appreciate ten years without much sunshine.'

It seemed Les got the message and it was passed along the group.

They waited and the usual sounds of the night crowded in: the shrieking howl of a fox seeking a mate, dogs barking and insects shuffling about and other clicking things. In the distance they could hear the odd car meandering along country lanes with the gear and engine tone changes that accompany winding lanes. A light rain started and once it had made them wet enough to be uncomfortable it cleared and the cloud disappeared to leave a bright full moonlit night. It was almost like daytime but in black and white.

The patrol waited in complete silence not moving an inch one hundred percent alert to any potential danger. Kevin used the starlight scope on the Bren to scan the area but nothing moved. At about 3am Steve felt a tug on the comms cord and then another one. This was serious as two meant it was not a mistake. The baddies were coming. Steve made a low noise that his team could hear but was barely noticeable more than a few feet away. They all gripped their weapons and got ready for action. At first one figure followed by another came into view about fifty yards down the track. They were walking quietly all holding weapons at the ready position. These guys were professionals, not your common or garden thug. Eventually Steve counted seven men about five yards spacing. They were all armed with a variety of weapons but at least three looked like AK47s. The remainder looked like World War Two vintage but dangerous all the same as bullets still come out the end. When they were smack in the middle of the killing zone Steve shouted at the top of his voice,

'HALT, STAND STILL, PUT DOWN YOUR WEAPONS WE ARE...' but that's as far as he got as two of the baddies turned and fired their automatic weapons in his general direction. Steve's entire team fired into the men. The terrorists kept firing for all the two or three seconds or so that it took for all to be killed outright. Kevin on the Bren had taken out three before the two guys who initially fired had taken their fingers off the trigger. Les had taken out one with a killing shot to the head. Eddie had shot one of them as he started to run away. Two had tried to escape and ran down the track but were taken down by the Black Watch cut off team. All of them were stone dead. Eddie and Les broke cover and ran down to the killing area. Les stood above the head of the first dead man and pointed his weapon at the man's head at point blank range. Eddie put his weapon down and examined the man to check he was dead. He crouched on the man with his knee in his back and rolled him over. Les checked the man for any grenades or booby-traps and shouted,

'Clear!' Eddie and Les cleared all the dead men one at a time.

Once done Steve shouted,

'AMMO AND CASUALTIES, INDIA ONE ONE?'

Steve's team all responded with their personal ammunition count and the fact that they were unharmed. Steve shouted again,

'INDIA ONE TWO?'

The Black Watch all responded in the same way.

'LEATHER, ARE THEY ALL DEAD?' Steve shouted what seemed to be a pointless question.

Les responded,

'AFFIRMATIVE.'

'INDIA ONE TWO ARE YOUR ENEMY DEAD?'

A slightly more distant voice responded in the same way Les had. Steve paused for a moment.

'INDIA ONE TWO ON ME – SECTION TO ALL ROUND DEFENCE!'

The four Black Watch guys doubled in to the immediate area and took up positions on the other side of the killing zone from Steve's team. Steve's team all turned around and faced outwards. The whole process had taken about four minutes from the first squeeze of the trigger. Now they'd wait and see if there was anyone else out there.

'Eddie, tell me you have been on the blower with all this back to our lords and masters?'

'All done, Steve, contact report, sitrep and ammo and casualty state sent. We are to stay in situ until assistance arrives. Acorn are of the opinion that it is unlikely that there are any others out there,' Eddie said matter-of-factly.

'Well let's not give them an easy one if there are, eh?' He shouted to the guys,

'STAND TO... STAND TO, I DON'T WANT ANY SUPRISES!'

Within twenty minutes two *Puma* helicopters had landed that were due to take away the dead terrorists for identification and post mortem, although with the number of holes in them cause of death would not be hard to determine. The OC and WOI Bruce came in on the first chopper and after examining the scene came over and warmly greeted the guys. He could see they were a bit strung out. He instructed the pilot of one *Puma* to take back both patrols ASAP. Initially the pilot objected but the OC reminded him that they had more responsibility to live soldiers who had just been in combat than dead terrorist scumbags. The pilot, noting the SAS wings high on the major's sleeve, agreed and within minutes they were in the *Puma* rattling back to Ballykinler. It landed on the main square and they all debussed with their Bergens, webbing and weapons. They moved away from the *Puma* as it lifted, turned one hundred and eighty degrees, and then flew noisily back to the scene of the action.

Steve put down his kit and sat on his Bergen placing his M16 between his legs, it was 6am. They all followed suit with their variety of weapons in a small circle.

They all paused for a moment or two, savouring the morning's silence, whilst one or two birds here and there punctuated the stillness with their ritual song.

Steve eventually broke the silence and said,

'Well, that's the end of that I suppose. End of tour, chaps! Day after tomorrow we'll all be on a three week leave and then back with our own guys again. I feel a bit like Donald Sutherland at the end of *The Eagle has landed,* when I say it's been a privilege to have served with you.'

They all stood up, picked up their weapons and Bergens and walked towards the block. Les said to no one in particular,

'I'm gonna have a good shit, shower and shampoo, eat a nice meal, have a couple of beers, a good shag… and then I'm gonna pack my fucking suitcase!'

Steve was coming to the close of his lecture and he felt the lesson had gone well. He loved teaching and had found that his disability did not get in the way of his current vocation. Steve was now a world class authority on medieval history, especially the crusades. A few more years and he'd probably be a professor. Not bad for an ex-grunt, he often thought. He did miss the Army though, not the stagging on, not the boredom or the occasional bullshit. He missed the camaraderie, the friendship and if he was honest, the danger and the risk. Life and mates were not quite the same in Civvie Street, it all seemed less intense. This was hard to explain to someone who had never been in the mob. When he did start to tell stories of his experiences they'd be the funny bits and the cock-ups, never the tragedies and the danger.

He summed up the lesson and started to take them through the homework that they would be required to do by Monday if they expected to pass his course. This class was typical of most he took and he knew all his students, especially the ones that just seemed to be a waste of space. Not because they were thick but because they were not there to learn. It seemed they thought that an education was their God given right and not a gift, something they should appreciate and nurture.

The Army had been less than generous with his compensation and made him wait what seemed to be forever. He was led to believe that he'd get enough out of the system to be able to at least get by. He was brought down to Earth very quickly by the petty thinking of the damned bureaucrat arseholes that just seemed to delight in trying to give a disabled serviceman as little as they could possibly get away with. Thinking about it made him feel bitter. Perhaps it was a blessing in disguise, he'd often think, as he would not be teaching if they had paid him handsomely for his lack of erections and the other embarrassments that he had to suffer daily.

He still saw some of his old buddies now and again but sometimes the talking got difficult. It had been hard enough when he was in the Army let alone now that he was in academia with a PhD to boot. He did try and avoid sophisticated subjects and tried to just be one of them. But he wasn't really, never was! He went to the Regimental functions and although he was treated well he often got the feeling that a lot of them felt guilty that they had gotten away with it whilst Steve was in a wheelchair. After the initial warmth of greeting old friends the talking became awkward with long pauses, as squaddies don't really know what to say to an invalid. So, they'd all just get drunk!

Steve finished giving out the assignment. It was a tough one and they'd be writing most of the weekend to get it done. Steve asked if there were any questions and immediately a few hands went up. He answered them with the air of someone who literally knows what they were going to ask, which was largely true as this was his tenth year doing this job and by now there were no new questions, until he came to Wilkes. Wilkes was a complete waste of space and effort, which really annoyed Steve because Wilkes was intelligent and had potential. However, as he came from a wealthy family he felt that education was just one of those inconveniences that you go through, to be overcome. Wilkes, with his serious face on, asked his question.

'Sir, I was planning on having a really sex filled weekend and I am wondering how, if I span the heights of sexual excess and, due to the stresses of my appetite in that direction, if I get too knackered to do this. Do you have any advice on how I could possibly get it all done?' Wilkes gave Steve a look of triumph as the others in the class giggled and laughed.

Steve looked coldly at Wilkes and waited for the noise to die down then said quietly,

'It's obvious, Wilkes, you use your other hand.'

Chapter 19

Beer Bellies & Double Chins

November 2017

Eddie arrived at the crematorium a touch early at ten past eleven. Whilst travelling there he had felt a bit self-conscious on the bus wearing his blazer with his regimental badge and his medals. He had been out of the Army some twenty-eight years now and was doing okay. He had somehow stumbled into IT and found out he actually understood some of it. He had managed to drag himself up to the level of a mid-manager and was fairly happy with his lot. However, Tony, one of his old comrades, had recently suffered a long and painful bout of cancer and eventually succumbed. He was an old Army mucker and friendship and protocol demanded that Eddie attended the funeral. Kevin arrived shortly after, then Pete, Les and finally Steve in his wheelchair. They huddled together and greeted each other warmly whilst commenting on the grey hairs of aging whilst complaining about the wife, the lack of money and sex. Other veterans arrived and were confronted by the usual swearing and vulgarity that ex-soldiers routinely expose each other to. Eventually the whole room was full of about sixty or seventy men of various ages, shapes and health all wearing the same design of blazer, badge and tie. The noise was loud and raucous laughter occasionally rang throughout the room.

The widow and the immediate family walked in, and someone shouted, 'Hup!' and the men present stood to and the room instantly became totally silent. She greeted the odd ex-squaddie she recognised or knew warmly whilst she was ushered quietly to the front.

The coffin of Tony, their departed comrade, entered and made its way down the aisle slowly, respectfully carried by grim looking comrades, his medals accompanied by a regimental peaked cap placed proudly on top. The coffin was placed with extreme reverence on the plinth whilst another veteran made a minor, almost invisible, adjustment to the deceased soldier's medals just to ensure they were perfect to the military eye. The current padre of their regiment had insisted on officiating and two buglers, one from the regiment and another from the Royal British Legion were in attendance. The padre paused for a moment before giving an address. It was the usual sort thing that is said over a dead body but, unlike a civilian, the speech attracted other qualities, things such as overpowering camaraderie, understated risks coupled with exemplary service to ones mates and country.

His closest friend, who had joined up at the same time as he had and served with him for twenty-two years, also gave a speech. He spoke of a gentle man, who at certain times and with huge regret had taken other people's lives but only when his mates or other innocents were under threat of losing theirs. It spoke of the trials of military life starting with basic training, the stress of combat and the loss of good mates at ages when they should not be considering death a threat. It also recalled the good times, getting drunk together and sharing the last few bob either of you had until the next payday. It was an undisguised expression of love from one man to another based on common experience of death and danger mixed with adventure, hardship and fun. It came from a deep emotional tie that can be and often is stronger than that between men and family. Suddenly, he stopped speaking as he was incapable for a few minutes to continue due to the emotion. A few old contemptibles in the room sniffed or fumbled with their glasses to discreetly wipe away a tear.

Eddie took the opportunity to look around especially at the civvie friends Tony had. He was always amazed at how uncomfortable they got as the emotional temperature at a military funeral rose. They could not understand why so many grown men could feel so close to one another. Civilians, especially men, who had never been in the armed forces, always felt a little bit lacking in the presence of those who had. Steve caught his eye and quietly mouthed,

'...and gentlemen in England now abed shall think themselves accursed they were not here...' His favourite line from Shakespeare's Henry V showed that Steve understood why Eddie was gazing at the civvies.

It was a common feature amongst ex-soldiers. Eddie, as a civvie, at any time when others in the workplace had been telling funny or memorable stories, would start saying, 'Yeah, I recall when I was in the Army...' in trying to relate a similar story, but the other men in the room would shuffle, look uncomfortable and change the subject. So Eddie stopped doing that and kept quiet the next time and the time after that until it became a habit. But at a funeral the civilians could not change the subject they had to listen and put up with it.

His friend continued with his eulogy reminding all about the odd weird, drunken and funny things that Tony had done. In due course he finished and the padre said a few more words and then hit a hidden button and the coffin started to lower itself down. The two buglers played the *Last Post* in honour of a fallen warrior, perhaps not in battle but he had faced that prospect and had earned that title. All the ex-soldiers present stood to attention and pondered absent friends of their own whilst struggling to maintain their dignity against the wave of raw emotions. Most managed it but some would not. Once out of sight it slowly but surely dawned on everyone that the funeral was now over so, after allowing the widow and family party to leave with dignity, they all shuffled to the door and ambled outside. The old soldiers mingled together shaking hands, hugging and giving ritual insults as is their way. In fine tradition they all went back to the residence of the deceased and spent a while there with the family in quiet reflection. After a while and without showing disrespect they slowly drifted off to a pub and the real wake began.

'Tony's wife's still good looking, I'd steal her knickers after a good shag any day,' said Kevin grabbing a pint and passing it to Steve. Les looked at him sternly and said,

'Look, Gus she'd need a better man than you, do you know the problems they had closing down his coffin?' Kevin shook his head in response looking concerned.

'No! What was the problem?'

'He died with an erection, Gus; it took four men to screw down the lid.' They all laughed loudly, Kevin in particular.

Pete launched into a story, one they'd all heard a million times before, about how Tony came to see him when he was a medic worried that he'd caught Gonorrhoea, or something worse, and launched into the gory details.

Eddie wasn't really listening, he looked at each of his friends in turn and saw all had their scars, some visible and some not. They were balding, going grey and more than one wrinkle was now in evidence. They shared pot bellies and the odd double chin. He watched them and smiled at the insults and swearing that they threw at one other, it was expected! He surveyed them all and found no fault. He noted they all held their heads high. They had an air about them that hinted they had been there and done that. They had a shared experience not matched by many people outside of the military. He recalled the fire fights, the explosions, being terrified and operating purely on adrenalin, the complete and utter exhaustion and weariness of endless hours on operations, digging in, patrolling, section attacks and stagging on. He remembered the agony of staying awake during ambushes when weary and exhausted. Fifty six ton Chieftain tanks screaming past mere feet away. The ten mile runs in full kit, the assault courses and the crippling weight of the Bergens he'd carried. The elation of helicopter operations and the eagle patrols. The fear of battle and the empty faces of the dead coupled with the terrified expressions of fear in the injured. The anger and the helplessness whilst tears and emotions are driven mercilessly out of the body whilst being held tightly, without shame or embarrassment, by his muckers until the weeping passed. He could recall the bellyaching laughter when some cock up had happened or the sheer stupidity of some of the tasks they'd be confronted with.

He glanced at their blazers proudly bearing the badge of their regiment and the campaign medals they wore carrying with them the guilt of living whilst others died, mingled with a self-conscious pride in what they had achieved. They may not have realised it, but they were, each and every one of them, heroes who had earned that title by virtue of the hardship and danger they had faced together. He knew that they'd all, to a man if asked, walk outside right now, pick up a weapon, Bergen and webbing, climb aboard a helicopter and fly into Hell to fight the Devil himself, but not for glory, not for honour and certainly not for their country… but for each other!

Eddie was suddenly brought back to the present by Les drunkenly bursting out as he held open the pub doors for them all to go to the next pub,

'When this fucking funeral's over I'm gonna have a shit, shampoo and a shower. I'm going to have a fucking huge meal, a few beers, a damn good shag and then I'm gonna…' but the last part was lost as the pub door swung shut behind them. Their laughter, however, would continue for a long, long time afterwards.

THE END

Appendices

1. Typical Equipment carried by an NIPG Patrol.

Weapons.

1 SLR 7.62 with 8 magazines with scope

2 M16s 5.56 with 8 magazines each

1 L1A4 Bren gun 7.62 with 15 magazines

1 L98 Sniper rifle with scope with 40 black spot rounds

1 M79 grenade launcher with 1 x 12 round HE bandolier

4 Browning Hi Power 9mm pistols with 2 mags each of 9 rounds

1 Remington semi-automatic shotgun with 30 rounds

1 White Phosphorous grenade

4 Coloured Signal Smoke grenades

12 L79 fragmentation grenades

1x L98 cleaning kit

1x M79 cleaning kit

1 x Bren cleaning kit

1 x SLR cleaning kit

1 x M16 cleaning kit

1 x Tripflare kit

Technical (Shared out)

4 x Practica SLR cameras

2 x 1000mm lenses

2 x 500mm lenses

4 x 55mm lenses

Various filters/x 2 adaptors for cameras

2 x Infrared searchlights

2 x Infrared goggles

2 x NITECH night vision scopes plus tripods and spare batteries (4)

1 x Teletron night scope with batteries (8)

1 x Starlight scope plus tripod plus spare batteries (8) – Bren attachment

2 x camera tripods

1 x Clansman 320 HF Radio

1 x battery generator hand cranked

2 x remote antenna kits

2 x 10' antennas

2 x headset assemblies

1 x handset

1 x Antenna Tuning Unit (ATU)

1 x remote handset kit

20 yards D10 cable

2 x 349 Clansman section level radios

4 x 320 antennas

2 x headsets for 349

1 x handset for 349

4 x batteries for 349

1 x UGS console unit

1 x recorder unit

4 x batteries

20 x various UGS detectors

2 x HP binos

1 x First Aid Pack – serious trauma wounds

40 x 35mm films of various ASA

Camera cleaning kit

More bloody batteries!

2 x prismatic compass

Personal Kit (each member)

1 x Bergen (Large SAS pattern)

1 x sniper/SAS smock

1 x 58 pattern webbing set

1 x mess tin

1 x multi-fuel cooker

8 x water bottles

1 x wash/shave kit/towel

1 x spare socks

1 x spare laces

1 x personal first aid kit/field dressing

1 x knife/fork/spoon

1 x notebook and pen

1 x map and case

1 x bayonet

1 x oil bottle

1 x spare shirt

1 x spare trousers

1 x cold weather top (wooly pully/Norgy)

1 x DPM/snow convertible waterproofs set

1 x poncho

1 x tents pegs and bungees (various)

1 x multifunction knife

1 x torch (right angled)

1 x mug

1 x aide memoire (SOPs)

1 x sleeping bag

4 x plastic bags (2 rubbish and 2 effluent)

1 x lighter/matches

Food (5-10 days' of food depending on operation)

1 x shovel/pick

5 x Hessian sacks for cammo

1 x cam cream

1 x cam scarf

1 x ghillie suit

1 x housewife (sewing kit)

1 x boot cleaning kit

1 x washing and shaving kit

1 x compass

Miscellaneous

1 x vehicle sized camouflage net
1 (2?) x water Jerry can – 5 gallons
100yds Comms cord (Para cord)
Maps and map cases

This when averaged out went to about 96lbs per person not including webbing, weapons and ammunition.